GREAT IRISH
TALES OF
FANTASY
AND MYTH

GREAT IRISH TALES OF FANTASY AND MYTH

Edited by
Peter Haining

BARNES
&NOBLE
BOOKS
NEW YORK

CONTENTS

INTRODUCTION

It is a curious fact that the first novel by an Irish author was also a fantasy—Jonathan Swift's *Gulliver's Travels* which he wrote in 1726. With this extraordinary tale the Dublin-born satirist initiated an imaginative tradition which later writers such as Standish O'Grady, W. B. Yeats, James Joyce, Eimar O'Duffy, James Stephens, Mervyn Wall and all the others represented in this book have turned into a body of work the envy of the world. Ireland has made a major contribution to so many literary genres, not least that of the unimaginable and the fantastic.

As the American master of fantasy, H. P. Lovecraft, observed in his important essay 'Supernatural Horror in Literature', written in 1927, 'Somewhat separate from the main British stream is the current of weirdness in Irish literature which came to the fore in the Celtic Renaissance of the late nineteenth and early twentieth centuries. Whilst on the whole more whimsically fantastic than terrible, such folklore and its consciously artistic counterparts contain much that falls truly within the domain of cosmic horror.'

All these Irish stories in their turn owe much to the nation's rich heritage of mythology—the gods, heroes and men and women of the sagas who, by their deeds of bravery, their shows of undying love or quests to the ends of the earth, provided the raw material from which the latter-day fabulists created their stories. It is a school of literature that was first properly formulated in the works of Standish O'Grady, the 'Father of the Irish Renaissance', in the closing decades of the nineteenth century, and has since been nurtured and developed to produce an entire group of landmark novels and influential short stories in the current century.

Storytellers have always been popular with the people of Ireland—the *seanchais*, *ollaves*, *files* and bards of the olden days—who were dedicated to satisfying audiences ranging from princes of the realm to ordinary men and women. Indeed, in order to meet the demand for this kind of entertainment, explained the historian P. W. Joyce in his authoritative study *Old Celtic Romances* (1894), these ingenious men had to compose stories that caught the popular fancy and so they often took legends or great events as their themes.

'In the course of time,' Joyce wrote, 'a body of romantic literature grew up consisting chiefly of prose tales which were classified according to subject into Gods and Heroes, Voyages and Expeditions, Tragedies and Courtships, Adventures, Visions & etc. Some of these tales were historical, i.e. founded on historical events and corresponded closely with what is now called the historical romance; while others were altogether fictitious—pure creations of the imagination. But it is to be observed that even in the fictitious tales, the main characters are always historical, or such as were considered so. The old ollaves wove their fictions around the legends of Cuculain, Oisin, Balor, Angus, the lovers Midir and Etain and the voyager Maildun, just like the Welsh legends of Arthur and his Round Table or the Arabian romances of Haroun-al-Raschid and his Court.'

Jonathan Swift was not the only eighteenth-century Irish writer to exploit this tradition ahead of the Renaissance. The Roscommon-born Oliver Goldsmith (1728–1774) was undoubtedly aware of the legend of the satirical poet Aithirne the Importunate, who demanded seven hundred white cows with red ears as tribute from the people of Naas, and he used this as his inspiration for the tale of the 'White Mouse with Green Eyes' in his story of Prince Bonbenin Bonbobbinet. Another contemporary, the Dubliner Samuel Derrick (1724–1769), who created an Ossianic saga in verse, 'The Battle of Lora', also drew on the belief expressed in some of the old legends that the heroes could fly to write his 'A Voyage to the Moon', which predated Jules Verne's classic by at least a century and established him as a pioneer of Science Fantasy—certainly in Ireland and probably in a large part of the rest of the world, too.

All the contributors to this volume have drawn on the nation's rich store of mythology and augmented these tales—some from ancient manuscripts and others purely from oral traditions—from their own imagination. I have therefore prefaced each story with details of the legends which were their inspiration, and have provided further relevant information about the people and places they feature.

The fact that tales of fantasy are now enjoying such popularity with modern readers—the younger generation in particular—should come as no great surprise: exactly one hundred years ago, W. B. Yeats wrote in his book *The Celtic Twilight*, published in 1893, a paragraph that the passage of time has done nothing to disprove and has, if anything, enhanced.

'It is perhaps, therefore, by no means strange that the age of "realism" should also be the harvest-time of folk-lore,' he said. 'We grow tired of tuning our fiddles to the clank of this our heavy chain, and lay them down to listen gladly to one who tells us of men hundreds of years old and endlessly mirthful. Our new-wakened interest in the impossible has been of the greatest service to Irish folk-literature.'

Welcome, then, to the world of the unimaginable that Yeats and his fellow writers offer for our entertainment, instruction and wonder.

Peter Haining
January 1994

1

GODS AND HEROES

THE HOUND OF ULSTER

Standish James O'Grady

Cuculain, 'The Hound of Ulster', is probably the most famous hero in Irish mythology, referred to by some as the 'Irish Achilles'. A man of great strength and bravery, known as the champion of all Ireland, he is best remembered for his single-handed defence of Ulster when it was under invasion from the forces of Connacht. Apart from his triumphs as a warrior, he had a magnetic attraction for women and among those who fell in love with him was Fand, the 'Pearl of Beauty', a goddess and wife of Mannanan Mac Lir, with whom he spent a time in the Otherworld. He possessed a number of mystical weapons including his sword, Caladin, and spear, the Gae-Bolg, and was accompanied on many of his adventures by his faithful charioteer, Laeg. His life was also tinged by tragedy, for he was forced to kill his best friend in combat, and he was finally slain for rejecting the love of Morrigan, the goddess of battles.

There are many accounts of Cuculain in Irish folklore, but his fame among modern readers owes much to the fictionalising of his legend by Standish James O'Grady (1846–1928) whose pioneer work earned him the title 'Father of the Irish Renaissance'. O'Grady, who spent years researching ancient Irish history, used the tales and legends he unearthed in a string of novels including The Coming of Cuculain *(1894),* The Flight of the Eagle *(1897) and* The Triumph and Passing of Cuculain *(1920)—all of which caused Benedict Kiely to declare of him in 1950, 'O'Grady brought the heroes into Irish literature.' It seems appropriate, therefore, that this collection should open with a story of Ireland's greatest hero by the nation's first modern teller of heroic tales. 'The Hound of Ulster' is a story of bloody combat and attempted supernatural intervention, a forerunner of the many very popular fantasy novels*

and stories of this kind which now crowd the shelves of libraries
and bookshops.

*   *   *

There was much foul play and unfairness practised against Cuculain by the men of Meave, but the Hound of Battle was always their better. Then amongst their number arose one named Lok Mac Favesh.

'Sufficient to me now,' he said, 'is the renown of Cuculain to render him a quarry worthy of my spear. Tomorrow, the host of Meave, released from this check, will cross the Avon Dia, invading the lands of Ulla and in my armoury the head of that brave stripling will be an ornament of my dun, and a boast to my posterity.'

In the morning his squires arrayed him in his battle-dress, his helmet and neck-piece and capacious leathern coat clasped round his breast and mighty waist, and over that they bound his strong breast-plate. To the ford he went like a moving tower, on legs like the trunks of trees, and though corpulent, and past the prime of his youth, nor very quick upon his feet, yet was his strength and power irresistible, which, indeed, all men knew. For, in the previous year, at the feast of Lunasa, held annually in honour to Lu Lamfada, on the plain of Tailteen, on that day which men in later times named the Kalends of August, he had broken in the skull of a bull with a single blow of his strong hand. Seven folds of tanned ox-hide stitched close together, o'er-ran the firm osier work of his shield, and above that was plating of brass two inches thick, and no man in the host of Meave could wield it, but on his arm it was lighter than the bratta which in sudden quarrel a man winds round his left arm, a defence against a knife. It, three brothers of the city of Limerick had made for him, and there was a painted device in the middle.

But, on the other side, came down Cuculain unarmoured, his linen tunic and crimson bratta soiled, and his brooch dulled with rust, his gold tresses tangled, and his countenance hollow and overcast. But harder than steel was his heart in his breast and the men of Meave were astonished and said: 'Is this, indeed, he who played at hurley with us?' for mighty seemed his stature, and terrible his advance, striding through the stunted willows to meet his enemy.

Then his feet splashed in the shallow water of the ford, but suddenly he shrieked, and his spears fell from his hand; for, above the head of Mac Favash he beheld the ghoul that had accompanied him unseen from the south, resting a bearded chin upon skinny knuckles, and it smiled at him. He, Cuculain, stood like one petrified, his eyes starting from their sockets, and his yellow hair stood out from his head. At this Lok Mac Favash advanced, and poising, cast his heavy spear at Cuculain's bare breast, but it erring, went lower towards the left, and passed through the shield at the upper rim, and entered the fleshy part of Cuculain's upper arm.

Dire agony took possession of Cuculain which was his safety, for it restored him to himself. Lok Mac Favash drew to him the spear by the haft, drawing the head out of Cuculain's flesh, but the shoulders held fast in the shield, wherefore he dragged the youth forward struggling and stumbling in the water, as the fisherman draws to land some noble fish, and the blood spurted out and reddened his white tunic and his legs. The men of Meave raised a shout, and that shout was heard in Emain Macha.

Meantime Lok Mac Favash was dragging Cuculain through the ford, and as he did so he laughed at and insulted him.

'Verily ere now, O men of Meave,' he said, 'have I had good sport in fishing. For in the sea below Limerick and in the harbour of Ilaun Ard Nemeth have I drawn into my boat fish, many and great that strongly resisted, and when I brought them into my boat, if troublesome I struck them on the head with a stick. But never till now have I drawn in a fish so vigorous, or that yielded such good sport. Nevertheless, him, too, will I mollify, stroking him down with my little stick.'

Therewith he drew his war-mace, the head alone seventy pounds, all brass, with spikes standing out upon it like the spikes of the sea urchin, and he shook it playfully backwards towards the men of Meave.

Then was there a respite for Cuculain, and very quickly and like the crooked track of the lightning, he drew his sword and smote the spear of Mac Favash just in front of the shield, and struck in twain the strong ashed tree. He recovered quickly the spears which had fallen from him, and with a cry leaped from the ford, strong and vigorous as a salmon springing over a cataract in early summer when he seeks the upper pools, and poising, was about to cast one of his spears at Lok, when, again, the spectre, breathing in his face an icy breath, confronted him, more hellish than before. Yet this time he shrieked not, nor was afraid, for despair and wrath had made him mad. Wherefore altering the direction he hurled at the ghoul the long spear, and it seemed as though it passed through a hollow eye socket.

A horrid cry penetrated the host, whereat the war-steeds and the beasts of burden ran together alarmed, and the whole host shuddered, and men saw some formless thing fall heavily into the ford. But, ere Cuculain could clutch his second spear, Mac Favash bore down upon him like a great ship that throws her billows on both sides from her broad prow, and beat him back into the ford, using both shield and club. Twice in succession he smote with his mighty club the shield of Cuculain, and shattered all the middle of that light shield; Cuculain stepped back nimbly, and again lifted his spear. Once more he cried out with mingled rage and fear, and he stood a moment as if glued to the spot, with his legs close together and working frightfully with his bloody knees.

Then as Lok Mac Favash was advancing to slay him, Cuculain sprang high out of the water, and around his ankles and below the calves of his legs was there coiled three times lapped, the twine of a great eel, blue, with glittering eyes and close-tapped tail. But as he sprang high in the air, Cuculain smote at it with his spear, using it like a staff, striking on the left side, and with a croak like a raven, the horrid thing unwound, and fell into the bloody water.

Cuculain poised once more his spear, and cast it at Lok Mac Favash, but the other held his round shield at an angle, and the spear screeched against the thick brass, grooving it as the ollav grooves the sand with his pen, teaching children to write. Once again Cuculain cried out, trampling wildly with his feet, and the spray went up and concealed the combat from the fierce trampling of the son of Sualtam, and the torn fragments of a strange water-weed floated down the stream from where Cuculain trampled, subduing the third transformation of the spectre.

While he was powerless Lok Mac Favash struck him on the left breast with his spiked club. Now all the middle of Cuculain's shield was broken away, and there was a ragged border all around, and with this border, the weakest part of the shield, he intercepted the blow, but the heavy mace broke through it and fell upon his breast, and the spikes tore his flesh. Then Cuculain staggered. Nevertheless he drew his sword and struck at Lok, but the other caught it on the very boss of the shield, where the brass was four inches thick, and the sword brake and showered about the stream.

Cuculain looked for a moment to the wide heaven and the sun, for it was blazing noon, and his lips moved, and, swerving swiftly to the right, he stooped. Now, a row of great pebbles crossed the ford, the work of some ancient king, and in a crescent-shaped line traversed the water and the dry land on each side, in order that, even in times of flood, there might be a passage for travellers, and below this was a chariot-ford where the heroes fought. Dropping the fragments of his shield, he laid his hands on the largest of these, smooth and white on the top, worn by many feet, but black and mossy upon the sides. A stone that two strong navvies, such as men are now, could with difficulty roll to the shore, using cowbars, but Cuculain raised it without difficulty. As a boy, eager to get at the sweet kernel, with ease lifts the strong-shelled fruit of the palm tree, and smashes it against the flagged basement, so Cuculain raised on high above his head the mighty pebble, standing with legs apart in the ford, and dashed it on the centre of the huge shield of Lok Mac Favish.

The great stone smashed through the broad shield of Lok, and smote him below the breast, and bore him to the ground, falling upon him, as one who wrestles with his enemy and falls with him to the ground, and it crushed him down under the water. But it wanted not water to slay him, for his body was broken from the impulse of the heavy missile. Cuculain seized the spear-tree of Lok's spear which was eddying around the place, and leant upon it, panting red all over as though he had ascended out of a bath of blood.

Then he drew himself together and sat down on one of the great pebbles, bowing his head between his hands, and vomited much blood into the stream. After which he rose and walked to the other shore, staggering as he went, and steadying his steps with the spear, and passed in between the willows. And the whole host of Meave was silent, and every eye watched him, warriors craning forward with raised hands, watching eagerly if he would fall. As when a sportsman and his beaters watch eagerly the flight of a bird which they deem is wounded, and one says he will fall, and another not, so the great host of Meave watched Cuculain as he went back, till the trees concealed him.

THE WISDOM OF THE KING

W. B. Yeats

When, in time, the ancient gods of Ireland were driven underground, they became known as the Sidhe—'the people of the hills'—and in folk memory as fairies. However, they have continued to influence the affairs of mankind in the nation ever since, and there are still a number of hills and mounds about the countryside which are reputed to be the dwelling places of the Sidhe. Standish O'Grady wrote several tales about these hidden gods, as did W. B. Yeats (1865–1939) who was inspired by the older man to devote himself to writing a series of short stories and novels featuring characters from Irish antiquity.

Yeats, whom T. S. Eliot later called 'the greatest poet of our time', maintained that O'Grady had 'started us all' in promoting the renaissance of interest in Irish mythology. As well as studying the ancient Gaelic records, he believed in magic and devoted more than fifty years of his life to occult experimentation. Curiously, this fascinating aspect of Yeats' life has received far less attention from critics and historians than his plays and poems, and many scholars have completely ignored his supernatural collections The Celtic Twilight *(1893),* The Secret Rose *(1897) and* The Stories of Red Hanrahan *(1897). In each of these books are to be found the same elements of Irish mythology that O'Grady had started to mine. 'The Wisdom of the King', written in 1897, is a timeless story of ancient wonders which, like those of O'Grady, has had a strong influence on modern fantasy fiction.*

*   *   *

The High-Queen of the Island of Woods had died in childbirth, and her child was put to nurse with a woman who lived in a hut of mud and wicker, within the border of the wood. One night the woman sat rocking the cradle, and pondering over the beauty of the child, and praying that the gods might grant him wisdom equal to his beauty. There came a knock at the door, and she got up, not a little wondering, for the nearest neighbours were in the dun of the High-King a mile away; and the night was now late. 'Who is knocking?' she cried, and a thin voice answered, 'Open! for I am a crone of the grey hawk, and I come from the darkness of the great wood.' In terror she drew back the bolt, and a grey-clad woman, of a great age, and of a height more than human, came in and stood by the head of the cradle. The nurse shrank back against the wall, unable to take her eyes from the woman, for she saw by the gleaming of the firelight that the feathers of the grey hawk were upon her head instead of hair. But the child slept, and the fire danced, for the one was too ignorant and the other too full of gaiety to know what a dreadful being stood there. 'Open!' cried another voice, 'for I am a crone of the grey hawk, and I watch over his nest in the darkness of the great wood.' The nurse opened the door again, though her fingers could scarce hold the bolts for trembling, and another grey woman, not less old than the other, and with like feathers instead of hair, came in and stood by the first. In a little, came a third grey woman, and after her a fourth, and then another and another and another, until the hut was full of their immense bodies. They stood a long time in perfect silence and stillness, for they were of those whom the dropping of the sand has never troubled, but at last one muttered in a low thin voice: 'Sisters, I knew him far away by the redness of his heart under his silver skin'; and then another spoke: 'Sisters, I knew him because his heart fluttered like a bird under a net of silver cords'; and then another took up the word: 'Sisters, I knew him because his heart sang like a bird that is happy in a silver cage.'

And after that they sang together, those who were nearest rocking the cradle with long wrinkled fingers; and their voices were now tender and caressing, now like the wind blowing in the great wood, and this was their song:

> Out of sight is out of mind:
> Long have man and woman-kind,
> Heavy of will and light of mood,
> Taken away our wheaten food,
> Taken away our Altar stone;

> Hail and rain and thunder alone,
> And red hearts we turn to grey,
> Are true till Time gutter away.

When the song had died out, the crone who had first spoken, said: 'We have nothing more to do but to mix a drop of our blood into his blood.' And she scratched her arm with the sharp point of a spindle, which she had made the nurse bring to her, and let a drop of blood, grey as the mist, fall upon the lips of the child; and passed out into the darkness. Then the others passed out in silence one by one; and all the while the child had not opened his pink eyelids or the fire ceased to dance, for the one was too ignorant and the other too full of gaiety to know what great beings had bent over the cradle.

When the crones were gone, the nurse came to her courage again, and hurried to the dun of the High-King, and cried out in the midst of the assembly hall that the Sidhe, whether for good or evil she knew not, had bent over the child that night; and the king and his poets and men of law, and his huntsmen, and his cooks, and his chief warriors went with her to the hut and gathered about the cradle, and were as noisy as magpies, and the child sat up and looked at them.

Two years passed over, and the king died fighting against the Fer Bolg; and the poets and the men of law ruled in the name of the child, but looked to see him become the master himself before long, for no one had seen so wise a child, and tales of his endless questions about the household of the gods and the making of the world went hither and thither among the wicker houses of the poor. Everything had been well but for a miracle that began to trouble all men; and all women, who, indeed, talked of it without ceasing. The feathers of the grey hawk had begun to grow in the child's hair, and though his nurse cut them continually, in but a little while they would be more numerous than ever. This had not been a matter of great moment, for miracles were a little thing in those days, but for an ancient law of Eri that none who had any blemish of body could sit upon the throne; and as a grey hawk was a wild thing of the air which had never sat at the board, or listened to the songs of the poets in the light of the fire, it was not possible to think of one in whose hair its feathers grew as other than marred and blasted; nor could the people separate from their admiration of the wisdom that grew in him a horror as at one of unhuman blood.

Yet all were resolved that he should reign, for they had suffered much from foolish kings and their own disorders, and moreover they desired to watch out the spectacle of his days; and no one had any other fear but that his great wisdom might bid him obey the law, and call some other, who had but a common mind, to reign in his stead.

When the child was seven years old the poets and the men of law were called together by the chief poet, and all these matters weighed and considered. The child had already seen that those about him had hair only, and, though they had told him that they too had had feathers but had lost them because of a sin committed by their forefathers, they knew that he would learn the truth when he began to wander into the country round about. After much consideration they decreed a new law commanding every one upon pain of death to mingle artificially the feathers of the grey hawk into his hair; and they sent men with nets and slings and bows into the countries round about to gather a sufficiency of feathers. They decreed also that any who told the truth to the child should be flung from a cliff into the sea.

The years passed, and the child grew from childhood into boyhood and from boyhood into manhood, and from being curious about all things he became busy with strange and subtle thoughts which came to him in dreams, and with distinctions between things long held the same and with the resemblance of things long held different. Multitudes came from other lands to see him and to ask his counsel, but there were guards set at the frontiers, who compelled all that came to wear the feathers of the grey hawk in their hair.

While they listened to him his words seemed to make all darkness light and filled their hearts like music; but, alas, when they returned to their own lands his words seemed far off, and what they could remember too strange and subtle to help them to live out their hasty days. A number indeed did live differently afterwards, but their new life was less excellent than the old: some among them had long served a good cause, but when they heard him praise it and their labour, they returned to their own lands to find what they had loved less lovable and their arm lighter in the battle, for he had taught them how little a hair divides the false and true; others, again, who had served no cause, but wrought in peace the welfare of their own households, when he had expounded the meaning of their purpose, found their bones softer and their will less ready for toil, for he had shown them greater purposes; and numbers of the young, when they had heard him upon all these things, remembered certain words that became like a fire in their hearts, and made all kindly joys and traffic between man and man as nothing, and went different ways, but all into vague regret.

When any asked him concerning the common things of life; disputes about the mear of a territory, or about the straying of cattle, or about the penalty of blood; he would turn to those nearest him for advice; but this was held to be from courtesy, for none knew that these matters were hidden from him by thoughts and dreams that filled his mind like the marching and counter-marching of armies. Far less could any know that his heart wandered lost amid throngs of overcoming thoughts and dreams, shuddering at its own consuming solitude.

Among those who came to look at him and to listen to him was the daughter of a little king who lived a great way off; and when he saw her he loved, for she was beautiful, with a strange and pale beauty unlike the women of his land; but Dana, the great mother, had decreed her a heart that was but as the heart of others, and when she considered the mystery of the hawk feathers she was troubled with a great horror. He called her to him when the assembly was over and told her of her beauty, and praised her simply and frankly as though she were a fable of the bards; and he asked her humbly to give him her love, for he was only subtle in his dreams. Overwhelmed with his greatness, she half consented, and yet half refused, for she longed to marry some warrior who could carry her over a mountain in his arms.

Day by day the king gave her gifts; cups with ears of gold and findrinny wrought by the craftsmen of distant lands; cloth from over sea, which, though woven with curious figures, seemed to her less beautiful than the bright cloth of her own country; and still she was ever between a smile and a frown; between yielding and withholding. He laid down his wisdom at her feet, and told how the heroes when they die return to the world and begin their labour anew; how the kind and mirthful Men of Dea drove out the huge and gloomy and misshapen People from Under the Sea;

and a multitude of things that even the Sidhe have forgotten, either because they happened so long ago or because they have not time to think of them; and still she half refused, and still he hoped, because he could not believe that a beauty so much like wisdom could hide a common heart.

There was a tall young man in the dun who had yellow hair, and was skilled in wrestling and in the training of horses; and one day when the king walked in the orchard, which was between the foss and the forest, he heard his voice among the salley bushes which hid the waters of the foss.

'My blossom,' it said, 'I hate them for making you weave these dingy feathers into your beautiful hair, and all that the bird of prey upon the throne may sleep easy o' nights'; and then the low, musical voice he loved answered: 'My hair is not beautiful like yours; and now that I have plucked the feathers out of your hair I will put my hands through it, thus, and thus, and thus; for it casts no shadow of terror and darkness upon my heart.'

Then the king remembered many things that he had forgotten without understanding them, doubtful words of his poets and his men of law, doubts that he had reasoned away, his own continual solitude; and he called to the lovers in a trembling voice. They came from among the salley bushes and threw themselves at his feet and prayed for pardon, and he stooped down and plucked the feathers out of the hair of the woman and then turned away towards the dun without a word. He strode into the hall of assembly, and having gathered his poets and his men of law about him, stood upon the daïs and spoke in a loud, clear voice:

'Men of law, why did you make me sin against the laws of Eri? Men of verse, why did you make me sin against the secrecy of wisdom, for law was made by man for the welfare of man, but wisdom the gods have made, and no man shall live by its light, for it and the hail and the rain and the thunder follow a way that is deadly to mortal things? Men of law and men of verse, live according to your kind, and call Eocha of the Hasty Mind to reign over you, for I set out to find my kindred.'

He then came down among them, and drew out of the hair of first one and then another the feathers of the grey hawk, and, having scattered them over the rushes upon the floor, passed out, and none dared to follow him, for his eyes gleamed like the eyes of the birds of prey; and no man saw him again or heard his voice.

Some believed that he found his eternal abode among the demons, and some that he dwelt henceforth with the dark and dreadful goddesses, who sit all night about the pools in the forest watching the constellations rising and setting in those desolate mirrors.

THE CALL OF OISIN

Lady Gregory

The great warrior Oisin (sometimes spelled Ossian) is said to have been, in his time, the most famous poet in Ireland, and the renowned Fenian Cycle about the deeds of the celebrated Fionn Mac Cumhail (usually anglicised as Finn Mac Cool) and the Fianna, is often popularly referred to as the Ossianic Cycle. He was the son of Finn and Sabd, the daughter of the god Bodb Dearg, and grew up to be a brave and fearless champion around whom many legends developed. The story of his adventure with a beautiful golden-haired stranger is retold in the following tale by Isabella Augusta, Lady Gregory (1852–1952).

Lady Gregory shared with her close friend W. B. Yeats a passion for mythology and the theatre, and apart from writing Gods and Fighting Men *(1904)—now acknowledged as another landmark in the renaissance of Irish fantasy fiction—she also helped Yeats to found the Abbey Theatre in Dublin and assemble the Irish Players, for whom she wrote several plays including* The Rising of the Moon *(1907). She made a special study of the Ossianic Cycle and here gives a vivid rendering of the young Oisin's fantastic adventure with its dramatic finale. Lady Gregory is credited with being the first writer to have linked the lives of Oisin and Ireland's patron saint, St Patrick.*

*　　*　　*

One misty morning, what were left of the Fianna were gathered together to Finn, and it is sorrowful and downhearted they were after the loss of so many of their comrades.

And they went hunting near the borders of Loch Lein, where the bushes were in blossom and the birds were singing; and they were waking up the deer that were as joyful as the leaves of a tree in summer-time.

And it was not long till they saw coming towards them from the west a beautiful young woman, riding on a very fast slender white horse. A queen's crown she had on her head, and a dark cloak of silk down to the ground, having stars of red gold on it; and her eyes were blue and as clear as the dew on the grass, and a gold ring hanging down from every golden lock of her hair; and her cheeks redder than the rose, and her skin whiter than the swan upon the wave, and her lips as sweet as honey that is mixed through red wine.

And in her hand she was holding a bridle having a golden bit, and there was a saddle worked with red gold under her. And as to the horse, he had a wide smooth cloak over him, and a silver crown on the back of his head, and he was shod with shining gold.

She came to where Finn was, and she spoke with a very kind, gentle voice, and she said: 'It is long my journey was, King of the Fianna.' And Finn asked who was she, and what was her country and the cause of her coming. 'Niamh of the Golden Head is my name,' she said; 'and I have a name beyond all the women of the world, for I am the daughter of the King of the Country of the Young.' 'What was it brought you to us from over the sea, Queen?' said Finn then. 'Is it that your husband is gone from you, or what is the trouble that is on you?' 'My husband is not gone from me,' she said, 'for I never went yet to any man. But O King of the Fianna,' she said, 'I have given my love and my affection to your own son, Oisin of the strong hands.' 'Why did you give your love to him beyond all the troops of high princes that are under the sun?' said Finn. 'It was by reason of his great name, and of the report I heard of his bravery and of his comeliness,' she said. 'And though there is many a king's son and high prince gave me his love, I never consented to any till I set my love on Oisin.'

When Oisin heard what she was saying, there was not a limb of his body that was not in love with beautiful Niamh; and he took her hand in his hand, and he said: 'A true welcome before you to this country, young queen. It is you are the shining one,' he said; 'it is you are the nicest and the comeliest; it is you are better to me than any other woman; it is you are my star and my choice beyond the women of the entire world.' 'I put on you the bonds of a true hero,' said Niamh then, 'you to come away with me now to the Country of the Young.' And it is what she said:

'It is the country is most delightful of all that are under the sun;

the trees are stooping down with fruit and with leaves and with blossom.

'Honey and wine are plentiful there, and everything the eye has ever seen; no wasting will come on you with the wasting away of time; you will never see death or lessening.

'You will get feasts, playing and drinking; you will get sweet music on the strings; you will get silver and gold and many jewels.

'You will get, and no lie in it, a hundred swords; a hundred cloaks of the dearest silk; a hundred horses, the quickest in battle; a hundred willing hounds.

'You will get the royal crown of the King of the Young that he never gave to any one under the sun. It will be a shelter to you night and day in every rough fight and in every battle.

'You will get a right suit of armour; a sword, goldhilted, apt for striking; no one that ever saw it got away alive from it.

'A hundred coats of armour and shirts of satin; a hundred cows and a hundred calves; a hundred sheep having golden fleeces; a hundred jewels that are not of this world.

'A hundred glad young girls shining like the sun, their voices sweeter than the music of birds; a hundred armed men strong in battle, apt at feats, waiting on you, if you will come with me to the Country of the Young.

'You will get everything I have said to you, and delights beyond them, that I have no leave to tell; you will get beauty, strength and power, and I myself will be with you as a wife.'

And after she had made that song, Oisin said: 'O pleasant golden-haired queen, you are my choice beyond the women of the world; and I will go with you willingly,' he said.

And with that he kissed Finn his father and bade him farewell, and he bade farewell to the rest of the Fianna, and he went up then on the horse with Niamh.

And the horse set out gladly, and when he came to the strand he shook himself and he neighed three times, and then he made for the sea. And when Finn and the Fianna saw Oisin facing the wide sea, they gave three great sorrowful shouts. And as to Finn, he said: 'It is my grief to see you going from me; and I am without a hope,' he said, 'ever to see you coming back to me again.'

*   *   *

It was a long time after he was brought away by Niamh that Oisin came back again to Ireland. Some say it was hundreds of years he was in the Country of the Young, and some say it was thousands of years he was in it; but whatever time it was, it seemed short to him.

And whatever happened him through the time he was away, it is a withered old man he was found after coming back to Ireland, and his white horse going away from him, and he lying on the ground.

And it was St Patrick had power at that time, and it was to him Oisin was brought; and he kept him in his house, and used to be teaching him and questioning him. And Oisin was no way pleased with the way Ireland was then, but he used to be talking of the old times, and fretting after the Fianna.

And Patrick bade him to tell what happened him the time he left Finn and the Fianna and went away with Niamh. And it is the story Oisin told: 'The time I went away with golden-haired Niamh, we turned our backs to the land, and our faces westward, and the sea was going away before us, and filling up in waves after us. And we saw wonderful things on our journey,' he said, 'cities and courts and duns and lime-white houses, and shining sunny-houses and palaces. And one time we saw beside us a hornless deer running hard, and an eager white red-eared hound following after it. And another time we saw a young girl on a horse and having a golden apple in her right hand, and she going over the tops of the waves; and there was following after her a young man riding a white horse, and having a crimson cloak and a gold-hilted sword in his right hand.'

'Follow on with your story, pleasant Oisin,' said Patrick, 'for you did not tell us yet what was the country you went to.'

'The Country of the Young, the Country of Victory, it was,' said Oisin. 'And O Patrick,' he said, 'there is no lie in that name; and if there are grandeurs in your Heaven the same as there are there, I would give my friendship to God.

'We turned our backs then to the dun,' he said, 'and the horse under us was quicker than the spring wind on the backs of the mountains. And it was not long till the sky darkened, and the wind rose in every part, and the sea was as if on fire, and there was nothing to be seen of the sun.

'But after we were looking at the clouds and the stars for a while the wind went down, and the storm, and the sun brightened. And we saw before us a very delightful country under full blossom, and smooth plains in it, and a king's dun that was very grand, and that had every colour in it, and sunny-houses beside it, and palaces of shining stones, made by skilled men. And we saw coming out to meet us three fifties of armed men, very lively and handsome. And I asked Niamh was this the Country of the Young, and she said it was. "And indeed, Oisin," she said, "I told you no lie about it, and you will see all I promised you before you for ever."

'And there came out after that a hundred beautiful young girls, having cloaks of silk worked with gold, and they gave me a welcome to their own country. And after that there came a great shining army, and with it a strong beautiful king, having a shirt of yellow silk and a golden cloak over it, and a very bright crown on his head. And there was following after him a young queen, and fifty young girls along with her.

'And when all were come to the one spot, the king took me by the hand, and he said out before them all: "A hundred thousand welcomes before you, Oisin, son of Finn. And as to this country you are come to," he said, "I will tell you news of it without a lie. It is long and lasting your life will be in it, and you yourself will be young for ever. And there is no delight the heart ever thought of," he said, "but it is here against your coming. And you can believe my words, Oisin," he said, "for I myself am the King of the Country of the Young, and this is its comely queen, and it was golden-headed Niamh our daughter that went over the sea looking for you to be her husband for ever." I gave thanks to him then, and I stooped myself down before the queen, and we went forward to the royal house, and all the high nobles came out to meet us, both men and women, and there was a great feast made there through the length of ten days and ten nights.

'And that is the way I married Niamh of the Golden Hair, and that is the way I went to the Country of the Young, although it is sorrowful to me to be telling it now, O Patrick from Rome,' said Oisin.

'Follow on with your story, Oisin of the destroying arms,' said Patrick, 'and tell me what way did you leave the Country of the Young, for it is long to me till I hear that; and tell us now had you any children by Niamh, and was it long you were in that place.'

'Three beautiful children I had by Niamh,' said Oisin, 'two young sons and a comely daughter. And Niamh gave the two sons the name of Finn and of Osgar, and the name I gave to the daughter was The Flower.

'And I did not feel the time passing, and it was a long time I stopped there,' he said, 'till the desire came on me to see Finn and my comrades again. And I asked leave of the king and of Niamh to go back to Ireland. "You will get leave from me," said Niamh; "but for all that," she said, "it is bad news you are giving me, for I am in dread you will never come back here again through the length of your days." But I bade her have no fear, since the white horse would bring me safe back again from Ireland. "Bear this in mind, Oisin," she said then, "if you once get off the horse while you are away, or if you once put your foot to ground, you will never come back here again. And O Oisin,' she said, 'I tell it to you now for the third time, if you once get down from the horse, you will be an old man, blind and withered, without liveliness, without mirth, without running, without leaping. And it is a grief to me, Oisin,' she said, 'you ever to go back to green Ireland; and it is not now as it used to be, and you will not see Finn and his people, for there is not now in the whole of Ireland but a Father of Orders and armies of saints; and here is my kiss for you, pleasant Oisin,' she said, 'for you will never come back any more to the Country of the Young.'

'And that is my story, Patrick, and I have told you no lie in it,' said Oisin. 'And O Patrick,' he said, 'if I was the same the day I came here as I was that day, I would have made an end of all your clerks, and there would not be a head left on a neck after me.'

'Go on with your story,' said Patrick, 'and you will get the same good treatment from me you got from Finn, for the sound of your voice is pleasing to me.'

So Oisin went on with his story, and it is what he said: 'I have nothing to tell of my journey till I came back into green Ireland, and I looked about me then on all sides, but there were no tidings to be got of Finn. And it was not long till I saw a great troop of riders, men and women, coming towards me from the west. And when they came near they wished me good health; and there was wonder on them all when they looked at me, seeing me so unlike themselves, and so big and so tall.

'I asked them then did they hear if Finn was still living, or any other one of the Fianna, or what had happened them. 'We often heard of Finn that lived long ago,' said they, 'and that there never was his equal for strength or bravery or a great name; and there is many a book written down,' they said, 'by the sweet poets of the Gael, about his doings and the doings of the Fianna, and it would be hard for us to tell you all of them. And we heard Finn had a son,' they said, 'that was beautiful and shining, and that there came a young girl looking for him, and he went away with her to the Country of the Young.'

'And when I knew by their talk that Finn was not living or any of the Fianna, it is downhearted I was, and tired, and very sorrowful after them. And I made no delay, but I turned my face and went on to Almhuin of Leinster. And there was great wonder on me when I came there to see no sign at all of Finn's great dun, and his great hall, and nothing in the place where it was but weeds and nettles.'

And there was grief on Oisin then, and he said: 'Och, Patrick! Och, ochone, my grief! It is a bad journey that was to me; and to be without tidings of Finn or the Fianna has left me under pain through my lifetime.'

'Leave off fretting, Oisin,' said Patrick, 'and shed your tears to the God of grace. Finn and the Fianna are slack enough now, and they will get no help for ever.' 'It is a great pity that would be,' said Oisin, 'Finn to be in pain for ever; and who was it gained the victory over him, when his own hand had made an end of so many a hard fighter?'

'It is God gained the victory over Finn,' said Patrick, 'and not the strong hand of an enemy; and as to the Fianna, they are condemned to hell along with him, and tormented for ever.'

'O Patrick,' said Oisin, 'show me the place where Finn and his people are, and there is not a hell or a heaven there but I will put it down. And if Osgar, my own son, is there,' he said, 'the hero that was bravest in heavy battles, there is not in hell or in the Heaven of God a troop so great that he could not destroy it.'

'Let us leave off quarrelling on each side now,' said Patrick; 'and go on, Oisin, with your story. What happened you after you knew the Fianna to be at an end?'

'I will tell you that, Patrick,' said Oisin. 'I was turning to go away, and I saw the stone trough that the Fianna used to be putting their hands in, and it full of water. And when I saw it I had such a wish and such a feeling for it that I forgot what I was told, and I got off the horse. And in the minute all the years came on me, and I was lying on the ground, and the horse took fright and went away and left me there, an old man, weak and spent, without sight, without shape, without comeliness, without strength or understanding, without respect.

'There, Patrick, is my story for you now,' said Oisin, 'and no lie in it, of all that happened me going away and coming back again from the Country of the Young.'

LAUGHING STRANGER

James Stephens

Lir is the most important sea-god in Irish mythology and his name appears in many places—not just in Ireland. Leicester in England, for example, evolved from Llyr-caster, while Shakespeare immortalised him as King Lear. Lir was eventually superseded as ruler of the seas by his handsome son, Manannan, who possessed magical powers to change his appearance and drive his chariot over the waves. He was married to Fand, the 'Pearl of Beauty'. Manannan Mac Lir appears in this next story, by James Stephens (1882–1950) whose book The Crock of Gold *(1912) has been described by Professor James M. Cahalan as 'the first great Irish fantasy novel and perhaps the best of its type'.*

Stephens, a very original and often whimsical writer who played an important role in the re-establishment of the Gaelic language in Eire, was physically a diminutive little man who looked rather like one of the characters from his own stories—a comical leprechaun. His novels based on the old Irish heroic cycles, such as The Crock of Gold, The Demi-Gods *(1914) and* In the Land of Youth *(1924), won him praise from W. B. Yeats, James Joyce and Frank O'Connor who declared he was a genius. These novels, and short stories such as 'Laughing Stranger' which he wrote shortly before his death, illustrate both his knowledge of Irish mythology and the reason why Professor Cahalan has written of him, 'No other Irish novelist outside of Joyce has achieved more in the realms of fantasy and mythology.'*

*   *   *

In the days of long ago and the times that have disappeared for ever, there was one Fiachna Finn the son of Baltan, the son of Murchertach, the son of Muredach, the son of Eogan, the son of Neill. He went from his own country when he was young, for he wished to see the land of Lochlann, and he wished that he would be welcomed by the king of that country, for Fiachna's father and Eolgarg's father had done deeds in common and were obliged to each other. He was welcomed, and he stayed at the Court of Lochlann in great ease and in the midst of pleasures.

It then happened that Eolgarg Mor fell sick and the doctors could not cure him. They sent for other doctors, but they could not cure him, nor could any one say what he was suffering from, beyond that he was wasting visibly before their eyes, and would certainly become a shadow and disappear in air unless he was healed and fattened and made visible.

They sent for more distant doctors, and then for others more distant still, and at last they found a man who claimed that he could make a cure if the king were supplied with the medicine which he would order.

'What medicine is that?' said they all.

'This is the medicine,' said the doctor. 'Find a perfectly white cow with red ears, and boil it down in the lump, and if the king drinks that rendering he will recover.'

Before he had well said it messengers were going from the palace in all directions looking for such a cow. They found lots of cows which were nearly like what they wanted, but it was only by chance that they came on the cow which would do the work, and that beast belonged to the most notorious and malicious and cantankerous female in Lochlann, the Black Hag.

Now the Black Hag was not only those things that have been said; she was whiskered and warty and one-eyed and obstreperous, and she was notorious and ill-favoured in other ways also.

They offered her a cow in the place of her own cow, but she refused to give it. Then they offered a cow for each leg of her cow, but she would not accept that offer unless Fiachna went bail for the payment. He agreed to do so, and they drove the beast away.

On the return journey he was met by messengers who brought news from Ireland. They said that the King of Ulster was dead, and that he, Fiachna Finn, had been elected king in the dead king's place. He at once took ship for Ireland, and found that

all he had been told was true, and he took up the government
of Ulster.

A year passed, and one day as he was sitting at judgment there
came a great noise from without, and this noise was so persistent
that the people and suitors were scandalised, and Fiachna at last
ordered that the noisy person should be brought before him to be
judged. It was done, and to his surprise the person turned out to
be the Black Hag.

She blamed him in the court before his people and complained
that he had taken away her cow, and that she had not been paid
the four cows he had gone bail for, and she demanded judgment
from him and justice.

'If you will consider it to be justice, I will give you twenty cows
myself,' said Fiachna.

'I will not take all the cows in Ulster,' she screamed.

'Pronounce judgment yourself,' said the king, 'and if I can
do what you demand I will do it.' For he did not like to be in
the wrong, and he did not wish that any person should have an
unsatisfied claim upon him.

The Black Hag then pronounced judgment, and the king had
to fulfil it.

'I have come,' said she, 'from the east to the west; you must
come from the west to the east and make war for me, and revenge
me on the King of Lochlann.'

Fiachna had to do as she demanded, and, although it was with
a heavy heart, he set out in three days' time for Lochlann, and he
brought with him ten battalions.

He sent messengers before him to Big Eolgarg warning him of
his coming, of his intention, and of the number of troops he was
bringing; and when he landed Eolgarg met him with an equal
force, and they fought together.

In the first battle three hundred of the men of Lochlann were
killed, but in the next battle Eolgarg Mor did not fight fair, for he
let some venomous sheep out of a tent, and these attacked the
men of Ulster and killed nine hundred of them.

So vast was the slaughter made by these sheep and so great the
terror they caused, that no one could stand before them, but by
great good luck there was a wood at hand, and the men of Ulster,
warriors and princes and charioteers, were forced to climb up the

trees, and they roosted among the branches like great birds, while the venomous sheep ranged below, bleating terribly and tearing up the ground.

Fiachna Finn was also sitting in a tree, very high up, and he was disconsolate. 'We are disgraced!' said he.

'It is very lucky,' said the man in the branch below, 'that a sheep cannot climb a tree.'

'We are disgraced for ever!' said the King of Ulster.

'If those sheep learn how to climb, we are undone surely,' said the man below.

'I will go down and fight the sheep,' said Fiachna.

But the others would not let the king go.

'It is not right,' they said, 'that you should fight sheep.'

'Some one must fight them,' said Fiachna Finn, 'but no more of my men shall die until I fight myself; for if I am fated to die, I will die and I cannot escape it, and if it is the sheep's fate to die, then die they will; for there is no man can avoid destiny, and there is no sheep can dodge it either.'

'Praise be to God!' said the warrior that was higher up.

'Amen!' said the man who was higher than he, and the rest of the warriors wished good luck to the king.

He started then to climb down the tree with a heavy heart, but while he hung from the last branch and was about to let go, he noticed a tall warrior walking towards him. The king pulled himself up on the branch again and sat dangle-legged on it to see what the warrior would do.

The stranger was a very tall man, dressed in a green cloak with a silver brooch at the shoulder. He had a golden band about his hair and golden sandals on his feet, and he was laughing heartily at the plight of the men of Ireland.

'It is not nice of you to laugh at us,' said Fiachna Finn.

'Who could help laughing at a king hunkering on a branch and his army roosting around like hens?' said the stranger.

'Nevertheless,' the king replied, 'it would be courteous of you not to laugh at misfortune.'

'We laugh when we can,' commented the stranger, 'and are thankful for the chance.'

'You may come up into the tree,' said Fiachna, 'for I perceive that you are a mannerly person, and I see that some of the venomous sheep are charging in this direction. I would rather protect you,' he continued, 'than see you killed; for,' said he lamentably, 'I am getting down now to fight the sheep.'

'They will not hurt me,' said the stranger.

'Who are you?' the king asked.

'I am Manannan, the son of Lir.'

Fiachna knew then that the stranger could not be hurt.

'What will you give me if I deliver you from the sheep?' asked Manannan.

'I will give you anything you ask, if I have that thing.'

'I ask the rights of your crown and of your household for one day.'

Fiachna's breath was taken away by that request, and he took a little time to compose himself, then he said mildly:

'I will not have one man of Ireland killed if I can save him. All that I have they give me, all that I have I give to them, and if I must give this also, then I will give this, although it would be easier for me to give my life.'

'That is agreed,' said Manannan.

He had something wrapped in a fold of his cloak, and he unwrapped and produced this thing.

It was a dog.

Now if the sheep were venomous, this dog was more venomous still, for it was fearful to look at. In body it was not large, but its head was of a great size, and the mouth that was shaped in that head was able to open like the lid of a pot. It was not teeth that were in that head, but hooks and fangs and prongs. Dreadful was that mouth to look at, terrible to look into, woeful to think about; and from it, or from the broad, loose nose that waggled above it, there came a sound which no word of man could describe, for it was not a snarl, nor was it a howl, although it was both of these.

It was neither a growl nor a grunt, although it was both of these; it was not a yowl nor a groan, although it was both of these: for it was one sound made up of these sounds, and there was in it, too, a whine and a yelp, and a long-drawn snoring noise, and a deep purring noise, and a noise that was like the squeal of a rusty hinge, and there were other noises in it also.

'The gods be praised!' said the man who was in the branch above the king.

'What for this time?' said the king.

'Because that dog cannot climb a tree,' said the man.

And a man on a branch yet above him groaned out, 'Amen!'

'There is nothing to frighten sheep like a dog,' said Manannan, 'and there is nothing to frighten these sheep like this dog.'

He put the dog on the ground then.

'Little dogeen, little treasure,' he said, 'go and kill the sheep.'

And when he said that the dog put an addition and an addendum on to the noise he had been making before, so that the men of Ireland stuck their fingers into their ears and turned the whites of their eyes upwards, and nearly fell off their branches with the fear and the fright which that sound put into them.

It did not take the dog long to do what he had been ordered. He went forward, at first, with a slow waddle, and as the venomous sheep came to meet him in bounces, he then went to meet them in wriggles; so that in a while he went so fast that you could see nothing of him but a head and a wriggle. He dealt with the sheep in this way, a jump and a chop for each, and he never missed his jump and he never missed his chop. When he got his grip he swung round on it as if it was a hinge. The swing began with the chop, and it ended with the bit loose and the sheep giving its last kick. At the end of ten minutes all the sheep were lying on the ground, and the same bit was out of every sheep, and every sheep was dead.

'You can come down now,' said Manannan.

'That dog can't climb a tree,' said the man in the branch above the king warningly.

'Praise be to the gods!' said the man who was above him.

'Amen!' said the warrior who was higher up than that.

And the man in the next tree said: 'Don't move a hand or a foot until the dog chokes himself to death on the dead meat.'

The dog did not eat a bit of the meat. He trotted to his master, and Manannan took him up and wrapped him in his cloak.

'Now you can come down,' said he.

'I wish that dog was dead,' said the king.

But he swung himself out of the tree all the same, for he did not wish to seem frightened before Manannan.

'You can go now and beat the men of Lochlann,' said Manannan. 'You will be King of Lochlann before nightfall.'

'I wouldn't mind that,' said the king.

'It's no threat,' said Manannan.

The son of Lir turned then and went away in the direction of Ireland to take up his one-day rights, and Fiachna continued his battle with the Lochlannachs.

He beat them before nightfall, and by that victory he became King of Lochlann and King of the Saxons and the Britons.

He gave the Black Hag seven castles with their territories, and he gave her one hundred of every sort of cattle that he had captured. She was satisfied.

Then he went back to Ireland, and after he had been there for some time his wife gave birth to a son.

BALOR AND THE WONDER-SMITH

Ella Young

Balor of the Evil Eye was the god of death whose one eye was said to be so malevolent that it could destroy anyone upon whom he gazed. A cunning and utterly ruthless man, he killed all those who threatened his rule—even attempting to slay his own grandson who was rescued and fostered by Manannan Mac Lir—and resisted numerous plots against his own life until his terrible eye was finally put out by a magic stone ball. As he died, 28 warriors who were unfortunate enough to be within sight of the eye also perished. But Balor did not outwit all his adversaries, as Ella Young (1865–1945) recounts in this story featuring another Irish hero, Gubbaun Saor 'The Wondersmith', who also appears in Norse and Teutonic folklore as Wayland the Smith.

Ella Young, who was born in Fenagh, Co.Antrim, was greatly influenced by Standish O'Grady and George William Russell, and embraced the mystical and mythological in much of her poetry and prose. She was associated with the Irish literary revival and the Nationalist movement between 1900 and 1925, after which she emigrated to America and there lectured on Irish literature at the University of California. While still living in Ireland, she toured Clare, Achill Island, Aranmore, the Curruan and many other places to collect at first hand the oral tales of mythology which later inspired her novels and collections like The Coming of Lugh *(1909),* Celtic Wonder Tales *(1910) and* The Weird of Fionvara *(1922). The following adventure of the Gubbaun Saor and his son and their grim encounter with Balor was published in the first issue of* The Dublin Magazine *in August 1923 and has not previously appeared in book form. It is a superb tale, full of the kind of strange mysteries and unimaginable monsters that any contemporary fantasist might envy.*

*   *   *

The oak-wood in the Gap of the Dragon was Summer-heavy: its branches held a murmurous stillness. Sunshine drowsed in it. The road through the Gap was sun-parched. The Son of the Gubbaun sat by the edge of the wood. He was cutting the ogham of a poem on a stave of holly, and he crooned the verse as he worked. Suddenly a strangling blackness clutched him, a breath as of Winter chilled him. The holly stave dropped from his hands. He rose stumblingly.

The road through the Gap was filled with strange creatures: monstrous uncouth animals straddled on it; dwarfs and giants, men that seemed deformed, crowded on it. They were cloaked and hooded. The two that stood nearest to the Son of the Gubbaun had robes that were stiff with gems. Their faces were masked in gold. Their towering headdresses glittered.

'We are come,' cried they, 'from the Court of Balor of the Mighty Blows, King of the Fomor. A fame and a rumour of the Gubbaun Saor, the Wonder-Smith, has come over the Black Waters into the country of Balor: it has stirred the mind of the king. He would have the Gubbaun build him a dun, a bulk, a rooted vastness that will be a weight upon the earth, a piled-up mountainous strength. To you, O Wonder-Smith, our king sends gifts and tokens. He will not stint the reward.'

'You do not speak with the Gubbaun Saor. I am his Son.'

'O Son of the Gubbaun Saor entreat your father for us: of you, too, a rumour has come. Our king be-speaks your countenance and help. Behold the gifts and tokens of Balor!'

Eight slaves blacker than charred wood led forward a pack-bearing beast: a beast to wonder at. He had horns that a bull could not carry: his hide was striped and barred like a tiger's, and a bush of hair, curling in twists, spread on his shoulders. He knelt heavily, and the slaves uncovered a world of riches before the Son of the Gubbaun Saor. They showed him cloths woven of gold and find-ruiny with patterned dragons coiling in their folds; drinking-cups crusted with gems; daggers hilted with narwhale tooth. The Son of the Gubbaun fingered emeralds as big as the egg of a gull and greener than a field of grass. Deep azurecoloured sapphires slipped through his hands; topazes that were rose-red; rubies like blood: stones very great and precious.

'Choose arles and earnest-money from amongst these,' said Balor's messengers, 'and at the Black Waters Balor's folk will await you.'

The Son of the Gubbaun chose a ruby, and a stone in which diver colours were spilt. His mind was tangled in the stones for a moment, and when he lifted up his eyes the road was emptiness. The gorgeous train, the fantastic beasts, the lords that had peacocked it, were gone! The sun was hot on his face.

It was with speed and with promptitude and with a fine energy of running that he set out for the house of the Gubbaun. The Gubbaun himself was on the threshold.

'Wonder-Smith,' cried the Son, 'I have seen a vision though it is not the Eve of Samhain. I have talked with lords from a far country. I have a token for you.'

He showed the precious stones and told what had befallen.

'I have worked for many kings,' said the Gubbaun, 'and was ever the kingliest myself. Balor is a blackener of the earth. He has one eye in the centre of his forehead that can devastate walled cities and blast a country-side. His breath freezes the sea-furrows. Why should I go to the country of Balor?'

'A strange land must Balor's country be,' said the Son, 'a land of chasms and deserts and icy fastnesses: the beasts of it are not like the beasts of the green earth: the skies have desolate lights in them: the lords of it hide their faces. Strange happenings wait for us in Balor's country. Are you not tired of the roads we know? Is not triumph sweet in an alien land? Let us go to the country of Balor I entreat you.'

'Because the green pastures have given you strength and lusti-hood,' said the Gubbaun, 'the desert delights you, and the road that dips under the sky-line entices your feet. But since it is so, let us start for the country of Balor with the rising of the sun tomorrow. There is no end to the hunger of the mind.'

Before the rising of the sun they rose. The Gubbaun took a gift to the Well of the Hazels. He cut a little rod from the Hazel Tree. He bathed his forehead. But the Son, too eager to start, did none of these things: he was choosing a travelling-cloak.

'May every day delight you till I come back bringing a gift from the Fomor!' he cried to Aunya, and ran out.

The Gubbaun Saor followed.

They had not gone far when the Gubbaun said: 'Son, shorten the road for me.'

'Put a shape of running on yourself,' said the Son, 'and your own two feet will shorten it.'

'Is that all the road-wisdom you have?' said the Gubbaun.

'It is,' said the Son.

'We may as well go back,' said the Gubbaun, 'It's little help you would be to me in Balor's country.'

Home they went. The Gubbaun shut himself up with his engines and secret contrivances, but the Son sat down by the hearth, and the Hound laid a head on his knee. The Gubbaun's Son caressed the Hound and he made a little rann for him. He said:

> *Hound*
> *My heart's delight*
> *Moon-white*
> *Sun-bright*
> *Hound from Under-the-Sea*
> *You left a King*
> *To follow me.*

And O Hound, and O Hound,' said the Gubbaun Saor's Son, 'if my wits were as nimble as your feet I wouldn't be sitting here now.'

'The Hound drank at dawn from the Sacred Well,' said Aunya, 'have you returned for a draught?'

'It was a misfortune that brought me back,' said the Son, 'My father bade me to shorten the road for him. I told him to put a shape of running on himself. He would have none of it. And since I am not a winged demon of the storm, or a gray hawk of the cliffs, I could think only of the swiftness that was in our feet. Back we came on every step we had taken.'

'Story-telling,' said Aunya, 'is the shortening of a road.'

'My blessing on the mouth that taught me!' said the Son, 'I have tales to last the life-time of a man; tales of scaly dragons and witches of the marshes; tales of deep whirlpools and piasts and spells of enchantment: with these I will shorten the road tomorrow.'

On the morrow the Son of the Gubbaun rose in the whiteness of dawn. He put a linen robe on his body. He crowned himself with a chaplet of arbutus that had fruit and blossom. Bare-footed he went three times round the Sacred Well, as the sun travels, stepping from East to West. Then he knelt and touched

the waters with his forehead and the palms of his hands. He
said:

> *'Well of the Sacred Hazels*
> *Heart of the Hidden Waters*
> *Well of Wisdom*
> *Be a deep coolness in my mind,*
> *Be hidden strength, O Well, in the hour of adversity,*
> *Show me the truth in the hour of deceit.*
> *Nourisher of the Rocks*
> *Life of Waters*
> *Eye that looks on the Stars*
> *Let there be love between us.'*

Aunya called to him:
'It is time to set out,' she said.
'It is not without advice and without a road-blessing that I am
setting out,' said the Son. 'The Well will give me a road-blessing.
Give me an advice.'
'Whoever you affront where you are going,' said Aunya, 'put
no affront on a woman: for women are the unlockers of secrets,
and a woman's hate hunts like the wolf. This is my counsel and I
add a gift to it.'
She gave him a rod of the hazel.
'It is likely,' she said, 'that this rod will help you!'
She turned to the Gubbaun.
'It is likely,' she said, 'that you have such a rod yourself.'
'It is more than likely,' said the Gubbaun.
They started.
The distance they had gone was not great when the Gubbaun
said:
'Son, shorten the road for me.'
'Story-telling,' said the Son, 'is the shortening of a road!
'The oak-wood in the Gap of the Dragon had the redness of
Spring on its branches. Midyir's queen came from the Sidhe-
Mound, lamenting—'
'Is the tale sorrowful?' asked the Gubbaun.
'It is sorrowful in parts, but the joyful parts are stronger than
the sorrowful parts: and the end is joyful.'
'Continue with it,' said the Gubbaun.

The Son continued. He continued till they came to the Black Waters.

*   *   *

At the edge of the Black Waters two of Balor's lords awaited the Gubbaun and his Son. They were cloaked and hooded and closely masked, yet it seemed to the Son of the Gubbaun that under the hood of one of them there was only half a face, and under the hood of the other the head of some strange animal.

'Salutation,' said the half-faced one, and as he spoke the sea of black waters reared itself in waves. 'Salutation to the Wonder-Smith and his son. I am Hrut of the many shapes, the son of Sruth, the son of Sru, the son of Nar, chief and man of might in the country of Balor—and lo, Balor's boat awaits us!'

Huddling against a stairway that Cyclops might have hewn, a boat lay blackly on the Black Waters. It had neither steersman nor galley-slave, neither sail nor oar. Unmoored it swung blankly like a drowned body cast up by the sea.

Without a word the Gubbaun stepped aboard. The Son followed. The hooded lords took their places. Hrut leaned over the stern. He lifted three handfuls of water and flung them against the sky. He gave a loud, piercing, horrible cry.

At that a sea-demon put his shoulder to the boat. He lifted the sea in a curved black foam-smoking precipice in front of the prow—he left it a gaping hollow behind! Short was their crossing.

Harsh was their welcome in Balor's country. A hard bleak desolate wilderness Balor's country was. The sun never lifted his forehead on it. The moon never showed herself. Every blade of grass in Balor's country was like a knife with a drop of venom on the point of it. The jagged stones were scimitar-edged.

'Will it please you, Wonder-Smith, to walk or ride?' asked Hrut.

'To ride,' said the Gubbaun.

Hrut gave a keen piercing cry.

Down THEY swooped out of the air; horribly toothed and clawed, with wings that made a storm about them. Fire came from their nostrils. They bit and clawed one another.

'Will you ride, Wonder-Smith?' asked Hrut.

'I will ride,' said the Gubbaun, 'put bridles on them.'

They put bridles on the biggest one for the Gubbaun, and on the second biggest one for the Son.

'Have you rods,' said the Gubbaun, 'to encourage them, or to chastise them?'

'They encourage themselves,' said Hrut, 'No rider has chastised them. Hold fast. As for us we will trust to our feet.'

The Gubbaun took a master-grip. The son copied him. They rose in the air.

'Oh!' cried the Son, 'it is nothing I have under me but a slanting icy wind, and that is thinning and spreading away—I am falling!'

'Give your fine steed the rod,' said the Gubbaun, 'the Hazel rod!'

The Son of the Gubbaun Saor drew a blow on the wind, and with that the scaly-writhing, fire-breathing, feathered monster took shape under him again. It was so till they struck the fastness of Balor.

Balor's devastating eye was close shut. Hugely the eye-lid weighed upon it, fleshy and sullen. Runes and spells and charms and incantations were on that lid to keep it shut. Balor's face was a blankness. His voice whipped the ears like sleet.

'Build me a dun,' he said, 'strong as the foundations of the earth; a dun with courts and passages and secret chambers; with carvings on the walls of it and carved monsters in the crevices of it; a dun that climbs and blossoms in spires and twists and flame-like billowing curves and fantasies; such a dun as never from the beginning of days shaped itself on the ridge of the world. Gold ye shall have in plenty, and rich jewels and cloaks of honour. Ye shall stagger under the load of your riches. I, Balor, have said it.'

'Such a dun,' said the Gubbaun, 'I can rear.'

The Gubbaun and his Son set to work. They had djinns, and dwarfs, and giants, and goat-footed men, and demons of the air, and fabulous animals, and monstrous beings, and strange beasts to help them. The dun took shape, it grew. There was great delight on the Son of the Gubbaun. He wished with all his heart for a reed flute, but Balor's country was bare of reeds. At length he fashioned a flute of metal, and as he played on it in an idle hour a woman of the Fomor drew close to him. She was poor. She had known hardship. Wrapped in her mantle she held a young child. It was a little while before she spoke. She said:

'For my little son I pray your good will with the music you make. There is a wasting sickness on him and he has no delight in life.'

'I will make a music of delight for him,' said the Gubbaun's Son. The child put his mother's cloak away from him and peered out. His face was dusky; he had prick ears like a faun; his hair was a black tangled bush standing up on his head; his eyes were golden-yellow and very bright like the eyes a goat has. His eyes pleased the Son of the Gubbaun Saor.

'I will play strength and joy,' he said.

Every day after that the Son of the Gubbaun made music for the Fomor woman and her child. He played away the sickness. He played till the child laughed and danced and tumbled over himself with delight. One day the woman was troubled.

'You have given life and delight to my child,' she said. 'Today he can repay you. My son has one gift from his birth—he can hear the stir of a bird's wing at the other end of the world! No walls can shut a whisper from him: and he has heard a whisper about you. Balor will put you and your father to death when ye have made an end of building the dun, lest a dun the like of it be reared for another. Take counsel therefore with what wisdom is in you and go unharmed from this country.'

The Son of the Gubbaun took that news to his father.

'I must think,' said the Gubbaun, and he sat down.

The djinns sat down. The goat-footed ones sat down. The fabulous animals stretched themselves and licked their paws. There was a marvellous, munificent, soul-gratifying cessation of labour.

Balor's voice split the stillness.

'Let the Gubbaun come before me,' he cried.

The Gubbaun came.

'The work has stopped;' roared Balor. 'Wherefore?'

'The work has stopped,' said the Gubbaun, 'because I am short of a tool that is lying under seven locks in my treasure-chest at home.'

'Give the tokens and signs of that tool,' said Balor, 'my swiftest messenger shall speed for it!'

'I trust no hand but my own on the tools of my trade.'

'Trust your own hand: my messenger shall bring the treasure-chest.'

'The chest is bedded with the foundations of the house: it cannot be moved!'

'If the house holds to the chest,' said Balor, 'my messenger will haul it hither as a net hauls the dog-fish with the salmon.'

He called to one of his most powerful djinns.

'Go,' he said, 'and bring the treasure-chest of the Wonder-Smith hither, though you should bring the ribs of the earth with it!'

'Live for ever, Magnificence,' said the djinn, and was gone.

'He will not come back,' said the Gubbaun Saor.

Balor writhed his lips in a scornful smile.

*   *   *

Cloaked in gold and vermilion, the sun was stepping into the western sea. The fragrant, amber-coloured air had stillness that was more than music. Aunya stood by the door of the Gubbaun's house. There was stillness and beauty in her face. She watched the sunset. Close to the threshold-stone a furry caterpillar clambered, picking his steps with solemnity and precision. He was a hairy-oubit to delight the heart; his skin like powdered velvet, his hair-tufts carmined and dusted with silver. His head, like an ebon mirror, gave back the sun light. Suddenly a murk of blackness caught the sky, a myriad-plumed gigantic world-engulphing blackness; a rushing, roaring, multitudinous tumult that whirled and spun upon itself; a pre-Cimmerian Cyclopian Centaurian blackness that neared in leaps and bounds and contortions and cataclysms.

Quick as thought Aunya put a shape of magic power on herself. She made herself a spear-point of light against that blackness. The blackness split on it and passed on either side of the house.'

'Messenger of Balor,' said Aunya, 'you have overshot the goal!'

The djinn was angered. He turned: he made himself a raging fire, a tongue of flame against Aunya. He writhed and licked devouringly.

Aunya raised herself in a thunderous-sounding, green, over-toppling wave of the sea.

Hiss-s-s-rt!!! The fire was quenched.

The djinn shook himself clear. He rose up, an icy scimitar-edged relentless-smiting wind of the desert. He smote the smoking sea-wave, he ripped it to shreds of foam: he flung himself flat-edged upon it: he leaned his weight in the thrust of an avalanche: his strokes were hammer-blows, his strokes were lightning-flashes. He howled outrageously, he tied himself into knots. Aunya made herself a drop of water and slid into the earth. The djinn collected himself and drew breath a moment— the wave had gone, no wetness of it glittered!

'Victory,' shouted the djinn. 'A great and utter destruction! I have been too strong.'

Laughter set his ears on edge. Aunya had taken her own shape again and was standing just out of hand-grip.

The djinn made himself an enormous, death-dealing, sickle-clawed, sabre-toothed, tigerish atrocity, and sprang for her! As he leaped, Aunya became a hawk crested with red gold and feathered with white silver. She hung motionless out of reach. She fluttered about his head, moth-like: moth-like she slid between his frantic paws: her talons gripped his shoulder: she buffetted him: she tweaked his tail: she pinched his ears: she tickled his nose: she was on both sides of him: she was above him, and below him, and beyond him, all at once. She was everywhere and nowhere.

At last the great beast rolled exhausted, with the foam of fruitless endeavour clogging and bitter in his mouth.

'Victory leans towards me,' said Aunya.

'Nay,' said the djinn, 'we are too evenly matched to contend thus. We waste time. Let us show each to the other in rivalry what power we are masters of. My power will out-bid yours.'

'So be it,' said Aunya; '*Wit is nimble-footed!*'

'*Cunning is more deep-rooted,*' said the djinn.

'*More to a thick skull suited,*' said Aunya.

'*Strength gives to wit the lie,*' said the djinn.

'*Only while strength is by,*' said Aunya.

'*Strength's claws are sharp and crooked,*' said the djinn.

'*But wit has wings to fly,*' said Aunya.

'Let's leave this rhyming,' said the djinn. 'It is fit only for women. Show me a wonder-feat.'

'I think,' said Aunya, 'that tree-splitting would delight you.'

'It would,' said the djinn.

Close to them was a giant yew-tree. It was older than the oldest ancestor of the eagle: old as the roots of the earth. A tough-knit, mighty-girthed, many-twisted trunk that tree had. Aunya struck it lightly with her hand. The yew-tree split from top to bottom: the redness at its heart was like the redness in a cleft pomegranate.

'Make the tree whole, O djinn,' said Aunya.

'I am a Force of Destruction and Ravage,' said the djinn; 'make it whole yourself'!

Aunya put her hand on the wound—the tree was whole as before.

'Split the tree,' said Aunya.

The djinn bent himself to the work. He made himself a flash of lightning—and slid through the leaves of the tree! He made himself a devastating whirlwind—and drew a singing note from the tree! He made himself a toothed weapon—he blunted, he shivered himself—and there was not a scratch on the tree!

'Does it out-task you, Son of Destruction?' asked Aunya.

'I could split a small branch,' said the djinn, 'if I tried!'

'You have not enough strength,' said Aunya, 'to hold two branches apart if you perched in a fork of the tree to get your breath again!'

The djinn made a leap for the tree and sat himself in a fork of it.

'Close! branches,' said Aunya.

They closed, and nipped the djinn: tighter and tighter they nipped him.

'My grief and my destruction,' cried the djinn: 'I am lost. Take victory, Aunya, and let me out.'

'I will give you room to sit at your ease,' said Aunya, 'but no more. Sit there till the Gubbaun Saor and his Son come home. When their feet cross the house-threshold I will give you freedom: and more than that, the length of your ears in two gold earrings for luck.'

'A swift home-coming to the Gubbaun Saor and his Son!' said the djinn:

'May the earth hasten their footsteps,
May water smooth the paths for them,
May the wind hustle them forward.'

'My own wish,' said Aunya: 'Sit there: you will see the sunrise: you will see the young crescent moon: you will see the greenness of grass.'

She left him.

'I'll put ears on me a mile long,' said the djinn to himself as he braced his shoulders in the fork of the bough, and took deliberately and with care the position of greatest ease.

*   *   *

Balor's country awaited the return of the djinn. The hours and days went by. A fury of expectancy wasted Balor. The Gubbaun Saor was calm.

''Twould be well for myself and my son to lose no more time,' said he; 'it would be well for us to set out now, for the bringing back of the tool.'

'My dignity would be lessened,' said Balor, 'if the compulsion of that errand were on you. I will send an embassy: like a conquering potentate, like a royal personage, that Tool shall enter my dominions!'

'To your son alone,' said the Gubbaun Saor, 'will I give the tokens of my wonder-tool: with him shall go the chief Vizier of your kingdom.'

'So be it,' said Balor; 'I will send my son: Powers and Principalities shall accompany him.'

The Gubbaun Saor gave the master-word to Balor's son.'

'The name of the tool is:

Cam 1.n-ᴀᵹᴀıᵹ ᴀn Cᴀım, coʀ 1 n-ᴀᵹᴀıᵹ ᴀn Cuıʀ, ᴀᵹus coʀ 1 n-ᴀᵹᴀıᵹ ᵹᴀnᵹᴀıᵹe.'

Balor's son said it over, nine times, to himself. He was satisfied then that he had it. He called for his robes of embassy, he marshalled the Powers and Principalities: he arranged their ranks for the White Unicorns and the Kyelins with tufted ears: he saw that the Green Dragons and the Scarlet and Purple Chimaeras were linked with chains of silver. Boastful were his words to the Fomorian Lords: 'Candles of Valour,' he said, 'do not grudge your transcendency to a country ignorant of Balor. Ye shall cast lustre upon it.'

With an earth-shaking sound of trumpets that ranked magnificence set forth.

Day rounded day till its return. Its return was an amazement. A sound of ullagoning went before it.

> *'Wye-hoo! Wye-hoo! Wye-hoo!*
> *Bal-a-loo! Bal-a-loo!*
> *Ai! Ai! Ai!*
> *Ul-a-loo! Ul-a-loo!*
> *Ul-a-loo!*
> *Kye-u-belick!'*

Wayside folk, hearing that lamentation, hastened to prostrate themselves and to cover their faces lest they might see how great lords of the Fomor beat their breasts and tore their hair, casting dust on their foreheads. Like a slow wounded snake the procession dragged itself onward.

> '*Wye-hoo! Wye-hoo! Wye-hoo!*
> *Bal-a-loo! Bal-a-loo!*'

That lamentation filled the courts of Balor. Laggard footsteps followed it. Balor's hand groped spearwards. He could not see the grief-dishevelled lords or the anguished abandonment of their prostrations. He dared not open that solitary terrible eye!

'Speak!' he thundered.

The Most Distinguished Personage in that distinguished train raised a dust-grimed head.

'O Balor, O Lord of Life,' he began, 'have pity on us! Misfortune has overwhelmed us: grief eats and gnaws upon us. Your Son, the Light of our Countenances, is in captivity: and the great Vizier likewise. Say the word, O Magnificence, that will rescue them from strait and bitter bondage, and from the terrible country of Ireland—a country where the mind is bewildered: a country where the eyes find no rest: for the earth is a glittering emerald and the sky a blinding sapphire, the sun is a scorching fire and the moon a blistering whiteness. A country where there is no solace for the heart'!

'Cease your lamentations,' said Balor,' 'and tell what has befallen.'

'We came,' O Dispenser of Fate, 'to the house of the Gubbaun. The woman of the house received us. The most illustrious and splendid Prince, your Son, recited to her the tokens of the Tool:

> Cam i n-aᵹaiᵭ an caim,
> Cor i n-aᵹaiᵭ an cuir,
> aᵹus
> Cor i n-aᵹaiᵭ an ᵹanᵹaiᵭe.

'True is the token,' said the woman of the house; 'I will unbar the treasury for you and the seven locks of the treasure-chest. Enter, Son of Balor; enter, Vizier of Balor.'

They entered, but they came not forth. The woman came forth. 'Go hence,' she said, 'and tell your king that in the treasure-chest of the Gubbaun his son is shut—a grip that will not loosen! With him is the Vizier, fastened down with seven locks. There they will measure time by the heart-beat and the shadow and fraction of a heart-beat till the Gubbaun Saor and his Son cross the threshold-stone of this house: whole and sound as they set out from it.'

'O Balor, O Mountain of Munificence, say the word. Let the Gubbaun Saor and his Son go for their Tool!'

The Most Distinguished Personage prostrated himself afresh.

'*Wye-hoo! Wye-hoo! Wye-hoo!*' sobbed the Unicorns and Chimaeras.

'Balor,' said the Gubbaun, 'the lid of my treasure-chest is heavy, the sides of it are straight and narrow. Let me and my son go for the tool.'

Balor made a frantic gesture with his hands. 'Go!' he cried.

Lords of the Fomor ushered forth the Gubbaun and his Son. Carefully they ushered them, like folk who guard a treasure, yet with an urgency of speed. Soon they stood on the terraced height of Balor's fortress. A sky pale as an ice-field was above their heads: a thousand fathoms below, a river pooled itself blackly. About them towered a wilderness of mountain-peaks; peaks, one-footed, craning upward, blind and insatiable; peaks like contorted monsters, inscrutable; peaks like a gigantic menace, dizzied to the fantasy of a nightmare—arid and hostile.

'Bring steeds for us'! said the Gubbaun.

Hrut, the son of Sruth, the son of Sru, the son of Nar, stepped forward. He flung his voice into the air in a shrill ringing cry—like colour spilt on ice it shivered on those monstrous pinnacles. The sky blackened. The air swirled and eddied to an impact.

Biting, clawing, tangled together, THEY descended.

'Bridle them!' said the Gubbaun.

Lords of the Fomor put bridles on them.

'Health and Prosperity be with you'! said the Gubbaun, his hand on a bridled neck.

'Health and Prosperity!' said the Son.

THEY rose, shaking storm from their wings, cavorting and hurtling, plunging and rearing through the steeps of air.

'Snails!' cried the Gubbaun, 'have ye no swiftness?'

It was thus that the Gubbaun Soar and his Son returned to Ireland.

*   *   *

When the Gubbaun Saor and his Son set foot again in Ireland the earth was glad at their coming: a Wave in the North reared itself and fell with a sound of clangorous bells and loud-voiced trumpets: a Wave in the East reared itself and fell with a sound of clashing cymbals and shrill-voiced flutes: a Wave in the South reared itself and fell with a sound of sweet singing voices, mingling with and over-mastering the sound of timpaun and cruit and bell-branch: and all along the islands of the West and the rocky inlets went a singing reedy whisper *'Mananaun! Mananaun'!*

The rhythm of that welcoming music was a pulse of joy in the flowering grasses: the strong oaks knew it: the white bulls of the forest moved to it, tossing their moon-curved horns: it set the sea-hawks sliding down the wind, stooping in circles: it was a hand-clapping and a shout of laughter in the mountain torrents.

'A noble land and good is Ireland,' said the Gubbaun, 'my thousand blessings on it!'

Aunya made a great Feast of Welcome for them. From the four corners of the world folk came to that Feast: some that had praise-mouthed names and a proud lineage, and some that had a virtue in them of such a strange and subtle essence that it escaped a clamorous recognition. Harpers came, and sweet-voiced women, and men of learning. Kings' sons came to it riding upon white stallions with their manes and tails dyed purple, bells and apples of gold on their bridle reins: the workers in brass and copper the proud makers of beautiful things came to it, and simple poor folk came with good-will in their hearts. The Chief-Poet of Ireland came, with thirty princes in his train, a slender dark-visaged man, his hair wound upon and bound with twists of gold, his singing-robe on his shoulders that only the Chief-Poet might wear: curiously wrought it was of the feathers of bright-coloured birds. There was a king from the North, blue-eyed and huge of limb, he that was lord of dragon-prowed ships: there was a queen from the South, a woman that had many lovers. She had a pale radiant face and eyes the colour of the sky when twilight purples it—she was everywhere the one Rose of Delight. And from the Faery Hills there came three Cup-Bearers so beautiful it was a heart-ache to look upon them for they had unwithering youth beautiful as light dancing on the sea-waves—beautiful as the apple-bough beyond our reach!

The Sheeoga came, the Little People, the Small Folk of the Mountains, they who put mortals astray, for a jest, covering the pathways: or crowd upon them like comrades, running before and behind, and on either side, most joyous of helpers, to show the gaps and pick safe footing through the quagmires—mindful of freshly-querned meal set in beechen bowls for them and porringers of sweet milk. They came in their multitudes and their multitudes, they joined hands and danced round the house, laughing. Aunya sent them out a silver cup brimmed with mead: as quickly as it was emptied it filled again. They never gave it back and it is likely that even to this day it is stravaguing the world in their company.

Within the Gubbaun's house the candles of a king's feast were lighted. The djinn was there—he had measured the length of his ears by the height of the door-lintel. The Great Vizier was there, uncobwebbed of the treasure-chest. Balor's Son was there, splendid in his robes of embassy. The Hound Failinis was there, and a Phoenix-Bird that came out of Tir-nan-oge.

The feast began: it went from lavishness to lavishness, it was jewelled with strangeness as a daggerhilt is crusted with gems. Towards the close the Gubbaun raised a great Cup of crystal in his hands. The wine in it shone like a ruby: it was wine from Moy-Mell.

'Drink!' he cried, 'Let each one drink to the measure of his thirst: the Cup is a well of plenty, it renews itself.'

The Cup went from guest to guest, and each one that held that Marvel in his hands drank to the thing he desired to honour. When the Cup came to Balor's Son he rose up and said:

'*To Balor the Munificent, and to the noble dun that is a-building!*'

The Cup flew into a thousand splinters. The wine ran down like blood.

'Dragon of Death!' cried Balor's Son, 'what evil omen is this?'

'The venom of untruth has shattered the Cup,' said the Gubbaun, 'Balor's munificence was treachery. But not for this thing shall the Cup be destroyed.' He gathered the fragments in his hand. 'Let truth make it whole:

'Balor plotted my death and the death of my Son when the dun was finished.'

The Cup became whole in the Gubbaun's hand.

'But,' said Balor's Son, 'in the presence of the lords and chiefs of the Fomor you named the Tool: you gave the Master-Word.'

'I named my Tool,' said the Gubbaun.

> 'The Crooked—against crookedness.
> The Twist—against a twist:
> and
> The Twist—against treachery:

That tool I needed: that tool my hands can handle now. *I drink to the time when Balor will know that gods are not jealous of godhead!'*

The Gubbaun drank till not a drop remained in the Cup.

'Tell Balor,' he said, 'that the envious heart drips poison on its own wounds, but munificence begets munificence. His mind imagined a palace: let him build it—he has the multitudinous centuries for leisure! But this one night is ours for joy and song. Let music sound, and let the jugglers now toss up the glittering balls.'

Tulkinna the Peerless One stepped forward. He had nine golden apples and nine feathers of white silver and nine discs of findruiney. He tossed them up. They leaped like a plume of sea-spray: they shone like wind-stirred flame: they whirled like leaves rising and falling. He wove them into patterns. He made them whirl like motes of dust. They danced like gauze-winged flies on a summer's eve. They tangled the mind in a web of light and darkness till at last it seemed that Tulkinna was tossing the stars.

Then came a burst of light-hearted music.

The djinn danced with the Phoenix-bird.

Aunya danced with Balor's Son.

The Chief Vizier danced with a woman out of Tir-nan-oge.

The Gubbaun Saor's Son danced with the queen from the South.

The sun and moon the stars and constellations danced to the measure of that dancing. The memory of it was honey in the mind of poets for a thousand years: it was riotous heady mead, it was wine in the veins of warriors for a thousand years, and to this hour it is laughter in the heart of the hills.

THE DEATH OF MACHA GOLD-HAIR

Dermot O'Byrne

Among the goddesses of Irish mythology there are few more terrible than Macha, who is said to personify battle and slaughter. She is one of the goddesses of war and is believed to hover over warriors, inspiring them with battle madness and urging them to cut off the heads of fallen enemies. These decapitated heads are known as 'Macha's acorn crop'. There are several versions of Macha's death, including one in which she was slain by Balor of the Evil Eye, but the version here by Dermot O'Byrne (1883–1953) may be rather closer to the truth.

Behind the small collection of books bearing the name 'Dermot O'Byrne', which were published in Ireland during the first quarter of this century, was the composer Sir Arnold Edward Trevor Bax (1883–1953) who was to become much better known as Master of the King's Music, a post which he held from 1942 to 1952, and then briefly under the present Queen until his death in 1953. Sir Arnold, who was knighted in 1937, although primarily a musician and composer, nursed a life-long interest in the mythology of Ireland which he used as the basis for his pseudonymous stories, writing under the family name of one of his Dublin friends. Strangely, he made no secret of this preoccupation in his entry in Who's Who, *listing his favourite recreation as 'a special interest in every aspect of Celtic life and history'. Among his musical compositions were* A Celtic Song-Cycle, St Patrick's Breast-Plate *and* In the Fairy Hills. *As 'Dermot O'Byrne' he published* A Ballad of Dublin and Other Poems *(1913),* Children of the Hills: Tales and Sketches of Western Ireland in the Old Times and the Present Day *(1915) and* Wrack and Other Stories *(1918). On the evidence of these books and 'The Death of Macha Gold-Hair' which was originally published in* The Irish Review *in 1917, Sir Arnold deserves recognition as a notable Irish fantasy writer.*

*   *   *

The harper Airbreach sat at Queen Macha's feet. He loved her and had been loved by her, but during this night of the great Beltaine feast his spirit was heavy within him. Occasionally he writhed impatiently on the low dragon-carved stool upon which he sat, and glanced up angrily and passionately into the lovely and mask-like face of the queen. Yet never once had she even looked at him. Perfectly motionless she sat on the great high-seat, whose cunning and beautiful fashioning was almost entirely hidden by the quantity of wolf- and deer-skins heaped about it that the fair body of the queen might recline in comfort during the feast.

Following a custom first ordained by herself, the harpers were ranged before the high-seat in the form of a half moon, for Macha liked to be girdled with music at all times. The ancient Muirteach, who crouched on his stool figured with grotesque fish and dragon-shapes immediately before the queen, had composed a rann:

'*As the foamy swift-footed milk-crested wave of the south*
Calls to the pleasant shores of smooth-sanded Eire
The desirous sweet-lipped surf of our singing
Is raining about the star-woman, the queen Macha of gracious
     words.'

This tribute had so greatly pleased the queen, that as a mark of her special favour she had bestowed upon the old bard a magnificent golden torque that was wont to circle her throat, and with her own hands had fastened it still glowing with the warmth of her sweet flesh about the neck of the aged minstrel. All the other bards had become inflamed with jealousy, and not content with criticising with rancour the technical merits of the rann, had made several attempts secretly to poison its author, though as yet without success.

From where Macha was seated she could see with ease every corner of the great dun. Though it was fashioned externally of clay and wattles rudely enough, the interior was, after the fashion of the time, not wanting in beauty and even splendour. New rushes had been strewn upon the floor and the damp walls were overhung with sumptuous skins and even in places with tapestries, many of which were already rotted and mildewed with the sticky ooze of the soaked clay beneath them.

The dun was lit with blazing rushes twisted tightly into a kind of plait, dipped in the fat of animals, and mounted in fantastically carven metal braziers. They burned badly, giving forth a very evil smell, and as they were continually going out with much hissing and sputtering several attendants had been set apart for the sole purpose of trimming and relighting them. The hour was late and the feasting was over long since, but still the flagons of mead passed precariously from hand to hand. Most of the 'ceanns' and nobles and many of the women were drunk and the floor was strewn with the inert bodies of warriors, ollavs, genealogists, amazons and maidens mingled almost indistinguishably, some rolling feebly alone among the soiled rushes, whilst others lay dully folded in one another's embraces, their heavy listless arms tightly interlaced, often as it seemed almost unconsciously.

The captain of the guard lay on his back in the middle of the floor, his glazed eyes staring without expression at the damp and oozing roof, and his right arm vaguely waving above him his drinking-cup, skilfully hammered out of the bleached skull of one of his foes. He mumbled quarrelsomely of his own exploits, whilst the paint and sweat dripped off his face into the rushes of the floor.

But the bards circled about the feet of the queen were sober to a man, not from inclination, but because they knew well that a false chord or a forgotten word meant instant death. All through the night they had sung almost unceasingly, but the queen was in very ill humour, and they were disheartened and ill-at-ease. Airbreach, close to Queen Macha's impatiently-tapping sandalled foot, glanced up again into her staring unfathomable face. The air in the dun was stifling, filled with the heavy odour of human bodies and the fumes of mead and wine.

Airbreach felt very dizzy, and he was not sure what thing might happen in the next moment. He drew a deep breath, and with that inhalation seemed to suck into his being a wandering flame that instantly set light to some primitive fury smouldering in the depths of his spirit. He shuddered slightly, and making a convulsive movement with his whole body leapt to his feet. His face was very pale, yet a red spot burned in the centre of each cheek. Tossing the long black hair out of his eyes, he smote several loud sour chords from his harp, and unheeding the fact that two of the strings had snapped beneath his fierce fingers sang:

'Woe to the sweet-tongued bard
And the hero skilled in combat,
He to be putting faith in the smiles of women,
And the honey talk of a high queen;

His soul to be trapped in the snare of desire,
In foolish and profitless things,
The poisonous net of her hair
And the pale mists of her flesh.

If I saw the hawks of the machair,
The fierce broad-winged eagles of western Sliabh Sneachta,
And I after gazing at the haughty queen,
My heart tormented in the bitter heat of the night,
I would say that those were gentle things.

I cry to the gerfalcons of the Red Gap,
The grey-backed very swift swallows of Dooish of the winds,
That they traverse the six roads of green Fodhla
And circle the winds with their strong flight,
My words scorching their tongues
Till they shower them over the world.

The wounds in my middle cry to you,
O wild birds, and this my message,
Macha, the comely queen
Of the glens of western Uladh,
The white-shouldered woman of Tír Conaill,
Is without gentleness, without honour,
Without warmth, without affection,
Without love of poet's words
And the roaring of the harps,
An empty flagon, a hollow reed,
A blasted birch-tree, a false string,
Blown foam on the shifting sands,

A whirl of dust on the dry roads of the world,
Vain as all vain things,
Vain with the vanity of women.'

Throwing the harp to the floor, Airbreach burst into a roar of bitter mocking laughter and stood before the queen, his breast heaving and his body swaying as though he were drunk.

When she had first understood the meaning of the the harper's song, Macha's face had flushed violently, but now she was very pale. She bit her lip, and her eyes seemed to search some icy distance. Then she smiled slightly. There were those in the dun who trembled seeing that smile.

'Cut out his tongue,' said Macha simply, and she smiled again, and then sat very still, though her bosom rose and fell like a stormy sea.

The kernes rushed upon the harper, and after binding him, seized his long dark hair and wrenched back his head. Then they battered on his mouth with the butt-end of a short spear until the teeth were driven in, and one of them drawing forth his sgian hacked out the tongue.

Macha sighed. 'Bring it to me,' she said. They laid the tongue on a silver dish and placed it before the queen. She looked at it curiously for a moment, and then a wave of fury appeared to flood her whole body. She trembled violently and her cheeks became more red than the wine-stains upon the rushes of the floor. Drawing a golden pin from her hair, many times with its delicate point she stabbed the tongue, about which the blood was already beginning to congeal. Then she rose to her feet, her chin thrust out, and her face lime-white even to the lips. She swept over the floor, the rushes hissing beneath her long scarlet robe, to the edges of which some of them clung. Laughing low and derisively, she stood before the harper.

'Airbreach, Airbreach,' she said softly, 'where now will you be finding any white woman to kiss those lips that a thousand windless nights among the dewy hills have lied so sweetly that the stars and the lake-waters have listened to thee even as thy love has listened? Between what fragrant breasts shall thy mouth that was beloved of queens whisper its music now in the secret corners of the house when lights are overturned?'

And she pointed her white forefinger, the nail dyed with a costly red spice, at the battered swollen bleeding thing that had once been the mouth of a great poet.

'Sing to me, Airbreach, my poet of the golden voice,' she went on with false tenderness, 'Sing to me one of thy songs that are more sweet than the music of the nightingales of Coillsheogue, and more heady than the red mead the rivers pour among the flowers of Magh Mell, the pleasant plain. Sing to me "The Waving of the Corn," with which men say the hearts of the proudest women are melted, as the snows of Errigal are melted in a single night by the warm honey-breath of golden-eyed Bel.' The eyes of the harper rolled expressionlessly in his bloodstained and contorted face. Even in his agony the queen seemed to hold him fascinated, as some lovely and evil she-snake fascinates her prey.

'Sing! sing! sing!' cooed Macha, relentlessly, 'I thirst for thy songs as a hero thirsts for battle, as the weary for sleep, as the night for the dawn.' She leaned forward, her eyes close to his staring and strained eyes, and suddenly she stamped her foot in simulated wrath.

'Thou wilt not sing,' she screamed savagely, and her eyes blazed. 'Cowherd! Mule! Clod! Ha, ha, ha! thou hast made very sweet music in thy day upon yonder harp, now shall thy harp make music upon thee!'

She made a sign to the chief of the kernes, pointing at the harp which lay among the tossed and trampled rushes, most of its strings already hanging tattered over the edges of the frame. But before any of them could make a movement an exulting cry rang out and from the listless and stupefied throng a woman leapt with the activity of a wild cat, trampling heedlessly on bare faces and arms in the fury of her wild rush. She was of abnormal height and clad in a single skin garment. Her muscular tanned legs were bare, and her thick black hair hung in matted dishevelled clusters over her eyes. Between her left eye and the corner of her mouth a long livid scar stretched, and the slipping aside of her loosely folded garment revealed the fact that her right breast had been burnt off according to the usual custom of warrior women, a practice which allowed the spear-arm greater freedom of action. Thrusting aside the blear-eyed staggering warriors, she snatched up the heavy clairseach with a sweeping movement of the arm as she ran.

The pain-clouded eyes of the doomed harper regarded her with a kind of dull surprise. For a moment she stood looking through her tangled hair into those eyes. Then she shook herself like some wild animal, and with a scream swung the clairseach above her like a battle-axe. As it fell one of the drunken women lying upon the floor cried out in terror and began to whimper, but the blows still continued to rain down. With the heavy embossed frame of the harp the amazon battered Airbreach's head until the bones of the skull were crushed and the blood spurted out upon the rushes. She laughed, feeling the hot dark drops dripping from the harp upon her hands and bare arms. And she chanted this rann:

> 'Aïa, Aïa, O—ro!
> Long shall the day be remembered
> In the dun of Cliath-na-Righ,
> In the goodly wide-spreading feast-house
> Of Macha of haughty eyebrows.
> Long shall this day be remembered,
> The night of the Bleeding of the Harp,
> The harp of Airbreach Honey-mouth
> Whose singing was a sword-edge,
> A moonlit drift of blossom,
> A wave on the shores of the heart.
> Long shall the day be remembered
> In the grianans of western Tír-Conaill,
> The day when the strings that were wont
> To stream with songs of passion
> Sweated with blood and death.'

When she had finished this chanting she dropped the harp and fell swooning as it seemed across the dead body of the poet, her face pressed into his breast.

Macha had regarded the scene with startled eyes that for the moment under the sway of astonishment appeared almost innocent and childlike, but the sudden silence which followed the amazon's chant broke the spell. The queen turned her head away contemptuously with a short laugh that seemed wrung from her throat almost involuntarily. There was a moment of silence, and then a strange sadness passed over the queen's face as a cloud floats across the hard blue midday sky. She stared abstractedly at the aged Muirteach's head, bent in some grievous reflection, his long silver hair falling forward among the strings of the *cruit* that rested on his knees. 'The waving of the corn!' she murmured slowly into the depths of her shining hair. She started with a gesture of irritation. 'I am weary,' she said fretfully, 'lead me to the grianan. I will that only women sleep with me tonight. I tire of men and their foolishness.'

The women led her down the length of the dun, the proud feet of the queen stepping delicately as those of a hind among the rushes stained with blood and wine. Her beautiful head, poised with marvellous grace on her white shoulders, was motionless, her eyes stared forward without expression. Already she seemed to have forgotten the tumultuous happenings of the evening. As she moved the little golden balls suspended to the ends of the four twisted plaits in which her yellow hair was dressed swayed languidly and rhythmically upon her graceful back, and the amethyst brooch that fastened the scarlet embroidered robe glittered now and again with unearthly and disturbing hues as the flickering gleam of the rush-lights fell momentarily upon it.

For a long time a profound silence had reigned in the dun. Then there was a very faint rustling somewhere among the rushes followed by a soft swift pattering sound. A rat ran across the skins on the floor and leaping upon the daïs began to gnaw one of the carven legs of the high-seat. Another half-hour passed, and then a pale shaft of moonlight stole through the single small opening that served the great dun as door and window. It moved slowly to the right, revealing for a moment perhaps the flushed face and swollen eyes of some sleeping reveller. It seemed to be searching for something, timidly, tenderly, as some fragile woman searches a star-lit battle-field for the body of her love. It swayed forward slowly and obliquely, every moment becoming more and more narrow, until finally, slender as the shaft of a spear, it fell upon the body of the dead Airbreach, on the blood, stiff, dark, and clotted about the wrecked milk-white face, on the obscure living shape stretched upon that lifeless shape, and the heavy hair spread about the pale breast like a thundercloud. The moonlight seemed to cling to those two for a moment and then stole softly away, leaving the dun in unfathomable darkness.

Towards morning Macha the queen awoke with a start, the grianan was strangely hot and she felt an unusual and painful sensation at her throat, as though wires were being twisted about it and were gradually biting into her flesh. She became furiously angry. With one hand she groped for the knife that was always her bedfellow in the darkness, whilst with the other she clutched her soft neck, but under her trembling fingers she felt nothing but the smooth firm flesh.

She opened her eyes, closed them again in terror, opened them once more. A heavy red glare smote upon them, and something smelling acrid and sour wreathed about her, flooding the glare in dense swelling clouds. Fire and smoke! She tried to scream, but those wires about her throat strangled the sound. She lifted herself upon her elbow with a supreme effort, for her body seemed turned to stone. She attempted to draw a full breath but was unable to do so. Something seemed to be straining and tearing her breasts, strange lights and darknesses swam before her eyes, there was a buzzing sound in her ears as though some bee had strayed into her brain and was striving to escape.

Through the smoke and the glare she could see the forms of her women lying as if in sleep, most of them quite still. Near to her one of them writhed languidly, heaving up her body for a moment and then falling back, as it seemed to the queen with a certain dreadful luxuriousness. She did not move again.

Macha was afraid of death, and the heat was becoming every moment more intense. It seemed that spears were piercing her eyes outward from behind and that they must fall from her head in the next instant. She tried to rise, but some force pinned her down to the bed. With a fearful struggle that seemed to tear the heart from her breast she gained her feet and stood reeling, the red glare wrapping like a lover her beautiful naked body, over which as it seemed to her a thousand envenomed tongues were sliding. She tottered this way and that, hiding her mouth in her hair, and seeking for some door of escape.

Suddenly she heard a sound of singing as it seemed at an immense distance. The queen's brain became confused. At times the singing melted into the flames, at others it seemed the flames sang, and again she thought that in those red-tongued darting things she was actually looking upon the very forms of those bitter passion-wrung sounds. It was indeed a bitter singing that night for Queen Macha Gold-hair.

'Hei-a! Hei-a! Hei-a-aha!
A red night for Cliath-na-Righ,
For the shining grianan of Macha Oir-cinn.
Sweet the song of the flames to the stars,
A music passing that of stately harps,
Masterful the red red lips
Kissing the breasts of the queen,
The tossing burning arms
That are wreathed in her tressy hair,
Hei-a! Hei-a!—Aro! Aree!
The four winds of green-pastured Eire,
The lean hungry winds
Furiously follow the fire,
The brown wind of the west, the moon in his hair,
The red wind of the east, his feet stained with the sun-blood,
The grey wind of the south, the rain in his eyes,
The black wind of the north, the storm froth on his mouth,
Ochone, ochone, aree!
The pale lips of the dawn
Will be crying after Macha the queen,
The blown sands in the dry sea-grasses
Shall answer with voices weak, faint, very thin.
The smooth very gracious body of her
That was as flowers that fall through foam,
The breasts that were apples on a sunny bough,
The hair that was ripe corn in the summer wind,
The mouth that was as the berry of the rowan,
All these are dust, a very little dust,
And it lying between the fingers of the four winds
In the sundered mists of the western world,
That cling to the four great mountains
Of surgy foam-worn Eire.
My grief for him that is the beloved
Of two pitiless fierce-eyed women!
Evil shall come to him from the sun,
And misfortune among the rains of the moon,
Neither shall he find peace in the hollow hills.
Aio, hei-a, aha! O Macha of the scornful brow,
My laughter leaps in the flames,
Sure I am after drowning you in the great fires of my mirth!'

The queen's head fell back, she clutched her breast with both hands. Dimly she heard a great crashing and splitting as the sides of the grianan fell in roaring. Through the glares and blacknesses circling giddily in her eyes she saw indistinctly the figure of a woman that leapt over the breach and was instantly lost in a wilderness of flame.

THE OUTLAW

Joseph O'Neill

The mighty Brian Boru who defeated the Norsemen at the Battle of Clontarf in 1014 at the cost of his own life, has a special place in the ranks of Irish heroes. He has been the subject of a number of fantasy tales, but few more ingenious than the novel Wind from the North *by James O'Neill (1873–1953), in which a modern-day Dublin clerk suddenly finds himself transported back in time and into the body of Olaf Ulfson, a would-be Norse hero who is pitted against Boru and his forces.*

O'Neill, who was a civil servant and spent much of his working life in the Irish Department of Secondary Education in Dublin (of which he was the head from 1923 to 1944), had begun his career as a Gaelic scholar, but perversely abandoned this only to fill his spare time writing novels about medieval Ireland. His interest in the subject brought him into contact with W. B. Yeats, but sadly did not give him the conviction to direct his undoubted talents wholly to writing. Because of this, O'Neill has tended to be dismissed by some critics as merely an educationalist who grew bored with his job and escaped by writing vivid fantasies about the past. Just how unfair this criticism is, and what an excellent fantasy writer Joseph O'Neill actually was, may be judged from the story 'The Outlaw', which was published in The Dublin Magazine *in 1934.*

*   *   *

Across the street to the right a man was being led out of the King's Borg by his guards. In front of the Borg, between it and the city gate a crowd had collected. As the man passed through it with hands bound behind his back he was a fair mark for them. Yells filled the air. Sticks and stones were flying. The guards drew away from the man leaving a space for the missiles.

'Come along,' Eric cried, dragging Olaf.

He was as excited as the crowd by the common fury against the man, though Olaf was sure he didn't know him. Olaf didn't wonder at this, though he himself felt nothing. Then the man's eyes, glancing round, rested on his. Immediately his feelings changed. He began to yell at him.

'Claim the right to run the gauntlet. You've the right to run the gauntlet—claim it. Claim it.'

The people round Olaf turned and stared at him, but he kept on shouting.

The man heard him, turned on his guards.

'The gauntlet!—the gauntlet! I claim the right to run it.'

'Let him run it—It will be better sport,' yelled a voice.

Then the whole crowd was yelling:

'Let him run it—let him run it.'

'He has to be brought to the doom-ring first. He must run the gauntlet from there,' said the Captain of the guards.

'Let him be brought there,' shouted the crowd.

'But he must be brought there uninjured. He must get his full chances.'

'Right! right!' they yelled.

The guards led the man towards the town-gate and through it. As he walked through the crowds he kept turning his head, looking at the women he was passing, the King's men in their red cloaks who were holding back the crowd, a ship tented-over which was floating out on the river opposite the town.

'He has the look of a man going to a festivity, not the look of a man going to the Doom-ring,' Olaf said to Eric.

'I've seen a lot of them that way as if they were looking forward to the unusual thing they were going to experience,' said Eric who had become calm again.

'Perhaps it's because he's to get a chance for his life.'

'It isn't. I've seen them like that when they had no chance. Those of them that weren't dead of anguish already were often looking forward to it, especially slow men. You'll find he's a slow sort of man, sluggish.'

'It's the resurrection they are looking towards, perhaps,' said Olaf.

'It isn't. I've seen as many heathens die that way as Christians, men who believed in nothing after death.'

'Then it's death itself they're looking forward to.'

'It can't be that. It's something else, an elation about something else. I've heard men confess it afterwards, some who escaped. I can see the same feeling in that fellow's face.'

'If I were going to be broken on the Doom-ring, I believe I would find the faces of the people I passed hard to understand, if they looked like the faces round us,' said Olaf. 'They would become things, not men or women any longer,' he added.

'I never think of death,' said Eric. 'Whenever I got a wound, even a deep one, it healed quickly.'

'You never even thought of dying well.'

'No. I never think of dying at all. Why should I? When they talk about dying like a Viking, I always say to myself "Why talk of things like that?"'

They were coming near the Doom-ring, a wide circular platform on the high ground near the mouth of the Dodder. The man was mounting the steps, looking down at the crowd. Behind the platform and the crowd on the river side, he could see rows of horses' faces. The country people had come to the town to see him being broken in the Doom-ring. There were also two bear-cubs at the Borg that a Norse trader had brought as a present to the King and they wanted to see them. Some of them also hadn't finished hiring their Spring workmen or collecting Winter debts. There were a good many reasons for coming in, and, as the country people had outspanned near the fiord, there was a big crowd on that side, as well as on the town side.

The man was standing on the Doom-ring mound, taking account of all this and drawing deep breaths. The double crowds made his chances less.

The guards freed him, untied his hands, led him to the edge of the Ring.

In front of him women who had been going through the crowd selling boiled eggs and cold fish, stood to stare up at him.

'He must get ten yards' grace,' the Captain said to the crowd.

They drew back, tense, waiting.

'Farther! Farther!' cried the guard. He freed the man.

'Now,' he said to him.

For a few moments the man still looked round at the crowd. Then he bounded towards the river. As he sprang, a roar went up from hundreds of throats. Sticks, stones flew at the flying figure.

He swerved, dodged. The shower of missiles was all round him, but it saved him from closer attack. A heavy stone struck him. He fell, got up again. The crowd was running towards the river to head him off.

'The Chapel! The Chapel beyond the South Wall,' Olaf yelled.

The man swung to the right, away from the river. The crowd swung round, yelling with the joy of the chase, but his change of direction had given him a breathing space.

Then Olaf remembered that there were men barking the oak-trees near the Chapel for his father's tannery.

'They'll cut him off,' he thought, 'drive him back to the crowd.'

He began to run. The man was to the left, running with long loping strides, towards the South City Wall. He had more than his ten yards' grace now, nearer fifty, and he was gaining on his pursuers. But the bark-cutters would get him, strike him down or head him back.

Olaf was in front of the crowd. If he could get to the bark-cutters before they harmed the man, they would be a help, as they were his own men and would take his orders.

He ran on breathlessly. He didn't know why he wanted to save this man. He had often hunted with the crowd when outlaws ran the gauntlet, but today there was some change in his mind, some feeling of comradeship when the man had looked at him.

They had rounded the corner of the city wall. The little chapel was in view, a man in priest's garb standing at the door, the bark-cutters standing in a bunch to the left looking towards them.

The fugitive swerved to the left. The bark-cutters began to run to cut him off.

'Don't cut him off—save him—save him,' Olaf yelled to them.

The men stopped, looking from Olaf to the fugitive.

'He's to be rescued!' Olaf shouted to them. 'Knui! Knui! To the rescue!'

He turned and faced the crowd. The bark-peelers came running up.

'Keep them back! Hold them back!' he cried to them.

The men spread out in a line facing the crowd. As they spread out they drew their knives.

The crowd halted, puzzled by what had happened.

'He's no kin to you or Ulf,' a man shouted to Olaf.

'He's my man!' Olaf cried back to him. 'Besides,' he said, 'He has got to sanctuary.'

He pointed towards the chapel. The man had reached the chapel door and was talking to the priest.

'He's a heathen,' cried a man. 'He has no right to Christian sanctuary.'

'The priest is accepting him,' cried another.

Aidan, the priest, had taken the man by the arm, was bringing him into the chapel.

'He hasn't any right to accept him,' cried a man.

'But he has the right,' shouted another.

Eric came up to Olaf.

'Why do you want to save him?' he asked.

'Because he has earned his life.'

'But they'll get him when he leaves the chapel.'

'They won't. The King can give him his liberty now that he has earned it by running the gauntlet.'

A light came into Eric's eyes.

'That Viking Captain down at the harbour is short of men. He'd take him if the King lets him go,' he said.

'I'll go to the King at once,' he added.

He was excited, as full of eagerness to save the man now as he had been before to hunt with the crowd.

'Stay beside the chapel,' he said. 'I'll be back in a short while.'

He went towards the crowd.

'I'm going to the King to see about it,' he said. 'You must wait for his decision.'

'You're taking a great deal on yourself, Eric Sorkerson,' said a man.

'I'm not taking it on myself. It's a matter only the King can decide,' Eric answered calmly.

'Eric Sorkerson is right,' cried several voices.

It was evident that the greater part of the crowd was in agreement. It began to break up into groups. The women with the hard boiled eggs and the fish had come up. It was midday. If the man hadn't run the gauntlet they'd have been getting near their dinners by now. So the women were welcome with their cold victuals.

There were other distractions in view also. A man had come from the rear with a brown stallion, a group of men round him.

'They're arranging a horse-fight. They won't trouble us for the

present, but keep where you are and don't let them come in,' said
Olaf to the bark-peelers, and went off to the chapel.

Before he went in he looked back at the crowd. They were in
two groups, round horses which they were bringing towards one
another.

Olaf walked to the chapel door, looked in. The man was talking
to the priest, telling him his story.

He was a curious-looking fellow, but as Olaf watched him he
knew why he had intervened to save him. It was the look in the
man's eyes, a curiously trustful look in a heavy old-fashioned sort
of face. He wondered how he had got to be an outlaw.

'I'm a man used to either field work or sea-work,' the man was
saying to the priest. 'Smith-work and carpenter work come handy
to me too, if you want them.'

Olaf looked at his clothes. They were old and worn, but the
coarse woollen jacket and the linen breeches were carefully darned
and the goatskin shoes were patched neatly.

'I won't hide from you that I'm a man with bad luck who brings
bad luck on others,' he was saying now.

'I couldn't employ you,' said the priest. 'Besides, you're a
heathen, but I'll save your life if I can.'

Olaf turned back to look at the crowd. The horses—a big brown
stallion and a grey with a black stripe on his back—were going
round one another trying to get a chance of biting. From the chapel
the man's voice came in a low murmur telling the priest about his
life; how he became an outlaw. Bits of it came to Olaf.

'Beside the shore, men were sitting round a fire built on stones.
On the fire a big kettle was hanging. I knew by the smell that they
were boiling fish. Out on the river they had a ship and a ten-oared
cutter. The cutter lay beside the rudder of the ship, and the oars
were in the loops.'

The yells of the crowd drowned his voice. The owner of the
brown stallion had joined in the fight, whipping his horse violently.
The horse responded by rising on his hind-legs and biting savagely
at the striped stallion's shoulder.

At the corner of the wood near the chapel a couple of tethered
goats, troubled by the noise, began to pull each other in different
directions. From the chapel, the voice became audible again: 'We
didn't plunder, as the land was poor, and we thought it better to
ask for a winter home there. It was there I met her. The early

winter slaughtering and salting was going on, the women going in and out all day, bringing honey and storing it in the shelves, men too with grain and malts—'

He paused, as if to picture the scene. Olaf could hear the priest's voice murmuring encouragement. Then the outlaw's words came clear again.

'Winter is a good herdsman, priest. She brings all creatures home. There was a woman there, a young woman with long hair down both sides of her bosom and the locks turned up under a belt that caught her scarlet kirtle round the middle. Her face was marked where she had fallen into the trench-fire when she was a child. Also she had little property—'

He stopped as if he was listening to the yells of the crowd. The owner of the striped horse had run under the rearing stallion and thrust at the other man with a stick.

The outlaw was continuing his story.

'I married her. Then one day a woman said to her: "You'd be well enough married if your husband had the name of courage." The eyes don't hide it, if a woman begins to think badly of a man. A little street runs in that town from the house we lived in down to the river and, as I was coming up one day, a woman said to another, "Every woman wants a man, not a mid-day ghost." So I knew what was happening to her.'

A group of riders appeared at the city gate, coming towards the chapel. Olaf recognised Eric amongst them. He went into the chapel and called out:

'The King's messengers are coming with the judgement.'

The man turned his face and Olaf saw that in his story he had forgotten why the King's men were coming. He turned back to the priest.

'I went to the mouth of the river. Fishermen came there,' he said, 'and it was a good place for tidings. It was there I learned about him and her.'

The trampling of horses was loud outside, Eric's voice calling out 'He is free. The Viking Captain is short of men and the King has agreed to let him go with him, if he gives a guarantee not to return.'

The man didn't seem to hear him.

'His courage wasn't so good after all, not as good as she thought,' he said to the priest.

'May God in His mercy pardon you, my son,' said the priest, 'And heal your mind,' he added.

Eric put his head in the door.

'The tide is on the ebb. The ship will be going out with the ebb-tide,' he cried.

The man turned.

'The ebb-tide,' he said, 'the ebb.'

He came out of the chapel.

'Let us get him back to the town while they're engaged with the horse-fighting,' said one of the King's men.

The man turned to the priest.

'If I ever can save a mass-priest, I'll save him, when we're plundering, Herra,' he said.

'Go and God be with you and bring you to His fold,' said the priest.

EARTH-BOUND

Dorothy Macardle

'Earth-Bound' is a tale that links a great Irish hero of the past, Red Hugh O'Donnell, with the unhappy political situation that affects the whole of Ireland today. A figure of mythology and a prisoner on the run from Mountjoy Prison both have the same dream—a dream of freedom. Like several other contributors to this section, Dorothy Macardle (1889–1958) was in her youth a friend of W. B. Yeats and George Russell, but her strong involvement in the Irish National Movement led to her arrest and imprisonment in Mountjoy Prison in 1922. Here she spent her time writing her first tales of fantasy which were later collected in a now rare little volume, Earth-bound (1924).

After her release from prison she still pursued her political activities, and these undoubtedly reduced the number of stories she might otherwise have written. However, two years after its publication her novel Uneasy Freehold (1942) was filmed by Paramount Pictures as The Uninvited, the first major horror picture since the 1930s, so starting a new wave of public interest in the genre. The film, about a brother and sister who rent a haunted house and try unavailingly to find a logical explanation for the ghost, starred Ray Milland and Ruth Hussey. It was infused with Dorothy Macardle's feeling for the supernatural, just as 'Earth-Bound' combines her knowledge of Ireland's fantasy tradition with her own grim experiences in Mountjoy.

* * *

'Do you think that people who are not Irish know what home-sickness is?' Una said. 'It is harder being away from a country that is in trouble,' Michael O'Clery answered, 'than from a country

that is at peace. It is not home-sickness only—it is that you want
to be in the fight.'

He spoke contentedly. It was his last night in Philadelphia;
tomorrow he was going home.

Una's pale little face looked sad in the dying fire-light; the
coming and going of Irish friends filled her, always, with joy and
pain. Even Frank's keen face grew wistful and, for myself, an
unbearable pang of *heim-weh* silenced me.

Una spoke again, after a pause.

'Do you know what I miss more than the people, more than
the dear places?' she said. 'It is that sense one has everywhere in Ireland—in the glens, and in Dublin—the old squares
on the north side, and the quays—of the companionship of the
dead.'

Frank laughed in brotherly mockery.

'They stay in Ireland, I suppose, sooner than go to Heaven? Or
is it doomed to it they are, instead of Hell?'

But Michael said seriously:

'I believe she's right.'

Michael had something to tell us: that could be felt. It was past
midnight but Una put coal on the fire.

Three weeks ago Michael had arrived, without a passport, in
Philadelphia, on some mission not to be disclosed, and, like most
friendly travellers from Ireland had found his way soon to the
young editors of the *Tri-Colour*, Una and Frank O'Carroll. Within
their hospitable studio his few idle hours were spent.

Nowhere outside Dublin have I known so shabby yet lovable a
room. It was perhaps their one treasure, Hugo Blake's glorious
'Dawn,' that made one seem to breathe there the air of home.
That picture is magical. There is nothing painted but the hills of
Clare-Galway seen from the water and daybreak in the sky behind,
yet it is the dawn of all that Ireland has been waiting for these
seven hundred years.

'You could go away from that picture,' Michael said once, 'and
die.'

There was little else—brown walls, three uncurtained windows
looking down on the square, at evening all blue shadow and amber
lights; faded draperies on the divans and many-coloured cushions
around the fire; it was enough, with Frank's iridescent, satirical
humour and Una's pleasure in her friends, to create an illusion

inexpressibly restful. It was the exiles' oasis of living waters at the end of each arid week.

It was late at night, as now, when all but a guest or two had gone, that the talk would grow full of reminiscences and omens and prophesies and dreams, and strange adventures would be told.

Not one word had Michael said, yet, of the perils that followed his escape, but Una's remark had started some deep train of thought in him. He repeated, in a tone of deep conviction:

'I believe she's right.'

'You think they stay—?' I asked.

'Some,' he replied. 'Some that died for Ireland, thinking more of Ireland than Heaven at the end.'

'And they're wanted,' he added gravely. 'They are surely wanted still.'

'Do you know Glenmalure?' he asked then.

I knew it, a deep valley of the Wicklow hills, shut out from life, compelling mournful thoughts.

'They might well be there,' I said.

'I'll tell you a thing happened there,' Michael went on, 'and you can explain it the way you please. It's there Donal and I were on our keeping after we escaped from Mountjoy.'

'Donal O'Donel?' asked Frank.

'Yes; he got a life-sentence, you know, and we were to be transferred to Pentonville. My own sentence was only two years, but I was fairly desperate for him. If you ever knew him you'd understand; he'd never been in a city a week together—a long-limbed mountainy lad, the quickest brain I ever met, extraordinarily confident and proud. He'd a kind of thirst for life for its own sake that you don't find often among the boys, yet the death-sentence seemed to give him a kind of joy; 'twas the commutation he couldn't stand—things looked fairly hopeless, you know, then— and Pentonville for life.

'We knew 'twould be a desperate chance; he had a damaged foot, he'd be hard to disguise too, with his fiery hair; but 'twas worth any risk and we had Pierce O'Donovan outside—the gaol was never built Pierce couldn't break; we made a plan you'd think crazy and got away.

'I'll not forget that night—the sky over us and a grand wind full of rain and a cruel moon and we driving like fury in an open car, clean through the city and over the hills! Half a dozen times we were halted, but Pierce had licences and all and we got through. He put us with an old couple in the last cottage in the glen—Glenmalure—who welcomed us like their own. We were to stay there till Donal's foot would be well, then we'd be sent for to join the column in the hills.

"Twas a strange land to us both—different altogether from Sligo or Donal's place, Donegal: a steep narrow valley in a wilderness of naked hills, all rocks, bracken and dead gorse, treacherous with spots of bog; the hills are channelled everywhere with torrents—you hear the noise of them night and day. Old Moran was forever warning us: "Many a one got lost here and was never found; the Glen doesn't like strangers," he used to say.

'I had no love for the Glen; 'twould be beautiful on the frosty mornings when Lugnacullia had a crest of snow, but in the after-noons—'twas December—when the sun fell behind Clohernagh and the whole place went chill and dark under a vast shadow, you felt drowned . . . I said to Donal it was too like Synge's play. Donal didn't know Synge's play; he never had much use for books; he'd rather be making history than reading it; he loved the Glen: "'Tis a grand place," he said, "heroic; it remembers the old times."

'His foot was better; he could hobble a good way with a stick and we explored the nearer hills on those bright cold mornings—Slieve Moan and Fananieran and Cullentragh. Donal was wild to climb to the Three Lochs, but old Moran made a scare: "There are bog holes you'd sink in and never rise," he said; "'twould be a good man would do it on a summer day, let alone in the snow"; and not a soul in the valley would guide us, so we gave it up.

'One day, though, we followed the torrent to Art's Loch; it was the longest climb Donal had done and he was pleased; a place like that exhilerated him. The sun was setting and there was a red stormy light on the water lying lost there in its hollow among the great hills. Dead solitary the loch is; I thought there was no life in it at all, but Donal was excited: "'Tis these places are haunted," he said, "by the old Chieftains and Kings." He looked like one of them himself standing there with the ruddy light on his face; predestined to victory he looked. A song Mrs Moran used to be quoting came into my head, about "The King of Ireland's son" and "the crown of his red-gold hair," but the sun sank and the shadow rose over him and a black thought crossed my mind—

"He is the sort England always kills." That place would make you afraid of death.

'There was trouble in the glens, we heard; it would likely be after Christmas before anyone would come for us; being ignorant of the country it would be useless setting off by ourselves. We got impatient waiting; maybe we went too freely about the hills; Donal was very heedless with strangers; they'd often stare at him as if wanting to remember his face. Anyway, on Christmas Eve the waiting came to an end.

"Twas a savagely cold day with a wind out of the north and a black sky and folks were staying at home. We sat all the evening with the Morans round a gorgeous fire talking, or rather listening to Donal's talk. He was in one of his keen, inventive moods when he'd plan laws and constitutions and lay out the whole government of Ireland the way you'd tell faery tales to a child. Some of his ideas would startle you, but he'd not let you off till you saw they were sound. He drew a map of Ireland on the bellows with a burnt stick and started planning a military defence; it was a great plan surely that he made. "We could face the nations of the world," he said, "if we had no traitors in our own. Ireland's a natural fortress, the best God made."

'"God keep you!" said Mrs Moran fervently: "God spare you, son!"

'There was a sharp knock at the door and we stood up; old Moran opened; it was a girl, a neighbour's girl, who worked at the hotel; she was wet and breathless and shivering with cold. The Black and Tans were drinking at the hotel; they had raided Glendaloch and Laragh; they were raiding Glenmalure, "For the two lads escaped out of Mountjoy." She had guessed suddenly and deserted her work to warn us—run all the way. "Beasts and devils they are! My God! if you heard the threats and curses! Into the hills with you," she pleaded, "for God's sake!"

'Donal looked at old Moran, "Where will we go?" The old man shook his head wretchedly: "If I could tell you that—" "If you could get to Reilly's at the Three Lochs," the girl said, "they'll not look as far as that; or O'Toole's of Granabeg, or Mr Barton's; but you'll not get so far; you'd have to pass Glendaloch."

'Mrs Moran was parcelling up food and sobbing, "My God! My God! the boggy hills and the snow, and he with a broken foot!" Snow was falling, steady and deliberate, out of the leaden sky;

Donal looked at it and smiled, the way you'd smile at an enemy; it was better than Pentonville. We thanked brave little Nannie and hugged poor old Mrs Moran and set out, facing north.

'There was the ford to cross, then the precipitous face of Lugduff Mountain to scale; by the time we had clambered to the ridge and looked down on Glenmalure again it was night. We saw through the snowfall white lights rushing along the road below, and shots sounding like volleys echoed among the hills.

'Our way lay over a rugged moorland, unbroken save for boulders and thwarted trees, a waste of bog and heather, stiff grasses and withered bracken all buried in snow; no light or outline of a house was visible; only the curves of the hilltops against the sky. We knew nothing of these regions; nothing of the direction in which any habitation lay; we could only push straight onward and trust to luck, keeping our faces to the wind.

'But there was no luck with us; the snow never ceased falling; not one star shone; each step was a separate labour; the snow drove in our faces; I grew heavy and numb with cold; Donal dragged forward steadily with the help of his stick, but he did not speak at all; I saw his face by the pale gleam of the snow; it was white and grim with pain. He refused angrily to take my arm.

'It comes back like a nightmare now: the two of us plodding on towards nothing, labouring up hill and down again, hour after painful hour, the desert around us looking forever the same; we might have been working in a circle for all I knew. At last Donal reeled and clutched my arm, then stood up, breathing through his teeth. I asked if his foot had given out. "If I could rest it a minute," he gasped; "it's only the lumpy ground . . ."

The snow had lightened a little and we could see: a black heaven and a white earth; sharp granite edges thrusting up through the snow; down hill, to our left, a clump of trees.

'My own feet were like lead, frozen: I was stupefied with cold and could think of nothing to do; I felt a monstrous weight was against us, compassing our destruction: the hills were malignant to us, and the wind, and God. Donal had his senses still; he whispered, "Make for the trees!"

'We reached the clump of firs at last and got a respite from the wind; Donal sank down on a fallen trunk, easing the tortured foot; I leaned against a tree, dizzy; I was afraid to sit down. Already that craving was over me that comes so fatally in snow, to abandon the forlorn, dreamlike struggle and lie down in the soft fleeciness and sleep. But Donal had risen, suddenly, as though called: "Come on," he said tensely, "we mustn't rest."

'We stood together in the open again, wondering which way to go; one way seemed as meaningless as another; all led to the same end. Donal looked at me for a moment remorsefully: "I'm sorry, Mike," he said, "you could have managed it alone."

'I was answering angrily, but he stopped me with "Hush! Look there!" pointing straight in front of him; then he started forward again whispering, "Come on!"

'He was following something; I followed him and at last, through the veil of blowing snow, I saw it too—a tall, dark, striding form.

'A crazy zig-zag course we made, following that far-off figure which never noticed us, never beckoned us, never turned.

'Down a steep rough hillside we went and far along the bank of a frozen stream; up a wooded slope and out once more on a white plain. Dizzied with swirling snow, choked and aching with the cold, we followed—no thought or will left to us of our own.

'Donal stopped short now and then for a moment, paralysed by pain, but limped on again; our guide never stopped; we never came near enough to call to him, never near enough to see more than the lithe, tall figure of a boy moving fearlessly through the night.

'We were travelling over a difficult, stony hillside, steering towards a black grove of trees, when Donal lurched sideways and leaned on my shoulder, his eyes closed. I saw he was done, exhausted, and I held him, looking for our guide. He had gone; he seemed to have disappeared into the trees. But below us lay the road: it would be easier going; it must lead to houses: hope—the hope of dear life—rose up in me, and Donal opened his eyes. "Come on," he said faintly, standing up and then, with a twisted smile, "I'll have to lean on you."

'We had not gone ten yards when the air rumbled with a familiar sound and below us from the right, round the turn of the hill they came driving—those lurching, malignant lights. We were in full view from the road, on the bare hill-side, and those were lorries below.

'I saw them crashing along and stopping, saw the rutty road splashed with brilliance from the headlights; saw the men dismounting and heard a hoarse voice shouting orders as they scattered to left and right.

'I looked at Donal. "Run," he commanded, "I'll follow," and at the first step he pitched headlong and lay on the snow.

'On the hillside opposite, the far side of the road, a searchlight from the lorry began to play. To rise, to attempt to drag or carry Donal would have betrayed us both; he was in a dead faint, his face like marble; I lay down, crouched over him in the snow.

'Men out of the lorries came swarming up, searching with flash lamps, cursing brutally as they came. Then the searchlight swung over and began to play along our side of the hill. The broad beam came creeping over the slope: I saw the intense black and white pictures leap out of the darkness one by one—saw every boulder, every bunch of stubble as it swept steadily towards where we lay. The searchers crossed it, reeling—they were drunk; they carried bayonets; they were Black and Tans. I pulled my gun out and held it at Donal's head—I meant to fire when the light touched us—God forgive me! what else was there to do?

'Then, suddenly, I saw our guide again; down from the cover of the trees he came leaping, between us and the path of light. I heard the triumphant yell of the searchers as the beam caught him full—a tall slim figure with lifted arms. He stood an instant, then ran, swift as a deer, clean across the shaft of light, away from us into the dark again; volleys of shots and a wild clamour of yells followed him as he ran.

'I staggered to my feet, dazed, half-believing I was in a dream; for I had seen him when the light fell on him—the long limbs and the high head and the red wind-blown hair; I would have sworn a hundred oaths that it was Donal, but Donal lay beside me on the snow.

'The shouts and firing followed the flyer and the sweeping light followed him over the hill. The lorries were turned and followed, driven madly along the road, and we were left in the empty night. I put my coat over him, chafed his hands and tried to warm his lips with my breath—nothing seemed any good. An awful memory came to me of the story of poor Art O'Neill, fugitive in those glens, frozen to death.

'I began to run blindly, for no reason, towards the trees.

'Out of the grove of trees a light shone; it was shining from an open door. I stumbled into the light and up the steps of a stone house; a grey-haired man stood there and a girl. "There's a man out there," I told them, "in the snow."

'They called servants and ran out with lanterns and a great dog followed them and found him and they brought him in.

'It took a long time to revive him, and his foot was lamed with frost-bite, but not much, and, but for that, he was soon well.

'We had come, I think, to the kindest folk in Ireland—the O'Byrnes of Glendasan. We must have travelled a dangerous way, they said, through Glenrigh, where King O'Toole is buried, past the grave of poor Art O'Neill—they knew the whole region—it was their own, and its histories, but they knew nothing about our guide.

'The Black and Tans caught nobody in the Glen.'

Amazed faces were turned to Michael as he ended his tale. Frank O'Carroll frowned but was silent; Max Barry, who is a rapacious historian, spoke eagerly: 'Art O'Neill? . . . Glenmalure! . . . Didn't Aodh Ruadh . . . wasn't it there?'

'Yes,' Una answered with glowing eyes, 'Aodh Ruadh O'Donal!—Red Hugh!'

Michael nodded, 'That is what Donal says.'

2

THE ROMANTIC
SAGAS

FLIGHT OF ANGELS

Austin Clarke

*The Irish god of love, Angus (spelt Aongus in Gaelic) is a beautiful
youth with four birds, each representing kisses, permanently fluttering around his head. One legend about him, 'The Dream of
Aongus', describes his pursuit of the lovely Caer and how he
managed to identify her while she was living in the shape of a
swan. The God of Love was also involved in the famous romance
of Diarmuid and Grainne and tried to help them with the aid of
magical devices.*

*It is now a well-established fact that the ancient Irish romantic
sagas frequently contained strong elements of erotic love running
through them, but it was only after centuries of suppression that
these elements began to be revived in new versions of the stories by
writers following in the footsteps of the renaissance begun by Standish O'Grady and, more especially, W. B. Yeats. In a number of
his poems Yeats made a point of emphasising the power of erotic
love, and he was directly responsible for inspiring the work of
Austin Clarke (1896–1974), a former literary teacher at University
College, Dublin, who apparently lost his job in 1921 'because he
had not been married in church'. Clarke took eroticism as the theme
of his first two novels,* The Bright Temptation *(1932) and* The
Singing-Men at Cashel *(1936), both of which were promptly banned
by the Irish censors. The first of these was a retelling of the story
of Diarmuid and Grainne in which two lovers are plagued with
guilt about the 'Evil One' whom their priest insists is motivating
their desire for each other.* The Singing-Men of Cashel *was centred
on the unfortunate Gorlia who has to endure two bad husbands—
one wanting no sex and the other nothing else—before finding true
love. In* The Sun Dances at Easter *(1952) Clarke drew directly on
mythology, in particular the influence of the love god Aongus on a
young wife named Orla who wants to conceive a child for her*

impotent husband, Flann, and goes on a pilgrimage to St Naal's Well. There she finds her solution with the help of a remarkable Otherworld lover, as the following extract from this now rare book reveals . . .

* * *

That night Enda told Orla the story of Congal More and the unfaithfulness of his wife, Fial, as revealed by Aongus.

When he had finished there was a silence between them for a while before the girl spoke.

'Never have I heard a merrier tale,' Orla exclaimed, 'and surely it would be banned by copyists in their holy schools, if they heard of it. There is much, however, that puzzles me, though I know these royal tales have more than one meaning. Indeed I was going to stop you almost at the very start to ask a question, but I remembered that you had put me under a little bond of silence.'

'What did you want to ask me?' said Enda, though he knew already.

'When you were telling about the comical cleric in the goatskin hood, I could not help thinking of my hermit, so alike were their tatters and tip-topping shoes. But I knew very soon that the stranger who came to the green of Tara that day, hundreds of years ago, was not a holy man.'

'Aongus has taken as many shapes as his Greek cousin, according to the poets, for love itself is like that, a solemn play in which there must be two comic parts, grave when it is gayest, gross and yet most delicate, when all that is beyond meaning has been grasped.'

She knew that his words were wise but the tone of his voice alarmed her.

'Enda, you cannot believe that it was Aongus I saw three days ago at Ardlahan? Say that it isn't true!'

Seeing his hesitation, she turned to him in distress, heedless of the firelight that went gladly around her gold wrist-bands.

'You do believe it, for I remember your startled look when I told you yesterday that the hermit seemed to have a birdflock about him. But it was only a foolish fancy of mine, because his raglets were astir in the breeze. I can see all clearly now . . . that was why you hurried to the Well, fearing I was in danger . . . that

is why you told me this story of Aongus tonight and asked me not
to say a word until it was over. You wanted me to guess your
intention.'

'Yes,' he admitted.

'It cannot be true,' she persisted. 'No, no, it cannot be true!'

But suspicions that she could not keep back came faster than
the storm outside . . . the fairy ring in the mist, this strange house
and the meal that had been prepared for them, the ancient mead-
cups, the unseen helpers. Both of them, in their agitation, must
have got up, for she was standing beyond the bench and within
arm's-reach of Enda. She could see behind his left shoulder the
intercrossings on the pillars as the fire-rays reached them, but the
bronze had changed into red gold. Another thought came into her
mind and she spoke slowly.

'We are not in Dun-da-lacha?'

'No.'

'Where are we, Enda?'

'We are under enchantment . . . we are in the invisible Ireland.'

'Behind the Faed Fiad?'

'Yes,' he said simply.

In her confusion she could not think rightly, yet, despite all
reason, she felt a wild exhilaration, as if her hidden self knew that
he spoke the truth. Was this, then, the meaning of her journey,
the meaning of her secret glances at him ever since she had seen
the love-spot on his cheek? They were alone together, beyond
violence and danger. No mortal could tell where they were or
what they did that night.

'And did you know all the time?'

'At first I was secretly bewildered, but when we were standing
near the door listening to the wolves far away in the storm, I knew
for certain. Then we turned, and I saw the empty table.'

'I saw it, too, but I thought it had been cleared by a servant.'

'I was just about to tell you everything, when you asked me for
a story.'

What was happening to them was as strange as the story he had
told her, as strange as all the stories she had ever heard at Ardlahan on winter nights. She stared into the fire as if it were not really
there and the adventures of Becfola, which had always delighted
her, came to her mind, came so fast that she could see them
occurring in the twinkle of a dream.

Early on a Sunday morning, Becfola left her husband's bed to go on a journey to Cluan-da-cailleach, for she wanted to fetch back seven dresses and seven brooches of gold which she had left there. It is unlucky to travel on a Sunday, but she was impatient to have them and set out at once with her maid. They journeyed all day without mishap, but at nightfall they became separated from each other in a wood. Becfola reached a great house and was alone in it with a fair-haired stranger. She gave her love to that youth and lay all night beside him without sin. At dawn she came back to the wood and found her maid asleep in a tree. But when she got home at last her husband was still abed, for it was the same Sunday morning on which she had left. 'Have you changed your mind?' he asked, and she knew, then, that she had been away less than a minute from his side. She undressed and went into the warmth of the bed again for her limbs had been chilled by the dews.

Orla looked up and the other adventures of Becfola vanished from her mind, for Enda was pointing at the table as if he guessed what she was thinking.

'Those candles!' he exclaimed. 'I watched them when I started to tell you the story of Congal and, though it must have taken more than an hour, they have not burned the ninth part of an inch.'

'Then we are beyond mortal time?'

'Yes.'

Orla could not help laughing at the failure of her own cleverness. She had got what she asked for, but did not really want, and this was the answer. All the merry or sad stories her young scholar had learned could not shorten the night, even if he told them again in Latin. Her eyes opened to him like a little primer and he knew at last why she had asked him to tell her a long story. Never had sight-reading been so fast or book shut so soon! She was certain that she had not stirred hand or foot, and yet Enda and she were together, their lips touching for the first time.

Full of wonder, she stirred from his arms.

'How am I here, Enda? I was over there just now and neither of us moved.'

'Darling, darling, we are in Moynell, where all that can be imagined is true.'

'And is every wish granted here?'

So great was her eagerness that he could not deceive her.

'Every wish that belongs to the present.'

She knew at once what he meant, but in her joy she wanted to forget the future. That wish was granted, for they were together again, kissing so wildly that soon her curls were mingling with his beard and she could no longer keep back her next wish. In obedience to it, the gold clasps unfastened from her hair, her sleeves began to bare at the armpits, as if impatient of so much unnecessary delay. Suddenly she was aware of what was happening and broke from his embrace in confusion. Already one of her breasts was trying firmly to show itself, but she caught back her shoulder-brooch before he had seen it. Although she was a married woman, it was clear to her that she could not trust herself to be as faithful as Becfola. She must resist the enchantment before it became too powerful. The fact that she had not felt it as soon as Enda proved that she could. She saw all clearly now, saw that they were among unworldly illusions cast by the fallen angels. Even the stories which Enda had related to her held a lesson. He had forgotten that lesson because of her and she was leading him into folly. But Saint Natalis would save them both from the last temptation of all, for she knew that if she yielded to it, the great wish of her life would never be granted.

'Enda, we must escape from here before it is too late.'

'But we cannot.' His voice was joyful.

'There must be a way, for we are taught that, as human beings, we have free will.'

'The theologians still dispute about that question!'

She did not heed his words, for she was suddenly inspired.

'Do you remember I told you of the strange happenings in the convent at Glan?'

'Your dream about the angels?'

'Yes, but I have discovered the explanation. Enda, it was no dream.'

She was sitting beside him on the bench as if they were at class. But he was her pupil now and she would instruct him in every detail, concentrate his entire attention on holy things.

'About an hour after the midnight vigil, I was wakened by a very bright ray of the moon. Then I heard a faint sound. I lay listening to it and soon heard other sounds, as of metal, stone and wood, but they were muffled. At first I thought that builders were

busy somewhere, but who could be working so cautiously at that
time of the night? I drowsed for a while, and when I opened my
eyes again the ray had changed to gold, and yet it could not be
sunlight. The sounds were coming from the same direction as the
strange moonbeam and they were regular. I could hear tap and
rap, clink and chink, keeping time with one another as if many
carpenters and chippers were at work. But each tool had a musical
note of its own and I fancied that they were all made of rare metals.
I was full of curiosity, and before I knew how it had happened I
was standing on the floor in the middle of the ray. Never was there
a lovelier light: when I spread my hands in it, they were shining:
when I glanced down at myself, I was all golden. I stole over to
the wall and listened, then I found a crack below the high sill and
peeped through it.'

Although Enda seemed attentive to all she said, the love-spot
on his cheek was so kissable that she had to talk faster lest it
distract her.

'I was looking straight into the open air and in the sky was a
large golden moon. It was shining so clearly that when I looked
down I could have counted the blades of grass, each separate,
sparkling as if with mica dust from granite blocks. At a little distance were wattled party-walls and the earth was cast up, here and
there, between the diggings. Nearby, a company of youths bent
over baulks, hammering and sawing, while others were climbing
ladders to a new wall, their head-curls and the very aprons they
wore, yellow as pollen. I thought they were the Sidhe at first and
was frightened, but I could not help taking another peep. Some
of the youths were coming and going with hods, but all their faces
were turned from me. In a corner, by themselves, heavenly-
looking chisellers were working, their hands glittering as if they
held wedge and mallet of pure crystal. I was certain, then, that
they had not come from ancient mound or rath, but were angels,
building a private chapel for the nuns. Suddenly a tall youth, who
seemed to be their supervisor, raised his head and I knew he was
aware that I was watching. He turned slowly and looked towards
the spy-hole and his face was a great jewel, so radiant that I fled
from it. I must have cried out, for Blanaid was bending over my
pillow. The next morning she found the wall-crack, but when we
looked through it, there was only a waste patch of weeds outside.'

'Then it was only a dream.'

'I thought so too, but now I know that Blanaid was mistaken, for I can remember clearly that the chink below the sill was in the east wall, and if we had gone to it we would have seen the holy foundations . . . And that is why the Abbess and the nuns prayed so much the next morning and rang all their handbells.'

'I don't quite follow you.'

'Many say the Abbess is a saint,' Orla explained, 'and so she must have felt the pagan influence which, in my ignorance, I brought with me into the holy house. But Saint Naal was protecting me and, as a sign of his intercession, I was granted that vision. I am not very good at argument, Enda, but surely all this proves that angels come to the aid of mortals. Therefore I believe that we have free will and can escape, if we truly desire it.'

Enda was moved by her words, remembering the religious doubts which had tormented him until he met her. But his mental training at Favoria as a celibate had not been sufficient. She was right—if they did not escape at once, it would be too late.

'Let us find out if we have free will,' he exclaimed.

Silently they willed themselves away, and as they did so they were in the shadowiness between the pillars: the candles had dimmed: the glow was fading on the hearth.

'We are escaping,' she whispered, 'keep close to me, so that we may not be separated from each other.'

Then the darkness was so intense that Orla could not tell what was happening to her. At first she thought she was back in her own bed again, miraculously safe at Ardlahan. But she was completely mistaken. The featherbed in which she lay was softer than the nests a thousand songbirds line with dainty down. The coverlet, on which her bare arm leaned, was prinked even to the touch and finer than any silk she had known. She stirred and was aware, then, that she had not been separated from Enda. They were still under the enchantment of Aongus and their real wish had been granted to them. How could she have any more scruples when she had failed to escape from the invisible Ireland, where all is happiness, and had no will of her own? She was certain, now, that the copyists had changed the story of Becfola in order to prevent scandal, but Enda would know the true version of those adventures. She was unable to ask that question, for never had mediaeval scholar turned to the love-book of Ovid to find his favourite passage so quickly and with such reverence as he turned to her.

Scarcely had he done so than she felt a sudden heavenliness and could not cry out.

But she rebelled against it and drew her arms closer around him lest he should discover what had happened. She was too late, for already he was sitting up.

'A flight of angels!' he exclaimed in awe. 'The miracle which I have sought so long has occurred and the summer storm is gone. Quick, quick, Orla! Let us follow the holy vision so that our folly, tonight, may be forgiven us.'

She did not dare to look towards the lintel, for the radiance of those heavenly hurriers was reflected on his face as he stood beyond the bedside. Clearly in that ray, and golden as her own the night before, she saw his naked body and thought in wonder that it had been glorified. She discovered her mistake at once, but, even in that exalted moment, she gazed with such admiration that his modesty must have known, for, snatching up his clothes in a bundle, he hid what belongs to the Devil. Her womanly curiosity was punished immediately, because all was dark again and she could hear him, in the distance, calling her to follow him.

*   *   *

Orla was so indignant with herself that she hid her face under the coverlet. She forgot even the flight of angels and could think of nothing but her own humiliation. The storm among the trees was over and Enda was gone for good. Indeed she was sure he was pelting as fast as he could to the nearest monastery, without the slightest regard for her. She hoped the way was pebbly as a penance, and that he had left his shoes behind him when he snatched up his clothes. He was just the same as any other Irishman, anxious always for the safety of his own soul. Having regained his will, he was afraid, no doubt, of damnation and would not look back lest she might be running after him. She was well rid of him and she did not care, even though she was left in the dark.

Despite her resentment, Orla really knew that she was lying to herself. She was to blame entirely for what had happened. She had wanted to escape, but when the doorway was illuminated she rebelled and refused to go with him, even though he was calling to her. Why should she be angry with him, when it was too late? He had believed everything she told him and, despite all temptation, was eager to respect her wish, however hard it might be. In her agitation she caught at the coverlet and it seemed to crumble under her touch. She grasped it again and, much to her astonishment, was left holding a handful of withered leaves.

Opening her eyes, Orla found that the moonlight was shining on her, between the loggings of a little doorway. The roof of wicker-and-clay was so low that she could almost reach it if she raised herself from the heap of dried bracken on which she was lying. She kept quite still for a while, wondering if this were a further punishment for her rebellion. But when she stirred again, the rustle of the bracken reminded her of something—and suddenly she knew. 'I am back in the hut . . . It is coming to me so clearly that it might have happened only a few minutes ago . . . Enda and I had taken shelter here from the downpour, both of us felt drowsy . . . and then we were out in the fearful darkness of the wood, running, as we thought, to Dun-da-lacha.'

Beyond the doorway the moonlight gleamed between bud and branch. Small mists, staying in the hollows, were paler than bushes. The very air was gentle where the angels had passed. As she thought of those heavenly sightseers, paying a flying visit to all the holy places in Ireland, she felt sad and lonely. Somewhere far away, Enda was watching them from a hillside. He had found what he wanted at last and was at peace.

A stray curl touched her cheek reproachfully and, putting her hand up to it, she found that she was wearing her hood. In her agitation she had not noticed that she was fully dressed and wrapped in her pilgrim's cloak. Only too quickly had she forgotten her journey. The miraculous Well was not more than a stroll from where she was, but it might have been a hundred miles away. She was unworthy to visit it in the morning and so the great wish of her life would never be granted to her. All she wanted was to have a baby and it was not her fault if she had failed to be good. She had done her best even when her will was not her own, but everything seemed to happen as in a dream. Curcog, her sister-in-law, had told her that the clergy had a pleasure-seeking dream once a month because they were not married, and if her betters were beguiled, what could she do? Suppose all that had happened was only a dream—that would explain why she was here now, with her clothes on. But there was no use in trying to deceive herself.

It was not a dream because she could remember very well the merry story which Enda told her by the fireside. Were there, then, happier states of consciousness in which all was different? How could she know, when even a scholar such as Enda was puzzled? The drowsier she became, the lovelier seemed all that had befallen her that night: and as she mused over it, her very senses were in a pagan swoon of tenderness. She understood at last why the heroes of old, for all their strength, could not resist the power of love. Even Cuchullin had taken to his sick-bed, so great was his longing for Fand, the wife of Mannanan, and lingered there until she sent messengers to him from the hidden world, and soon after that he spent a month with her in Moymell. Thinking of other lovers, Caer and Etain, Midir and many more, and remembering their dear words to one another, Orla sighed.

She was sitting up, wide-awake, for she was certain that she had heard an answering sigh to hers. She turned in the bracken and could scarcely believe the delight of her own eyes. Within arm's reach of her, Enda was lying fast asleep.

He must have been there all the time while she was blaming him in her vexation. His face was shadow-pale in the moonlight and she thought of the first time she had seen him on the hillside beyond Glen Nephin. She had wondered, as she stood by the mountain ash, if he were a young theological student on his way to the summer classes, then she was sure, because of his wild curls, that he was a poet with a headful of stories. In her joy at finding him again, she bent over the withered fronds and gazed at him. His breathing was so quiet, he might have been under enchantment. She shook him gently by the shoulder but he did not stir: then, in alarm, she shook him again, with little words of entreaty.

Enda wakened slowly and she was happy once more.

'Where are we?' he exclaimed in a bewildered tone.

She smiled because she knew more than he did this time.

'We are in the hut.'

He glanced towards the doorway.

'The rain has gone as quickly as it came! Forgive me . . . I . . . I must have dropped off asleep for a few minutes, while we were waiting for it to stop . . . and I've had a strange dream. Do you remember I told you how I saw Saint Maelisa, when I was a child, crossing the bay from Inish Meadhon, and the waves were many-coloured around his boat because of their holy reflections?'

'Yes.'

She could not help smiling a second time.

'Well, I've just dreamed about the flight of angels that escorted him. I turned to call you, for I thought you were somewhere near me, but there was no answer. Then all was dark and . . .'

He forgot what he was saying, for her face was shadow-pale beneath her hood and he knew, then, that he was in love with her. But she looked so aloof in her pilgrim's cloak that he did not dare to tell her. A dim recollection of what had happened in Moymell came back to him, and believing he had dreamed it, he turned away in embarrassment. He began to search for something in the bracken.

'What have you lost, Enda?'

'My satchel . . . but I've found it again. We must be off now to Dun-da-lacha.'

She could not resist a mirthful answer.

'We might be led astray again!'

'What do you mean?'

'Have you forgotten our meal in the strange hostel?'

'The wheaten bread, so pure and white,' he murmured, as if to himself . . .

'. . . that Ceasan could have found it in the faery-tree!'

'The cress and—'

'. . . the salmon he might have caught, when Eithne sent him to the river that night long ago!'

He turned to her in astonishment.

'But how could you know?'

'Because I was there.'

He did not seem to comprehend her.

'I can remember now, that, in my dream, you reached your hand into the shadows . . .'

'. . . and took the basket-dish of wintered apples!'

'And then I did the same—'

'. . . and found something Ceasan and Eithne had not got!'

'What was it?'

'A flagon of mead.'

'Yes, yes!' he cried excitedly. 'Then it was all true and not a dream!'

'We marvelled at everything about us.'

'We stood at the doorway after that, watching the storm, then we went back to the fire, for the night was chilly. You asked me for a story—'

'. . . and you told me *The Only Jealousy of Congal More.*'

She was delighted with that little game of discovery, but suddenly becoming alarmed lest he should remember too much, she stopped it.

'How could it have really happened, if we are here now, Enda?'

'We must have been together there in spirit.'

'Perhaps it was all illusion.'

'Some say that the invisible is all around us, in and out of thought and time, close as mind. When Bran was sailing across the ocean in search of the hidden land, Mannanan Mac Lir appeared to him, telling him he was already there.'

'What did he mean, Enda?'

'The ocean to Mannanan was a flowery plain on which he was travelling by car. We learn in the ancient poems that what seem lake and mountain to us are . . .' He stopped suddenly.

'What is it?' she asked anxiously.

But he was questioning her.

'Darling, I remember more now. We were standing between the firelight and the shadow. Neither of us moved . . . and yet we were in each other's arms. Have you forgotten our kisses?'

'How could I, Enda, when I gave you at least fifty!'

'But they were spiritual kisses and your will was not your own.'

'Neither was yours.'

'Suppose, for the sake of argument, it was.'

'Then, so was mine.'

'Prove your proposition!'

'How can I, sweet scholar?'

'*Solvitur osculando!*'

Love taught her Latin for an instant and she knew what he asked of her. Besides, her curiosity was as great as his own and she wanted to find out whether a spiritual kiss was better than a real one.

Although both of them found out at once, their kiss was so prolonged that they might have been in Moymell once more. Orla's hood had slipped back, but the gold clasps in her hair were secure and the gay hems beneath the pilgrim-cloak did not stir from her wrists. Only too soon, however, was she aware from his closer embraces that Enda had remembered all the happenings of the night. Never could anyone have been in such a dilemma as she was. Had Aongus brought them back, knowing that the wish of her life could not be granted while they were bodiless? He gave lovers so much and yet so little when they implored his protection—wrack of a sea-cave, a bed in bracken, a night's lodging under a cromlech, like Diarmuid and Grainne. Suppose she was wrong, suppose it was Saint Natalis who wanted to test her worthiness. If so, this was her last chance. In the old days, a hermit had put Liadain and Currither to the same test, but they had not been spirited back from Moymell. It was most unfair, and never had anyone been in such a dilemma as she was. Only of two things was she certain: she had free-will and she must make her choice in less than a minute.

*   *   *

The leaf-tips were sunning themselves, though shadows were thick-set among the trees, when Orla ventured from the hut early the next morning. In the stillness beyond the near branches she could hear a gentle chirping as if the smaller birds did not want to waken their young too soon. Wrapping her dew-dipped cloak around her, she hurried along the track, past fern and wood sorrel, resolving at every turn not to look behind her. She had left Enda fast asleep, sighed to herself and slipped out without saying farewell to him. She knew it was mean of her, but what could she do? She must be sensible again and find her way, as quickly as she could, to the Well before she was missed. Blanaid was sure to be there in good time.

As she went, her resolve was less and she could not help stopping for a few moments to gaze back at the hut. There it was between two oaks, rough-barked as them and twiggy-brown. How unlike the summer-house in which Fial Fairbrow met her lover, with its gaily pinioned roof and glass-beaded windows! In fancy she could see into that summer-house, so clearly had Enda described it, when he was telling her the story of Congal More, could see the red-yew furniture, fair naps and bronze fittings. But for all its plainness, she loved that hut more than if it had been a saint's refuge and it would be dear to her in memory. She hurried on, still thinking of it, but when she turned to look for the last time, it was hidden among leaves.

Orla felt so lonely then, she scarcely knew where the path was leading her until she found herself at the edge of a grassy clearing. Sunshine was warmer there and so quiet, the birds must be waiting in the thickets for her to go by. She was sure they came there, first thing in the morning, before the rabbits went back to their burrows. She thought she heard a light step on the track behind her and her heart beat fast. Enda had wakened and, finding her gone, was hurrying after her. She closed her eyes for a few seconds: they would be together always like lovers in the stories which he had not time to tell her. They would wander southward beyond the Shannon and the great lakes that she had never seen. No, no, they would not go south, for it was there that he had been acquainted with those other women. But why should she be jealous of them, when she alone had been in Moymell with him? She listened to her heart, but she knew she was mistaken: there was no sound of hurrying footsteps on the track. The birds were becoming impatient at her delay and were fluttering in the thickets. It had only been her fancy and she would not be safe from herself until she was at the Well. Enda was sure to sleep for hours, for when she bent over him in the dim dawn, he seemed tired out: and by the time the sunlight wakened him, Blanaid and she would be on their homeward journey, and if they travelled at a good pace they would . . . She was out of the wood, running down a slope; then she stood in perplexity. There were two tracks in front of her, one to the left, the other to the right.

It was the happiness of the bird-companies that made her take the path on her right, for never had she heard so many linnets, thrushes, blackbirds, all singing together. They were just beyond the ridge in front of her. No sooner was she between heather and bramble than the very larks went up, and, hastening beneath the airy thrills, she could hear a dozen notes for every step she took. The track brought her into a little glen and she stopped in surprise, seeing that the may was out. As she gazed at all that white blossoming, the hidden birds were so loud that she could not hear her own cry of pleasure. She remembered how she had lingered by the shore of Lough Guillinn, on the first morning of her pilgrimage and dreamed of the months when she would be expecting. She had touched the hawthorn buds, closing her eyes, as if she felt the pressure of her own delicate milk. In a little while the birds would be as busy here as at Lough Guillinn. Already in her fancy she could see the blackbirds running across the grass, green finch and gold-crest swaying on the taller stalks, hill-birds that were strange to her, all fetching and carrying titbits through the air. Soon there would be scores of tiny parents on the wing, and, after that, the fledglings would fluff themselves and get ready for their first lesson in flying. Never had she heard so many birds singing all together and soon she could see a few of them, here and there, on the bushes. Opposite her was perched a thrush, shaking with notes that were as copious and variegated as the mighty speckles on his chest, and then the linnets went by. Suddenly in the sunlight she seemed to see the hermit, more tattered than ever, as he laughed and beckoned her to come: then she could no longer see him, but she knew by the linnets going in front of her that Aongus was hidden among them in the sunlight. Enda seemed to be beside her and they were studying together the augury of the birds. Then she started from her daydream and ran out of the white glen. She was certain, now, that she had taken the wrong turn.

Orla did not pause until she had gained the other track and could not hear the bird-songs any more. It was among these round-ish hills, these sheep pasturages, that Enda and she went astray the night before, so she glanced around anxiously lest she should see the pale stone. She had come to the bent and a sea-breeze was touching her brow: then between two hills, she saw the clearness of the morning tide. The Well must be hidden among those trees under the bigger hill, less than a quarter of a mile away. When she reached it, she would be safe at last.

Orla had scarcely any breath left as she went under the trees. Her heart sank, for there was no well there. Then she noticed a clump of older trees by the hillside, near the shore. She came to that damp place before the sun had reached it and knew at once that she was no longer astray. Reverently she stood before the thorns, gazing at the ancient branches, behung with weather-worn rags from which the dyes had long since fled. Year after year, barren women had come there and each left one of those simple pledges. It fluttered there, in wind and sun, until it, too, was dust. Moved by the pious belief of centuries, Orla watched the scraps until she could scarcely see them because her eyes were filled with tears. Then she pulled up her skirt, and tore off a small strip near the hem. She tied it to the highest branch she could reach. On that bare thorn-tree, it looked like a last green leaf.

Slowly she turned towards the steps which led to the Well beneath the rock. Never had she prayed so fervently in her young life as at this moment when she besought Saint Natalis to intercede for her. Many things had happened that she would never understand. But her wish had been answered partly for she was the first at the Well that morning and her side was quick with hope. She rose from her knees and, seeing the circle of shale, she made the rounds, widdershins, and seven times, for she remembered all Blanaid's instructions. As she turned for the last time, the sun entered the wood and something shone with life from the Well and disappeared again in a splash.

It was the blessed trout.

Joyfully, Orla ran to the pool, and, scooping her hands, she drank of the ripple. Her mouth was dry and feverish, but she could feel the water chilling her inside and dreamed her wish was already granted. Then she heard the distant murmur of a crowd: the pilgrims were coming along the seashore to the Well. She must not be seen, so she ran, and waited behind a rock.

In a long procession, the women approached, their heads covered with black shawl or weather-hood. A few were sobbing, but those beside them prayed louder as they turned slowly towards the trees. At a respectful distance, their menfolk waited humbly and Orla glanced in a little dread towards them as she thought of the frenzied sport the night before, but she could not see her assailant. The women were beginning their rounds and she joined them quietly. As she did so, she found Blanaid looking for her and drew her aside.

'I was a little late, lady, and couldn't find you at the hostel.'

'It would have been difficult,' Orla smiled.

'You mean . . . you were the first at the Well?'

Orla nodded.

'But it's wonderful! You must have stayed up all night.'

'I didn't.'

She whispered something and Blanaid's eyes opened wider.

'And you saw the holy jumper?'

'Yes.'

'And drank the water and made the rounds?'

'Everything you told me.'

'Then you will surely have your wish.'

Suddenly Orla swayed a little and leaned against a tree.

'What is it?' exclaimed Blanaid anxiously.

'It's nothing . . . my stomach felt a little sick just now. But I'm all right again.'

'It's the cold spring water; you've been fasting too long. But it's a good sign!'

As they were leaving the prayerful wood, Blanaid showed her the basket she had brought with her.

'I'll cook breakfast for you at the hostel. I've a couple of heathpoult's eggs here, fresh butter and an oaten cake, warm from the griddle. I made it myself this morning and that is why I was a little late.'

'The sight of that good food has given me an appetite already. We'll hurry and be miles away before all these people start for home.'

At that moment Orla turned pale for she was certain that she saw through the branches the red curls of Enda as he came in search of her. Before she could stir, Blanaid had turned with a giggle.

'Well, I never! Look who is coming!'

She whispered and Orla, turning round, met her husband.

'Thank Heaven you're safe!' exclaimed Flann as he clasped her hands.

'Of course I am safe,' she smiled bravely, 'and I've been at the Well already. But why did you come?' she wondered.

'I had such a dreadful dream about you the night before last and thought you were in danger.'

'That was when we were at the convent.'

She turned to Blanaid.

'I was so uneasy,' he went on, 'that I left the next morning with a few men, hoping to overtake you. But we went astray in a great mist that came from the sea yesterday and wandered for hours without meeting a soul. Then we came on a ragged old man sitting under a turf stack, watching a flock of little birds nearby. He said he was a bird charmer, and laughed so much we could scarcely get a word of broken Irish from him. But to make a long story short, the wicked rascal put us on the wrong road.'

Orla could not help thinking it was the stranger who had delayed Blanaid with his cunning conversation beyond Nephin, while he was mending his bird-snares. She knew, now, who he was, but she kept her thoughts to herself.

'And what happened after that, Flann?'

'We found our way at last to Dun-da-lacha and stayed the night there.'

Orla gave a start but said nothing. She was pleased that Flann had come for her, despite all he said when she told him for the first time about the holy well. She took his arm and talked happily as they went back along the shore to the hostel.

So far, then, the pilgrimage of Orla.

Her wish was granted and in due course she presented her husband with a fine bouncing boy. Little Flann had one red-gold curl, and whenever his mother suckled him she looked down at it, knowing that he would soon have as many of them as his daddy.

MIDIR AND ETAIN

Sir Shane Leslie

The love story of Midir, the proud and handsome son of the Dagda, the father of the ancient gods, and the beautiful Etain, is probably the most famous romance in Irish mythology. There are numerous versions of the tale in which the supernatural intervenes in the affairs of the couple who have subsequently become fairies in the minds of the people—but few more fantastic adaptations than the following one by Sir Shane Leslie (1885–1971), the larger-than-life writer, scholar, editor, world-traveller and investigator.

Sir Shane Leslie was a one-man phenomenon. For some years he was a friend of Leo Tolstoy, then for a time lived as a tramp. He brilliantly edited the Dublin Review *before moving to America where he lectured at the University of Pennsylvania. He was, however, most deeply driven by a fascination with mythology and the supernatural, and for many years carried out painstaking investigations into tales of hauntings in Britain and Ireland, which formed the basis of his famous* Ghost Book *(first published in 1955 and still in print). He devoted similar energy to studying the heroic legends of his native land for collections such as* Masquerades *(1924) and* Fifteen Odd Stories *(1935). His unique version of 'Midir and Etain' is taken from the first of these now rare volumes.*

*   *   *

Once upon a time the Kingdom of Meath was as rocky and stone-bound as the fields of Connaught today. Etain the girl fairy lived with Midir the King of the Elf-mounds of Ireland. She was the most beautiful of her kind, for the folk of Ireland judged beauty ever afterward by Etain the beautiful, but she was unstable and fitful. She had a mind and a half-memory, as well as a full memory. It was out of her half-memory that Midir heard her speak in her sleep of other lovers beside himself. With brooding on her strange-ness he became a stranger to her in his own mind. With that he left her and went riding upon his coal-black horse. A snow-white hound ran for shadow by its side, for no fairy horse can throw a shape upon the ground.

It was a second wife he brought home. She was also of the fey, and her jealousy was more terrible than the jealousy of women born. She dealt secretly with her Druids to ply Etain with spells. They made Etain as a butterfly that eateth flowers. Etain fluttered vainly into Midir's sight, but his eyes were cast elsewhere and the Druids' wind blew Etain like a silken leaf across moor. Seven years she was carried hither and thither by the king-winds of Ireland until she lighted in the palace of Midir's dear foster-son by the Boyne water. He knew her for woman under fey and built her a little house with windows instead of doors, and fed her with bog myrtle and rowanberries. At evening she would assume her ancient beauty. For the Druid spell was by the Sun and by the Moon and lost power in the twilight, which is neither of sunshine nor moonlight. Midir's Druids knew she was come by Boyne water and hastened till they found her bower hanging like a swallow's room to the palace walls. Etain was drying her wings in the light. With a magic blast they tossed her again upon the elements, and for seven years she floated like a little satin cloud hither and thither.

A lesser wind dropped her into the court where the people of Ulster sucked sweet hydromel from methers. Etain fell into the cup beside the King's wife. It was a woman's cup and white with milk, so that she swallowed Etain for a white curd. In earthly shape was Etain reborn and then was she called Etain, for her fairy name was not revealed then or thereafter by dream or Druid. With Ulster's princely daughters she was reared till the noon of maidenhead. One day they bathed together in the blue speckled sea. A strange horseman rode by upon a coal-black horse, and a seagull sailed for silvery shadow under its hoofs. All but Etain slipped into the waves, but she stood, caught in her half-mind. The stranger said, so that she heard:

'She was so delicate that a Queen quaffed her unwitting. Her place is not with earth children. For her sake Meath shall be smoother than sea and the Elf-mounds of Ireland laid in ruin. The men of Ireland shall measure beauty by her name for ever.'

He said, and slipped behind air and was unseen. Hither and thither the princely maidens of Ulster waded for wonder and for fear of his words. But Etain stood trembling like a winged thing in a draught of fire.

Eochy was King of Ireland and lived in the demesne of Meath. For the man of Meath is the ruler of the men of Ireland. But the rocks of Meath gave no place to his horses, and the rushes no milk to his cows. He was wont to ride round Ireland visiting every King and Kingling of his allegiance. His loneliness for one was not healed by the company of the many. He stayed unwedded, not finding mate among the royal women of Ireland. Harpers he had sent upon horses and wizards upon air to find one willing and worthy to queen Ireland. Lastly he rode out with only a favourite harper alone with him. Toward evening they found Etain. A purple mantle stitched with silver hung across her shoulder. With a silver comb she drew her hair into plaits. Her cheeks were red as the sun upon the West, and her arms were whiter than the snow falling at dawn. Her teeth were pearls dashed in the foam of the sea. Her eyebrows were darker than the wing of the bright beetle.

The King asked her name. 'I am Etain of the Elf-mounds,' she said; for by dreaming she had happed upon the place she came from. He asked if she were betrothed, and she told him that the Kings and noblemen of the Faery came wooing her by all the wells and waterways of Ireland. To forsake all the women of the world the King promised, if she would but come with him to Meath. But for love of the World-under-wave she would not queen Ireland.

Eochy returned to his home. By day he lay him down, and by night he rode and swam. Love of Etain let him not enjoy the life and valour of the world. Druid and harper could not quell the pangs of his pain nor the sorrow of his sickness. A leech came, who could tell the disease in the house from the smoke curling on the roof-top. 'No need to lament,' quoth he, approaching the palace, 'this man is undone by one of the two peerless plagues which afflict the men of Ireland. It is envy or it is love.' He saw the King and said: 'It is not envy. It is beyond the dream of Druid and the healing of harpers. The herb of the physician cannot attain thereto.' The King rose and said: 'My disease hath run deeper than my covering of skin. My love is a kingdom of strength and I am held therein. I am wrestling with a spectre. I am tossed to

Heaven and I am thrown into the sea. I am enamoured of an echo.'

'Better seek the rock that gave you the echo,' said the leech, and the King set riding again with his harper. When they approached the dwelling of Etain, the King sent his harper to play in her hearing while he waited the distance of the sound away. Etain saw the King passing and took no notice, for she saw the darkness of his horse's shadow upon the rocks. But of his sweetest the royal harper harped. When he played of the wonders and wooings of Meath, Etain listened and the Boyne river passed from her memory, and the Kingdom of the Elf-mounds from her half-memory. She rose to reward the harper. Nothing would he take but to tell her his story. He told her of Eochy, High King of Ireland, wasting away for her sake, until she took pity and told him to send the King to tryst at dawn that he might live and not die of her.

At dawn of dawn one drew near to her, and courted her with tales of the beauty and bravery of Meath. She soothed his love and went her way in the twilight. In the true dawn came the King, and when he found her gone he wished to lie down and die. His harper found Etain and persuaded her to tryst with the King at the dawn of the morrow. Once again it was the wraith that came to Etain in the twilight of dawn, but with the likeness and the voice of Eochy. The wraith told her that the women of Meath had lost all beauty in the night. Etain said: 'It is with Eochy and not with you that I trysted at dawn lest he should come to his death.' The wraith replied: 'It were better that you should court me than the sick King, for I was your lover in the aforetime.'

Ever was Etain remembering, and the wraith spoke to her by the fairy name that lay in her half-memory, and said: 'I am Midir and by the sorcery of Druids we were driven apart. Again have I found thee as ever of enduring beauty and faithless mind. When I prattled to thee of the Methians thou thoughtest I was their King. King am I only of those who pass under wave and beyond world.' Then was Etain divided between her love for Faery and her anger at the trick which Midir had played against her, and she made pretence that she would marry the man who had Meath for his own. Answered Midir: 'Can I not give thee all the may-meadows and well-waters of Ireland for bride gift?' Answered Etain: 'Even so would I not exchange the Methian royalty for thy lineage, which

is none that men know.' 'True said,' replied Midir, 'for there is
no lineage where there is neither birth nor death.' Fiercely he
pressed her to return with him to the Elfmounds, saying: 'Thou
shalt live for ever with the primrose-haired. Thou shalt be Queen
of the tribes who pass all-seeing and unseen through the hills of
Ireland. Pleasant are the plains of Ireland, but there is a Plain
which is beyond pleasure. Delicious to the minds of men is the
sweet hydromel that the women of Ireland brew in vats, but the
drink of my country enchanteth every sense together.'

Etain would have laid away her pretence then and gone with
Midir, but Eochy drew near with his harper, and the earthly harper
drowned the dream of Faery. For a year and a moon and a night
Etain lived with Eochy in the Kingdom of Meath, and theirs were
all the boundaries of all Ireland. Whoever is Lord of Meath king-
eth every bound of Ireland. 'The Setting is with the Jewel,' as the
Brehons have said. Their allotted time passed and they chanced
to sit in the hall of banquet. The inner gates were closed. The
armed men were withdrawn from the ramparts, for it was against
the chivalry of Ireland to make attack after nightfall. The porter
stood alone in the court. A warrior was seen passing within the
gates. The porter knew not his face nor his accoutrements and
still-stood with fright. His knees kissed and his heels fled from
each other. Eochy heard the clinking of his knees and cried aloud
to the porter: 'Who knocks?'

'Midir of the Elf-mounds,' was the reply, 'and I am come to
play against the royal harpers for a fee.'

The King of Ireland consented, both for his love of harmony
and for his love of the hazard. Now the best harpers in Ireland
are they who have learnt their tunes from the herdsmen who listen
at the holes of the Elf-mounds, and Midir made sure that no harper
of Eochy would play other than echoes of his own music. Very
cunningly he played the music of challenge, and sang of the youth
and beauty of the world that is ever young, until the old wine in
the casks stored under the roof became fresh wine of the grape
and poured down the walls. When he had finished, the very
warriors and poets of Eochy cried: 'Victory indeed!'

Then the King called his favourite harper, who had been stolen
out of his cradle by a water-wench, and had heard better music
under wave than ever upon earth. Long he played and all listened,
Midir most of all. It was no music of Elf-land or echo of the elfin

tune, but the music of the cities which have been drowned in the Western sea. The night winds carried the music into the trees outside the royal rath of the King and, though it was winter, they burst into bloom. When he had ended, all present cried: 'Victory over victory!' Midir asked the fee he should pay to the royal harper of Ireland. 'Clear the plains of Meath smooth of stone!' said the harper, who knew whence Midir came. Midir went as he came.

At dawn the royal steward went out and found the fields as smooth as the face of the clouds, and a great host with fairy oxen carrying away every stone except the magic stones of the Druids, and sinking them into the bogs and waterholes of Ireland.

But Midir was unsatisfied and came to the King the next night, passing porter and portals into the room of banquet. The King asked his need, and he said: 'A game of royal chess.' The board was set of gold and silver squares, and the King slew half of Midir's chessmen. Midir pretended anger, and bade the King choose whatever stake he would. 'Rid the fields of Meath of every rush,' said the King. At dawn the royal steward went out and reported that a multitude of small folk were hewing down the last rushes as men destroy a forest.

The next night Eochy came again and asked another game. The King gladly consented to show his skill. Midir played with the wisdom of his own people, and he left no piece but his own standing upon the board, and the King's kingpiece. The King inquired his stake. 'To hold Etain the beautiful in my arms for a moment of time,' said Midir. The King was troubled and bade him return after the month.

At the end of the month Eochy filled his halls with chosen warriors and trim swordsmen, and sent men riding to and fro upon the ramparts. Midir passed through them all. 'A debt is due to me,' he said. 'I have not considered yet,' said the King. 'Etain the beautiful thou hast promised me.' 'But only for a moment of time,' said Eochy. Fear came upon Etain, for the year of her forgetfulness was passing from her. To the King she clung, saying: 'Until thou resign me I will not go from thee.' 'I will not resign thee,' said Eochy, 'but he may take thee in his arms for a moment of time as thou art, and in the midst of my warriors, and while my horsemen gallop the battlements.' 'Well said,' quoth Midir, 'for a moment of love time is longer than all time.' To Etain then he whispered her fairy name.

She withdrew not from his arms, but passed away with him as she had come, through the lattice of the roof. Eochy the King rose and cried aloud as a sheep shouteth to an eagle bearing away her lamb. When the warriors in the court heard the cry of the King, they leaped against each other with their swords in their hands and shame in their eyes. And the riding men spurred to and fro upon the ramparts. Yet no one was seen to pass, and though the King of Ireland rode into the night with his harper and his Druid he never came by Etain the beautiful. But the fields of Royal Meath to this day are smooth of stone and rid of rush.

A PRINCE IN DISGUISE

Sinead de Valera

At least three kings named Cormac have featured in Irish romances: Cormac Cond Longes, who had a famous affair with the wife of Craiftine of Leinster; Cormac Mac Art, the High King, whose daughter Grainne eloped with the warrior Diarmuid, giving rise to the legend of 'The Pursuit of Diarmuid and Grainne'; and Prince Cormac of Ulster whose courtship of Etain is the subject of this story by Sinead de Valera (1889–1975).

Mrs de Valera, the wife of the former President of Ireland, was a highly regarded writer of folk stories and had a special interest in retelling the ancient myths in books such as The Stolen Child *(1965), for young readers, and* The Four-Leaved Shamrock *(1968), a collection of legends for adults. Her books have played a significant part in promoting among Irish readers a love of their ancient heritage, but stories such as 'A Prince in Disguise', which has only previously been available in a limited Irish edition, are undoubtedly worthy of wider circulation.*

*　　*　　*

Prince Cormac was the only child of King Oriel and Queen Aoife.

The great desire of the parents' hearts was to see their son happily married. They determined to speak to him about choosing a wife.

'Cormac,' said the King, 'you must marry. Surely you will not allow the throne to descend to a stranger.'

'And,' added the Queen, 'our great possessions to pass out of the family.'

'But, Mother, I am content as I am. Where could I find a wife I would love as I love you? And where could I find one with such beautiful raven hair and sparkling eyes as yours?'

'You, yourself, Cormac, have inherited your mother's beautiful eyes and hair,' said the King.

Cormac possessed many natural gifts. He was handsome and brave and had won the affection of his people by his kindness and charm.

Among his many manly qualities was his skill as an athlete. He was almost tired of receiving homage and praise for his achievements on the sports field.

'Fergal,' he said one day to his best friend, 'it is because I am the Prince that such great tribute is paid to my athletic triumphs.'

'Nonsense,' said Fergal, 'the applause is thoroughly deserved.'

'Well, I intend to put the sincerity to the test. I want you to help me to disguise myself and I shall play as an ordinary hurler.'

'And how will you arrange all that?'

'The players will be waiting for the arrival of the Prince and when he does not appear I in my disguise will offer to fill the vacant place so that the game may be played.'

'Well, you have always enjoyed jokes and pranks. I hope this one will turn out to your satisfaction.'

The day for the contest arrived. The players on both sides were ready for the game, but where was the Prince?

'The match must proceed,' said the captain on one side.

'Yes,' agreed the other captain. 'It would be unlucky to postpone it. It must be played today for the new moon will appear tonight and our matches are timed for the first appearance of the new moon.'

At this point in the conversation Cormac, wearing a wig and cleverly disguised, came forward and spoke in a foreign language. Fergal answered in the same language.

'The game may go on as usual,' he said, 'if this player is allowed to take the vacant place.'

'By all means he will be allowed to play,' said one of the captains.

'And indeed,' said the captain of the other side, 'we are all very thankful to him for enabling us to proceed with the game.'

Opposite the ground where the match was to be played there was a beautiful castle. It had belonged to a chieftain named Niall who lived there with Maeve his wife and their daughter Etain.

Maeve had died and after some years Niall had married a widow named Sorcha who had a daughter, Grainne.

The second wife seemed at first to be very kind.

'I will be a mother to Etain, your dear child,' she said, 'and though Grainne is some years older than your daughter they will love each other like sisters.'

There is a proverb in Irish which says 'Time is a good story-teller.' It had a sad story to tell about poor Etain. Her father died.

After his death Sorcha and Grainne showed themselves in their true colours. They were very cruel to Etain. Grainne hated her.

'Mother,' she would say, 'how is it that Etain looks more beautiful in her old clothes than I do in all my grandeur?'

'Never mind, my dear. We will keep her out of the way and no one will know how beautiful she is.'

Poor Etain had a very unhappy life.

Sorcha and Grainne were among the spectators at the great match. From a small hillock on the side of the field they watched the play.

Etain longed to see the game. She managed to steal out of the house and got a place among the crowd. Like all the onlookers here eyes were fixed in admiration on one of the players who outshone all the others. His movements were swift and accurate and it might be said that the game centred round him.

Suddenly a ball whizzed towards him. There was a wail from the crowd as it struck him. He fell to the ground just near the place where Etain stood.

In her excitement she rushed towards him and raised his head. As she did so the fair wig fell away and the black, curling hair was revealed.

'Prince Cormac, Prince Cormac,' came the shout from the crowd.

For a moment Cormac opened his eyes and gazed at the fair face bending over him. Then he became unconscious.

'Let the Prince be brought to my house,' said Sorcha, 'and send at once for medical aid.'

To the joy of all concerned the doctor said the injury was not serious. Rest and quiet were all that was necessary for complete recovery.

Sorcha and Grainne were delighted to have the Prince for their guest.

'Dress in your finest clothes, my daughter, and sing your sweetest songs,' said Sorcha. 'Do your best to charm and entertain the Prince.'

Now Cormac was particularly musical. The harsh, out-of-tune singing that he was forced to listen to nearly drove him mad. News of the accident, had, of course, been sent to the palace.

The King was absent from home when the message arrived but the Queen set out at once to go to her son.

There was much delay on the journey. A rain storm had come on and travelling was very difficult. Shortly before the end of the journey the weather changed and the sun shone brightly.

As the carriages approached the castle, beautiful singing was heard from inside the orchard.

'Stop the carriages for a while,' ordered the Queen.

The singing ceased but out from the orchard came a lovely girl. Her fair hair had come loose and had fallen on her shoulders like a golden fleece.

The Queen could not restrain her admiration.

'Fair maiden, what is your name?' she asked.

'Etain is my name, your Majesty.'

Just then a huge, tall man came running towards Etain.

'Hurry, hurry, asthore,' he said. 'Your step-mother is calling and you know the sort of temper she has.'

When Queen Aoife reached the castle Sorcha and Grainne went down on their knees to welcome her.

'I am thankful,' said the Queen, 'for the hospitality and kindness you have shown to the Prince, my son.'

'Oh, your Majesty, it has been a privilege and an honour to have him with us.'

The Prince was delighted to see his mother.

After some time the Queen said:

'As we were passing the orchard I heard most beautiful singing.'

'It must have been Grainne, my daughter, your Majesty heard,' said Sorcha. 'She has a wonderful voice.'

'Yes, Mother,' said Cormac with a slight wink, 'she has indeed quite a wonderful voice.'

'When we reached the entrance to the orchard a lovely girl came out. I thought perhaps she was the singer.'

'Oh! Not at all,' said Grainne, 'she was merely one of the servants.'

'Though she was poorly dressed,' said the Queen, 'she looked very beautiful with the sunshine gleaming on her golden hair.'

'Mother,' exclaimed Cormac, 'I have seen a girl like that in my dreams.'

'Your Majesty,' said Sochra, 'the Prince has been delirious nearly all the time since the accident. Nothing soothes him but a drink which I prepare for him.'

Cormac looked at the Queen and said, 'Is it not strange, Mother, that I feel bright and strong till I take the drink. After having it I become dull and listless.'

The Queen turned to Sorcha, saying: 'Thank you for your hospitality and kindness, which I hope to repay. I shall have arrangements made to take the Prince home as soon as possible.'

The Queen departed but soon returned to take Cormac home.

Sorcha and Grainne were determined that neither Cormac nor the Queen would see Etain. They had the girl locked in a room at the top of the house. No one was allowed to go near her.

There was only one person in the household who dared to befriend Etain. This was poor, simple Conn, who did most of the slavish work round the kitchens. He was a huge, strong fellow, but for all his size and strength he was very gentle and kind. All the animals round the house loved and trusted him.

Conn had a great affection for Etain. She told him all her troubles.

Very shortly before the departure of the Queen and Cormac, Conn rushed upstairs to the locked room.

'Are you there, my girl?' he asked through the keyhole.

'Yes, Conn,' came the reply.

Conn hurled his great body against the door. The lock broke and he was soon in the room.

'Come quietly, asthore. They are getting ready for the journey. We will slip out by the back door.'

Etain followed Conn. Before long they were out on the road. The moon was shining brightly.

'Now,' said Conn, 'when we come to the orchard gate stand still. Leave the rest to me.'

Queen Aoife, Cormac and their retinue left the castle to the great disappointment of Sorcha and her daughter.

When the carriages were approaching the orchard, Conn rushed in front of them waving his hands.

'Stop, stop,' he said. 'Look towards the orchard gate.'

All eyes turned to where Etain stood in the moonlight. Her beautiful hair stirred lightly in the faint breeze.

'Mother,' exclaimed Cormac, 'that is the face I have seen in my dreams.'

Conn came to the carriage door.

'Oh, Queen,' he said, 'take pity on a poor, tortured girl and save her from the cruelty of a heartless pair.'

'Mother,' said Cormac, 'please take the girl into the carriage.'

'Oh,' said Etain, 'I cannot go without Conn, my best friend.'

'There is room for all,' said the Queen.

Etain remained silent after she told why and how she had escaped from the castle.

Not so Conn.

'Won't there be hunger and thirst in the castle tonight?' he said, chuckling and rubbing his hands.

'You know, your Majesty,' he continued, 'Sorcha and her ugly daughter have fine appetites and like a good meal.'

'And will they not have one tonight?' asked Cormac.

Conn shock with laughter as he said:—

'Hardly, your Highness. I collected all the hungry cats I could find and shut them in the pantries. How will it be when the cooks go to look for the milk, cream, beef, fish and all the good things that the cruel pair will be expecting for their evening meal?'

Not one of the company could refrain from joining in the hearty laughter.

The end of the story was that King Oriel and his Queen got their wish when their valiant son was married to beautiful Etain.

LEGEND FOR A PAINTING

Julia O'Faolain

Dragons are a recurring feature in Irish romances, and the familiar scene of a beautiful maiden held prisoner by a monstrous serpent as she awaits rescue by some valiant knight is to be found in any number of stories. Curiously, despite the surfeit of these creatures in such tales, legend has it that St Patrick drove out all the serpents from the land—although in fact there have never been any venomous reptiles in Ireland. This has done nothing to remove the dragon-and-the-lady concept from fantasy fiction, however, as this next story by Julia O'Faolain (1935-) clearly demonstrates.

Julia O'Faolain, the daughter of the famous novelist and short story writer, Sean O'Faolain, has proved herself as talented and inventive a writer as her father in a number of novels and short story collections published since the appearance of her first work, Two Memoirs of Renaissance Florence, *published in 1967. She has drawn on her rich Irish heritage for several stories, but none quite match the dark fantasy and humour of 'Legend for a Painting'.*

*　　*　　*

A knight rode to a place where a lady was living with a dragon. She was a gently bred creature with a high forehead, and her dress—allowing for her surroundings—was neat. While the dragon slept, the knight had a chance to present himself.

'I have come,' he told the lady, 'to set you free.' He pointed at a stout chain linking her to her monstrous companion. It had a greenish tinge, due the knight supposed to some canker oozing from the creature's flesh.

Green was the dragon's colour. Its tail was green; so were its wings, with the exception of the pale pink eyes which were embedded in them and which glowed like water-lilies and expanded when the dragon flew, as eyes do on the spread tails of peacocks. Greenest of all was the dragon's under-belly which swelled like sod on a fresh grave. It was heaving just now and emitting gurgles. The knight shuddered.

'What,' the lady wondered, 'do you mean by "free"?'

The knight spelled it: 'f-r-e-e', although he was unsure whether or not she might be literate. 'To go!' he gasped for he was grappling with distress.

'But where?' the lady insisted. 'I like it here, you know. Draggie and I'—the knight feared her grin might be mischievous or even mad—'have a perfect symbiotic relationship!'

The knight guessed at obscenities.

'I clean his scales,' she said, 'and he prepares my food. We have no cutlery so he chews it while it cooks in the fire from his throat: a labour-saving device. He can do rabbit stew, braised wood pigeon, even liver Venetian style when we can get a liver.'

'God's blood!' the knight managed to swear. His breath had been taken away.

'I don't know that recipe. Is it good? I can see,' the lady wisely soothed, 'you don't approve. But remember that fire scours. His mouth is germ free. Cleaner than mine or your own, which, if I may say so with respect, has been breathing too close. Have you perhaps been chewing wild garlic?'

The knight crossed himself. 'You,' he told the lady, 'must be losing your wits as a result of living with this carnal beast!' He sprinkled her with a little sacred dust from a pouch that he carried about his person. He had gathered it on the grave of Saint George the Dragon Killer and trusted in its curative properties. 'God grant,' he prayed, 'you don't lose your soul as well. Haven't you heard that if a single drop of dragon's blood falls on the mildest man or maid, they grow as carnal as the beast itself? Concupiscent!' he hissed persuasively. 'Bloody! Fierce!'

The lady sighed. 'Blood does obsess you!' she remarked. 'Draggie never bleeds. You needn't worry. His skin's prime quality. Very resistant and I care for him well. He may be "carnal" as you say. We're certainly both carnivores. I take it you're a vegetarian?'

The knight glanced at the cankered chain and groaned. 'You're mad!' he ground his teeth. 'Your sense of values has been perverted. The fact that you can't see it proves it!'

'A tautology, I think?' The lady grinned. 'Why don't you have a talk with old Draggie when he wakes up? You'll see how gentle he can be. That might dispel your prejudices.'

But the knight had heard enough. He neither liked long words nor thought them proper in a woman's mouth. *Deeds not words* was the motto emblazoned on his shield, for he liked words that condemned words and this, as the lady could have told him, revealed inner contradictions likely to lead to trouble in the long run.

'Enough!' he yelled and, lifting his lance, plunged it several times between the dragon's scales. He had no difficulty in doing this, for the dragon was a slow-witted, somnolent beast at best and just now deep in a private dragon-dream. Its eyes, when they opened, were iridescent and flamed in the sunlight, turning, when the creature wept, into great, concentric, rainbow wheels of fire. 'Take that!' the knight was howling gleefully, 'and that and that!'

Blood spurted, gushed, and spattered until his face, his polished armour and the white coat of his charger were veined and flecked like porphyry. The dragon was soon dead but the knight's rage seemed unstoppable. For minutes, as though battening on its own release, it continued to discharge as he hacked at the unresisting carcass. Butchering, his sword swirled and slammed. His teeth gnashed. Saliva flowed in stringy beardlets from his chin and the lady stared at him with horror. She had been pale before but now her cheeks seemed to have gathered sour, greenish reflections into their brimming hollows.

Abruptly, she dropped the chain. Its clank, as it hit a stone, interrupted the knight's frenzy. As though just awakened, he turned dull eyes to her. Questioning.

'Then,' slowly grasping what this meant, 'you were never his prisoner, after all?'

The lady pointed at a gold collar encircling the dragon's neck. It had been concealed by an overlap of scales but had slipped into view during the fight. One end of the chain was fastened to it.

'He was mine,' she said. 'But as I told you he was gentle and more a pet than a prisoner.'

The knight wiped his eyelids which were fringed with red. He looked at his hands.

'Blood!' he shrieked. 'Dragon's blood!'

'Yes,' she said in a cold, taut voice, 'you're bloody. Concupiscent, no doubt? Fierce, certainly! Carnal?' She kicked the chain, which had broken when she threw it down and, bending, picked up a link that had become detached. 'I'll wear this,' she said bitterly, 'in token of my servitude. I'm your prisoner now.' She slipped the gold, green-tinged metal ring on to the third finger of her left hand. It too was stained with blood.

THE KISS

Michael Scott

According to the ancient romances, Irishmen have been falling in love with the enchanting members of the fairy race, the Sidhe, since time immemorial. Chief among these beguiling women is Grian— named after the dazzling splendour of grian, *the sun—who is said to be the Queen of the Sidhe, and dwells in a palace on top of Cnoc Greine near Pallas Green in Co. Limerick. Her story has been told in a number of the old legends, but is here revived in a modern version by Michael Scott (1943-).*

Scott, a former Dublin antiquarian bookseller, is now one of the pre-eminent Irish writers of folk stories and fantasy fiction: he has published three volumes of Irish Folk and Fairy Tales *(1982);* A Celtic Odyssey: The Voyage of Maildun *(1985); and* Irish Myths and Legends *(1992). His short stories are also notable for their authentic background and historical accuracy, as well as the evocative nature of their telling—all elements which will be found in this tale of four young men who go hunting and track down a most unexpected prize . . .*

*   *   *

The four brothers had been pursuing the enormous boar for the best part of two days now. But the huge beast was cunning, and its scarred body and chipped tusks bore mute testimony to the many hunters who had tried and failed to take the creature. It had left half a hundred dead men in its wake and scores more crippled. It was generally agreed that it was a magical beast, but because it had assumed a physical form, it was vulnerable to physical weapons . . . at least in theory.

Niall, youngest son of Eochu Muigmedon, raised his hand and his three elder brothers, who were riding single file several paces behind him, stopped, waiting patiently while he scouted the land ahead. Though not yet nineteen summers, Niall had already proven himself a brave warrior and a tracker of extraordinary ability in the previous summer when he had traced a serpent-like peist to its lair in one of the smaller rivers and then slain it himself. When the local people had dragged the creature from the bloody river and laid it out on the ground, they had found it to stretch to eight man-lengths. Niall now wore a jerkin made of the creature's skin.

The dark-haired young man slid off his mount and examined the ground which had been baked hard by an unremitting summer. Already many of the rivers had run dry, crops had burnt in the fields, and a disastrous fire had raged across the boglands in the heart of the country, which had destroyed several villages and claimed scores of lives. Niall ran his hand across the ground, but the dry, dusty, cracked earth showed no signs and he sat back on his haunches, allowing his thoughts to roam, trying to think himself into the mind of the boar, looking at the lie of the land from the creature's perspective, trying to visualise how it would see the surrounding terrain.

There was a break in the bushes there!

Niall scuttled over to the gap in the flaking hedgerow, and then he nodded in triumph. There were a dozen of the boar's black hairs scattered on the ground where it had squeezed through. Still on his hands and knees, he pushed his way through the bushes, eyes squinting in the sunlight, head turning slightly from side to side, nostrils flaring as he tested the air for scent.

The boar had come through the hedge . . . and gone that way!

Niall Mac Muigmedon straightened slowly, shading his clear blue eyes from the glare of the mid-morning sunshine. With the landscape shimmering and twisting before him in a heat haze that had draped itself across the countryside like a shifting curtain of gauze, it was difficult to distinguish details, but he thought he could make out a grey thread of smoke spiralling upwards into the metallic sky.

Fethchu and Fethmac, the twins, dismounted and joined their younger brother. They were identical, dark-haired, with the pale blue eyes they had inherited from their northern mother, and so alike that even Niall had difficulty telling them apart. Both were armed with short, stout boarspears. Maolan, the eldest brother, remained on his horse, watching the trio impassively. Though there were nearly ten years between Maolan and the twins and five more between them and Niall, there was no animosity between them, a trait they had learned from their father who had managed to weld the numerous northern and western clans together into a tribe to resist the blond, blue-eyed invaders from the Cold Lands beyond the sea.

'What do you see?' Niall asked, pointing to a pile of stones rising up in the centre of the field.

The twins squinted into the distance.

'It looks like . . .' Fethchu began.

'. . . smoke,' Fethmac finished.

The young man nodded slowly. 'I thought so. The boar took that direction also.'

'How long ago?' Fethchu asked.

'Not long past; since the dawn perhaps.'

The twins turned as one as they raced back for their mounts, Niall following more slowly. He had seen what the boar was capable of doing; they had been following its swath of destruction across the country. He knew how defenceless lightly armed villagers were against the primeval strength of the creature, and he had no desire to look at more gored and torn bodies. In the last village they had been shown a young man—not much older than Niall—who had been gored in the belly by the beast. Though wracked by agony, the young man had managed to give a description of the beast and the direction it had taken, before finally begging them to release him from his suffering. Maolan had examined the wound, but it had already begun to putrefy. Without a word he had plunged his dagger into the youth's heart.

'The trail leads yonder, brother,' Niall said, looking up at Maolan. The eldest of the brothers nodded slightly; he rarely spoke and was nicknamed 'the Silent'.

The four brothers rode on. They moved in single file, with plenty of space between their mounts. If the boar charged, it would only be able to concentrate on one of them, leaving the others time to attack it.

They rode across a flat open countryside, scorched amber and gold and without signs of life: neither deer nor cattle roamed the fields and no birds flew in the heavens. Without the benefit of any shade, the sun was unbearably hot and Niall could feel hot sweat moving down along the length of his spine. He was wearing a heavy leather cuirass, which was uncomfortably heavy, but, as Maolan had pointed out, better to be hot than dead.

The young man dug the heel of his hand into his eyes, and brushed away the salt sweat, blinking furiously. The grey thread that rose straight up into the cloudless, windless sky was indeed smoke, and was issuing from a tumbled pile of stones that was half buried in the ground. If he hadn't seen the smoke, they would probably have ridden past, assuming that it was nothing more than a natural outcropping of rock.

The four brothers stopped well back from the rock. While Niall and Maolan examined it closely, the twins deliberately turned away, keeping watch on their surroundings: there were more dangerous beasts than wild boars in the countryside.

'Can you see any sign of the beast's spoor?' Maolan asked.

Niall dismounted and dropped flat on the ground, his hands brushing at the burnt grass, seeking any sign. The grass was crisp beneath his fingers and, as he pressed downwards, it slowly straightened, leaving no visible mark. Resting his chin on the ground, he stared intently on the earth, finally spotting a series of indentations in the earth. Coming easily to his feet, he nodded at the tumbled pile of stones. 'It went that way.'

The four brothers moved towards the stones. There was a deeply shadowed opening close to the ground, through which the grey-white wisp of smoke was escaping. They had spread out into a long line, being careful not to bunch up. Niall stopped and pointed with his spear. An enormous boar-print was clearly visible in the dust beside a flat stone.

Maolan looked at Fethchu and Fethmac and pointed left and right. They were to go around the stones. With his spear, he indicated that Niall should go up on to the stones, above the entrance. Maolan waited until the twins had reappeared on the far side of the stones; they were both shaking their heads, indicating that there was no other entrance. Moving in closer to the island of stones, they took up positions to the left and right of the dark entrance. When his three brothers were in position, Maolan grounded his spear, butt first, on the hard earth and called out, 'You, within! Come forth. Face me.'

Niall heard a scrabbling sound from inside the heaped stones and jerked his thumb downwards, warning his brother that the primitive dwelling was occupied.

'I have tracked a savage beast to this place,' Maolan continued. 'That is all I am hunting this day.'

A shape appeared in the doorway, a bundle of grey rags, mingled with leaves, twigs and matted filth. Niall, who was above the figure, recoiled with the stench that wafted up from the creature.

'I am the son of Eochu Muigmedon . . . ,' Maolan began.

'Where are your brothers, Maolan, son of Eochu Muigmedon?' The cracked voice was undoubtedly female, though the features were hidden beneath a mass of twisted, tangled hair. 'All Erin knows the sons of Eochu Muigmedon are inseparable.'

'Who are you, old woman?' Maolan asked. 'What are you: witch, sorceress?'

'Neither,' the old woman cackled, 'and not so old as you might think,' she continued. Using a twisted stick, the old woman hobbled up from what was obviously her dwelling in the heart of the stones. She looked left and right, immediately spotting the twins, and then raised her head slightly to look up at Niall. 'Are the sons of Eochu Muigmedon so frightened of one woman?'

Niall slid down the stones to stand beside the creature. Though he was the smallest of the brothers, the woman only came to his chest. 'It was not you we feared,' he said easily, 'but rather what else might be within.'

'There is nothing within but memories.'

Niall nodded, concentrating on breathing through his mouth. The woman was indescribably filthy and, in the intense heat, her odour had assumed an almost physical presence. He could feel his eyes watering with the smell and he knew he'd be smelling that stench for days to come. He would have to wash at the first opportunity. 'We have been chasing a fearsome giant boar for days now. Every town, village and farm we've encountered has some evidence of its passage . . . usually a dead or wounded body,' he added. 'We were afraid we'd find another such here.'

The old woman nodded. 'The boar passed this way earlier this morning. But there was nothing here to tempt it to linger.'

Niall nodded. 'We'll head on then. We must stop this beast before it wreaks more destruction and claims more lives.'

'You'll quench your thirst first though,' the old woman said and, without waiting for a reply, slipped back into the dark interior of the pile of stones. Niall looked at Maolan, who shook his head quickly. They all knew the dangers of accepting food or drink in this fashion.

When the woman reappeared, she was carrying an enormous stone jar and four polished wooden goblets. She set the goblets down on a flat stone and poured thick sweet-smelling mead. Niall felt his mouth water with the sweet richness of it. 'We must push on,' he said reluctantly, 'we are determined to catch this boar.'

'The mead is good,' the old woman said, her voice sounding suddenly tired. 'Will you not accept my hospitality?' She held out a brimming goblet.

Niall looked at his elder brother again. 'It is not that we do not appreciate your hospitality . . . ,' he said eventually

'You fear me,' the woman said suddenly. 'You fear me because of my appearance. Thus am I cursed. Thus am I doomed.'

'Niall,' Maolan said softly, 'we must away.'

The young man looked closely at the woman, seeing her deep brown eyes for the first time beneath the matted tangle of hair. Her eyes were magnified with unshed tears.

Before his brothers could object, Niall reached out suddenly, snatched the goblet and drank deeply. The mead tasted like nectar.

'Niall!' Maolan hissed angrily.

The young man passed back the goblet, his head reeling from the powerful drink. 'My brother worries too much,' he said softly.

'Caution is always admirable, but sometimes one has to trust one's instincts,' the old woman murmured.

'True,' Niall whispered. 'We must away,' he said, and then, leaning forward, brushed the old woman's hair off her face and kissed her lightly on the cheek. 'Take care.'

He had turned away and was walking back towards Maolan when the twins screamed a warning. Niall turned back . . . and then stopped in horror.

Something was happening to the old woman . . . she was changing, altering, her body twisting, turning, convulsing. She fell to the ground, and the rags that covered her frail body crawled and moved with a life of their own as her body spasmed. A stick-like claw bit into the hard earth, blackened ragged nails tearing grooves in the dust.

Maolan's screamed warning jerked Niall around again: the boar had appeared from around the stones and was racing toward them, head lowered, strings of saliva dripping from the gaping jaws. He realized then he had put down his spear when he'd taken the goblet of mead. The beast was enormous, its head was on a level with his chest, its eyes burning with an evil intelligence. Its paws bit deeply into the hard earth as it charged towards him, snorting in a deep bass bellow.

The twins threw their spears at the beast. Fethchu's went high over the boar's back, while Fethmac's bit into the ground in front of it. The boar didn't even slow as it trampled over it, snapping it in two.

Maolan's spear thudded into the ground beside Niall. Wrenching it free, the young man turned to face the creature that was almost upon him. He knew there was no way he could stand the boar's charge: even with the heavy boar spear in his hands, the beast would simply impale itself on the spear and then run him down.

He had one desperate chance . . .

Niall raced towards the beast, the bizarre action shocking his brothers speechless. At the last moment, he grounded the spear in the hard earth and used it to launch himself up and over the boar's back. He hit the ground with enough force to knock the wind from him.

Confused, the boar skidded to a halt in a cloud of red dust. It spun around and spotted the bundle on the ground. Lowering its head, its razor-sharp teeth winking in the sunlight, it charged Niall. He managed to stagger to his feet, at least determined to die like a man.

The beast bore down on him, the sunlight turning its coarse red hair to a burnished copper that also seemed ablaze in the afternoon light . . . and then Niall realized the hair was alight. The beast was burning!

The boar stopped, tossing its head in confusion. Blue flames were dancing across its skin, the coarse hair crisping, curling. It opened its mouth and bellowed, and disgorged a column of flame. It staggered a few final steps towards Niall, before crashing over on its side less than half-a-dozen paces in front of Niall. It writhed in silent agony. The stench of burning hair and flesh tainted the dry air.

Niall retrieved Fethchu's spear which had missed the beast.

Approaching as close as possible to the wildly thrashing animal, feeling the skin on his face and arms sear in the incredible heat, he plunged the spear deep into its body, ending its torment.

Fethchu and Fethmac helped him away from the carcass. Maolan appeared, holding the horses. He embraced his younger brother, touching blunt fingers to the young man's hair and eyebrows which had been singed by the flames. 'You were lucky,' he said simply.

'But what happened . . . ?' Niall asked, surprised to find that his voice was hoarse and raw. There was a taste of smoke and burnt meat in his mouth and nostrils.

The three brothers looked beyond Niall. He turned slowly to face the same direction.

There was a woman standing before the tumbled stone dwelling. A tall golden-haired, brown-eyed woman, with pale, delicate features. In his bemused state it took him a few moments to realise she was wearing the grey rags of the evil-smelling old woman. Shaking off his brother's hands, he walked forward to stand before her. He guessed she was only a few summers older than himself.

'You saved me,' he said simply.

'You saved me,' she replied.

'I did nothing.'

'Five hundred summers and more ago, I refused the attentions of an old lord. He was powerful though and versed in magic and, whilst he had once been great, he had grown spiteful in his old age. He condemned me to live ageing but alive until someone accepted something willingly from me. I've waited and tried and, over the seasons, many people came and went and none would ever accept anything I offered. Most people feared me, loathed me for what I had become, despised me for the state in which I lived, but, you see, I had been placed under a geasa—a spell— never to leave my tower. However, the same lord had had my tower pulled down and then compelled me to live in the ruins.' She smiled at Niall and reached out with her long fingers to touch his face. 'And now you have broken that spell.'

'You set fire to the boar.'

'I once kept the fire that is sacred to the sun alight. My element is fire; my magic is drawn from that power.'

'Who are you?' Niall asked. 'And who was the lord who condemned you thus?'

The woman smiled. 'I am Grian, whom you now know as legend, and the lord was Fionn, son of Cumhal, who was once man, but is now legend. Do not condemn him. When Dermot took Grainna away from him, he lost much of his capacity to love. When his son Oisin was taken away into the Tir na nOg, he became bitter indeed. Remember him instead as a hero.'

'And you?' Niall whispered. 'What will become of you now?'

'Now?' The woman's smile was radiant. 'Now I can go and die in peace.'

THE WOMAN WITHOUT MERCY

Maurice Walsh

Irish mythology has its share of black-hearted and evil women, as many as any other nation—although they have a tendency to be more intriguing and certainly more memorable, as the next two stories will demonstrate. The title of 'The Woman Without Mercy' almost speaks for itself, and to say much more than that it pits brother against brother for the love of the same woman would spoil the enjoyment of reading it. The story is an example of the exceptional talent of Maurice Walsh (1879–1968), the novelist who was born in Listowel, Co.Kerry, and was once described by the American magazine Life *as 'an articulate Irishman with the heart of a poet'. After the success of his early novels,* The Key above the Door *(1926),* The Small Dark Man *(1929) and* Thomasheen James *(1941), he became world-famous when his story* The Quiet Man *was brought to the screen in 1953, starring John Wayne. 'The Woman Without Mercy' was written in 1923 for the* Dublin Magazine, *and I am delighted to be restoring it to print in these pages.*

* * *

Delgan walked the road all by himself, but Delgan was not lonely. Behind him as he walked was a stupendous wide plain, and, a million miles beyond the far-away curve of it, loomed the blue-grey of mountains. And the same stupendous plain stretched away in front of him, slowly lifting its grey-green like the sea, until, like the sea, it rolled starkly over the horizon, beyond which were no mountains, but splendid, serene white towers of cloud lifting themselves out of the void beyond the world's edge. The immense arch of the sky did not touch the horizon, but went unbelievably beyond it on every hand, so that the towering white clouds seemed to be in the foreground, and the plain, that went from horizon to horizon, no more than an unstable palm's-breadth thrust up into the voids of space. An imaginative man might have a fear that this plot of earth would at any moment reel and topple and fall forever through that void.

But Delgan did not walk as if he were on the edge of an abyss. His stride was long and supple, and in his own mind he towered into the sky and looked abroad over worlds. He was at one with sky and mountain and plain, and the austere morning light he evolved out of himself. But whatever he was in his own mind, in fact he was no more than a bright speck on that weary plain— that overawed, shallow crater of grey-green sloping up to the horizon and falling off into the deeps of the sky.

He was a tall man and a lean one, with a clean, set, blue-shaven face and black hair cut straight across above black brows and coming far down at the back of the neck. He was dressed in an orange tunic, gathered loosely at the waist by a green girdle, and leaving neck, arms, and legs brown and bare. A film of silken, black hair covered arms and legs, and as he strode forward one would have noticed that he was abnormally long of thigh and unduly short between bony knee and lean ankle. On his feet he wore leather sandals, and his toes were spaced widely. He carried a long, smooth staff of ash, but he did not use it as a staff. Sometimes it was over one shoulder and sometimes over the other, and again at the back of both and bending stiffly as his arms strained it, and now and then, when he was thinking, one end of it rested on the ground and his chin rested on the other over his clasped hands.

Delgan did not seem to be walking of any set purpose. He strolled, he loitered, he zig-zagged aimlessly. He gazed open-mouthed, narrow-eyed at the tremendous sky, wide-eyed at the ghost-mountains outside the world, frowningly at the dust of the road. He whispered words to himself, he whistled a bar of a tune, he hummed the verse of a song. Evidently the song was his own, for he smiled with some vanity, recited the verse with gusto, changed a word or two, shook his black head, and grew vacant-eyed with the inner travail of creation.

> Though death doth dog my steps
> With threat of hell hereafter,

I'll season life with love
And love with laughter.

That is what he declaimed, and thereafter frowned with the doubt of the creator.

'Death,' said he, to his toes, 'does not dog my steps, but only waits to welcome me at the end of pleasant roads, and hell has been quenched these thousand years. Moreover, I have small acquaintance with love, but, from what I have seen of it, it has many attributes, and laughter is not one of them. There is my brother Urnal now. If the tales be true, love has dealt hardly by him and by many good men through him.'

He strode on, still frowning, and the frown had not left his brow when he came suddenly on a fault in the plain and looked down into a little valley. He halted abruptly.

'Talk of the devil,' he said. 'There is Urnal himself and the woman with him.'

That valley was one of the surprises of that plain. From horizon to horizon stretched the plain, desolate, lifeless, infinitely austere: a smooth, unlined, slowly-lifting floor, where nothing moved but the cloud shadows, where nothing could cower away from the terrible immobility of the void. Yet across all its vast space it was seamed with little valleys such as this: shallow, narrow, verdant: pleasant places, with a stream loitering and hasting in the hollow, a cluster of shielings at every wimpling ford, hand-tilled gardens running up one slope and, running up the other, terraced vineyards facing the sun.

Delgan dipped down over the rim of the valley, and there was no longer a bright speck on the plain; there was nothing but grey-green grass undulating faintly in the wind, and cloud shadows running under the sun. Down there the very atmosphere was different: quiet instead of immobile, secure instead of uncaring, human instead of timeless, serene instead of austere. In an open space near the water, where a dark alder leant over a pool, sat a man and woman at food, and Delgan went directly to them by a path between the garden strips. The man rose to meet him. He was a younger man than Delgan, but he was as like him as any man could be: a little taller perhaps, a little wider in the shoulder, a little less lean of flank, but with the same swing and the same litheness. His black hair was cut in line with his black brows, and he has a dour, set, blue-shaven face. His tunic was orange also and girdled with green.

'At last, Urnal, I have found you,' said Delgan.

They placed affectionate hands on each other's shoulders, but in Urnal's touch there was, besides affection, some little hint of allegiance.

'I am glad you have found me, brother,' said Urnal in a slow voice that rumbled like a drum. 'Why, were you looking for me?'

'That can wait,' said Delgan lightly. 'I am looking now for breakfast.'

'Come, then,' invited Urnal. 'We have plenty.' He turned to where the woman sat, her back against the tree, and: 'Alor,' he said, 'this is my brother Delgan.'

'I knew that he was your brother,' said the woman. 'You are alike and yet unlike.'

'I have heard of you, Alor,' said Delgan. 'Men speak of you in all the valleys and in all the hills.'

'And I have heard much of Delgan,' said she.

'Only from his brother Urnal,' said Delgan.

'Only from your brother, indeed,' she admitted, 'but he speaks greatly of you.'

'That is my brother's way. But it is true that no one knows of Delgan, and that all the world knows of Urnal and his woman Alor.'

'I am not Urnal's woman,' said Alor quietly.

'And never will be,' said the heavy voice of Urnal.

'Let us eat,' said Delgan, and he and Urnal sat on the ground opposite Alor, who served them with brown bread and soya-bean cheese, and moved a great crystal jug of amber wine near their hands. As they ate they talked.

'It was up near the ice-line,' began Delgan, and, pausing, went off on an aside. 'Know ye that the ice-line is already down on the Cymbri, and I have been across to Eireann dryshod? The northern seas are all shallows these days.'

'I know,' said Urnal. 'All the people are drifting south.'

'Not all. There are some in Eireann who persist in living on the edge of the ice—men and women—all in the same tribe too, already eating flesh and evolving a god.'

'What else did you find at the ice-line?' questioned the woman.

'Tales of my brother Urnal and a woman Alor,' replied Delgan.
'If they were tales of blood they were true tales,' said Urnal.
'They were tales of great sword-work,' said Delgan.
'And why were you seeking your brother?' That woman was
not afraid of any question.
'A man must do what he can for his own,' half-evaded Delgan,
'and I am Urnal's elder brother.'
He ate slowly, his eyes on the ground and his face very still.
Urnal had finished eating, and he sat clasping his knees, his eyes
on Alor, and his face a stone.
'When you are still,' said the woman, 'I find it hard to tell which
is Urnal and which Delgan.'
'I am Urnal,' said Delgan.
'No. You have a face like doom, and Urnal the face of one
already doomed.'
'You should know that,' said Delgan to the ground. He lifted
his eyes and looked at his brother and his brother looked at
him.

'I saw pale kings and princes too,
    Pale warriors, death-pale were they all;
Who cried, "The Woman Merciless
    Hath me in thrall."

'It was a singer of the old days, ten thousand years ago, that
made that song,' said Delgan. 'He made many songs, they say,
but only that and another live.'
He turned slow, musing eyes on Alor.
'Are you that woman without mercy?' he asked simply.
She flushed red to her red hair.
'I am only a woman,' she said, a little bitterly, 'and I use no
wiles.'
And that protest Delgan did not question. He leant aside and
put a hand over Urnal's clasped hands.
'What is your trouble, brother?' he asked, and there was grieving
in his voice.
'I love that woman,' said Urnal heavily, 'and she does not know
love at all.'
'But, indeed, I do,' denied the woman, but without heat. 'I shall
know love when love comes. It is what I seek.'

'It is not wise to seek love,' chided Delgan. 'Why did you not stay in the place of women and let love seek you there?'

'I stayed in that place and the men came. There was no man amongst them. I do not think there is any man in all the world.'

'There is Urnal. He comes of a good stock. Is he not a fit mate for you?'

'The father of my son will not be Urnal,' was all she would say.

'Why not send him away then?'

She threw her hand towards Urnal in an expressive gesture.

'I cannot leave her, Delgan,' said that man, 'and she knows that I will not take what she will not give. She goes in many strange places, and to kill for her in her need is a great reward. Killing grows on one.'

'You know your rights, Alor,' said Delgan, not seeming to heed his brother. 'The people in all the twenty valleys would rid you of this man if you spoke the word.'

'I am no coward,' she said, 'and I am not yet afraid of Urnal, though he is a killer.'

'Are you not afraid at all?' wondered Delgan.

She looked at him, and as she looked his face froze, became stone, became implacable as fate, and a glaze went over his eyes. Her shoulders shrank a little as in a cold wind, and her eyes flickered, though they held.

'I am afraid of you,' she said simply.

'That fear will abide,' he said in a voice of brass, and turned to his brother.

'This woman will never be your woman,' he said. 'Killing does grow on one, brother. In time it ousts all other passions, even that of love, and in the end the killer is himself the killed. Until that end, Urnal, you will be but heaping pain on pain, for this woman has no mercy, and soon you, the killer, will have no mercy either. The woman is not to blame. She is older than all the tales, and all the great tales have been about her. All men desire her, and she, all desire, desires no one. Let her go her own road, brother, and let you and me go back to my father's house above the marshes of Rem. Come.'

'I will not come,' said Urnal slowly, but unhesitatingly. 'I am not unhappy, and I think that Alor is not unhappy either. I will go on until a better man kills me, or till Alor meets the man of her desire.'

'And him you will kill, too,' added Delgan.

Urnal made no reply to that.

'I was afraid that that would be the way of it,' said Delgan. 'I am too late for anything but the one thing,' and he rose to his feet and looked about him.

Two horses, long-tailed, rough-coated, medium-sized cayuses of the plains, saddled, but loose-girthed, grazed some distance up stream, and towards them Delgan walked slowly. Behind one saddle hung a long, straight sword in its sheath, and Delgan, with a quieting word to the horse, fingered the cross of the hilt. The horse swished a long tail and went on cropping.

'Drinker of blood,' he murmured, 'my father made you; guard you the life of his son Urnal, if you can, this day. Will you tell me if death is the only cure for some things—and I the killer or the killed? Will you tell me to go my own road out of this place and leave Urnal to his? You will say nothing that are always ready for your own work. Tell me, then, that Urnal is a man dogged by fate, running in a narrow groove, and not to be helped but by blow of blade. Tell me that I must kill the woman too, O sword! You will not. To kill her is not permitted, but some day the people, for their own sake, will decide that she must die. You and I will abide that day.'

He drew the sword, long and thin and with a blue sheen on it, and went back to the woman and his brother. He laid the sword at Urnal's feet.

'Brother,' he said quietly, 'I am taking the woman Alor.'

Urnal said nothing, but a small cold flame came into his eyes as they rested on the blade.

Delgan lifted his ashen staff and ran a hand down its smooth surface.

'You were splendid company on every road,' he said, 'and pleasant thoughts your aim. You whispered wisdom to me when you were under my chin, and when you whistled through the air you brought me the words of many a song. Go now on a voyage of your own.'

And javelin-like he threw it in the pool, where it dipped and floated and drifted aslant towards the shallows and the distant sea. Then he turned and strode down the valley to the hamlet by the ford.

The woman came across to Urnal and knelt by him.

'Kill that man for me,' she whispered in his ear.

Urnal had not changed his posture, and his eyes were still on the sword.

'I will not,' he told her. 'There is no need. Delgan is not a swordsman, and he does not yet desire you. I will but disarm him and send him on his road.'

Her breast pressed against his shoulder and her hands touched his neck.

'Kill him for me,' she whispered, 'and I will be the mother of your son.'

He lifted his head and looked at her, and the stone of his face quivered and broke.

*   *   *

When the people—it was a man's valley and there were no women—had assembled in the talk-ground above the ford Delgan made his demand.

'I have a quarrel,' said he, 'that only the sword can decide. Will the people lend me a sword?'

'Who are you and whom would you fight?' questioned the head-man.

'I am Urnal from Rem, of whom you may have heard, and I would fight the man who sits yonder with Alor.'

'There is dust on your feet,' said the other. 'Urnal rode in with Alor last evening and he had a sword hanging at his heel. He showed the young men some of his sword-play.'

'Yet I am Urnal.'

'And who is the other?'

'The other is already dead. He has no name any more.'

'So would Urnal speak,' said an old man, 'and you have the face of a killer. Why would you fight?'

'For the same reason that Urnal always fought.'

'What do Alor and the man say?' queried the head-man.

'Ask Alor and the man,' cried a young man impatiently. 'Give him a sword and we shall see if he can use it. Urnal of Rem can, and so can the man yonder, whoever he is.'

The head-man could not think of any more questions at that time.

'Bring the swords,' he said.

The impatient young man brought the swords. There were five of them shining wickedly on the grass.

'That is the best one,' pointed out the young man, 'and it is the best sword in the twenty valleys.'

Delgan lifted and hefted it.

'It is a good sword,' he agreed, 'but I will ride out of this valley with a better sword at my heel. Come now and see this one kill.'

He went up the valley, and all the people trooped after him and wondered.

The two blades clanged and held, and Urnal found that Delgan knew swording. He could not get his blade away from Delgan's— he never did get it away. The swords lifted into the air and screamed and writhed, and it was Urnal's arm that was forced up, and it was Urnal who yielded a step. The clinging blades came down in a wide swoop, and the blade of Delgan was inside the other. Close to the ground the steel wisps bent and writhed and groaned, and again it was Urnal who gave ground.

To the woman, leaning sombrely against the tree, weary of this work, to the half-circle of men intently watching, that sword-play looked no more than a supremely easy exhibition of skill—a small display of the art of engaging before the real work began. Instead of that it was a supreme effort of nerve and sinew. The tensed muscles stood out on forearms and on necks, the lithe bodies swayed and stiffened, the bony knees bowed and trembled, the sandal edges crushed the grass and bit deep into the firm soil, and the feet, that seemed to shift and leap with feather ease, met the ground with the stamp of iron. And always the blades remained locked.

After minutes the first blow was struck. It was the last blow also. At the very supreme moment of effort, before Urnal could yield the step he needed for balance, Delgan disengaged like lightning, and, as Urnal came in a stride, got in the blow he had played for: a sharp, crisp thud on the back of the neck. And on that instant Urnal was dead.

Delgan for a space looked down on the still body of his brother lying face-down at his feet. The people watched him silently, awesomely, and as one man they started when, suddenly, he swung on them. His face was frozen into something implacable as fate, a glaze was over his eyes, and his sword was held point forward in a stiff right hand.

'Who of you will take the woman Alor?' he challenged in a voice of brass.

No man there said one small word.

*   *   *

Alor and Delgan rode out over the rim of the valley, and his father's sword hung at Delgan's heel. The great plain smoothed itself out behind them, hiding beyond all guessing the little lives that moved subduedly within it. Delgan had come out of that valley a man changed in some subtle way, and, in his own mind, that change should have shaken the heavens. But the void had not changed at all. The cloud-shadows still ran, the wind blew forlornly out of desolate space, the void remained austerely immobile. It took no notice of Delgan; it took no notice of life; it was not concerned with man; it was concerned with Nothing.

THE BEWITCHING OF FURSEY

Mervyn Wall

*The theme of erotic love inspired by the old sagas, which W. B.
Yeats and Austin Clarke had pioneered, was taken a step further
by Mervyn Wall (1908-), a one-time Dublin civil servant whose
biting and satirical fantasies are now regarded as classics of their
kind.* Indeed, The Unfortunate Fursey *(1946), a picaresque novel
about a medieval monk, has been described by the American his-
torican Everett F.* Bleiler in his Guide to Supernatural Fiction
*(1983) as 'a landmark book in the history of fantasy'. It stands out
as another crowning achievement for Irish fantasy, equal to James
Stephens'* The Crock of Gold, *published just over thirty years
earlier.*

*Unlike Austin Clarke, Wall managed to avoid a confrontation
with the censors by giving no obvious descriptions of sex, although
he did still manage to satirise the Church's attitude towards eroticism
with biting effect (to such a degree that, in the case of* The Unfortunate Fursey, *one Dublin bishop actually sent an emissary round
the local bookshops 'requesting' the proprietors not to sell it!). The
success of these books enabled Wall to leave the Civil Service, and
after a period working for Radio Eireann, he became Secretary of
the Arts Council until his retirement in the mid-70s. Brother Fursey
is certainly his greatest creation and his influence can be seen in the
spate of recent best-selling novels which feature medieval monks as
amateur detectives. 'The Bewitching of Fursey' is fantasy and
humour brilliantly combined as the little monk finds himself
embroiled in a terrible misadventure with an old witch . . .*

* * *

Fursey stood motionless, gazing out over the flood of brown, bog-
stained water that moved by impassively. At this point a narrow

mudbank extended into the river forming a backwater in which the water circled ever so slowly, eddying slightly as it rejoined the main stream. Nothing was to be heard but the tiny flap-flapping of the wavelets against the bank on which he stood.

'There's nothing here at all,' he said to himself. 'This is very remarkable.'

His eye fell suddenly on a rope lying along the grass, and trailing over the bank into the river. Beyond the rope a stream of bubbles rose delicately and broke on the surface of the water. This seemed to him even more remarkable, so he hurried over and began to haul in the rope. It was heavy work, especially when one was trying at the same time to maintain an upright position on a pair of crutches; so after he had tripped himself twice, he abandoned the crutches and, seating himself on the grass, pulled at the rope as if his life depended on it. He was greatly amazed when a little old woman tied in a ball, bobbed up on to the surface and came drifting towards him. At first he couldn't reach her; but he hit on the expedient of passing the armpit of one of the crutches over her head, and so by hooking her under the chin, he was able to yank her up on to the bank. His strong, rough fingers quickly untied the ropes that bound her feet and hands. She lay to all appearances dead, and the ex-monk, not knowing what to do, gazed down at her in mingled pity and horror. He did not for a moment doubt but that this was more of the Devil's work, and he was swept by a flood of fierce indignation against that suave personage.

All at once he remembered an incident that had occurred at Clonmacnoise the previous year. On the feast day of the blessed Kieran, after the usual banquet at which ale and mead had been consumed in great quantities, little Brother Patrick had insisted on going for a walk along the bank of the River Shannon. The great river flowed past the settlement, and the diminutive monk insisted that he wanted to look at the full moon, which, he said, reminded him of his mother. Brother Fursey and a few laughing lay-brothers went with him. It was a good thing they did, for the voluble Patrick had not gone very far before he fell into the river. His frightened brethren managed to fish him out and carry him back unconscious to the monastery. Father Sampson, who was knowledgeable in such matters, had immediately swept them all aside and, seizing the damp and bedraggled Patrick, had flung him across the gatepost where he worked on the lay-brother's back with a see-saw motion to the vast admiration of the group of half-tipsy monks. In a few minutes Brother Patrick had come back to life, laughing uproariously and still talking about his mother.

The recollection of this event had no sooner crept across Fursey's mind than he seized The Gray Mare and laid her across a granite boulder so that her head and legs hung down on either side. After a moment's thought he placed hands carefully on her back below the ribs, and began to exert pressure, rhythmically swaying himself back and forward on his crutches. Nothing happened for a long time. Fursey's difficulty was to remain awake. He had not had a full night's rest since the awful evening when the legions of Hell had first ambled into his cell at Clonmacnoise; and the see-saw motion of artificial respiration induced sleepiness. Twice he tumbled backwards, but he picked himself up and resumed his good work without even pausing to examine his bruises. At long last he was rewarded by a low cry from the old woman. He redoubled his efforts, and she began to scream. Fursey paused and carefully turned her over. She was a strange sight with her old grey locks plastered to her head. She looked up at him with bleary eyes.

'I'll admit anything you want,' she gasped. 'Why don't you burn me and have done with it?'

While Fursey was wondering what this strange speech could mean, she lapsed once more into unconsciousness. He began immediately to chafe her hands and feet vigorously. When he looked at her face again he was delighted to see that her eyes were open and were fixed upon him. He began to laugh immoderately.

'What are you trying to do?' she asked savagely. 'Rub the skin off me?'

This surprised Fursey greatly, and he was looking down in wonder at his large rough hands when she struggled feebly into a sitting position and aimed a blow at him. The startled Fursey retreated a few paces and stood looking at her with dumb reproach. A lump came into his throat; he felt that his eyes were about to fill with tears: he bowed his head, and turning, started to hobble away. A cracked voice called after him:

'Where are you going?'

Fursey turned. 'I don't know,' he answered.

'Who are you?' she asked.

'Just a stranger who brought you out of the water and back to life.'

The Gray Mare turned this over in her mind for a few moments, and when she spoke again, her voice was more gentle.

'You're some class of a monk?'

'No. I was once, but not now.'

'They thrun you out?' queried The Gray Mare.

'Yes,' answered Fursey, the pink blood gliding into his cheeks. The old woman emitted a throaty cackle.

'Was it creepin' after some high-steppin' young female you were?'

'Certainly not,' replied Fursey indignantly. When he remembered all the high-stepping young female demons that had crept after him, his indignation increased.

'Certainly not,' he repeated. 'Nothing of the sort.'

The Gray Mare seemed to have lost interest in his affairs. She was peering short-sightedly to left and right.

'Are they all gone?' she asked in a loud whisper.

'I don't understand,' said Fursey. 'There's no one here, if that's what you mean.'

'Dirty pack of murderers,' muttered the old woman. 'They'd have left me to drown.'

'Well, you're not drowned,' said Fursey. 'May God and the blessed Kieran have you in their keeping,' and he turned away once more.

'Mister monk,' called out the old woman.

'Yes?'

'You can't leave me here to catch my death of cold in my damp habiliments,' she said coaxingly. 'You've a kind face, mister man. Do me another kindness, and I won't forget it to you. Would you ever carry me up to my little house beyond on the hill? I doubt if I could get there by myself, I'm that weak.'

'Certainly,' said Fursey.

It was a nightmare journey. It is bad enough to have to climb a hill on crutches, but it is infinitely worse to have to do so with an old woman on one's back. The Gray Mare seemed to think it was all a great game. She belaboured Fursey with her fists pretending he was a horse, all the time crowing and cackling and exhorting him to 'gee-up.' The unfortunate Fursey stumbled on his way, gasping and grunting, sometimes choking and sometimes weeping from sheer misery. At length he stood at her door: how he got there he never knew.

'Carry me in,' commanded the old woman.

Fursey ducked his head and struggled in through the low doorway. It was an ordinary kind of cabin with a great hole in the centre of the roof to let out the smoke. The Gray Mare slid off his back and leaned against the table, her wet garments clinging to her skinny frame. She shivered violently as she began to speak. Fursey did not hear what she said. He half-closed his eyes as the walls of the room swayed sickeningly: he saw the floor coming up to meet him, and he was conscious of falling heavily.

When he awoke he was in darkness and lying on a hard pallet covered by a ragged blanket; but he did not mind how hard his bed was, provided he was allowed to lie still and rest his aching legs and back. He was conscious of distant crooning and muttering: while he was wondering about it vaguely, he fell asleep again. And so for an interminable period he slept and awoke and dozed, blissfully at peace. He was fully awakened at last when a door was opened, and the light from another room fell across his face. The Gray Mare was standing in the doorway grinning in at him.

'Are you awake, mister man?' she croaked.

'Yes,' said Fursey, sitting up. 'I'm awake.'

'Maybe you're hungry and would like something to eat?'

'Yes,' said Fursey eagerly. 'I'm hungry.'

'Well, come and get it,' she said, and she went back into the far room.

Fursey got off the bed wonderfully refreshed, and followed her. It was only when he was standing by the table in the outer room that he remembered that he had forgotten his crutches. He staggered and held on to the table with both hands.

'What's wrong with you?' queried The Gray Mare. 'You're not going to go unconscious on me again?'

'I've forgotten my crutches,' said Fursey. 'I can't walk without them.'

'Nonsense,' replied the old woman. 'You've just walked in here without them. You don't need crutches.'

'I assure you that I do,' replied Fursey earnestly. 'My hip was smashed by a poltergeist.'

'Arrah what,' said the old lady, 'the lad only sprained it. I cured you while you slept. You did me a kindness, and I told you I wouldn't forget it to you. Just try, and you'll see that you're able to walk.'

Fursey was accustomed to obedience, so he immediately relaxed his grip on the table and essayed a few steps across the floor. To his huge delight he found that he could walk. To convince himself of the genuineness of this astounding miracle he started to run up and down the kitchen.

'I can walk,' he cried. 'I can walk.'

'Stop running,' said the old woman. 'You'll upset the pot. Sit down there and have something to eat. You should be hungry. You slept the whole night through and most of today. It's already late in the afternoon.'

As Fursey seated himself he observed on the table what appeared to be a small wax image of a man. The light from the smoke hole in the roof fell directly upon it, so that he could see it clearly. A little tuft of white hair was tied to the head, and it was partly wrapped in a piece of thick brown material similar to the habit he was wearing. A dead snail pierced by a thorn lay on its hip. While Fursey was still gazing at the image The Gray Mare suddenly snapped it from the table and turned her back. A moment later she went to the fire and threw something in. Then she kneaded the image between her skeleton-thin hands until it was just a lump of shapeless wax, which she put away carefully on a shelf. She seated herself at the table opposite Fursey and sneezed once or twice. In answer to his polite enquiry, she explained that she had caught cold as a result of her immersion in the river. Fursey looked from her to the bare board between them and then back at her again, wondering with a sinking heart whether there was any food in the house. She seemed to guess his thoughts.

'What would you like to eat?' she asked.

'Whatever you're having yourself,' replied the ex-monk politely.

The Gray Mare stretched up her hand, and Fursey noticed for the first time a rope which hung from the rafters. Raising his eyes he saw that the end of it hung loosely over a beam in the roof. The Gray Mare jerked the rope three times, and to Fursey's astonishment a flagon of ale, two loaves of bread and four pounds of choice beef slid down the rope, apparently from nowhere, and settled themselves in a neat pile on the table. While he was still gaping up at the rafters, thinking that it was a very inconvenient place to keep the larder, The Gray Mare arose and, going to a hole in the wall, took out a couple of wooden goblets, which she brought over to the table. She shook a family of red spiders out of one of them and placed it in front of Fursey. The spiders ran hell-for-leather over the table in all directions, but she recovered them without difficulty and carefully stowed them away in an old stocking that hung from a hook in the wall. Fursey realised with a sigh that he had lived so long in the cloister that he was quite unaccustomed to the ways of ordinary people, so he carefully suppressed any manifestation of surprise.

Before long they were eating and drinking merrily. Fursey thought she was the pleasantest person he had ever met. Women as they had existed in his imagination, and as he had seen them from afar, were creatures endowed with an evil comeliness in order to tempt men; but this amiable old lady was so hideous that she was not like a woman at all. He could converse easily with her and found it pleasant to do so, as conversation with a woman was a new experience for him. Never, he felt, had he met such kindliness and understanding in a human being. Before he had finished his first goblet of ale, he had told her of his incredible experiences in Clonmacnoise and his resultant misfortunes. She listened with the greatest interest, punctuating his monologue occasionally with a murmur of sympathy or with a violent sneeze.

'One of the things I wonder at most,' he said, 'is the fact that while I was in Clonmacnoise I had the most awkward impediment in my speech; but now it's gone, and I can speak with reasonable fluency.'

The Gray Mare nodded her head sagely.

'That's easily accounted for,' she said. 'The impediment was frightened out of you. You went through so much that it's doubtful if anything can ever frighten you again.'

It made him uncomfortable, however, to hear her uttering harsh words about his late brethren in Clonmacnoise, as she did on hearing how he had been finally expelled from the monastery. He shifted uneasily on his stool, knowing that it was unlucky to speak ill of the clergy. In any case it was the demons who were to blame. In this strange world things like that just happen to a man; no one can help it. What else could the monks do but get rid of him? He was glad when she launched into a mumbling and toothless account of her own trials and sufferings.

He was appalled at human depravity when he heard of the bitter enmity which the sexton of the neighbouring churchyard bore her on account of such a small matter as a wandering goat. He crossed himself when she assured him that the sexton was undoubtedly a sorcerer. He could scarcely believe his ears when she told him how the wicked sexton had actually had the effrontery to denounce her to the authorities for crimes which he had himself committed. He became frightened when he heard how human beings had 'walked' her up and down for three days and nights without sleep, how human beings had taken her and thrown her into the river, and how human beings, even when her innocence had been fully demonstrated, had nevertheless picked up stones to kill her. It frightened him to think of the kind of world it was in which he must in future live, and he longed to be back in the quiet and safety of the cloister. It was with an aching heart that he told himself that he must put Clonmacnoise forever out of his thoughts.

The Gray Mare was muttering to herself as she gathered a little pile of crumbs together with her skinny fingers.

'And you were really innocent all the time?' asked Fursey.

She shot a quick look at him.

'Didn't you find me at the bottom of the river,' she replied gratingly. 'Isn't that sure proof that I'm not a witch?'

'Yes,' said Fursey. 'I've always heard that that's sure proof.'

She started up suddenly.

'The sexton,' she said. 'He'll be renewing his attack, and here I am wasting my time gabbling, instead of making preparations to meet him.'

She hurried over to the fire and began to stir a huge pot that hung over the embers. Then she lifted down a cob-webbed jar from the shelf and, taking from it a handful of amber grains, she threw them into the liquid, which began at once to bubble and spit angrily. Bending over the cauldron she began a low chant. At that moment there was a clatter of horses' hooves on the track outside the door.

'Hallo there!' shouted a loud voice.

'Who's that?' hissed the old woman.

Fursey went to the door and opened it. Three horsemen had reined their steeds on the road about fifty paces from the door. To his astonishment Fursey recognised the Abbot Marcus, who was being helped from his horse by a huge red-faced friar. On a bony nag sat an ecclesiastic in the dress of a bishop. He was gaunt and sallow, and he gazed at Fursey sourly. At a little distance stood a band of serving men loaded down with books of exorcism, bells and stoups of holy water. They were looking thoroughly frightened, as if they might take to their heels at any moment.

The first thought that came into Fursey's mind was that the Abbot Marcus had come for him to take him back to Clonmacnoise. He ran down the road and flung himself on his knees at the Abbot's feet. Marcus raised his hand and laid it gently on Fursey's head in blessing. The ex-monk gripped the Abbot's robe and gazed up at the grave face, lined with study. The far-away eyes that were bent on him were kind.

'You're going to take me back?' said Fursey.

The Abbot turned away his face.

'Get up, Fursey,' he said.

Fursey rose to his feet and glanced from one to the other. The big friar was looking at him with great interest, but the Bishop's eyes were as cold as ice, and a sneer was trembling about his mouth. Fursey instinctively knew that in the trio he had only one friend. He turned again to the Abbot Marcus.

'Father Abbot, are you not going to let me go back?'

The Abbot's eyes shifted uncomfortably. 'No,' he said at last.

Fursey stood an abject figure, looking from one to the other. Then he looked at the road and up at the wide sky. He saw everything blurred and dim through a film of tears.

'Come now, my man,' said the Bishop bitingly. 'Weeping won't help you. I am too good a judge of human nature not to know reality from fake.'

'Please, my lord bishop,' interposed the Abbot. 'I've already explained to you the circumstances under which Fursey left Clonmacnoise. I made it clear that he was in no way to blame.'

'Where are the demons he was consorting with yesterday?' snapped the Bishop. 'Let him tell us that.'

'They're gone,' said Fursey.

'Gone where?' asked the Bishop quickly, as if to startle Fursey into an admission.

'I don't know. They just disappeared.'

There was a moment's silence, then Father Furiosus interposed.

'They're certainly not here now,' he said mildly. 'We've rung bells and sprinkled holy water over an area of two square miles. No demon could stand up to that.'

'Did you see any sign of an old woman?' asked the Bishop.

'Yes,' replied Fursey surprised. 'I pulled an old woman out of the river, and brought her up here to the house. She's in there now.'

He turned and pointed to the little cabin behind him.

'What did you do that for?' asked the Bishop sharply. 'Why did you have to meddle?'

'Because,' interjected the Abbot with some heat in his voice, 'it was what any Christian would be expected to do.'

'Even if the object of his misplaced charity was a witch?' queried the Bishop.

'She's not a witch,' said Father Furiosus with some exasperation. 'God clearly demonstrated that she was innocent.'

The Bishop was silent, but he continued to watch Fursey with baleful eyes.

'Father Abbot,' pleaded Fursey, 'let me go back with you to the monastery.'

'That is impossible,' said the Abbot with finality. 'You must understand, my poor Fursey, that the gates of Clonmacnoise and every other religious settlement are closed against you. Be reasonable, Fursey. For nearly two weeks you have consorted with demons. For all we know you may have even formed friendships. No abbot could risk taking you in. These goblins that you know would be likely to return to renew the acquaintance. The fact that you appear to have recovered the free use of your speech and are in a position to challenge them, is no safeguard. That would be a small impediment to imps and demons of the wilier sort. In any case, if I took you back to Clonmacnoise, it's very likely that the whole community would leave in a body.'

'I see,' said Fursey, hanging his head.

A sudden thought seemed to strike Bishop Flanagan.

'Where did you spend the night?' he asked sharply.

'In the cottage,' replied Fursey.

'With the Gray Mare?'

'With the old woman,' answered Fursey innocently.

A sharp intake of breath was heard from Father Furiosus. The thunderclouds gathered on the Bishop's forehead.

'The two of you were alone?' he asked in tones of doom.

'Yes,' said Fursey haltingly.

'In my diocese!' said the Bishop in a horrified whisper. 'An unmarried man and woman spend the night together in the one house without chaperon, and he stands there and has the effrontery to tell me so to my face! Do you know, my man,' he continued, his voice rising to a shout, 'that what you have done is a reserved sin in this diocese? What do you think of such conduct, Father Furiosus?'

Furiosus had tightened his grip on his blackthorn, and he was looking at Fursey menacingly from beneath his ginger eyebrows.

'He must marry the woman,' said Furiosus.

'Of course he must,' replied the Bishop. 'There's no other way to avert the scandal.'

'Marry?' said Fursey faintly.

'And if he doesn't,' continued the Bishop, 'I'll put a penance on him that will cripple him in this life and in the next.'

'Let us discuss this new turn of events,' said the Abbot. 'Oblige us, Fursey, by stepping aside for a few moments.'

Fursey walked some paces down the road and leaned against a tree for support. Meanwhile the three ecclesiastic approached more closely to one another and conversed in grave whispers.

'It mightn't be a bad idea at all,' said Abbot Marcus. 'The plight of this wretched man weighs somewhat on my conscience, and I should like to see him fixed in life. No monastery will admit him, and as he hasn't the wit to earn a living, he will certainly starve on the roadside unless something is done for him. Moreover,' he added thoughtfully 'you tell me that this woman, tho' not a witch, is nevertheless a great sinner who never goes to Mass. Union with such a godly man as Fursey cannot but have a profound effect on her character. By good example he is very likely to win her back to God and Holy Church.'

Father Furiosus seemed impressed.

'Yes,' he said, 'and you have told us that this Brother Fursey is a man of notable piety. He can, therefore, be trusted to report to the authorities should she at any time be tempted to engage in the black art.'

'This is all irrelevant,' said the Bishop hotly. 'I would remind you that I am in authority in this diocese. The point is simply this—that the unfortunate woman has been compromised by this blackguard, and that wrong can only be righted by marriage. He must marry her. I insist.'

'There is no need to raise your voice,' said the Abbot coldly. 'We are all agreed, tho' perhaps for different reasons.'

He turned to where Fursey was leaning against the tree gaping vacantly out over the countryside, and called him by name, but Fursey did not appear to hear. He had been trying to assemble his thoughts so as to understand what was about to happen to him, but his mind insisted on remaining an obstinate and tumultuous blank. Father Furiosus went down the road and taking Fursey by the arm, led him back to where the others were standing.

'Now listen carefully, Fursey,' began the Abbot kindly. 'We are all agreed that you must marry this lady. It is your duty, because by your incautious behaviour you have cast a reflection on her honour. From a material point of view you will be making a good match. She appears to have a tidy little property, and you will enjoy economic security for the rest of your life.'

'She has only a broken-down cabin and a goat,' replied Fursey bleakly.

The Abbot looked at him severely.

'I didn't expect to find in one of my monks a sordid greed for material goods,' he replied.

'But I'm a monk,' said Fursey, his voice rising in an hysterical squeal. 'I can't marry.'

'Your vows are simple vows,' said the Abbot smoothly, 'and it's in my power to release you. I shall immediately do so; it would be most unfair to hold you to them.'

'But she is far from comely,' objected Fursey feebly.

'I'm surprised at you,' said the Abbot. 'There will be all the less temptation to desires of the flesh.'

'It's better to marry than to burn,' said the Bishop.

'But I don't feel myself burning,' said Fursey.

'Don't be impertinent,' said the Bishop. 'It's all settled.'

Fursey looked up appealingly at Abbot Marcus.

'What will I do?' he asked.

'Do as I say, marry her,' replied the Abbot, 'and may God bless you both.'

Fursey bowed his head.

'Whatever you say, Father Abbot,' he muttered brokenly. 'I suppose it's for the best.'

'Now we must tell the woman,' said Furiosus.

There was a moment's hesitation as none of the ecclesiastics was anxious to approach a cottage which had been held in such abominable repute. At last Father Furiosus went and called on The Gray Mare to come out. She had been watching the proceedings from the dark interior of her cottage inasfar as her defective eyesight would permit, and she now emerged hesitantly. She glanced to left and right as if considering flight, but Father Furiosus took her gently by the arm and began to lead her down the road, assuring her with a rough kindness that she had nothing to be afraid of. As she came hobbling towards them, the Bishop retreated a pace and made the sign of the cross in the dust of the road with the point of his pastoral staff. She stood before them, a frail bowed figure, making a smacking sound as she sucked at her toothless gums. She looked down at the cross traced in the dust, then up at the Bishop malevolently.

'Haven't youse done enough to me?' she asked bitterly.

Father Furiosus hastened to explain that byegones were byegones and that they were all meeting on a friendly footing. He propounded the proposition to her. At first she was incredulous; but when she realised that he was in earnest, she was overcome by a fit of cackling. She threw a gamey eye across at the blushing Fursey.

'So the rascal wants to marry me,' she croaked. 'He's not a bad-looking fellow, with his white head and his young face.'

'I'm forty,' said Fursey, hoping dimly to dam her rising enthusiasm.

'Sure that's only young,' she replied. 'You'd be useful around the house, milking the goat and the like.'

'Well, what do you say?' enquired Abbot Marcus.

'It's not what I'd call a romantic wooing,' she replied, 'but I suppose we could do our courting afterwards. It will always keep.'

She gave Fursey a girlish nudge with her elbow. A wintry smile flickered across his face.

'Well, are you agreed?' asked the Bishop impatiently.

'Yes,' said The Gray Mare. 'I'll try anything once.'

'Well, go down on your knees,' said the Bishop.

The Gray Mare was helped into the required position by Father Furiosus. She complained of her rheumatics, and requested him to stand by to help her up again. Two serving men were summoned to act as witnesses. The Gray Mare delayed the ceremony for some minutes by her insistence on combing her hair with her long, skinny fingers, and by her efforts to get it to curl over each ear. The Abbot formally released Fursey from his vows, stumbling occasionally over the words, for he was embarrassed by Fursey's dumb, dog-like gaze that was rivetted all the time on his face. Then the Bishop approached and placing The Gray Mare's lank claw in Fursey's plump fist, he read through the marriage ceremony in clipped and hurried Latin. The little band of serving men had drawn near to watch the proceedings. A bird yelped an occasional note from the single rowan tree standing before The Gray Mare's cabin; and the red sun, half below the distant slate-grey mountains, rolled his last laughing beams on the happy couple.

A FABLE

Mary Lavin

One of the great influential figures in Irish fantasy fiction was Lord Dunsany whose contribution to this collection appears in the third section of the book. Among many writers he has inspired over the years can be listed Mary Lavin (1912-), who actually grew up near Dunsany's estate in County Meath and whose interest in folklore and mythology was fostered by the nobleman-writer. Since writing her very first tales under his guidance, Mary Lavin has developed into a consummate storyteller about Ireland, its people and history, and she has been widely praised on both sides of the Atlantic, frequently being discussed in the same breath as such leading Irish short story writers as Sean O'Faolain and Frank O'Connor. 'A Fable' is a moving story about a fabulously beautiful woman and her impact upon a small community; it is also as timeless in its way as the oldest Irish romantic saga still extant . . .

*   *   *

She was the most beautiful woman they had ever seen and so they hated her. The women feared that she would dim their own glory, and the men disliked her because they felt she was inaccessible, even to the strongest and most fierce of them. The women need not have feared for the orchid does not take from the beauty of the bluebell. The men need not have disliked her because they could not possess her body, for, had they been wiser men than they were they would have realised that a woman of such incandescent beauty belonged to every eye that looked on her. So the beauty of Helen had belonged to every man in Greece and Menalaus had no greater desire to drag her back from Troy across the coiling waters than had the least man among the men of Greece, hammering the curved boards, banging the singing rivets. But the men in the village where this beauty came to live were not wise men, nor were they generous, nor yet were they kind.

There is no need to try and describe her face for faces such as hers cannot be described, except by some idea like the idea we have been given of the face of Helen by the man who said that it launched a thousand ships. You may say of her, if you wish, that she was like a bough of apricot blossoms. She came to the village quietly one evening after dusk, to live in the house of her fathers that had been shut up for nearly a generation. She came without warning and that in itself was a mark against her with the people of the countryside. The first they saw of her was on the top of a long and insecure ladder climbing up on to the roof of her house and poking at the lichen cushions on the tiles with a little cane. She wore trousers, like a man, and the lines of her lovely body were seen in silhouette against the blue breast of the sky. Her face was framed in the gold-lace of her hair. She was beautiful every hour of the day, but, in the early sunlight she was perhaps most beautiful, and the villagers got the full impact of her starshining beauty upon their shrinking and unprepared eyes. They all saw her. The demesne was on a hilly ridge of the valley and so they all saw her. They felt a shock run through their bodies at the sight of her. They did their work badly all that day, as men and women do who work after the gusts of a great emotion have subsided and left an inexpressible lassitude of spirit and of body.

Next day they were themselves again, with energy to satisfy their curiosity about the newcomer. There was not much to be found out except that she intended to live in the old house permanently. She was going to have the house redecorated. That meant to the minds of the people in the valley that she was a spendthrift. They further decided that, as like as not, she would give big parties when the house was ready and that they would be attended by young and very gay people. That meant that she was fast. And so the legend grew that this exquisite creature was hateful in mind and heart. It was indeed a pity that she did not have one small flaw, even one. If one little ivory shell of her teeth were only turned or crooked they might have found her more human. If once in a while, even once in the April of every year when the chemist in the valley put sarsparilla on his windows, if, even then, she had one spot on her skin they would not have been so grudging of praise whenever she passed them on the roads. But not one single flaw had she, and as she cantered over the fields the wind and rain could only blush and never redden her cheeks; they could cluster and tangle, but never untidy, her hair.

Every day she rode along the roads and if she sometimes shyly smiled at one of the people she met on the wayside they hurried home to tell their friends how she had sneered at them. Her own friends came from the city, and the windows in the big house on the hill were lit all night and patterned over with the passing and repassing of human figures. Presumably her friends were fond of her, although when their cars came careering into the market square, and they wanted to know the way to her house, they were not always careful, nor just, in the description they gave of her in order to show who they meant and whose house they sought. Some of these friends were very pretty too. The postmistress who lived just in the square and who always rushed out into the dusty road to tell the drivers the way, before the wife of the haberdasher across the street could open her door to get out, gave it as her opinion that there was one very handsome girl among her friends. This girl was dark-haired with soft peach-skin cheeks. She had a clearcut profile and she would have been perfect only for a small cast in her left eye. The whole village was interested in the beautiful girl with the cast in her eye. When they saw her at the Meet of the Harriers they were delighted with her. The poor girl. It was such a pity about her eye, because she was so beautiful. They stood around the Town Hall to watch the riders and the hounds pass by, into the copse behind the demesne. They noticed with satisfaction that there were more gentlemen talking to her than to any other woman, and that there was always one ready to slip from his mount and do her a service, light her cigarette, tighten her girth-strap or pick up her fallen whip. There was one other girl who was very popular and she also was a guest from the big house. The gentlemen from the surrounding county seemed to be very attentive to her also. And she was very pretty too. As the postmistress said, she would have been nicer than the dark girl if only her nose were not a little too long. And she had a lovely expression too. On that they were all agreed. In fact it was doubtful whether those who were mounted or those who were watching their performances had the greater enjoyment that morning at the first Meet of the year. The enjoyment of the villagers, and perhaps that of an odd person here and there among the members of the

Hunt, was increased by an added pleasure later in the day, when the beautiful owner of the big house on the hill was forced to dismount at one point of the road and open a gate for herself. There had seemed to be no one on the spot at the moment, or no one looking her way. No one looking her way, I think. When she was on the ground and pulling off her yellow string gloves to open the wire knot that served as a lock, one or two of the gentlemen rode up and were about to help her, but she had opened the gate and was already leading the mare through. It did not seem worth while to knot up the wire for her, anyway she was nearly finished doing it up herself. What extraordinary hands she had, like the unbelievable unflawed plaster hands of the draper's dummies. And watching the swiftly moving hands the men thought of the hands of wives and sweethearts that they had kissed and caressed, and strangely enough those hands were either red or slightly chapped or, indeed, definitely stubby. To tell the truth the perfection of this fabulously beautiful girl was really beginning to get on the nerves of the whole neighbourhood. If only she had managed to look tired after those energetic rides across country the spell might have been broken earlier than it was, but when she looked tired her eyes were deeper than the pools of the bog, and the blue veins that faintly beat in her forehead made her skin more like porcelain than ever. The veins were like the blue mark of the potter's under-glaze. She looked more lovely than ever, but of course by this time what had unconsciously irritated everyone was the one thing that they would not admit to exist. In short, before very long, no one for miles away from the big house was aware that a face such as only forms in flesh once every hundred years had come to gaze on, and be gazed upon, by them.

Then one day when the Hunt was once more meeting at the square and the beautiful girl came riding down the hilly lawn from her house an accident occurred. It was very slight, but it had a deep effect on the hearts and minds of the people who witnessed it. She had ridden down the hill and those who had seen her coming through the branching trees were preparing to stare at her insolently as she sailed over the ditch that divided her own demesne from the tree-shaded village street where the horses and riders, the hounds and the spectators were gathered. She rose in the air and with sure feet the mare brought her forelegs clear of the thorny bank. It was, as usual, a clean and graceful jump and no one was prepared for the unexpected way the high hanging strand of bramble switched her face.

The branch of briar switched her face and its thorns tore into her flesh. With the force of the slashing twig she was thrown from her mount and with the pain of its lashing sting she lay where she fell, silent, still, face-upward in the grassy tangled ditch. Her eyes were closed like the eyes of an old-fashioned china doll and her lashes lay flat on her cheeks in an adorably old-fashioned way. Her hair was spread around her seemingly sleeping face like a fine gold filigree fan, and some strands still clung upwards caught on the thorns of the undergrowth, taut wires of finely spun whitegold.

Everyone in the street seemed to see the accident in its least details. And perhaps the momentousness of her beauty and the momentousness of it having come among them dawned on their slow and dull-eyed minds for they acted with a dignity beyond the power of prophecy to foresee in their heavy faces one moment before this moment. They did not rush. They did not shout, or scream. Slowly they came over towards the ditch where she lay like figures in a play acting at the will of some artistic producer rather than at the cat-call of their instinct to stare at blood.

For the blood that had crept into the scratches and weals on her face had come slowly too, but with more sinister advance from cut to cut, until, on the pale white porcelain cheek there was a blood etching of the briar branch itself.

After the first moments of unnatural calm, the wonder in the eyes of the villagers gave place to a sudden pity in their hearts and that gave way to the skill and strength of their limbs as they lifted her up on strong shoulders and wordlessly carried her back to her house on the hill.

All day the image of her face as they had last seen it stayed in the minds of those people and the colours and contours of things habitually in their minds ran together all day long to make images of what they had seen in slightly different forms. So, when the postmistress pressed down the deckle-edged, and bright red, stamp upon a glossy white envelope she shivered. For her mind had made a new image of the porcelain skin with the briar etching on the face of a girl so beautiful that the postmistress let her tears fall freely on an envelope that had cost more to the dozen than her own black blouse. And when the gardener at the convent was picking a red lady-bug from the frail white petals of a winter cyclamen he sighed and thought he had never seen a more beautiful thing in all this world and in all his life than this white cyclamen petal, and nothing more cruel or more frightening than this redbacked insect that he flung to the ground in disgust. For, although he did not know it himself, he was thinking of a face in a ditch. And the schoolmaster went to his book case that day and took down Macbeth although he did not particularly like it and could not say to save his soul why he wanted to read it again. But when he came to the description of Duncan's death he surprised himself by exclaiming 'Ah . . . here it is . . .' as he drew a pencil mark along the famous lines that tell how Duncan's silver skin was laced with his golden blood. He left the book open at that page and took out a cambric handkerchief to wipe his glasses. And the draper's wife who had wrung the neck of a pure white pullet and seen the jet of red spurt over the silken feathers, had said that life was very cruel. The whole village felt that life was very cruel and so they lined themselves up as allies of its most pitiful victim.

For the beautiful girl was pitifully scarred. After staying in a shaded room for three weeks she had come out one day determined to ignore the markings on her skin. It happened, for life is full of unrelated coincidences, that she had long been threatening to go up on the roof and see if she could whether or not there was room for a skylight between the two chimneys on the east side of the library. And for the first time since her fall the people down in the streets saw her, and it might almost have been the first day that she came among them, for they paused to look up at her figure against the blue and they said they had never seen any one or any thing more beautiful and that she would be the most beautiful girl in the world if it were not for her scarred face. And the postmistress called a messenger boy and told him to go up to the big house and tell the mistress that the letter she had sent to be posted that morning, the letter to the doctor in Vienna, was not sufficiently stamped. It was none of her business of course, but she was sure that the young lady wouldn't want such an important letter to be understamped. It must be important. It was probably a letter about her face to some clever foreign doctor. As the boy went up the hill she watched the figure on the distant roof. She was curling around the chimney pots like a great cat, light, deft, lithe, sleek and lovely. Those were the words of the schoolmaster and not the postmistress, for he too, was watching her. He wondered how she managed for books, his were old of course, but at any rate he'd mention it to her house steward, would say to him that she was welcome to any of his, he could make out a list of them some night, or perhaps if she was passing the schoolhouse some day he could give the children transcription, or perhaps she'd come after school hours? . . . But no . . . Better when the children would be there because it would not be right that any breath of shame should fan such a lovely creature. It was really too bad about her face, only for that . . .

Her face was worse than might be imagined from the nature of the accident, but there were two reasons for this: firstly, the force with which she rode against the lash of the thorn was so great that the skin was displaced and had to be sewn, secondly, fine porcelain cracks easier than delph and shows the mark of its mending. But if the villagers had been unable to bear the beauty of her unscarred face they seemed to long for the sight of her now. If a farmer's lad delayed and dallied with his fork or harrow when he saw her coming to a closed gate, it was not in order to humiliate her into opening it herself but in order that she might be forced to alight and be nearer to him as he ran with well timed speed to fumble the wire-lock and mumble his regrets at not being quicker. And if he did not get there in time he would have a little spray of violets or a soft showery branch of pussy willow in his hat and he would pull it out and offer it to her as naturally as if she were his sweetheart and they had lain in the hay together. And that evening he would say to his mother that she was a very civil lady and that if it wasn't for that mark on her face she'd be the finest lady in the land. And his mother would ask how her cheek looked and the boy would say there was no sign of blood on it now at all, but her skin was all puckered up. 'I know,' his mother would assure him, 'like the grooves in a carving dish.' 'See,' she would say and take one down from the dresser and show him the way a branching rill was made in the china to let the gravy flow into one well. And he had nodded that it was exactly like that but whether he meant the colour and smoothness of the skin or the scar on the skin he did not really indicate. And he would tell his mother how he had given her the flowers and his mother would boast about it to the rest of the villagers, for they all loved her dearly and were glad to serve her. Were it not for the scar on her face, would she not be the most beautiful girl in the country?

For two years she lived quietly in the valley, beloved by all those who dwelt in it with her. Then one day she got a letter from the doctor in Vienna (and, although it is not important, let it be recorded that it was insufficiently stamped) saying that he was of the opinion that by now an adequate length of time had been let lapse since the wounds had been made, and that the time had come when it would be safe and advisable to have new skin grafted over the scars. She told the people in the valley and they were glad and they lit candles for her safety in the chapel on the hill. They went to the station to see her off and one little cripple boy threw white heather into the smoky little carriage of the train as it left the station, noisily and fussily. Her pale and serene face was pressed to the plate glass window to see the last of the kind but stupid folk and they thought how beautiful she would be were it not for the unfortunate mark on her cheek.

All the time that she was away they kept candles lighting before the shrine of the Beautiful Virgin, who was indeed very beautiful and would be more so still were it not for the fact that the paint from her blue mantle had run a little and stained her face a rather dark colour. They prayed that she would not be hurt by the foreign nurses and the foreign doctor, and they prayed that she would not be scarred worse when she returned. But for her return to beauty and perfection they did not pray because they did not believe that such a thing were possible, and furthermore they did not remember what she looked like when she was perfect, and still furthermore they had loved her as she was. So, when, one day and unexpected, she arrived at the little station and walked up the street the people ran out of the shops and the children ran out of the schools and her mare put its bay head over the wall of the demesne and all with excited clamour welcomed her home. But as in all public demonstrations of this kind they spoke more to each other than to her and looked almost exclusively at each other rather than at her; she had passed in her own gates and up to her own hall-door and had entered the house and been seen in silhouette against her bedroom blind by the crowd of kind and happy people before anyone noticed whether or not she had been cured. They consulted each other, and none of them, not even the postmistress, not even the schoolmaster, not even the station-master and not even the harbourmaster (this was a purely honorary appointment in the inland valley) had noticed whether or not the scars were healed and concealed. Somehow they thought that they were not, and lulled themselves with this decision so that they were enabled to rest all through that summer night and rise refreshed the next morning. She was not on the roof this morning, but she rode courageously out over the ditch where she had fallen and they had all been so impressed by her spirit and bravery that of course they forgot to look at her face that day too. On the third day she sent a messenger down to the chandler for some candles for her dinner table and the messenger had returned to say there were no candles to be had in the village. That is absurd, she thought, but she could not remedy matters by saying so and she merely sent the messenger to the church to borrow a few unblessed candles with the promise of returning a dozen for every one she borrowed. The clergy were disappointed to lose the opportunity of closing such a friendly, uncommercial and profitable deal, but the fact was they had no candles. That really was absurd. She put on a very becoming hat and went down to the village. The first person she met was the postmistress, but the draper's wife came over with her daughter and the daughter's fiancé the chemist, before they had spoken two words. So there was quite a crowd there when she asked about the shortage of candles. They all agreed with her that it was a ridiculous state of affairs but they could not suggest any reason for it. Suddenly the postmistress clapped her hands together, but they did not ask her what she had remembered, because they knew she would tell them. Before they had time to go away she was reminding them that there were no candles because there had been so many burned in the chapel for the last month. That explained the shortage of candles but when the beautiful woman asked why they were burning all those candles there was not one who could remember. They called over the farmer's boy, who was sneaking by at the moment behind a wagon of hay in order that they would not notice the big bunch of bluebells in his hat, and they asked him if he could remember why they had lit so many candles before the Virgin last month. And he had said quite simply that they had lit them for the safety of the operation. The woman from the big house had been grieved to hear that someone had been operated on in the village, but they assured her that no one in the village had been operated on at all. Then she suddenly remembered her own operation and asked if it could possibly be that out of their kindness they had

. . . but she didn't get time to finish for, of course, they all remembered with a rush and began to tell her together. But they stopped as suddenly as they began and stared into her face. She was cured. She was completely cured and there was not the least trace of her scars. In fact, her sufferings had made her an impossible bit more lovely. She was indeed the most beautiful woman they had ever looked upon. And they hurried away with brief excuses to tell their husbands and children, for it will be remembered that she had not been up on the roof this time and they had not all seen her. And as they hurried along the streets they began to wonder if her manner was exactly the same? If her clothes were in as perfect a taste as they had been when she was going away. For the force of the unendurable quality of perfect beauty was working in their minds already. The farmer's boy got suddenly impatient with his sentimental bouquet and was about to throw them in the hedge when he pondered on all that had happened. As they went their various ways they all pondered on what had happened and next minute they were coming back with their husbands and children to ask the beautiful woman to be their Harvest Queen in the Autumn of the year. For just as the unendurable pain of her perfect beauty was entering the heart of these people there entered also the steel and iron of a faint suspicion and it grew with every step they took towards her where she stood at the stone trough in the market square while her bay mare with the cream coloured mane drank the sunwarm water. For these people who were stupid did not believe in beauty and so they did not believe either that the operation was really successful. They believed that after a time the scars would show out through the new skin again. They believed this so firmly that they loved her more than ever before. And the girls with moles on their faces and the men who had married women with double chins, were one in secretly pitying her as she stood there lovely as the water in which she was reflected. The gods were good to these stupid people for some reason of their own and permitted many of them before they died to have their vision without in any way spoiling the beauty of the beautiful woman. For after many, many years had passed and she had married and borne children and held her grandchildren in her arms Time at last cracked the porcelain skin into the faint red lines of broken veins. And the gappy gums of men who were old when she was young who was now old, muttered that they had lived to see the prophecies of their fathers come true and that the brambly briar had shown out through the new skin after all. But if they were stupid they had gained some grain of wisdom and they said before they put their arms into the outheld shroud that they didn't know why she had bothered to go away and have new skin grafted over the brambly, briary patches on her cheeks, for indeed, they said, she was more beautiful with than without them.

3

THE
WONDER-QUESTS

THE VOYAGE OF MAILDUN

P. W. Joyce

Irish mythology contains a number of accounts of quests in search of great treasures in far-off lands, or of voyages of wonder to the ends of the earth. There is, for instance, the tale of Bran, the son of Febal, who discovered the 'Land of Joy'; and the legendary quest of the three courageous sons of Tuireann, which has been compared to the more famous story of Jason and the Argonauts. Brendan the Navigator, from County Kerry, also undertook a fabulous voyage in the sixth century, when he found an island populated by spirits in bird form and landed accidentally on a giant whale. Stories of sea expeditions to find a mythical island in the Atlantic called Hy-Brasil—named after the High King of the World—are a feature of Irish tradition.

But the most famous of all these tales is 'The Voyage of Maildun', based on the Ancient Book of the Dun Cow *(written about 1100), which was first made available to the general public in 1894, in a popular version by the Dublin scholar and historian P. W. Joyce (1827–1914). Joyce, who lived in Rathmines, wrote a string of authoritative histories of Ireland as well as several studies of Irish music and language. Maildun (sometimes transcribed as Mael Dun) is recognised as one of the major figures of Irish mythology. The hero's fabulous voyage is the oldest so far identified and is believed to have inspired Brendan to set out on his later mission. Joyce's transcription of Maildun's dramatic adventures—now referred to as the 'Irish Odyssey'—not only inspired Lord Alfred Tennyson's epic poem, 'The Voyage of Maeldune', but also, as I shall explain later, significantly influenced the creation of* Ulysses, *the great novel of his namesake, James Joyce.*

*   *   *

There was once an illustrious man of the tribe of Owenaght of
Ninus, Allil Ocar Aga by name, a goodly hero, and lord of his
own tribe and territory. One time, when he was in his house
unguarded, a fleet of plunderers landed on the coast, and spoiled
his territory. The chief fled for refuge to the church of Dooclone;
but the spoilers followed him thither, slew him, and burned the
church over his head.

Not long after Allil's death, a son was born to him. The child's
mother gave him the name of Maildun; and, wishing to conceal
his birth, she brought him to the queen of that country, who was
her dear friend. The queen took him to her, and gave out that he
was her own child, and he was brought up with the king's sons,
slept in the same cradle with them, and was fed from the same
breast and from the same cup. He was a very lovely child; and
the people who saw him thought it doubtful if there was any other
child living at the time equally beautiful.

As he grew up to be a young man, the noble qualities of his
mind gradually unfolded themselves. He was high-spirited and
generous, and he loved all sorts of manly exercises. In ball-playing,
in running and leaping, in throwing the stone, in chess-playing, in
rowing, and in horse-racing, he surpassed all the youths that came
to the king's palace, and won the palm in every contest.

One day, when the young men were at their games, a certain
youth among them grew envious of Maildun; and he said, in an
angry and haughty tone of voice:

'It is a cause of much shame to us that we have to yield in every
game, whether of skill or of strength, whether on land or on water,
to an obscure youth, of whom no one can tell who is his father or
his mother, or what race or tribe he belongs to.'

On hearing this, Maildun ceased at once from play; for until
that moment he believed that he was the son of the king of the
Owenaght, and of the queen who had nursed him. And going anon
to the queen, he told her what had happened, and he said to her—

'If I am not thy son, I will neither eat nor drink till thou tell me
who my father and mother are.'

She tried to soothe him, and said, 'Why do you worry yourself searching after this matter? Give no heed to the words of
this envious youth. Am I not a mother to you? And in all this
country, is there any mother who loves her son better than I love
you?'

He answered, 'All this is quite true; yet I pray thee let me know who my parents are.'

The queen then, seeing that he would not be put off, brought him to his mother, and put him into her hands. And when he had spoken with her, he asked her to tell him who his father was.

'You are bent on a foolish quest, my child,' she said; 'for even if you knew all about your father, the knowledge would bring neither advantage nor happiness to you; for he died before you were born.'

'Even so,' he replied, 'I wish to know who he was.'

So his mother told him the truth, saying, 'Your father was Allil Ocar Aga, of the tribe of Owenaght of Ninus.'

Maildun then set out for his father's territory; and his three foster brothers, namely, the king's three sons, who were noble and handsome youths like himself, went with him. When the people of his tribe found out that the strange youth was the son of their chief, whom the plunderers had slain years before, and when they were told that the three others were the king's sons, they gave them all a joyful welcome, feasting them, and showing them much honour; so that Maildun was made quite happy, and soon forgot all the abasement and trouble he had undergone.

Some time after this, it happened that a number of young people were in the churchyard of Dooclone—the same church in which Maildun's father had been slain—exercising themselves in casting a hand-stone. The game was to throw the stone clear over the charred roof of the church that had been burned; and Maildun was there contending among the others. A foul-tongued fellow named Brickna, a servant of the people who owned the church, was standing by; and he said to Maildun—

'It would better become you to avenge the man who was burned to death here, than to be amusing yourself casting a stone over his bare, burnt bones.'

'Who was he?' inquired Maildun.

'Allil Ocar Aga, your father,' replied the other.

'Who slew him?' asked Maildun.

'Plunderers from a fleet slew him and burned him in this church,' replied Brickna; 'and the same plunderers are still sailing in the same fleet.'

Maildun was disturbed and sad after hearing this. He dropped the stone that he held in his hand, folded his cloak round him, and buckled on his shield. And he left the company, and began to inquire of all he met, the road to the plunderers' ships. For a long time he could get no tidings of them; but at last some persons, who knew where the fleet lay, told him that it was a long way off, and that there was no reaching it except by sea.

Now Maildun was resolved to find out these plunderers, and to avenge on them the death of his father. So he went without delay into Corcomroe, to the druid Nuca, to seek his advice about building a curragh, and to ask also for a charm to protect him, both while building it, and while sailing on the sea afterwards.

The druid gave him full instructions. He told him the day he should begin to build his curragh, and the exact day on which he was to set out on his voyage; and he was very particular about the number of the crew, which, he said, was to be sixty chosen men, neither more nor less.

So Maildun built a large triple-hide curragh, following the druid's directions in every particular chose his crew of sixty, among whom were his two friends, Germane and Diuran Lekerd; and on the day appointed put out to sea.

When he had got only a very little way from the land, he saw his three foster brothers running down to the shore, signalling and calling out to him to return and take them on board; for they said they wished to go with him.

'We shall not turn back,' said Maildun; 'and you cannot come with us; for we have already got our exact number.'

'We will swim after you in the sea till we are drowned, if you do not return for us,' replied they; and so saying, the three plunged in and swam after the curragh.

When Maildun saw this, he turned his vessel towards them, and took them on board rather than let them be drowned.

They sailed that day and night, as well as the whole of next day, till darkness came on again; and at midnight they saw two small bare islands, with two great houses on them near the shore. When they drew near, they heard the sounds of merriment and laughter, and the shouts of revellers intermingled with the loud voices of warriors boasting of their deeds. And listening to catch the conversation, they heard one warrior say to another:

'Stand off from me, for I am a better warrior than thou; it was

I who slew Allil Ocar Aga, and burned Dooclone over his head; and no one has ever dared to avenge it on me. Thou hast never done a great deed like that!'

'Now surely,' said Germane and Diuran to Maildun, 'Heaven has guided our ship to this place! Here is an easy victory. Let us now sack this house, since God has revealed our enemies to us, and delivered them into our hands!'

While they were yet speaking, the wind arose, and a great tempest suddenly broke on them. And they were driven violently before the storm, all that night and a part of next day, into the great and boundless ocean; so that they saw neither the islands they had left nor any other land; and they knew not whither they were going.

Then Maildun said, 'Take down your sail and put by your oars, and let the curragh drift before the wind in whatsoever direction it pleases God to lead us;' which was done.

He then turned to his foster brothers, and said to them, 'This evil has befallen us because we took you into the curragh, thereby violating the druid's directions; for he forbade me to go to sea with more than sixty men for my crew, and we had that number before you joined us. Of a surety more evil will come of it.'

His foster brothers answered nothing to this, but remained silent.

For three days and three nights they saw no land. On the morning of the fourth day, while it was yet dark, they heard a sound to the north-east; and Germane said:

'This is the voice of the waves breaking on the shore.'

As soon as it was light they saw land and made towards it. While they were casting lots to know who should go and explore the country, they saw great flocks of ants coming down to the beach, each of them as large as a foal. The people judged by their numbers, and by their eager and hungry look, that they were bent on eating both ship and crew; so they turned their vessel round and sailed quickly away.

Again for three days and three nights they saw no land. But on the morning of the fourth day they heard the murmur of the waves on the beach; and as the day dawned, they saw a large high island, with terraces all round it, rising one behind another. On the terraces grew rows of tall trees, on which were perched great numbers of large, bright-coloured birds.

When the crew were about to hold council as to who should visit the island and see whether the birds were tame, Maildun himself offered to go. So he went with a few companions; and they viewed the island warily, but found nothing to hurt or alarm them; after which they caught great numbers of the birds and brought them to their ship.

They sailed from this, and on the fourth day discovered a large, sandy island, on which, when they came near, they saw a huge, fearful animal standing on the beach, and looking at them very attentively. He was somewhat like a horse in shape; but his legs were like the legs of a dog; and he had great, sharp claws of a blue colour.

Maildun, having viewed this monster for some time, liked not his look; and, telling his companions to watch him closely, for that he seemed bent on mischief, he bade the oarsmen row very slowly towards land.

The monster seemed much delighted when the ship drew nigh the shore, and gambolled and pranced about with joy on the beach, before the eyes of the voyagers; for he intended to eat the whole of them the moment they landed.

'He seems not at all sorry to see us coming,' said Maildun; 'but we must avoid him and put back from the shore.'

This was done. And when the animal observed them drawing off, he ran down in a great rage to the very water's edge, and digging up large, round pebbles with his sharp claws, he began to fling them at the vessel; but the crew soon got beyond his reach, and sailed into the open sea.

After sailing a long distance, they came in view of a broad, flat island. It fell to the lot of Germane to go and examine it, and he did not think the task a pleasant one. Then his friend Diuran said to him:

'I will go with you this time; and when next it falls to my lot to visit an island, you shall come with me.' So both went together.

They found the island very large; and some distance from the shore they came to a broad green race-course, in which they saw immense hoof-marks, the size of a ship's sail, or of a large dining-table. They found nut-shells, as large as helmets, scattered about; and although they could see no one, they observed all the marks and tokens that people of huge size were lately employed there at sundry kinds of work.

Seeing these strange signs, they became alarmed, and went and called their companions from the boat to view them. But the others, when they had seen them, were also struck with fear, and all quickly retired from the place and went on board their curragh.

When they had got a little way from the land, they saw dimly, as it were through a mist, a vast multitude of people on the sea; of gigantic size and demoniac look, rushing along the crests of the waves with great outcry. As soon as this shadowy host had landed, they went to the green, where they arranged a horse-race.

The horses were swifter than the wind; and as they pressed forward in the race, the multitudes raised a mighty shout like thunder, which reached the crew as if it were beside them. Maildun and his men, as they sat in their curragh, heard the strokes of the whips and the cries of the riders; and though the race was far off, they could distinguish the eager words of the spectators: 'Observe the grey horse!' 'See that chestnut horse!' 'Watch the horse with the white spots!' 'My horse leaps better than yours!'

After seeing and hearing these things, the crew sailed away from the island as quickly as they were able, into the open ocean, for they felt quite sure that the multitude they saw was a gathering of demons.

They suffered much from hunger and thirst this time, for they sailed a whole week without making land; but at the end of that time they came in sight of a high island, with a large and very splendid house on the beach near the water's edge. There were two doors—one turned inland, and the other facing the sea; and the door that looked towards the sea was closed with a great flat stone. In this stone was an opening, through which the waves, as they beat against the door every day, threw numbers of salmon into the house.

The voyagers landed, and went through the whole house without meeting any one. But they saw in one large room an ornamented couch, intended for the head of the house, and in each of the other rooms was a larger one for three members of the family: and there was a cup of crystal on a little table before each couch.

They found abundance of food and ale, and they ate and drank till they were satisfied, thanking God for having relieved them from hunger and thirst.

After leaving this, they suffered again from hunger, till they came to an island with a high hill round it on every side. A single apple tree grew in the middle, very tall and slender, and all its branches were in like manner exceedingly slender, and of wonderful length, so that they grew over the hill and down to the sea.

When the ship came near the island, Maildun caught one of the branches in his hand. For three days and three nights the ship coasted the island, and during all this time he held the branch, letting it slide through his hand, till on the third day he found a cluster of seven apples on the very end. Each of these apples supplied the travellers with food and drink for forty days and forty nights.

A beautiful island next came in view, in which they saw, at a distance, multitudes of large animals shaped like horses. The voyagers, as they drew near, viewed them attentively, and soon observed that one of them opened his mouth and bit a great piece out of the side of the animal that stood next him, bringing away skin and flesh. Immediately after, another did the same to the nearest of his fellows. And, in short, the voyagers saw that all the animals in the island kept worrying and tearing each other from time to time in this manner; so that the ground was covered far and wide with the blood that streamed from their sides.

The next island had a wall all round it. When they came near the shore, an animal of vast size, with a thick, rough skin, started up inside the wall, and ran round the island with the swiftness of the wind. When he had ended his race, he went to a high point, and standing on a large, flat stone, began to exercise himself according to his daily custom, in the following manner. He kept turning himself completely round and round in his skin, the bones and flesh moving, while the skin remained at rest.

When he was tired of this exercise, he rested a little; and he then began turning his skin continually round his body, down at one side and up at the other like a mill-wheel; but the bones and flesh did not move.

After spending some time at this sort of work, he started and ran round the island as at first, as if to refresh himself. He then went back to the same spot, and this time, while the skin that covered the lower part of his body remained without motion, he whirled the skin of the upper part round and round like the movement of a flat-lying millstone. And it was in this manner that he spent most of his time on the island.

Maildun and his people, after they had seen these strange doings, thought it better not to venture nearer. So they put out to sea in great haste. The monster, observing them about to fly, ran down to the beach to seize the ship; but finding that they had got out of his reach, he began to fling round stones at them with great force and an excellent aim. One of them struck Maildun's shield and went quite through it, lodging in the keel of the curragh; after which the voyagers got beyond his range and sailed away.

Not daring to land on this island, they turned away hurriedly, much disheartened, not knowing whither to turn or where to find a resting-place. They sailed for a long time, suffering much from hunger and thirst, and praying fervently to be relieved from their distress. At last, when they were beginning to sink into a state of despondency, being quite worn out with toil and hardship of every kind, they sighted land.

It was a large and beautiful island, with innumerable fruit trees scattered over its surface, bearing abundance of gold-coloured apples. Under the trees they saw herds of short, stout animals, of a bright red colour, shaped somewhat like pigs; but coming nearer, and looking more closely, they perceived with astonishment that the animals were all fiery, and that their bright colour was caused by the red flames which penetrated and lighted up their bodies.

The voyagers now observed several of them approach one of the trees in a body, and striking the trunk all together with their hind legs, they shook down some of the apples and ate them. In this manner the animals employed themselves every day, from early morning till the setting of the sun when they retired into deep caves, and were seen no more till next morning.

Numerous flocks of birds were swimming on the sea, all round the island. From morning till noon, they continued to swim away from the land, farther and farther out to sea; but at noon they turned round, and from that to sunset they swam back towards the shore. A little after sunset, when the animals had retired to their caves, the birds flocked in on the island, and spread themselves over it, plucking the apples from the trees and eating them.

Maildun proposed that they should land on the island, and gather some of the fruit, saying that it was not harder or more dangerous for them than for the birds; so two of the men were sent beforehand to examine the place. They found the ground hot under their feet, for the fiery animals, as they lay at rest, heated the earth all around and above their caves; but the two scouts persevered notwithstanding, and brought away some of the apples.

When morning dawned, the birds left the island and swam out to sea; and the fiery animals, coming forth from their caves, went among the trees as usual, and ate the apples till evening. The crew remained in their curragh all day; and as soon as the animals had gone into their caves for the night, and the birds had taken their place, Maildun landed with all his men. And they plucked the apples till morning, and brought them on board, till they had gathered as much as they could stow into their vessel.

After rowing for a long time, their store of apples failed them, and they had nothing to eat or drink; so that they suffered sorely under a hot sun, and their mouths and nostrils were filled with the briny smell of the sea. At last they came in sight of land—a little island with a large palace on it. Around the palace was a wall, white all over, without stain or flaw, as if it had been built of burnt lime, or carved out of one unbroken rock of chalk; and where it looked towards the sea it was so lofty that it seemed almost to reach the clouds.

The gate of this outer wall was open, and a number of fine houses, all snowy white, were ranged round on the inside, enclosing a level court in the middle, on which all the houses opened. Maildun and his people entered the largest of them, and walked through several rooms without meeting with any one. But on reaching the principal apartment, they saw in it a small cat, playing among a number of low, square, marble pillars, which stood ranged in a row; and his play was, leaping continually from the top of one pillar to the top of another. When the men entered the room, the cat looked at them for a moment, but returned to his play anon, and took no further notice of them.

Looking now to the room itself, they saw three rows of precious jewels ranged round the wall from one door-jamb to the other. The first was a row of brooches of gold and silver, with their pins fixed in the wall, and their heads outwards; the second, a row of torques of gold and silver; and the third, a row of great swords, with hilts of gold and silver.

Round the room were arranged a number of couches, all pure white and richly ornamented. Abundant food of various kinds was spread on tables, among which they observed a boiled ox and a roast hog; and there were many large drinking-horns, full of good, intoxicating ale.

'Is it for us that this food has been prepared?' said Maildun to the cat.

The cat, on hearing the question, ceased from playing, and looked at him; but he recommenced his play immediately. Whereupon Maidun told his people that the dinner was meant for them; and they all sat down, and ate and drank till they were satisfied, after which they rested and slept on the couches.

When they awoke, they poured what was left of the ale into one vessel; and they gathered the remnants of the food to bring them away. As they were about to go, Maildun's eldest foster brother asked him:

'Shall I bring one of those large torques away with me?'

'By no means,' said Maildun; 'it is well that we have got food and rest. Bring nothing away, for it is certain that this house is not left without some one to guard it.'

The young man, however, disregarding Maildun's advice, took down one of the torques and brought it away. But the cat followed him, and overtook him in the middle of the court, and, springing on him like a blazing, fiery arrow, he went through his body, and reduced it in a moment to a heap of ashes. He then returned to the room, and, leaping up on one of the pillars, sat upon it.

Maildun turned back, bringing the torque with him, and, approaching the cat, spoke some soothing words; after which he put the torque back to the place from which it had been taken. Having done this, he collected the ashes of his foster brother, and, bringing them to the shore, cast them into the sea. They all then went on board the curragh, and continued their voyage, grieving for their lost companion, but thanking God for His many mercies to them.

On the morning of the third day, they came to another island, which was divided into two parts by a wall of brass running across the middle. They saw two great flocks of sheep, one on each side of the wall; and all those at one side were black, while those at the other side were white.

A very large man was employed in dividing and arranging the sheep; and he often took up a sheep and threw it with much ease over the wall from one side to the other. When he threw over a white sheep among the black ones, it became black immediately; and in like manner, when he threw a black sheep over, it was instantly changed to white.

The travellers were very much alarmed on witnessing these doings; and Maildun said:

'It is very well that we know so far. Let us now throw something on shore, to see whether it also will change colour; if it does, we shall avoid the island.'

So they took a branch with black-coloured bark and threw it towards the white sheep, and no sooner did it touch the ground than it became white. They then threw a white-coloured branch on the side of the black sheep, and in a moment it turned black.

'It is very lucky for us,' said Maildun, 'that we did not land on the island, for doubtless our colour would have changed like the colour of the branches.'

So they put about with much fear, and sailed away.

On the third day, they came in view of a large, broad island, on which they saw a herd of gracefully shaped swine; and they killed one small porkling for food. Towards the centre rose a high mountain, which they resolved to ascend, in order to view the island; and Germane and Diuran Lekerd were chosen for this task.

When they had advanced some distance towards the mountain, they came to a broad, shallow river; and sitting down on the bank to rest, Germane dipped the point of his lance into the water, which instantly burned off the top, as if the lance had been thrust into a furnace. So they went no farther.

On the opposite side of the river, they saw a herd of animals like great hornless oxen, all lying down; and a man of gigantic size near them: and Germane began to strike his spear against his shield, in order to rouse the cattle.

'Why are you frightening the poor young calves in that manner?' demanded the big shepherd, in a tremendous voice.

Germane, astonished to find that such large animals were nothing more than calves, instead of answering the question, asked the big man where the mothers of those calves were.

'They are on the side of yonder mountain,' he replied.

Germane and Diuran waited to hear no more; but, returning to their companions, told them all they had seen and heard; after which the crew embarked and left the island.

The next island they came to, which was not far off from the last, had a large mill on it; and near the door stood the miller, a huge-bodied, strong, burly man. They saw numberless crowds of men and horses laden with corn, coming towards the mill; and when their corn was ground they went away towards the west. Great herds of all kinds of cattle covered the plain as far as the eye could reach, and among them many wagons laden with every kind of wealth that is produced on the ridge of the world. All these the miller put into the mouth of his mill to be ground; and all, as they came forth, went westwards.

Maildun and his people now spoke to the miller, and asked him the name of the mill, and the meaning of all they had seen on the island. And he, turning quickly towards them, replied in few words:

'This mill is called the Mill of Inver-tre-Kenand, and I am the miller of hell. All the corn and all the riches of the world that men are dissatisfied with, or which they complain of in any way, are sent here to be ground; and also every precious article, and every kind of wealth, which men try to conceal from God. All these I grind in the Mill of Inver-tre-Kenand, and send them afterwards away to the west.'

He spoke no more, but turned round and busied himself again with his mill. And the voyagers, with much wonder and awe in their hearts, went to their curragh and sailed away.

After leaving this, they had not been long sailing when they discovered another large island, with a great multitude of people on it. They were all black, both skin and clothes, with black headdresses also; and they kept walking about, sighing and weeping and wringing their hands, without the least pause or rest.

It fell to the lot of Maildun's second foster brother to go and examine the island. And when he went among the people, he also grew sorrowful, and fell to weeping and wringing his hands, with the others. Two of the crew were sent to bring him back; but they were unable to find him among the mourners; and, what was worse, in a little time they joined the crowd, and began to weep and lament like all the rest.

Maildun then chose four men to go and bring back the others by force, and he put arms in their hands, and gave them these directions:

'When you land on the island, fold your mantles round your faces, so as to cover your mouths and noses, that you may not breathe the air of the country; and look neither to the right nor to the left, neither at the earth nor at the sky, but fix your eyes on your own men till you have laid hands on them.'

They did exactly as they were told, and having come up with their two companions, namely, those who had been sent after Maildun's foster brother, they seized them and brought them back by force. But the other they could not find. When these two were asked what they had seen on the island, and why they began to weep, their only reply was:

'We cannot tell; we only know that we did what we saw the others doing.'

And after this the voyagers sailed away from the island, leaving Maildun's second foster brother behind.

The next was a high island, divided into four parts by four walls meeting in the centre. The first was a wall of gold; the second, a wall of silver; the third, a wall of copper; and the fourth, a wall of crystal. In the first of the four divisions were kings; in the second, queens; in the third, youths; and in the fourth, young maidens.

When the voyagers landed, one of the maidens came to meet them, and leading them forward to a house, gave them food. This food, which she dealt out to them from a small vessel, looked like cheese, and whatever taste pleased each person best, that was the taste he found on it. And after they had eaten till they were satisfied, they slept in a sweet sleep, as if gently intoxicated, for three days and three nights. When they awoke on the third day, they found themselves in their curragh on the open sea; and there was no appearance in any direction either of the maiden or of the island.

They came now to a small island, with a palace on it, having a copper chain in front, hung all over with a number of little silver bells. Straight before the door there was a fountain, spanned by a bridge of crystal, which led to the palace. They walked towards the bridge, meaning to cross it, but every time they stepped on it they fell backwards flat on the ground.

After some time, they saw a very beautiful young woman coming out of the palace, with a pail in her hand; and she lifted a crystal slab from the bridge, and, having filled her vessel from the fountain, she went back into the palace.

'This woman has been sent to keep house for Maildun,' said Germane.

'Maildun indeed!' said she, as she shut the door after her.

After this they began to shake the copper chain, and the tinkling of the silver bells was so soft and melodious that the voyagers gradually fell into a gentle, tranquil sleep, and slept so till next morning. When they awoke, they saw the same young woman coming forth from the palace, with the pail in her hand; and she lifted the crystal slab as before, filled her vessel, and returned into the palace.

'This woman has certainly been sent to keep house for Maildun,' said Germane.

'Wonderful are the powers of Maildun!' said she, as she shut the door of the court behind her.

They stayed in this place for three days and three nights, and each morning the maiden came forth in the same manner, and filled her pail. On the fourth day, she came towards them, splendidly and beautifully dressed, with her bright yellow hair bound by a circlet of gold, and wearing silver-work shoes on her small, white feet. She had a white mantle over her shoulders, which was fastened in front by a silver brooch studded with gold; and under all, next her soft, snow-white skin, was a garment of fine white silk.

'My love to you, Maildun, and to your companions,' she said; and she mentioned them all, one after another, calling each by his own proper name. 'My love to you,' said she. 'We knew well that you were coming to our island, for your arrival has long been foretold to us.'

Then she led them to a large house standing by the sea, and she caused the curragh to be drawn high up on the beach. They found in the house a number of couches, one of which was intended for Maildun alone, and each of the others for three of his people. The woman then gave them, from one vessel, food which was like cheese; first of all ministering to Maildun, and then giving a triple share to every three of his companions; and whatever taste each man wished for, that was the taste he found on it. She then lifted the crystal slab at the bridge, filled her pail, and dealt out drink to them; and she knew exactly how much to give, both of food and of drink, so that each had enough and no more.

'This woman would make a fit wife for Maildun,' said his people. But while they spoke, she went from them with her pail in her hand.

When she was gone, Maildun's companions said to him, 'Shall we ask this maiden to become thy wife?'

He answered, 'What advantage will it be to you to ask her?'

She came next morning, and they said to her, 'Why dost thou not stay here with us? Wilt thou make friendship with Maildun; and wilt thou take him for thy husband?'

She replied that she and all those that lived on the island were forbidden to marry with the sons of men; and she told them that she could not disobey, as she knew not what sin or transgression was.

She then went from them to her house; and on the next morning, when she returned, and after she had ministered to them as usual, till they were satisfied with food and drink, and were become cheerful, they spoke the same words to her.

'Tomorrow,' she replied, 'you will get an answer to your question;' and so saying, she walked towards her house, and they went to sleep on their couches.

When they awoke next morning, they found themselves lying in their curragh on the sea, beside a great high rock; and when they looked about, they saw neither the woman, nor the palace of the crystal bridge, nor any trace of the island where they had been sojourning.

One night, soon after leaving this, they heard in the distance, towards the north-east, a confused murmur of voices, as if from a great number of persons singing psalms. They followed the direction of the sound, in order to learn from what it proceeded; and at noon the next day, they came in view of an island, very hilly and lofty. It was full of birds, some black, some brown, and some speckled, who were all shouting and speaking with human voices; and it was from them that the great clamour came.

At a little distance from this they found another small island, with many trees on it, some standing singly, and some in clusters, on which were perched great numbers of birds. They also saw an aged man on the island, who was covered thickly all over with long, white hair, and wore no other dress. And when they landed, they spoke to him, and asked him who he was and what race he belonged to.

'I am one of the men of Erin,' he replied. 'On a certain day, a long, long time ago, I embarked in a small curragh, and put out to sea on a pilgrimage; but I had got only a little way from shore, when my curragh became very unsteady, as if it were about to overturn. So I returned to land, and, in order to steady my boat, I placed under my feet at the bottom, a number of green surface sods, cut from one of the grassy fields of my own country, and began my voyage anew. Under the guidance of God, I arrived at this spot; and He fixed the sods in the sea for me, so that they formed a little island. At first I had barely room to stand; but every year, from that time to the present, the Lord has added one foot to the length and breadth of my island, till in the long lapse of ages it has grown to its present size. And on one day in each year, He has caused a single tree to spring up, till the island has become covered with trees. Moreover, I am so old that my body, as you see, has become covered with long, white hair, so that I need no other dress.

'And the birds that ye see on the trees,' he continued, 'these are the souls of my children, and of all my descendants, both men and women, who are sent to this little island to abide with me according as they die in Erin. God has caused a well of ale to spring up for us on the island: and every morning the angels bring me half a cake, a slice of fish, and a cup of ale from the well; and in the evening the same allowance of food and ale is dealt out to each man and woman of my people. And it is in this manner that we live, and shall continue to live till the end of the world; for we are all awaiting here the day of judgment.'

Maildun and his companions were treated hospitably on the island by the old pilgrim for three days and three nights; and when they were taking leave of him, he told them that they should all reach their own country except one man.

When they had been for a long time tossed about on the waters, they saw land in the distance. On approaching the shore, they heard the roaring of a great bellows, and the thundering sound of smiths' hammers striking a large glowing mass of iron on an anvil; and every blow seemed to Maildun as loud as if a dozen men had brought down their sledges all together.

When they had come a little nearer, they heard the big voices of the smiths in eager talk.

'Are they near?' asked one.

'Hush! silence!' says another.

'Who are they that you say are coming?' inquired a third.

'Little fellows, that are rowing towards our shore in a pigmy boat,' says the first.

When Maildun heard this, he hastily addressed the crew:

'Put back at once, but do not turn the curragh: reverse the sweep of your oars, and let her move stern forward, so that those giants may not perceive that we are flying!'

The crew at once obey, and the boat begins to move away from the shore, stern forward, as he had commanded.

The first smith again spoke. 'Are they near enough to the shore?' said he to the man who was watching.

'They seem to be at rest,' answered the other; 'for I cannot perceive that they are coming closer, and they have not turned their little boat to go back.'

In a short time the first smith asks again, 'What are they doing now?'

'I think,' said the watcher, 'they are flying; for it seems to me that they are now farther off than they were a while ago.'

At this the first smith rushed out of the forge —a huge, burly giant—holding, in the tongs which he grasped in his right hand, a vast mass of iron sparkling and glowing from the furnace; and, running down to the shore with long, heavy strides, he flung the redhot mass with all his might after the curragh. It fell a little short, and plunged down just near the prow, causing the whole sea to hiss and boil and heave up around the boat. But they plied their oars, so that they quickly got beyond his reach, and sailed out into the open ocean.

After a time, they came to a sea like green crystal. It was so calm and transparent that they could see the sand at the bottom quite clearly, sparkling in the sunlight. And in this sea they saw neither monsters, nor ugly animals, nor rough rocks; nothing but the clear water and the sunshine and the bright sand. For a whole day they sailed over it, admiring its splendour and beauty.

After leaving this they entered on another sea, which seemed like a clear, thin cloud; and it was so transparent, and appeared so light, that they thought at first it would not bear up the weight of the curragh.

Looking down, they could see, beneath the clear water, a beautiful country, with many mansions surrounded by groves and woods. In one place was a single tree; and, standing on its branches, they saw an animal fierce and terrible to look upon.

Round about the tree was a great herd of oxen grazing, and a man stood near to guard them, armed with shield and spear and sword; but when he looked up and saw the animal on the tree, he turned anon and fled with the utmost speed. Then the monster stretched forth his neck, and, darting his head downward, plunged his fangs into the back of the largest ox of the whole herd, lifted him off the ground into the tree, and swallowed him down in the twinkling of an eye; whereupon the whole herd took to flight.

When Maildun and his people saw this, they were seized with great terror; for they feared they should not be able to cross the sea over the monster, on account of the extreme mist-like thinness of the water; but after much difficulty and danger they got across it safely.

When they came to the next island, they observed with astonishment that the sea rose up over it on every side, steep and high, standing, as it were, like a wall all round it. When the people of the island saw the voyagers, they rushed hither and thither, shouting, 'There they are, surely! There they come again for another spoil!'

Then Maildun's people saw great numbers of men and women, all shouting and driving vast herds of horses, cows, and sheep. A woman began to pelt the crew from below with large nuts; she flung them so that they alighted on the waves round the boat, where they remained floating; and the crew gathered great quantities of them and kept them for eating.

When they turned to go away, the shouting ceased; and they heard one man calling aloud, 'Where are they now?' and another answering him, 'They are gone away!'

From what Maildun saw and heard at this island, it is likely that it had been foretold to the people that their country should some day be spoiled by certain marauders; and that they thought Maildun and his men were the enemies they expected.

On the next island they saw a very wonderful thing, namely, a great stream of water which, gushing up out of the strand, rose into the air in the form of a rainbow, till it crossed the whole island and came down on the strand at the other side. They walked under it without getting wet; and they hooked down from it many large salmon. Great quantities of salmon of a very great size fell also out of the water over their heads down on the ground; so that the whole island smelled of fish, and it became troublesome to gather them on account of their abundance.

From the evening of Sunday till the evening of Monday, the stream never ceased to flow, and never changed its place, but remained spanning the island like a solid arch of water. Then the voyagers gathered the largest of the salmon, till they had as much as the curragh would hold; after which they sailed out into the great sea.

The next thing they found after this was an immense silver pillar standing in the sea. It had eight sides, each of which was the width of an oar-stroke of the curragh, so that its whole circumference was eight oar-strokes. It rose out of the sea without any land or earth about it, nothing but the boundless ocean; and they could not see its base deep down in the water, neither were they able to see the top on account of its vast height.

A silver net hung from the top down to the very water, extending far out at one side of the pillar; and the meshes were so large that the curragh in full sail went through one of them. When they were passing through it, Diuran struck the mesh with the edge of his spear, and with the blow cut a large piece off it.

'Do not destroy the net,' said Maildun; 'for what we see is the work of great men.'

'What I have done,' answered Diuran, 'is for the honour of my God, and in order that the story of our adventures may be more readily believed; and I shall lay this silver as an offering on the altar of Armagh, if I ever reach Erin.'

That piece of silver weighed two ounces and a half, as it was reckoned afterwards by the people of the church of Armagh.

After this they heard some one speaking on the top of the pillar, in a loud, clear, glad voice; but they knew neither what he said, nor in what language he spoke.

The island they saw after this was named Encos;[1] and it was so called because it was supported by a single pillar in the middle. They rowed all round it, seeking how they might get into it; but could find no landing-place. At the foot of the pillar, however, down deep in the water, they saw a door securely closed and locked, and they judged that this was the way into the island. They called aloud, to find out if any persons were living there; but they got no reply. So they left it, and put out to sea once more.

The next island they reached was very large. On one side rose a lofty, smooth, heath-clad mountain, and all the rest of the island was a grassy plain. Near the sea-shore stood a great high palace, adorned with carvings and precious stones, and strongly fortified with a high rampart all round. After landing, they went towards the palace, and sat to rest on the bench before the gateway leading through the outer rampart; and, looking in through the open door, they saw a number of beautiful young maidens in the court.

After they had sat for some time, a rider appeared at a distance, coming swiftly towards the palace; and on a near approach, the travellers perceived that it was a lady, young and beautiful and richly dressed. She wore a blue, rustling silk head-dress; a silver-fringed purple cloak hung from her shoulders; her gloves were embroidered with gold thread; and her feet were laced becomingly in close-fitting scarlet sandals. One of the maidens came out and held her horse, while she dismounted and entered the palace; and

1 Encos means 'one foot'.

soon after she had gone in, another of the maidens came towards Maildun and his companions and said:

'You are welcome to this island. Come into the palace; the queen has sent me to invite you, and is waiting to receive you.'

They followed the maiden into the palace; and the queen bade them welcome, and received them kindly. Then, leading them into a large hall in which a plentiful dinner was laid out, she bade them sit down and eat. A dish of choice food and a crystal goblet of wine were placed before Maildun; while a single dish and a single drinking-bowl, with a triple quantity of meat and drink, were laid before each three of his companions. And having eaten and drunk till they were satisfied, they went to sleep on soft couches till morning.

Next day, the queen addressed Maildun and his companions:

'Stay now in this country, and do not go a-wandering any longer over the wide ocean from island to island. Old age or sickness shall never come upon you; but you shall be always as young as you are at present, and you shall live for ever a life of ease and pleasure.'

'Tell us,' said Maildun, 'how you pass your life here.'

'That is no hard matter,' answered the queen. 'The good king who formerly ruled over this island was my husband, and these fair young maidens that you see are our children. He died after a long reign, and as he left no son, I now reign, the sole ruler of the island. And every day I go to the Great Plain, to administer justice and to decide causes among my people.'

'Wilt thou go from us today?' asked Maildun.

'I must needs go even now,' she replied, 'to give judgments among the people; but as to you, you will all stay in this house till I return in the evening, and you need not trouble yourselves with any labour or care.'

They remained in that island during the three months of winter. And these three months appeared to Maildun's companions as long as three years, for they began to have an earnest desire to return to their native land. At the end of that time, one of them said to Maildun:

'We have been a long time here; why do we not return to our own country?'

'What you say is neither good nor sensible,' answered Maildun, 'for we shall not find in our own country anything better than we have here.'

But this did not satisfy his companions, and they began to murmur loudly. 'It is quite clear,' said they, 'that Maildun loves the queen of this island; and as this is so, let him stay here; but as for us, we will return to our own country.'

Maildun, however, would not consent to remain after them, and he told them that he would go away with them.

Now, on a certain day, not long after this conversation, as soon as the queen had gone to the Great Plain to administer justice, according to her daily custom, they got their curragh ready and put out to sea. They had not gone very far from land when the queen came riding towards the shore; and, seeing how matters stood, she went into the palace and soon returned with a ball of thread in her hand.

Walking down to the water's edge, she flung the ball after the curragh, but held the end of the thread in her hand. Maildun caught the ball as it was passing, and it clung to his hand; and the queen, gently pulling the thread towards her, drew back the curragh to the very spot from which they had started in the little harbour. And when they had landed, she made them promise that if ever this happened again, some one should always stand up in the boat and catch the ball.

The voyagers abode on the island, much against their will, for nine months longer. For every time they attempted to escape, the queen brought them back by means of the clew, as she had done at first, Maildun always catching the ball.

At the end of the nine months, the men held council, and this is what they said:

'We know now that Maildun does not wish to leave the island; for he loves this queen very much, and he catches the ball whenever we try to escape, in order that we may be brought back to the palace.'

Maildun replied, 'Let some one else attend to the ball next time, and let us try whether it will cling to his hand.'

They agreed to this, and, watching their opportunity, they again put off towards the open sea. The queen arrived, as usual, before they had gone very far and flung the ball after them as before. Another man of the crew caught it, and it clung as firmly to his hand as to Maildun's; and the queen began to draw the curragh towards the shore. But Diuran, drawing his sword, cut off the man's hand, which fell with the ball into the sea; and the men gladly plying their oars, the curragh resumed her outward voyage.

When the queen saw this, she began to weep and lament, wringing her hands and tearing her hair with grief; and her maidens also began to weep and cry aloud and clap their hands, so that the whole palace was full of grief and lamentation. But none the less did the men bend to their oars, and the curragh sailed away; and it was in this manner that the voyagers made their escape from the island.

They were now a long time tossed about on the great billows, when at length they came in view of an island with many trees on it. These trees were somewhat like hazels, and they were laden with a kind of fruit which the voyagers had not seen before, extremely large, and not very different in appearance from apples, except that they had a rough, berry-like rind.

After the crew had plucked all the fruit off one small tree, they cast lots who should try them, and the lot fell on Maildun. So he took some of them, and, squeezing the juice into a vessel, drank it. It threw him into a sleep of intoxication so deep that he seemed to be in a trance rather than in a natural slumber, without breath or motion, and with the red foam on his lips. And from that hour till the same hour next day, no one could tell whether he was living or dead.

When he awoke next day, he bade his people to gather as much of the fruit as they could bring away with them; for the world, as he told them, never produced anything of such surpassing goodness. They pressed out the juice of the fruit till they had filled all their vessels; and so powerful was it to produce intoxication and sleep, that, before drinking it, they had to mix a large quantity of water with it to moderate its strength.

The island they came to next was larger than most of those they had seen. On one side grew a wood of yew trees and great oaks; and on the other side was a grassy plain, with one small lake in the midst. A noble-looking house stood on the near part of the plain, with a small church not far off; and numerous flocks of sheep browsed over the whole island.

The travellers went to the church, and found in it a hermit, with snow-white beard and hair, and all the other marks of great old age. Maildun asked who he was, and whence he had come.

He replied, 'I am one of the fifteen people, who, following the example of our master, Brendan of Birra, sailed on a pilgrimage out into the great ocean. After many wanderings, we settled on this island, where we lived for a long time; but my companions died one after another, and of all who came hither, I alone am left.'

The old pilgrim then showed them Brendan's satchel, which he and his companions had brought with them on their pilgrimage; and Maildun kissed it, and all bowed down in veneration before it. And he told them that as long as they remained there, they might eat of the sheep and of the other food of the island; but to waste nothing.

One day, as they were seated on a hill, gazing out over the sea, they saw what they took to be a black cloud coming towards them from the south-west. They continued to view it very closely as it came nearer and nearer; and at last they perceived with amazement that it was an immense bird, for they saw quite plainly the slow, heavy flapping of his wings. When he reached the island, he alighted on a little hillock over the lake; and they felt no small alarm, for they thought, on account of his vast size, that if he saw them, he might seize them in his talons, and carry them off over the sea. So they hid themselves under trees and in the crannies of rocks; but they never lost sight of the bird, for they were bent on watching his movements.

He appeared very old, and he held in one claw a branch of a tree, which he had brought with him over the sea, larger and heavier than the largest full-grown oak. It was covered with fresh, green leaves, and was heavily laden with clusters of fruit, red and rich-looking like grapes, but much larger.

He remained resting for a time on the hill, being much wearied after his flight, and at last he began to eat the fruit off the branch. After watching him for some time longer, Maildun ventured warily towards the hillock, to see whether he was inclined to mischief; but the bird showed no disposition to harm him. This emboldened the others, and they all followed their chief.

The whole crew now marched in a body round the bird, headed by Maildun, with their shields raised; and as he still made no stir, one of the men, by Maildun's directions, went straight in front of

him, and brought away some of the fruit from the branch which
he still held in his talons. But the bird went on plucking and eating
his fruit, and never took the least notice.

On the evening of that same day, as the men sat looking over
the sea to the south-west, where the great bird first appeared to
them, they saw in the distance two others, quite as large, coming
slowly towards them from the very same point. On they came,
flying at a vast height, nearer and nearer, till at last they swooped
down and alighted on the hillock in front of the first bird, one on
each side.

Although they were plainly much younger than the other, they
seemed very tired, and took a long rest. Then, shaking their wings,
they began picking the old bird all over, body, wings, and head,
plucking out the old feathers and the decayed quill points, and
smoothing down his plumage with their great beaks. After this
had gone on for some time, the three began plucking the fruit off
the branch, and they ate till they were satisfied.

Next morning, the two birds began at the very same work, picking and arranging the feathers of the old bird as before; and at
midday they ceased, and began again to eat the fruit, throwing
the stones and what they did not eat of the pulp, into the lake,
till the water became red like wine. After this the old bird plunged
into the lake and remained in it, washing himself, till evening,
when he again flew up on the hillock, but perched on a different
part of it, to avoid touching and defiling himself with the old
feathers and the other traces of age and decay, which the younger
birds had removed from him.

On the morning of the third day, the two younger birds set
about arranging his feathers for the third time; and on this occasion
they applied themselves to their task in a manner much more
careful and particular than before, smoothing the plumes with the
nicest touches, and arranging them in beautiful lines and glossy
tufts and ridges. And so they continued without the least pause
till midday, when they ceased. Then, after resting for a little while,
they opened their great wings, rose into the air, and flew away
swiftly towards the south-west, till the men lost sight of them in
the distance.

Meantime the old bird, after the others had left, continued to
smooth and plume his feathers till evening; then, shaking his
wings, he rose up, and flew three times round the island, as if to

try his strength. And now the men observed that he had lost all the appearances of old age: his feathers were thick and glossy, his head was erect and his eye bright, and he flew with quite as much power and swiftness as the others. Alighting for the last time on the hillock, after resting a little, he rose again, and turning his flight after the other two, to the point from which he had come, he was soon lost to view, and the voyagers saw no more of him.

It now appeared very clear to Maildun and his companions that this bird had undergone a renewal of youth from old age, according to the word of the prophet, which says, 'Thy youth shall be renewed as the eagle.' Diuran, seeing this great wonder, said to his companions:

'Let us also bathe in the lake, and we shall obtain a renewal of youth like the bird.'

But they said, 'Not so, for the bird has left the poison of his old age and decay in the water.'

Diuran, however, would have his own way; and he told them he was resolved to try the virtue of the water, and that they might follow his example or not, whichever they pleased. So he plunged in and swam about for some time, after which he took a little of the water and mixed it in his mouth; and in the end he swallowed a small quantity. He then came out perfectly sound and whole; and he remained so ever after, for as long as he lived he never lost a tooth or had a grey hair, and he suffered not from disease or bodily weakness of any kind. But none of the others ventured in.

The voyagers, having remained long enough on this island, stored in their curragh a large quantity of the flesh of the sheep; and after bidding farewell to the ancient cleric, they sought the ocean once more.

They next came to an island with a great plain extending over its whole surface. They saw a vast multitude of people on it, engaged in sundry youthful games, and all continually laughing. The voyagers cast lots who should go to examine the island; and the lot fell upon Maildun's third foster brother.

The moment he landed he went among the others and joined in their pastimes and in their laughter, as if he had been among them all his life. His companions waited for him a very long time,

but were afraid to venture to land after him; and at last, as there
seemed no chance of his returning, they left him and sailed away.

They came now to a small island with a high wall of fire all round
it, and there was a large open door in the wall at one side near
the sea. They sailed backward and forward many times, and always
paused before the door; for whenever they came right in front of
it, they could see almost the whole island through it.

And this is what they saw: A great number of people, beautiful
and glorious-looking, wearing rich garments adorned and radiant
all over, feasting joyously, and drinking from embossed vessels of
red gold which they held in their hands. The voyagers heard also
their cheerful, festive songs; and they marvelled greatly, and their
hearts were full of gladness at all the happiness they saw and
heard. But they did not venture to land.

A little time after leaving this, they saw something a long way off
towards the south, which at first they took to be a large white bird
floating on the sea, and rising and falling with the waves; but on
turning their curragh towards it for a nearer view, they found that
it was a man. He was very old, so old that he was covered all over
with long, white hair, which grew from his body; and he was
standing on a broad, bare rock, and kept continually throwing
himself on his knees, and never ceased praying.

When they saw that he was a holy man, they asked and received
his blessing; after which they began to converse with him; and
they inquired who he was, and how he had come to that rock.
Then the old man gave them the following account:
'I was born and bred in the island of Tory.[1] When I grew up to
be a man, I was cook to the brotherhood of the monastery; and
a wicked cook I was; for every day I sold part of the food intrusted
to me, and secretly bought many choice and rare things with the
money. Worse even than this I did; I made secret passages underground into the church and into the houses belonging to it, and
I stole from time to time great quantities of golden vestments,
book-covers adorned with brass and gold, and other holy and
precious things.

1 Tory Island, off the coast of Donegal, where there was a monastery
dedicated to St Columkille.

'I soon became very rich, and had my rooms filled with costly couches, with clothes of every colour, both linen and woollen, with brazen pitchers and caldrons, and with brooches and armlets of gold. Nothing was wanting in my house, of furniture and ornament, that a person in a high rank of life might be expected to have; and I became very proud and overbearing.

'One day, I was sent to dig a grave for the body of a rustic that had been brought from the mainland to be buried on the island. I went and fixed on a spot in the little graveyard; but as soon as I had set to work, I heard a voice speaking down deep in the earth beneath my feet:

'"Do not dig this grave!"

'I paused for a moment, startled; but, recovering myself, I gave no further heed to the mysterious words, and again I began to dig. The moment I did so, I heard the same voice, even more plainly than before:

'"Do not dig this grave! I am a devout and holy person, and my body is lean and light; do not put the heavy, pampered body of that sinner down upon me!"

'But I answered, in the excess of my pride and obstinacy, "I will certainly dig this grave; and I will bury this body down on you!"

'"If you put that body down on me, the flesh will fall off your bones, and you will die, and be sent to the infernal pit at the end of three days; and, moreover, the body will not remain where you put it."

'"What will you give me," I asked, "if I do not bury the corpse on you?"

'"Everlasting life in heaven," replied the voice.

'"How do you know this; and how am I to be sure of it?" I inquired.

'And the voice answered me, "The grave you are digging is clay. Observe now whether it will remain so, and then you will know the truth of what I tell you. And you will see that what I say will come to pass, and that you cannot bury that man on me, even if you should try to do so."

'These words were scarce ended, when the grave was turned into a mass of white sand before my face. And when I saw this, I brought the body away, and buried it elsewhere.

'It happened, some time after, that I got a new curragh made, with the hides painted red all over; and I went to sea in it. As I sailed by the shores and islands, I was so pleased with the view of the land and sea from my curragh that I resolved to live altogether in it for some time; and I brought on board all my treasures— silver cups, gold bracelets, and ornamented drinking-horns, and everything else, from the largest to the smallest article.

'I enjoyed myself for a time, while the air was clear and the sea calm and smooth. But one day, the winds suddenly arose and a storm burst upon me, which carried me out to sea, so that I quite lost sight of land, and I knew not in what direction the curragh was drifting. After a time, the wind abated to a gentle gale, the sea became smooth, and the curragh sailed on as before, with a quiet, pleasant movement.

'But suddenly, though the breeze continued to blow, I thought I could perceive that the curragh ceased moving, and, standing up to find out the cause, I saw with great surprise an old man not far off, sitting on the crest of a wave.

'He spoke to me; and, as soon as I heard his voice, I knew it at once, but I could not at the moment call to mind where I had heard it before. And I became greatly troubled, and began to tremble, I knew not why.

'"Whither art thou going?" he asked.

'"I know not," I replied; "but this I know, I am pleased with the smooth, gentle motion of my curragh over the waves."

'"You would not be pleased," replied the old man, "if you could see the troops that are at this moment around you."

'"What troops do you speak of?" I asked. And he answered:

'"All the space round about you, as far as your view reaches over the sea, and upwards to the clouds, is one great towering mass of demons, on account of your avarice, your thefts, your pride, and your other crimes and vices."

'He then asked, "Do you know why your curragh has stopped?"

'I answered, "No" and he said, "It has been stopped by me; and it will never move from that spot till you promise me to do what I shall ask of you."

'I replied that perhaps it was not in my power to grant his demand.

'"It is in your power," he answered; "and if you refuse me, the torments of hell shall be your doom."

'He then came close to the curragh, and, laying his hands on me, he made me swear to do what he demanded.

' "What I ask is this," said he; "that you throw into the sea this moment all the ill-gotten treasures you have in the curragh."

'This grieved me very much, and I replied, "It is a pity that all these costly things should be lost."

'To which he answered, "They will not go to loss; a person will be sent to take charge of them. Now do as I say."

'So, greatly against my wishes, I threw all the beautiful precious articles overboard, keeping only a small wooden cup to drink from.

' "You will now continue your voyage," he said; "and the first solid ground your curragh reaches, there you are to stay."

'He then gave me seven cakes and a cup of watery whey as food for my voyage; after which the curragh moved on, and I soon lost sight of him. And now I all at once recollected that the old man's voice was the same as the voice that I had heard come from the ground, when I was about to dig the grave for the body of the rustic. I was so astonished and troubled at this discovery, and so disturbed at the loss of all my wealth, that I threw aside my oars, and gave myself up altogether to the winds and currents, not caring whither I went; and for a long time I was tossed about on the waves, I knew not in what direction.

'At last it seemed to me that my curragh ceased to move; but I was not sure about it, for I could see no sign of land. Mindful, however, of what the old man had told me, that I was to stay wherever my curragh stopped, I looked round more carefully; and at last I saw, very near me, a small rock level with the surface, over which the waves were gently laughing and tumbling. I stepped on to the rock; and the moment I did so, the waves seemed to spring back, and the rock rose high over the level of the water; while the curragh drifted by and quickly disappeared, so that I never saw it after. This rock has been my abode from that time to the present day.

'For the first seven years, I lived on the seven cakes and the cup of whey given me by the man who had sent me to the rock. At the end of that time the cakes were all gone; and for three days I fasted, with nothing but the whey to wet my mouth. Late in the evening of the third day, an otter brought me a salmon out of the sea; but though I suffered much from hunger, I could not bring myself to eat the fish raw, and it was washed back again into the waves.

'I remained without food for three days longer; and in the afternoon of the third day, the otter returned with the salmon. And I saw another otter bring firewood; and when he had piled it up on the rock, he blew it with his breath till it took fire and lighted up. And then I broiled the salmon and ate till I had satisfied my hunger.

'The otter continued to bring me a salmon every day, and in this manner I lived for seven years longer. The rock also grew larger and larger daily, till it became the size you now see it. At the end of seven years, the otter ceased to bring me my salmon, and I fasted for three days. But at the end of the third day, I was sent half a cake of fine wheaten flour and a slice of fish; and on the same day my cup of watery whey fell into the sea, and a cup of the same size, filled with good ale, was placed on the rock for me.

'And so I have lived, praying and doing penance for my sins to this hour. Each day my drinking-vessel is filled with ale, and I am sent half a wheat-flour cake and a slice of fish; and neither rain nor wind, nor heat, nor cold, is allowed to molest me on this rock.'

This was the end of the old man's history. In the evening of that day, each man of the crew received the same quantity of food that was sent to the old hermit himself, namely, half a cake and a slice of fish; and they found in the vessel as much good ale as served them all.

The next morning he said to them, 'You shall all reach your own country in safety. And you, Maildun, you shall find in an island on your way, the very man that slew your father; but you are neither to kill him nor take revenge on him in any way. As God has delivered you from the many dangers you have passed through, though you were very guilty, and well deserved death at His hands; so you forgive your enemy the crime he committed against you.'

After this they took leave of the old man and sailed away.

Soon after they saw a beautiful verdant island, with herds of oxen, cows, and sheep browsing all over its hills and valleys; but no houses nor inhabitants were to be seen. And they rested for some time on this island, and ate the flesh of the cows and sheep.

One day, while they were standing on a hill, a large falcon flew by; and two of the crew, who happened to look closely at him, cried out, in the hearing of Maildun:

'See that falcon! he is surely like the falcons of Erin!'

'Watch him closely,' cried Maildun; 'and observe exactly in what direction he is flying!'

And they saw that he flew to the south-east, without turning or wavering.

They went on board at once; and, having unmoored, they sailed to the south-east after the falcon. After rowing the whole day, they sighted land in the dusk of the evening, which seemed to them like the land of Erin.

On a near approach, they found it was a small island; and now they recognised it as the very same island they had seen in the beginning of their voyage, in which they had heard the man in the great house boast that he had slain Maildun's father, and from which the storm had driven them out into the great ocean.

They turned the prow of their vessel to the shore, landed, and went towards the house. It happened that at this very time the people of the house were seated at their evening meal; and Maildun and his companions, as they stood outside, heard a part of their conversation.

Said one to another, 'It would not be well for us if we were now to see Maildun.'

'As to Maildun,' answered another, 'it is very well known that he was drowned long ago in the great ocean.'

'Do not be sure,' observed a third; 'perchance he is the very man that may waken you up some morning from your sleep.'

'Supposing he came now,' asks another, 'what should we do?'

The head of the house now spoke in reply to the last question; and Maildun at once knew his voice:

'I can easily answer that,' said he. 'Maildun has been for a long time suffering great afflictions and hardships; and if he were to come now, though we were enemies once, I should certainly give him a welcome and a kind reception.'

When Maildun heard this he knocked at the door, and the door-keeper asked who was there; to which Maildun made answer.

'It is I, Maildun, returned safely from all my wanderings.'

The chief of the house then ordered the door to be opened; and he went to meet Maildun, and brought himself and his companions into the house. They were joyfully welcomed by the whole household; new garments were given to them; and they feasted and rested, till they forgot their weariness and their hardships.

They related all the wonders God had revealed to them in the course of their voyage, according to the word of the sage who says, 'It will be a source of pleasure to remember these things at a future time.'

After they had remained here for some days, Maildun returned to his own country. And Diuran Lekerd took the five half-ounces of silver he had cut down from the great net at the Silver Pillar, and laid it, according to his promise, on the high altar of Armagh.

THE HERO OF MICHAN

James Joyce

As I have already mentioned, 'The Voyage of Maildun' very probably played a significant part in the creation of the nation's most famous modern novel, Ulysses, by James Joyce (1882–1941), which was first published in Paris in 1922. There are several examples in Joyce's earlier short fiction that reveal his interest in Irish mythology, as well as Finnegan's Wake (1939) in which the great hero, Finn MacCool, makes an appearance. The title itself embodies several puns, including one calling upon Finn to rise again from his deathlike sleep—'Finn Again Wake'.

Although Joyce's work undoubtedly developed from a number of elements of Irish tradition, there is strong evidence that he had read 'The Voyage of Maildun', and that at least one major section of the book—the 'Cyclops' episode which is full of 'mock epic material', to quote several Joycean scholars—was actually inspired by it. This idea was first suggested by Vivian Mercier and then expanded in an article, 'An Old-Irish Model for Ulysses' by Stanley Sultan in the James Joyce Quarterly in 1968. In his essay, Sultan pinpoints a number of similarities between the travel epic and Ulysses. 'Joyce refers to "the solid man" Muldoon,' he writes, 'and "The Voyage of Maildun" includes features that are found in Ulysses and not in the Odyssey: a horse race; a division into untitled sections; a similar name for the hero (Maildun in Irish means "chief of the fort", Leopold in German "bold for the people"), and perhaps most interestingly of all, Maildun's refusal (like Leopold's) to take revenge on his worst enemy.' Sultan is convinced that at the very least the earlier epic was 'an invisible contributor to the great novel'. This is a view that I share, and you are now invited to draw your own conclusions by reading the episode below from the 'Cyclops' section of Ulysses, which I have entitled 'The Hero of Michan'.

*   *   *

In Inisfail the fair there lies a land, the land of holy Michan. There rises a watchtower beheld of men afar.There sleep the mighty dead as in life they slept, warriors and princes of high renown. A pleasant land it is in sooth of murmuring waters, fishful streams where sport the gunnard, the plaice, the roach, the halibut, the gibbed haddock, the grilse, the dab, the brill, the flounder, the mixed coarse fish generally and other denizens of the aqueous kingdom too numerous to be enumerated. In the mild breezes of the west and of the east the lofty trees wave in different directions their first class foliage, the wafty sycamore, the Lebanonian cedar, the exalted planetree, the eugenic eucalyptus and other ornaments of the arboreal world with which that region is thoroughly well supplied. Lovely maidens sit in close proximity to the roots of the lovely trees singing the most lovely songs while they play with all kinds of lovely objects as for example golden ingots, silvery fishes, crans of herrings, drafts of eels, codlings, creels of fingerlings, purple seagems and playful insects. And heroes voyage from afar to woo them, from Elbana to Slievemargy, the peerless princes of unfettered Munster and of Connacht the just and of smooth sleek Leinster and of Cruachan's land and of Armagh the splendid and of the noble district of Boyle, princes, the sons of kings.

And there rises a shining palace whose crystal glittering roof is seen by mariners who traverse the extensive sea in barks built expressly for that purpose and thither come all herds and fatlings and first fruits of that land for O'Connell Fitzsimon takes toll of them, a chieftain descended from chieftains. Thither the extremely large wains bring foison of the fields, flaskets of cauliflowers, floats of spinach, pineapple chunks, Rangoon beans, strikes of tomatoes, drums of figs, drills of Swedes, spherical potatoes and tallies of iridescent kale, York and Savoy, and trays of onions, pearls of the earth, and punnets of mushrooms and custard marrows and fat vetches and bere and rape and red green yellow brown russet sweet big bitter ripe pomellated apples and chips of strawberries and sieves of gooseberries, pulpy and pelurious, and strawberries fit for princes and raspberries from their canes.

I dare him, says he, and I doubledare him. Come out here, Geraghty, you notorious bloody hill and dale robber!

And by that way wend the herds innumerable of bell-wethers

and flushed ewes and shearling rams and lambs and stubble geese and medium steers and roaring mares and polled calves and long-wools and storesheep and Cuffe's prime springers and culls and sowpigs and baconhogs and the various different varieties of highly distinguished swine and Angus heifers and polly bullocks of immaculate pedigree together with prime premiated milchcows and beeves: and there is ever heard a trampling, cackling, roaring, lowing, bleating, bellowing, rumbling, grunting, champing, chewing, of sheep and pigs and heavyhooved kine from pasturelands of Lush and Rush and Carrickmines and from the streamy vales of Thomond, from M'Gillicuddy's reeks the inaccessible and lordly Shannon the unfathomable, and from the gentle declivities of the place of the race of Kiar, their udders distended with superabundance of milk and butts of butter and rennets of cheese and farmer's firkins and targets of lamb and crannocks of corn and oblong eggs, in great hundreds, various in size, the agate with the dun.

The figure seated on a large boulder at the foot of a round tower was that of a broadshouldered deepchested stronglimbed frank-eyed redhaired freely freckled shaggybearded widemouthed largenosed longheaded deepvoiced barckneed brawnyhanded hairylegged ruddyfaced, sinewyarmed hero. From shoulder to shoulder he measured several ells and his rocklike mountainous knees were covered, as was likewise the rest of his body wherever visible, with a strong growth of tawny prickly hair in hue and toughness similar to the mountain gorse (*Ulex Europeus*). The widewinged nostrils, from which bristles of the same tawny hue projected, were of such capaciousness that within their cavernous obscurity the fieldlark might easily have lodged her nest. The eyes in which a tear and a smile strove ever for the mastery were of the dimensions of a goodsized cauliflower. A powerful current of warm breath issued at regular intervals from the profound cavity of his mouth while in rhythmic resonance the loud strong hale reverberations of his formidable heart thundered rumblingly causing the ground, the summit of the lofty tower and the still loftier walls of the cave to vibrate and tremble.

He wore a long unsleeved garment of recently flayed oxhide reaching to the knees in a loose kilt and this was bound about his middle by a girdle of plaited straw and rushes. Beneath this he wore trews of deerskin, roughly stitched with gut. His nether extremities were encased in high Balbriggan buskins dyed in lichen purple, the feet being shod with brogues of salted cowhide laced with the windpipe of the same beast. From his girdle hung a row of seastones which dangled at every movement of his portentous frame and on these were graven with rude yet striking art the tribal images of many Irish heroes and heroines of antiquity, Cuchulin, Conn of hundred battles, Niall of nine hostages, Brian of Kincora, the Ardri Malachi, Art MacMurragh, Shane O'Neill, Father John Murphy, Owen Roe, Patrick Sarsfield, Red Hugh O'Donnell, Red Jim MacDermott, Soggarth Eoghan O'Growney, Michael Dwyer, Francy Higgins, Henry Joy M'Cracken, Goliath, Horace Wheatley, Thomas Conneff, Peg Woffington, the Village Blacksmith, Captain Moonlight, Captain Boycott, Dante Alighieri, Christopher Columbus, S. Fursa, S. Brendan, Marshal Mac- Mahon, Charlemagne, Theobald Wolfe Tone, the Mother of the Maccabees, the Last of the Mohicans, the Rose of Castille, the Man for Galway, The Man that Broke the Bank at Monte Carlo, The Man in the Gap, The Woman Who Didn't, Benjamin Franklin, Napoleon Bonaparte, John L. Sullivan, Cleopatra, Savourneen Deelish, Julius Caesar, Paracelsus, sir Thomas Lipton, William Tell, Michelangelo, Hayes, Muhammad, the Bride of Lammermoor, Peter the Hermit, Peter the Packer, Dark Rosaleen, Patrick W. Shakespeare, Brian Confucius, Murtagh Gutenberg, Patricio Velasquez, Captain Nemo, Tristan and Isolde, the first Prince of Wales, Thomas Cook and Son, the Bold Soldier Boy, Arrah na Pogue, Dick Turpin, Ludwig Beethoven, the Colleen Bawn, Waddler Healy, Angus the Culdee, Dolly Mount, Sidney Parade, Ben Howth, Valentine Greatrakes, Adam and Eve, Arthur Wellesley, Boss Croker, Herodotus, Jack the Giantkiller, Gautama Buddha, Lady Godiva, The Lily of Killarney, Balor of the Evil Eye, the Queen of Sheba, Acky Nagle, Joe Nagle, Alessandro Volta, Jeremiah O'Donovan Rossa, Don Philip O'Sullivan Beare. A couched spear of acuminated granite rested by him while at his feet reposed a savage animal of the canine tribe whose stertorous gasps announced that he was sunk in uneasy slumber, a supposition confirmed by hoarse growls and spasmodic movements which his master repressed from time to time by tranquillising blows of a mighty cudgel rudely fashioned out of paleolithic stone.

Who comes through Michan's land, bedight in sable armour?
O'Bloom, the son of Rory: it is he. Impervious to fear is Rory's
son: he of the prudent soul.

THE RETURN OF CUCHULAIN

Eimar O'Duffy

The concept of an ancient Irish hero being brought to life in modern times which James Stephens initiated in The Crock of Gold *and James Joyce developed further in* Ulysses, *reached its apogee in three novels known as the 'Cuandine Trilogy', written in the late Twenties and early Thirties by another civil servant turned writer, Eimar O'Duffy (1893–1935).* King Goshawk and the Birds *(1926),* The Spacious Adventures of the Man in the Street *(1928) and* Asses in Clover *(1933) are little known outside Ireland, but represent an achievement of satiric fantasy worthy of comparison with the best of Flann O'Brien and Samuel Beckett.*

O'Duffy, who worked in the Irish Department of External Affairs until he lost his job in 1925, was clearly as influenced by the myths and traditions of his native land as was James Joyce, and it has been pointed out that it was probably no coincidence that he set the action of the best volume of his trilogy, King Goshawk and the Birds, *in the area of Barney Kiernan's pub where the fantasy elements of Joyce's 'Cyclops' episode are recounted. Moreover just as* The Crock of Gold *ends with Angus, the god of love, about to leave for Dublin to free a philosopher, so* King Goshawk *describes the arrival in the city of another god, Cuchulain.*

Critic James M. Cahalan has called King Goshawk and the Birds *'a comic and satiric masterpiece'. It relates what happens when King Goshawk, a vulgar American capitalist living in Ireland, threatens what little romance there remains in life by buying up all the song birds and charging admission to hear them sing. A venerable 'Philosopher of Stoneybatter' determines to right this terrible wrong by journeying to Tir na nOg (the Land of Youth) to recruit the aid of the 'sleeping' hero, Cuchulain. The impact of an ancient warrior on the twentieth century, as told in 'The Return of Cuchulain', is not unlike that of Gulliver among the Lilliputians, and may well have been intended to be so by O'Duffy who greatly admired his fellow countryman and forerunner in Irish fantasy fiction.*

*   *   *

The Philosopher came upon the spirits of the heroes walking in the meadows of asphodel in Tir na nOg. They were not like the spirit of Socrates, which resembled a still flame; but they had the forms of men, glorious and ethereal. A hero is a person of superabundant vitality and predominant will, with no sense of responsibility or humour, which makes him a nuisance on earth; but he is in his element in the third heaven. There the heroes take themselves and one another at their own valuation, regarding their weaknesses as strength, their defects as merits. Their life is in their fame: every time an earthly orator recites their names they experience thrills of pleasure; if they are forgotten they die.

The Philosopher recognised many of the heroes as they walked in golden sunlight over the meadows of asphodel: Hector and Achilles arm in arm; Horatius in friendly colloquy with the Tusculan Mamilius; Henry V. of England; Patrick Sarsfield and Shane O'Neill; Bertrand du Guesclin; Garibaldi; and there were many more whom he did not know, mighty men of every race and nation that has shed blood on the green fields of earth. To none of these did the Philosopher address himself, but ever kept a watch for the one that seemed to him best suited for his purpose: namely, Cuchulain of Muirthemne, son of Dechtire and of Lugh of the Long Hand, of whom it was said in his time that there was none to compare with him for valour and truth, for magnanimity and courtesy, for strength and comeliness among the heroes of the world. In the crowd that went by there was none that resembled him. The Philosopher therefore passed on, and crossing another field he came to a glade, and saw before him a bush spangled with blossoms of ever-changing colours, that played sweet music in the breath of the wind. In the shadow of the bush reposed a youth of exceeding beauty. Three colours were in his hair: brown at the skin, blood-red in the middle, golden at the ends. Snow-white was his skin; as seven jewels was the brightness of his kingly eyes. Seven fingers had he on each hand; seven toes on each foot; and if you doubt it, go straightway and poke your misbelieving nose into the pages of the Book of Leinster or the Book of the Dun

Cow or the Yellow Book of Leccan, where all these things are faithfully recorded, with a good deal more that I spare you. Certain it is that it was by these marks that the Philosopher knew that the youth in front of him was Cuchulain.

By the hero's side lay a woman, with her head resting amorously on his shoulder. Very fair she was, with two plaits of hair of the rich hue of marigolds, eyes as blue as the wood anemone, and her naked body as white as the foam of the sea. The Philosopher took her at first to be Emer; but presently in their love talk, which held him entranced as by celestial music, he heard Cuchulain call her Fand; at which the Philosopher was moved to indignant speech. Said he:

'I thought that affair was over since Manannan Mac Lir shook his cloak of forgetfulness between you. And surely it were only just to render to Emer in heaven that faithfulness you denied to her on earth.'

'You forget,' said Cuchulain, 'that in heaven there is no marrying nor giving in marriage. As for this'—looking down at the woman—'I am tired of it,' whereupon he cast her from him, and she vanished. 'She was but the figment of my imagination,' said he, 'made with a wish; unmade with another: for heaven is but the fulfilment of the heart's desire.'

'I do not care for this heaven,' said the Philosopher.

'Your desire is nobler,' said Cuchulain. 'You should seek a higher heaven.'

'I am not a spirit,' said the Philosopher. 'I am the mind of a man, and I have come all the way from Earth to find you.'

'What is your errand?' asked Cuchulain.

'Man,' said the Philosopher, 'is full of wickedness and folly.'

'True,' said Cuchulain. 'Tell me what wickedness and folly he has done since I left the earth.'

'In the first place,' said the Philosopher, 'he is never done fighting and killing.'

'That,' said Cuchulain, 'is foolish, but it is not wicked. I fought and killed many in my time on earth. I am since convinced of folly, but I am clear of guilt.'

'In those days,' said the mind of the Philosopher, 'men fought with men in hot blood, hand to hand, strength against strength, feat against feat, and knowing well what it was they were fighting for. But for many centuries they have been possessed of a devilish powder which enables them to kill at a distance; and by labouring hard at its improvement they have learnt how to kill without seeing one another at all. So that now when countries are at war they do not send forth armies, but each hurls millions of missiles over mountains and seas at the other, destroying lands and cities, men, women, and children, until one or other is utterly overwhelmed. Some of these missiles are so cunningly devised that when they hit they divide up into thousands of particles which riddle and macerate the body; others contain deadly poisons; others scatter the contagion of leprosy and such foul diseases through the air; others on bursting are converted into a fine dust which is borne on the wind and blinds every eye in which it finds lodgement. They inflict on each other besides a thousand more abominations of which I cannot tell you, for already I grow weaker and must soon yield to the earthward pull of my body. But you must know this also, that nobody ever knows the real cause or meaning of these wars, and that if any one asks he is immediately put to silence.'

Said the spirit of Cuchulain: 'This is indeed a most iniquitous way of fighting. But is the tale of man's wickedness and folly complete?'

'No,' said the Philosopher. 'That is only the beginning. While the many are thus fighting, the few are contriving against their liberties, and robbing them of their bread and their homes, so that all the wealth of the world has now passed into the hands of usurers. And at last, infamy of infamies, these have begun to covet the beauty of the world as well.' Then he told Cuchulain of the bird-purchase of King Goshawk; and at that the hero was thrown into a rage surpassing even that of Socrates.

'Enough!' said he. 'I will rest here no longer. Let us to earth at once.'

*   *   *

So the Philosopher's mind returned to him in the little room in the back lane off Stoneybatter; and having rubbed his natural eyes he saw the spirit of Cuchulain standing before him, glorious and resplendent as a flame in a dark place, as a fountain among stagnant waters.

'Welcome to Earth and to my humble abode,' said the Philosopher. 'And pray pardon me if I leave you for a moment: for I must find you a body, in order that you may go inconspicuously among men, and see for yourself the folly and wickedness from which you would redeem them.' And at that he took himself off, leaving the hero gazing in bewilderment at the strange habitation of the heir of the ages.

Now there was a man dwelling on the same floor as the Philosopher who thought life was not worth living; for he had to spend most of it making up pounds and half-pounds of tea, sugar, flour, butter, cheese, bacon, sausages, and the like into parcels, and being polite to the fools that bought them; and he had to subsist himself on the same commodities, which he hated with the same intensity and for the same reason as the slaves who built the Pyramids must have hated the architecture of Ancient Egypt. He felt that it was no life for a man to rise in the morning before the sun had taken the chill from the air, to be at every one's beck and call during the best hours of the day, and not to be free till its tag end when there was nothing to do but sit in a stuffy picturehouse puffing fags. Of course there were also Saturday afternoons and Sundays: but what could you do with a half-day beyond killing time at the pictures or a football match? and most of a Sunday was gone by the time you had heard Mass and finished dinner, and the picture-houses didn't open till eight o'clock. Oh, it was a hard life and a dull life to be doomed to, very different from the life of his dreams. He would have liked to be rich, to be exquisitely dressed, to live in a gorgeous house, to have abundance of leisure, to have silent, smoothlygliding servants and automobiles always at his command, to be loved and won by glorious shining women— in short, to live like the heroes of his favourite film dramas. Instead of that he had to work, to obey orders, to loiter aimlessly between whiles, to wear cheap ready-made suits, to dodge other people's motors and serve their servants with sugar and sausages, and every hour of the day to be tempted by the sight of women customers and passers-by with pretty ankles and swelling hips and bosoms, that would stir up hot tormenting passions which he could only satisfy by risking damnation to eternal brimstone, or else by getting married—which he couldn't afford, and besides the girl he was walking out with was no great marvel, with her pale lips and her flat chest and her thin legs that didn't properly fill her stockings. Oh, a very dull life, thought Mr Robert Emmett Aloysius O'Kennedy.

It was to this man that the Philosopher came seeking the loan of a body. He was standing before his mirror wondering whether he ought to wash his neck that morning when he heard the Philosopher's knock.

'Come in and sit down,' he said hospitably, for he liked the Philosopher, thinking him an amusing old ass. 'You don't mind if I go on washing?' he added. 'Because I'll be late if I don't,' and, having decided to spare his neck for yet another day, he began vigorously to sponge his face.

'You told me the other day,' said the Philosopher, 'that you didn't consider life worth living.'

'I did,' said Mr O'Kennedy.

'Do you still think the same?' asked the Philosopher.

'I do,' said Mr O'Kennedy, and began to dry his face in an exceedingly dirty towel.

'Would you like to quit it for a time?' asked the Philosopher.

'I'd like to quit it for good,' said Mr O'Kennedy emphatically.

'For ever is a long time,' said the Philosopher. 'But I think we could manage a month.'

Mr O'Kennedy would have winked here if there had been anybody to wink at. The old boy was certainly more cracked than usual this morning.

'What is your body worth?' asked the Philosopher.

'Couldn't be sure,' said Mr O'Kennedy. 'The boss pays me three quid a week for the use of it, but I think he includes my soul in the bargain.'

'Your body is all I want,' said the Philosopher. 'What do you say to two pounds ten? And while I'm using it your soul can go off to heaven for a rest.'

'Done,' said Mr O'Kennedy, who thought he had a yarn that would keep his friends in stitches for a week.

Then the Philosopher put Mr O'Kennedy sitting in a chair; and he made three passes with his hands; at which the body of the young man became fixed and immovable, and his soul was filled with fear.

'Stop!' he cried. 'You are killing me.'

'You said that was what you wanted,' said the Philosopher.

'I didn't mean it,' said Mr O'Kennedy.

Then the Philosopher made three more passes; and the soul of the young man departed from him, and went wandering into space.

But the Philosopher took his body, and stripped it, and washed it thoroughly, and brought it to his own room, where he set it down before Cuchulain, saying:

'Come, now. Here is a body: a poor thing; a pitiful thing; not too well made, and somewhat marred in use; but still a semblable human body. Put it on.'

Cuchulain looked at the body and did not like it at all; for it was meanly shaped, without sign of beauty or strength. The muscles were small and flabby; the spine curved; the feet distorted fantastically by ill-fitting boots: a body unsuited to a hero. Cuchulain picked it up distastefully, as one might handle another's soiled combinations. Then he gave it a shake and clasped it to him; the spirit seemed to melt and blend with the body; and presently the heart of Robert Emmett Aloysius O'Kennedy began to beat, his lungs to breathe, his eyes to open, and his limbs to stretch themselves, as if the soul within were testing its new tenement. For some minutes after the figure stood motionless, with introspective eyes, like one in contemplation. Then came a lightning change: convulsions seized upon the body of Mr O'Kennedy, and in an instant Cuchulain had cast it from him with a cry of horror.

'O pitiful brain of man,' he said. 'What fears, what habits, what ordinances, what prohibitions have stamped you slave. I thought just now that I was in a very sweat of terror of some dreadful being named the Boss, who held over me mysterious powers, and from whom I anticipated chastisement if I were late in his service today, as I most assuredly expected to be. At the same time I felt a certain small satisfaction in remembering that yesterday I had done him some underhand injury which he would be unable to trace to my account. It was but a small weed of joy in a forest of fears. I had a fear that a man I knew might have heard that I had spoken ill of him that day; and another fear that a man I had lied to might find me out. I had also a fear that my clothes were not quite the same as were worn by every one else, and a fear of what all the people I knew might be saying or thinking of me at the moment. Then there was in me a fear that had been inspired some time ago by a play I had seen, which made me seem to myself a mean, stupid, and malicious creature; and of that fear there was born in me a hatred of the play and of the man who wrote it. I hated him for using the theatre, where I went to enjoy myself, as a means of making me hate myself. And that recalled to my memory the worst fear of all those that beset me. For in the same theatre a few days before I had watched some women dancing, and my eyes had feasted on the roundness of their limbs, and my body had been bathed in warm desires. For that sin I was damned eternally to a pit of flame unless I should repent and confess. I was afraid to confess, for fear of what the druid should think of me: and I was afraid not to confess for fear of the pit of flame. Then I began to make excuses for myself, saying that I had not looked very long and that after all there had not been much to see, so that I had not sinned mortally, and had earned only some temporary fire. But I could not make myself feel quite sure of that; nor could I decide whether I was more afraid of the confession or the pit of fire. Then I began to wonder whether there was really a God or a pit of fire at all. But I dared not let myself think of that, lest I should be struck dead and buried in the pit of fire forthwith: whereupon I—even I, Cuchulain—was seized with a loathsome terror, to escape which I cast the foul body from me. And let you, O Philosopher, remove it now; for I swear by the sunlight of Tir na nOg that I will not take to me such a horror again.'

'That is not spoken like Cuchulain,' replied the Philosopher, 'who in the olden times, when he was a man and a hero, was never known to look back from a task that he had once undertaken. It is clear, however, that the spirit is affected by the condition of the somatic substrate on which it depends for expression, so I will clean it up and let you try it on again.'

So saying the Philosopher took scalpel and forceps, and, having opened the skull of Robert Emmett Aloysius O'Kennedy, and carefully reflected the membranes, he exposed the brain to the full glare of the morning sun. Then in a bottle he compounded a lotion of carbolic acid, cold horse sense, and common soap, with which he thoroughly scoured and irrigated both the psychical centres of the cerebral cortex and the association fibres connecting them with each other and with the sensory centres: for, as Halliburton or another hath it, *Nihil est in intellectu quod non prius in sensu fuerit*. After this operation, Cuchulain entered again into the body, which straightway began to glow with a divine beauty. The skin glistened like white satin; great muscles swelled and rippled beneath it; the chest expanded to a third as much again as it was; the back straightened like a spring released; the eyes flashed fire; and the sheepish countenance of Robert Emmett Aloysius O'Kennedy shone like that of a hero in his feats. Again Cuchulain began to test the strength of his borrowed frame, stretching the arms above his head, expanding the chest, stamping the feet on the ground: until at last the Philosopher cried:

'Hold now! Enough! Do you not remember all the war-chariots and the swords and spears you broke in the testing the day you first took arms and went foraying against the Dun of Nechtan's sons? This bag of bones is too frail for such experimenting, and if you wreck it I cannot get you another. Besides it is only hired by the week.'

Then sounded the voice of Cuchulain from the vocal chords of Robert Emmett Aloysius O'Kennedy like a symphony of Beethoven from the brass trumpet of a cheap gramophone, saying: 'Excellent advice, O Sage, and none too soon, for already I feel my shoulders crack. I will forbear in other respects, but the ghosts of my seven toes are most uncomfortably crammed into the warped and etiolated extremities of this starveling here, so that I seem to tread on dried peas: therefore stretch them I must.' So he sat down, and began bunching his toes as one might do to expand a shrunken stocking; and with the effort the metatarsal bones straightened out, the phalanges uncurled, a shower of corns and bunions fell on the floor, and the two feet, which had hitherto looked more like the bleached rhizomes of some unknown plant than any part of an intelligent animal, assumed a healthy shape and hue, and heroic proportions. Even so Cuchulain was not yet comfortable in his corporeal tenement, but presently said to the Philosopher, very wry in the face: 'I fear I can never wed myself peaceably to this flesh. Lo, I have here'—pointing to his belly— 'a most woeful and disturbing sensation, as of a griping emptiness, and unless it is soon relieved I will abandon this carnal vesture yet again and return to Tir na nOg.'

'That is most unfortunate,' said the Philosopher. 'I had hoped you would be free of the human frailties and the physical needs which hamper us. This pain you feel is called hunger, and it is the prick of the goad with which King Flesh reminds us that we are his slaves, forcing us to cram ourselves with bread and meat, which we metabolise into energy, which we must use to procure more bread and meat, thus remaining in a vicious circle of uselessness, eating to live and living to eat, instead of turning our minds to the pursuit of wisdom. And now that I come to think of it, I am hungry myself, and no wonder, for I have forgotten how long it is since my last meal. Have patience now, and in a moment both our pangs shall be assuaged.'

The Philosopher then went out, and in a shop at the corner of the street he bought a loaf of bread, a piece of cheese, and a quart of milk; on which provender he and Cuchulain fared right joyously, charging their batteries with peptone and the other approved albuminoids, not forgetting a due proportion of vitamins as prescribed by the medical columns of the Sunday papers. Believe me, bread and cheese and milk is the best food in the world for hungry men, when you can trust your dairyman and beer is under a ban: the proof of which is that when Cuchulain had finished he rose from his chair, and, stretching himself, put a foot through the floor and both hands through the ceiling.

'Steady!' said the Philosopher. 'This is not Bricriu's Palace. It is time your limbs were fettered with the garments of civilised society.' So saying, he took out some spare ones of his own and showed Cuchulain how to put them on. Be sure that Cuchulain in donning the trousers and tucking in the shirt showed no more grace or dignity than your mortal man—poet, priest, politician, soldier, average fool, or father of ten. I wish, indeed, that all men who hold position or notoriety could be compelled to put on their trousers publicly at least once a year: by which means we should rid ourselves of a vast quantity of that humbug and hero-worship which make the world intolerable for honest and self-reliant men. For, as the proverb says, no man is a hero to his valet: the reason being that the valet sees the hero getting into his trousers.

*   *   *

Thus clothed and fed, Cuchulain set forth with the Philosopher to explore the city. What a sight was here for eyes accustomed to the splendours of Tir na nOg. Come, O Muse, whoever you be, that stood by the elbow of immortal Zola, take this pen of mine and pump it full of such foul and fetid ink as shall describe it worthily. To what shall I compare it? A festering corpse, maggot-crawling, under a carrion-kissing sun? A loathly figure, yet insufficient: for your maggot thrives on corruption, and grows sleeker with the progression of putridity (O happy maggot, whom the dross of the world trammels not, had you but an immortal soul how surely would it aspire heavenward!). But your lord of creation rots with his environment; so the true symbol of our city is a carrion so pestilent that it corrupts its own maggots.

What ruin and decay were here: what filth and litter: what nauseating stenches. The houses were so crazy with age and so shaken with bombardments that there was scarce one that could stand without assistance: therefore they were held together by plates and rivets, or held apart by cross-beams, or braced up by scaffoldings, so that the street had the appearance of a dead forest. (Was it not a strange perversity that slew the living tree to lengthen the days of these tottering skeletons?) Many of the houses were roofless; others were inhabited only in their lower storeys; some had collapsed altogether, and squatters had built them huts of wood or mud or patchwork on the hard-pounded rubble. The streets were ankle-deep in dung and mire; craters yawned in their midst; piles of wrecked masonry obstructed them. Rivulets ran where the gutters had been. Foul sewer smells issued from holes and cracks.

Fit lairage was this for the tragomaschaloid mob that jostled the celestial visitor to the realms of earth. What stink of breath and body assailed his nostrils; what debased accents, raucous voices, and evil language offended his hearing; what grime, what running sores, what raw-rimmed eye-sockets, what gum-suppuration and tooth-rot, what cavernous cheeks, what leering lips and hopeless eyes, what pain-twisted faces, what sagging spines, what streeling steps, what filthy ragged raiment covering what ghastly-imagined hideousness of body sickened his beauty-nurtured sight.

Yet with all this putridity and squalor there were not wanting, even in those bygone days, many signs of progress and private enterprise. At every street corner there were loud-speakers which yelled forth news and advertisements. Airplanes circled like great dragon-flies in the sky, squirting out smoke-signals such as: 'Read Cumbersome's Papers', 'Why have a Bad Leg? Try Popham's Pills', 'Trust the Trusts that Feed You', 'Vote for Coddo', '*To him that hath shall be given.* Scripture backs the Trusts', 'Are you Languid? Try Peppo'. But these were but superficial signs of civilis-ation. If the hero had taken the pains to inquire, he would have learnt that every foot of land in the neighbourhood was worth fabulous sums of money; and that by a miracle of organisation every square inch of rag on the backs of the people, and every crust fermenting in their bellies had helped to make millions for somebody. Cuchulain, however, was too preoccupied with the uglier side of things to make any such inquiries. Was he not a morbid ghoul and gloomy pessimist thus to nose and grope in the dark for hidden horrors, with the best of life dancing before him in the warm sunshine?

In the pother and hurly-burly I have described, owing to the celestial vigour of Cuchulain, which was chafed rather than impaired by his catatheosis, and to the enfeeblement of the Philosopher, in whom the milk and cheese had not yet replenished the loss of tissue occasioned by his fast, the two became separated, Cuchulain pursuing his way alone, and the Philosopher, after a vain attempt to overtake him, returning to his lodging. Cuchulain, however, not perceiving the loss of his companion, strode onward with more than earthly vigour, to the grave detriment of his borrowed body, which was thereby shaken up, loosened, and derivetted, like a cheap car fitted with a too powerful engine, so that soon the stomach of Robert Emmett Aloysius O'Kennedy began to clamour for more nutriment.

Just as this clamour was beginning to be unbearable, Cuchulain espied a shop window most alluringly arrayed, with a cargo more varied and of more diverse origins than ever was carried by Venetian argosy or Corinthian trireme or galley of Tyre or ancient Sidon. There were oranges there from Jaffa and Seville, and little golden tangerines from Africa nestling in silver tinfoil. There were lemons from Italy and Spain; olives and currants from the land of Hellas; raisins from the Levant, and sultanas and muscatels. Figs were there from Smyrna, and dates from Morocco, Tripoli, and Cyrenaica; bananas, the long straight kind, from Jamaica, and short curved ones from the Canaries; and pineapples and cocoanuts from the islands whose palm-trees fan the Pacific. Then there were cheeses of a hundred species: great Stiltons like mouldy casks from a tangle of jetsam; Gorgonzola streaked like marble; rich yellow English Gloucester; Dutch cheeses like bloated beetroots; hygienic cheeses done up in jars to keep in the vitamines; evanescent-flavoured Gruyère and sharp-fanged Roquefort; simple chaste Cheddar, and sensuous Camembert. There were teas also from China, India, and Ceylon, coffee from the East

Indies, cocoa from Brazil and Ecuador, and sugar from five conti-
nents and a hundred isles. Rice was there from many lands—
China and Japan, Persia and Siam; and with it were pearly sago
and slippery tapioca. There were tinned sardines there from
France and Scotland; tinned salmon and potted meat from
America. From Canada there was shredded wheat and macaroni;
and macaroni also from Italy. Great pyramids of apples there
were, from England and from the home orchards: some red as the
blush of a country maiden, some yellow like shining taffety; with
pale Newtown pippins and quiet green baking apples. Over all
hung fine well-smoked hams and bacon flitches from Denmark
(with a few from Limerick), and American bacon like greasy tal-
low. And there were biscuits and chocolates and candied fruits
and nuts and odds and ends from the Lord knows where. All these
things came as tribute to the men of Eirinn: they made nothing
for themselves.

Here, therefore, Cuchulain turned in that he might find the
wherewithal to appease the revolt of the baser nature he had put
on; but he had scarce set foot in the shop before he was accosted
by a large and ferocious person with stand-up hair and waxed
moustaches, who, hauling him forward by the lapel of his coat,
bawled into his face: 'What's the meaning of this, you blasted
young slacker? An hour late! You can leave this day week; and
go behind the counter this minute and make up the orders or I'll
smash your face in.'

'Sir,' said Cuchulain, 'I know not what your rank is, nor what
you take me for. Howbeit, I am not used to being handled thus,
or being spoken to in such fashion as you have assailed me withal.
Loose me, therefore, lest the grossness of this body which I am
wrapped in should foul my spirit with thoughts of anger.'

The Manager, however, had not in all his life been conscious
of the image of God in any shop boy: neither were his eyes opened
now. Therefore, taking a stronger hold of Cuchulain, he would
have thrust him ignominiously before him, had not the hero, by
a sudden exertion of his muscles, maintained himself as if rooted
to the floor.

'Come on, now, you obstinate young devil!' cried the Manager,
giving him a flip on the ear with his great fat hand.

Anger came on Cuchulain at that, and a terrible appearance
came over him. Each hair of his head stood on end, with a drop

of blood at its tip. One of his eyes started forth a hand's-breadth out of its socket, and the other was sucked down into the depths of his breast. His whole body was contorted. His ribs parted asunder, so that there was room for a man's foot between them; his calves and his buttocks came round to the front of his body. At the same time the hero-light shone around his head, and the Bocanachs and Bananachs and the Witches of the Valley raised a shout around him. For such was his appearance when his anger was upon him; as testify the Yellow Book of Leccan and the other chronicles; which, if any man doubt, let him search his conscience whether he have not believed even stranger things printed in newspapers. For myself, I think the chroniclers are the more trustworthy, as they are certainly the more entertaining; for, if they lie, they lie for the fun of it, whereas the journalists lie for pay, or through sheer inability to observe or report correctly.

Now when the Manager of MacWhatsisname's grocery saw Cuchulain facing him in the same dreadful guise wherein he overcame Ferdiad at the ford and drove Fergus before him from the field of Gairech, the strength went out of his limbs, and the corpuscles of his blood fled in disgraceful rout to seek refuge in the inmost marrow of his bones. Dreadful were the scenes that were then enacted in the arched and slippery dark purple passages of his venous system. Smitten with a common panic, Red Cells, Lymphocytes, and Phagocytes rushed in headlong confusion down the peripheral veins, which soon became choked with swarming struggling masses of fugitives. Millions of smaller Lymphocytes and Mast Cells perished in the crush, but the immense mobs poured on towards the larger vessels. Yet even here there was no relief: for as each tributary stream ingurgitated its protoplasmic horde, these too became stuffed to suffocation; so that, though every corpuscle strove onward with all his strength, the jammed and stifled cell mass could scarce be seen to move. Here and there bands of armed Phagocytes, impatient of delay, tried to cut themselves a passage through the helpless huddled mass of Lymphocytes and Platelets: but they succeeded only in walling themselves up with impenetrable mounds of slaughtered carcases. Still more frightful scenes occurred when two mobs, travelling by anastomosing vessels, met each other head to head: for while those in front fought in grim despair for possession of the road until it was totally blocked and thrombosed with their bodies, the cells behind, still harried by fear, pressed onward as vigorously as ever, to the great discomfiture of the dense crowds packed between, who, thus driven by an irresistible force against an impenetrable obstacle, perished in millions.

Thus was the Manager's blood very literally curdled. And straightway Cuchulain made his salmon-leap and fisted him a smasher under the third waistcoat button, breaking four of his ribs, and hurling him backwards against the counter with enough force to crack the front of it; yet he was so well covered behind that he took no further hurt, though by his screams you would have thought he had been dumped upon the hob of hell. Then, having wrecked the shop and all it contained, Cuchulain went forth into the street, breaking a thigh or a collar-bone for any that attempted to stop him: for all which he was most soundly rated by the Philosopher when he returned to him at the close of the day.

'What have I done?' said the Philosopher. 'Old footling dunderhead that I am. What have I fetched out of heaven to show mankind his wickedness and folly? Have you no respect for our civilisation that you must sally forth, as fiery-wild as upon that first foray of yours in the barbarous youth of the world, and the first grocer's shop you come to, must leave your sign of hand upon it as though it had been the Dun of Nechtan's sons. This will never do. If two thousand years of heaven have not tamed your soul, you must tame it now; or if it is the body of Mr O'Kennedy that is at fault, then you must bring it into subjection right rapidly: for this sort of thing cannot be done in these days.'

'What,' said Cuchulain, 'have you no such pests now as these sons of Nechtan whose Dun lay athwart the road out of Ulster into Meath, and they took toll of blood and treasure of all that came by? A right strong place it was, not to be easily taken; and the sons of Nechtan were protected by magic also, so that Foill, the eldest, could not be killed with edge of sword or point of lance; and Tuachel, the second, if he were not killed by the first thrust or the first cut, could not be killed at all; and the youngest, Fandall, was swifter in the water than a swallow in the air: yet I slew them all, and gave their Dun to the winds to howl in, and to the wild beasts of Sliabh Fuaith for a lairage. Have you no such pests now?'

'A many!' said the Philosopher. 'Their duns lie across all the ways of the men of Ireland, and none may eat or drink or walk abroad without paying them toll. But they cannot be brought low by such tactics as these: for they are more cunningly fenced in, and protected by more potent magic, than ever were the sons of Nechtan. This Goshawk that I told you of is one of them: and I wish you would learn to control yourself, lest you find yourself in a gaol before you can cross swords with him. But, come now. When you had vindicated your honour by thrashing the grocer, what was your next exploit? Tell me all.'

'When I had left the grocer,' said Cuchulain, 'I walked farther up the street until I came to an eating-house, which I entered very gladly, as I was feeling the pangs of my adopted stomach more keenly than ever. Here I was received at first more courteously than in any other place in this earth of yours. The master of the house bowed low to me, gave me a chair by a table clothed with fine linen, and summoned a servant to attend to my wants. Right generous and goodly fare was then put before me, and I fed full, to the manifest enjoyment of this voracious body. Afterwards, when I had rested me a while, I sought out the master of the house that I might thank him for his hospitality: but in the midst of my speech I was interrupted by the aforesaid servitor, who thrust a piece of paper into my hand, saying, "Your bill, sir," whereat the master of the house said, "Good morning, sir; much obliged; pay at the desk." Then there came upon me a most noble rage, not this time out of the spleen of O'Kennedy, but out of my own soul; and I said: "Pay! Thou kindless, impious, inhospitable boor! What shall I pay?" for I had thought the place to be a hostelry for the free entertainment of strangers, such as they have in all the planets I have ever visited, and as they had in Eirinn in the olden time. Then said my host: "I don't know what part of the world you come from, stranger: but in this benighted country you don't get nothing for nothing." "Very well, then," I said, " I will pay. But not now, since I have not the wherewithal. Good day to you, therefore. I will return anon." So saying, I would have departed in peace, but the fellow laid hand on my shoulder, saying that he would not suffer me to go until I had paid what I owed. By my hand of valour, my word never was doubted before. Therefore I smote him, yet not very hard: only so as to lay him senseless at my feet, but with the life still in him.' (Here the Philosopher groaned.) 'After that,' said Cuchulain, 'two warriors, twins, clad both alike in blue, and their helmets embossed with shining steel, came to his assistance. To these I would willingly have explained the justice of the case, but before I could speak they seized upon me, so that I was compelled to defend myself. Yet, pitying their ignorance, I did them no injury, only binding them back to back with their own harness.'

The Philosopher groaned again, and said: 'How many people altogether have you maimed and killed? Speak out. Let me know the worst at once.'

'Venerable sir,' said Cuchulain, 'I maimed no more; neither did I kill any. After that I went to a picture-house, but seeing that there was a charge for admission, I did not enter. And by my hand of valour, there is no other planet in the universe—not even among the savage seventy that revolve around the Dog Star—that acts so scurvily: for pictures were meant to elevate the soul, and therefore cannot be priced.'

'What a pity you had no money,' said the Philosopher.

'After that,' said Cuchulain, 'I entered a car driven by electricity. What do you call them?' 'Trams.' 'Trams. I thank you. Your trams are tolerable. Nay, I have seen worse, but I have forgotten where. In this tram there were seventeen people, whom I observed with great interest. Nine of them wore discs of glass before their eyes, held in place by a band of metal fixed to the nose. Why did they do that?'

'To enable them to see,' said the Philosopher. 'Their eyes were bad.'

'Why?' asked Cuchulain.

'Civilisation,' said the Philosopher.

'Twelve of them,' said Cuchulain, 'had strange looking teeth of a most unnatural aspect.'

'They were false teeth,' said the Philosopher.

'What became of their own?' asked Cuchulain.

'Rotted,' said the Philosopher.

'Why?' asked Cuchulain.

'Civilisation,' said the Philosopher.

'Ten of them,' said Cuchulain, 'had complexions of a pale green colour, with dull eyes and drooping lips. What was the meaning of this?'

'They were poisoned,' said the Philosopher, 'by eating too much preserved food.'

'Why did they do that?' asked Cuchulain.

'They could afford no better.'

'Why?' asked Cuchulain.

'Civilisation,' said the Philosopher.

'Eight of them,' said Cuchulain, 'had sores on their faces; and there were two that could not sit straight, but balanced themselves tenderly on half a rump. What was wrong with them, venerable sir?'

The Philosopher, with all commendable delicacy, gave explanation of the phenomenon.

Said Cuchulain: 'The bottom of your civilisation is in no better case. Never have I seen so many and such strange diseases as upon this little planet. Yet you have learned and charitable physicians to cure these ills, whose advice was written plain upon the windows of the tram; as, for instance: *Are you jaded, weary, dispirited? Have you that tired feeling? Then try Peppo;* and, *Is your Liver bad? Mixo will set you right;* and again, *You feel well today. But who knows what loathsome diseases the Future may bring in its train? If you want to* KEEP *well, dose yourself daily with Absoluto.* How is it, then, that these diseases persist?'

'These were no physicians' prescriptions,' said the Philosopher. 'They were but the advertisements of the Patent Medicine Trust. All these sick people you saw were sick because they were poor, and so had to stint themselves in food. To pay for these pills and bottles they must stint their food again, and so again become ill.'

'I begin to understand your world,' said Cuchulain. 'While I was making these observations the Guardian of the tram came to me and held out his hand in a manner that I had at last come to know the meaning of. Can you get nothing in this world without money, my friend?'

'No,' said the Philosopher.

'Therefore,' said Cuchulain, 'I got up to leave the tram quietly, whereupon the Guardian laid hand on me as though to detain me. Nevertheless I smote him not, but, stopping, held his arm a moment, so that he paled and offered no further hindrance. Having dismounted from the tram, I accosted one who passed, asking him to direct me to Stoneybatter. Very quickly he gave me a description that I could not understand, and would have hurried away had I not detained him by the shoulder, saying: 'What, churl! is this your courtesy to a stranger? I have a mind to slay thee, but lead me on straight to Stoneybatter, and perhaps I may pardon thee.' Said the man of Dublin: 'What sort of a joker are you? Do you know who I am?' I said I did not.

'I am Solomon Beetlebrow,' quoth he, 'Minister of the Interior.' 'Your humble servant,' said I, bowing. 'But time presses, therefore lead on.' At that I took him by the ear, and in this wise he led me to Stoneybatter, but not without exciting some admiration in our course.'

THE END OF THE RAINBOW

Lord Dunsany

Many Irishmen have dreamed of finding Tir na nOg and the other fabled lands of mythology such as Tir fo Thuinn (Land under the Waves), Tir Tairnigiri (Land of Promise), Tir na mBeo (Land of the Living) and Tir na mBan (Country of Women). All these have featured frequently in the old legends and are said to equate with the Otherworld. However, the road to the Land of Youth has probably attracted more seekers than any of the others and is the focus of this next story by Lord Dunsany, in which a dying man determines to set his eyes on the wonder-world before breathing his last.

Lord Dunsany (1878–1957), the highly versatile poet, playwright and novelist who lived a life of high adventure as exciting as anything he described on paper, has been called the 'father' of the invented fantasy world in short story form; making him not only an important figure in Irish fantasy fiction but in the genre as a whole. Dunsany was a big-game hunter, a soldier in the Boer War and World War One, and was wounded in the Easter Rebellion of 1916. He escaped from captivity in Greece during the Second World War and was for a period the Chess Champion of Ireland. He began to write fantasy fiction in 1903 and drew indirectly on the Irish tradition of myths and heroes for his famous collections of stories such as Time and the Gods *(1906),* The Sword of Welleran *(1908),* The King of Elfland's Daughter *(1924),* The Man Who Ate the Phoenix *(1949) and many more. The following story of the quest for the road to Tir na nOg (or Tir-nan-Og as it is sometimes translated) was written in 1933 for* The Curse of the Wise Woman.

*   *   *

There was a conference only two days ago in my sitting-room between two gentlemen that were members of the government of this State, though I doubt if really they were anything more than the members' secretaries; and in any case we decided nothing, and I only mention it for the sake of a curious comparison, which is that the memory of the details of that conference is less vivid in my mind today than the things that I heard and saw on a morning fifty-two years ago when I drove over to see Marlin, hoping that, after all, Dr Rory may have been wrong. I went to Clonrue first, to see the doctor, impatient for some better news than what he had given me only the day before, and I even got it, for he had seen Marlin again, later that day. 'He's walking about a good deal,' he said.

'Then he'll live longer than you thought?' I asked.

'Ah, I think he will,' said the doctor.

And from that I tried to get him to say that perhaps he was wrong after all, and that Marlin would yet recover. What he said I cannot remember. But what does it matter? I was only asking him to echo my hopes. Dr Rory's words could not turn Fate back to walk the way that I wished. Yet neither he nor I ever guessed the end of Marlin.

'What way are you going?' he said to me then.

'There's only one way,' I answered.

'Ah, but you can't get down the bohereen,' he told me.

'Can't get down the bohereen?' said I.

'No,' said Dr Rory, 'they are making a road along it.'

'A road?' I exclaimed.

'Yes,' said the doctor.

'What ever for?' I asked.

'The Peat Development (Ireland) Syndicate,' he replied.

Then it was true. What had almost seemed like ravings, when Mrs Marlin told me, was mere accurate information. They were going to spoil the bog.

'But did my father ever give them leave?' I asked, clinging to a last hope, for it was not like him to allow syndicates and such things from towns to make a mess of the countryside.

'They bought an option for fifty pounds,' said the doctor. 'And now they've taken it up. You'll get a rent from them.'

'I don't want their rent,' I said. For it seemed like selling Ireland piecemeal, if they were going to cut the bog away. One did not feel like that about the turf-cutters, who all through the spring and summer had their long harvest of peat, that brought the benignant influence of the bog to a hundred hearths, and that filled the air all round the little villages with the odour that hangs in no other air that I know. Indeed the very land on which the Marlins' house was standing had been once about twenty feet higher, and had been brought to that level by ages of harvests of peat, or turf as we call it. And the land that was left was still Ireland. But now it was to be cumbered with wheels and rails and machinery, and all the unnatural things that the factory was even then giving the world, as the cities began to open that terrible box of Pandora.

'Why did my father do it?' I asked.

'He only sold them the option,' said the doctor. 'He never thought they'd come here with their nonsense. And fifty pounds is fifty pounds.'

'What are they going to do?' I enquired.

'Compress the turf by machinery and sell it as coal,' he answered.

'What nonsense,' I exclaimed.

'Of course it is,' he replied. 'But there's a lot of money to be made out of a company. And when it's got an address beside a bog, and is actually working there, it will look much more real to investors than when it's only in a prospectus. Not that it doesn't catch some of them even then.'

'I wish my father hadn't done it,' I said. But that was no use.

'They'll be broke in a few years,' said the doctor.

In a few years: that seemed terribly long to a boy.

'They'll ruin the bog,' I said. 'Can no one stop them?'

'I'm afraid not,' he answered.

It seemed so wrong that all that wonderful land, so beautiful and so free, should be brought under the thraldom of business by a city so far away, that my thoughts in their desperation turned strangely to Mrs Marlin.

'Could Mrs Marlin do anything?' I asked.

'I'm afraid not,' he said.

'Couldn't she lay a curse on them?' I continued.

'She might curse their souls a bit,' said the doctor reflectively, 'but they'd think more of business.'

In despair I left him then, and went on to see Marlin.

'We'll go by the other road,' I said to Ryan. 'They're spoiling the bohereen.'

And Ryan muttered something, as though he were cursing the

Peat Development Company, but with an amateur's ill-trained curses; not like Mrs Marlin. So down the road we went, the other road from Clonrue. And, if it is not too late, why does not some museum preserve a few yards of an old road, as it used to be before even bicycles came to cover it with their thin tracks? It's clear enough in my memory, with its wandering wheel-tracks, its pale-grey stone bright in the sunlight, and the cracks that ran through it everywhere from its unstable foundation, as soon as it neared the bog; but when I and my memory are gone and all my generation, who will remember those roads? I suppose it will not matter. They will lie sleeping, deep under tarmac, those old white roads, like the stratum of a lost era for which nobody cares. But who cares aught for the past? That pin-point of light called The Present, dancing through endless night, is all that any man cares for.

So we drove down the other road, and along the side of the bog; and the little cracks were running among the wheel-tracks as though the bog had often whispered a warning, telling that he was amongst the ancient powers, of which the earthquake was one, and that he suffered roads as all these powers suffer the things of man, which is grudgingly and for a while. And half a mile or so from the Marlins' cottage, at the nearest point to which this road came to them, I got out of the trap. My walk lay over the level land from which the bog had receded, or rather from which it had been pushed back by man: on my left, all the way as I went, the cliff of the bog's edge stood like a wave of a threatening tide, dark and long and immanent. Square pools of sombre deep water lay here and there under the cliff, with a green slime floating in most of them, and the green slime teeming with tadpoles. I sat down by the brink of one of these pools and looked at it, for the sheer joy of being home again. I looked and saw little beetles navigating the dark water like bright pellets of lead, and rather seeming to be running than swimming. Then an insect with four legs skipped hurriedly over the surface, going from island to island of scarlet grass, and a skylark came by singing. Above me in the mosses beyond the top of the bog's sheer edge the curlews were nesting, their spring call ringing over the pools and the heather. Beside me a patch of peat was touched with green as though it had gone mouldy, and up from it went a little forest of buds, each on its slender stalk, for spring had come to the moss as well as the curlews. In amongst the soft moss grew what looked like large leaves, but so fungoid was their appearance that it was hard to say whether they belonged to the moss, or were even vegetable at all: rather they seemed to haunt the boundary of the vegetable kingdom as ghosts haunt the boundary of man's. Strangely ill-assorted were those gross leaves and the fairy-like slenderness of the stalks. I could have sat there long, watching the activity of the two kinds of insect that scurried over that water, or looking at the history of the ages in the coloured layers of the peat, which is always written wherever an edge of Earth is exposed, if only one can read it; and all the while the skylark sang on. I could have sat there idly all day in deep content, only that an anxiety thrilled through my content, and drove me on, urging me to hasten to hear the worst about Marlin. And so I walked on, under the bog's edge, with peaty soil underfoot, on which sometimes rushes grew, now all in flower, and sometimes heather, young and very green, and sometimes, almost timidly, the grass; for the grass came mostly along the tracks of the turf-carts, and where the earth was most trodden, and by little bridges across tiny streams, as though only in the immediate presence of man could it dare to usurp that land where the bog so recently reigned. And all the way as I went over that quiet land there went beside me a chronicle of the ancient shudders of Earth, old angers that had stirred and troubled the bog; for the long layers, tawny and sable, ochre, umber and orange, that were the ruins of long-decayed heather and bygone moss, went in waves all the way, sometimes heaving up into hills, the mark of some age-old uprising, sometimes cracked by clefts that sundered them twenty feet down, as though they still threatened the levels so lately stolen by man. And even that land that man had won for himself faintly shook as I trod it, making the threat of the bog all the more ominous. I passed innumerable little ditches, dug to run off the water that came down from the bog, so that the things of man might grow there and not the things of the wild. And over all of them were little bridges for the turf-carts to cross with their donkeys, for a man on foot could step over the ditches anywhere; trunks of small trees heaped over with peat and sods; but the trunks were all rotting away, so that only a prophet could tell whether man would hold that land, or whether the damp and the south-west wind and the bog would one day claim their own again.

Presently I came on turf-cutters at their work, digging out of the brown face of the soft cliff their foot-long sections of peat, four or five inches thick and wide, with an implement that seemed a blend between a spade and a spear. I don't suppose that has altered since I was living in Ireland, nor for some centuries before that. And another thing that can scarcely ever have altered is the little turf-cart in which the pieces of fresh wet peat are drawn away by donkeys, for it has the air of having been there for ever, and I do not see what it can ever have altered from, for it is so simply primitive that it must have been nearly the first. The superstructure was like that of the wheel-barrow and little larger, but it was the wheels that had been left behind by receding ages from man's very earliest effort at drawing loads. These were merely two trunks of trees, hollowed a little where the axles should be and leaving a pair of crude wheels at the ends. An iron bar ran through the core of each trunk, connecting it to the cart, and on these the trunks revolved. Two donkeys dragged the little load away to be stacked and to dry in the spring weather, with a little heather on top to keep off the rain. In those stacks the long, brick-like pieces of chocolate-coloured turf would dry to pale ochre and be carried to the cottages to take their part in the struggle against the next winter. Two men with long black hair were working the face of the bank as I came by, cutting in level lines, as though they were taking bricks layer by layer off a wall; so that when they had come to the blacker layers underneath, and had gone as low as they could and met the water, the edge of the bog would have receded along the width of their working a distance of four inches. We greeted each other as I passed, and I went on over grass and bare peat and rushes, and over the little bridges, till I saw far off the willows that grew near the Marlins' house, shining like sunlight coming through greenish smoke. I saw the willows that I knew so well, now glorying in the spring, but I saw with a pang light flashing on roofs that were strange to me: mean buildings had come already, with the swiftness of an encampment, to that land that had always seemed to me as enchanted as any land can be. And what would come of that enchantment now? So elusive a thing, among that cluster of huts, could never survive the noise, the ugliness, the ridicule and the greed. I felt sick at heart at the sight of them; and in my despair I knew nothing that could protect the ancient wildness that was such a rest and a solace to any cares that one brought to it from the world; and, feeling helpless myself, I placed no confidence in any help that could come from Mrs Marlin.

*   *   *

When I saw the willows shining I hurried on, for anxiety drove me on over the little bridges to hear the news of Marlin. The curlews uttered their curious cry on my left, beyond the wavy strata, while above me a skylark sang on and on and on; and, amongst all the cries of the birds and the gleam of the willows, my melancholy deepened, standing out all the blacker against the splendour of spring.

And then I saw Mrs Marlin, far off, in her garden. She was not hurrying, she was not wailing; and I knew how grief would have racked that dark woman, giving a wild movement to her strides and a certain terror to every line of her. Or if I did not know to what fury grief would have urged her spirit, I saw at least, and even at that distance, that no great passion was driving her; although later, when I came nearer, I saw often a quick uneasy turn of her head towards the new huts and the dam that was building across the stream, as though a malevolence smouldered in her, or she rested from recently cursing; but at least Marlin was not dying; and, suddenly relieved of that fear, I walked towards her with all my anxieties gone.

'How is Marlin?' I asked, when I got within call of her.

'He's all right, sir,' she said.

I came a few paces nearer.

'I am delighted to hear that,' I said to her. 'The doctor gave a very bad account of him.'

And she laughed at that, with rather a sly look.

'Ah, what does he know?' she said.

'Where is he?' I asked.

'Ah, he's gone,' she replied.

'But Marlin, I mean,' said I.

'Aye. Sure, he's gone,' she answered.

'Gone?' I said. 'Where?'

'Over the bog,' she said.

'But what way?' I asked.

'A rainbow showed him,' she said.

'A rainbow?' I muttered.

And she went to the door and opened it for me, and we went in. And she offered me a chair before her great fireplace and sat down a chair herself and gazed into the red embers of the turf, which never break into flame. And then she said: 'He was very ill. Ill as the doctor said. But, sure, what does he know of anything, only of the affairs of that world?' And she pointed away from the bog.

'He was lying there in his bed yesterday evening, ill as the doctor said, and I was trying to get him to take some medicine, when he turned to me and says: "Mother, I must go. For if I stop any longer I'll be dying. And I'll not die in this earth." And I says to him: "Ireland's a good enough land for any man to die in." And he says: "Not when it's Hell you'd have to go to; and it's where I'd go from here." And at that he rises up from his bed and puts on his boots, and gives one look round at the cottage. Then he gives me a kiss and sets off, and there was a rainbow shining. And no sooner had he climbed up by the bank of turf and set his foot on the bog, but the rainbow begins to go further and further off. And he follows it all the way to the everlasting morning.'

I don't exactly know what she meant by that, but she pointed through a window as she spoke, in the direction in which the sun usually brightened far patches of water, away by the bog's horizon, all the morning; the direction in which so often I had seen Marlin's eyes stray.

'But how far did he go?' I asked.

'To Tir-nan-Og,' she said.

'But how did he know the way?' said I.

'The rainbow showed him,' she answered.

What had happened to Marlin? I wondered. Where had he gone?

'How far did you see him?' I asked.

'Away and away,' she said. 'And the rainbow before him.'

'But he couldn't walk out of your sight,' I said. 'A sick man couldn't have done it.'

But still she pointed away to the far horizon, where the water shone and no hills bounded the bog.

'The night came on,' she said, 'after the rainbow left him.'

Her words frightened me. You can't walk the bog out there in the night; or it is very nearly impossible.

'You should have called him back,' I said.

'Call back a rainbow!' she exclaimed, with a gust of laughter.

'No, Marlin,' I explained.

'Nor him, either,' she said. 'They were both of them going away to the glory of Tir-nan-Og, the rainbow from the dark world and the coming of night, and my son from damnation. Little they know the rainbow from his few visits to these fields, little they know it that have not seen it glorying in its home, entwined with the apple-blossom of the Land of the Young; and little they know of a man till they have seen him in the splendour of his youth among the everlastingly youthful in the orchards of Tir-nan-Og.'

For a moment I feared she would try to go after him, and drown herself, thinking she could not go very far in safety, at her age, over the bog.

'You're not going, too?' I asked.

'I'll never see him there,' she said. 'God knows I'll never see him there, having stayed on Earth too long, till my feet are slow with its weeds and my soul with its cares. Though I'll say nothing harsh against Earth, for the sake of Ireland. And I have one thing more to do upon Earth yet. For I have to speak with the powers of bog and storm and night, and to learn their will with the men that are harming the heather.'

'Show me the way he went,' I said, and got up from the chair; for I felt sure that a man as sick as he was could never have walked far over the bog. And she rose and came with me out of the door and we walked to the bog's edge, I impatient to find Marlin and trying to hurry her, she without any anxieties and only concerned with her reflections, which she uttered as we went.

'It's by the blessing of God,' she said, 'that mothers never see their sons grow old; bent and wrinkled and haggard. It's the blessing of God. And they should not see them die. A few days more and Tommy would have died, there in his bed beside me; and no art of mine could have hindered it; for I have no power against the splendour of death. But he rose and walked away out of the world, where age cannot overtake him, and where death is only known from idle stories told in the orchards by those that are young for ever, for the sake of the touch of sadness that gives a savour to their immortal joy. Weakness and wrinkles and dying, they are the way of this world, and the shadow of damnation creeping nearer. But he has walked away from the world and away from the shadow.'

All the while I was trying to hurry her, picturing Marlin lying a mile away out in the bog, for I feared he could scarce have got further; and how would a sick man fare, out there all night?

'Was there any frost?' I asked her; for we still had a touch of frost sometimes at night, and she was nearer to these things than I in our large house.

But she only answered: 'Aye, the world's cold,' and gazed away before her with happy eyes as though she went to her son's wedding.

'Hurry,' I said, for she would not quicken her pace. 'Or we'll find him dead.'

'Ah, no,' she said. 'He would not wait for death. And why would he, with damnation prepared for him by those that are jealous of the land of the morning?'

I don't know whom she meant; and, God knows, these are no words of mine, but only hers still haunting my memory, where I fear they should not be, and would not be if I could banish them.

And so we came to the steep edge of the bog and she climbed agilely up, and I after her; and for a while we walked in silence over the rushes. The moss lay grey all round us, crisp as a dry sponge, while we stepped on the heather and rushes, the heather all covered with dead grey buds, the rushes a pale sandy colour. I had never walked the bog in the spring before, and was surprised at the greyness of it. But some bright mosses remained, scarlet and brilliant green; and along the edge of the bog under the hills lay a slender ribbon of gorse, and the fields flashed bright above it, so that the bog lay like a dull stone set in gold, with a row of emeralds round the golden ring. A snipe got up brown, and turned, and flashed white in turning. A curlew rose and sped away down the sky with swift beats of his long wings and loud outcry, giving the news, 'Man, Man,' to all whose peace was endangered by our approach, and a skylark shot up and sang, and stayed above us, singing. The pools that in the winter lay between the islands of heather, and that Marlin used to tell me were bottomless, were most of them grey slime now, topped with a crust that looked as if it might almost bear one. We knew the way to go; the way that I had so often seen Marlin's eyes gazing, the way that Mrs Marlin said straight out was the way to Tir-nan-Og: I could see the water flashing over there, though the grey moss was dry about us. The fear that I had had that Mrs Marlin would come to harm in the bog I had now entirely forgotten, for she stepped from tussock to tussock surely and firmly, with a stride that seemed to know the bog too well to falter even with age. We came, with the skylark still singing, to pools that were partly water and partly luxuriant moss: strange grasses leaned along them and burst into flower. More and more pools them we met, and less grey moss, and presently the wide lakes lay before us, to which Marlin had looked so often. I stood on a hummock of heather and stared ahead, then looked at Mrs Marlin. There was nothing but water and rushes and moss before us. We were as far as a sick man could have walked, apart from the danger and difficulty of all that lay ahead. If Marlin had come this way there was no hope for him.

'You are sure he went this way?' I asked, and knew that the question was hopeless even as I asked it.

Her face all lighted up, looking glad and young, and with shining eyes she gazed over the desolate water, and said: 'Aye, he went this way, this way; away from the world and the shadow cast by damnation, black as tar on the cities. Aye, he went this way.'

And then I knew that Marlin shared with the Pharaohs that strange eternity of the body that only Egypt and the Irish bog can give. Centuries hence, when we are all mouldered away, some turf-cutter will find Marlin there and will look on a face and a figure untouched by all those years, even as though the body had obeyed the dream after all.

*   *   *

Then I brought Mrs Marlin back from the bog, thinking she had gone far enough, and knowing that the part of it to which we had come was dangerous walking even for a young man. For these were the waters that Marlin called 'the sumach,' or some such word that I do not know how to spell, a mass of stored rains that grew heavier every year, till it flooded in under the roots of whatever growth gave a foothold, and floated the light surface of mosses and peat, till everything trembled round one as one walked: one called it the shaky bog, the most dangerous of all the kinds of bog that one walks. These waters were the source of the stream that ran past the Marlins' house; but, as more rain came with the storms than left with the stream, the whole weight of the bog was increasing.

'We must get all the men we can find, and search the bog for him,' I said, when I got her back to the safe grey moss and the heather. And at that she laughed with peals of her strange wild laughter.

'Aye, search the world for him,' she said. 'But he will not be there. And it's not the world that wants him, but Hell. And Hell will not have him either. It's the orchards of Tir-nan-Og that have him now, with the morning dripping from their branches in everlasting light, golden and slow, like honey. Aye, and the evening too, and both together; for Time that troubles us here comes not to those gleaming shores. Age, desolation and dying; that's the way of these fields; and not one wrinkle, nor sigh, nor one white hair, ever came to Tir-nan-Og.'

'We must look for him,' I said. For it was a duty to do all that one could, even if the search seemed hopeless; and I did not wish her words to turn me away from it, as I feared that they soon would.

'Aye, search for ever,' she said, 'and you'll never see him. But I shall see him often.'

'Where?' I said.

'Where would it be,' she answered, 'but about his mother's house and over the heather that he knew as a child, and on mosses by pools where he played? Where else would he go when he comes from Tir-nan-Og, and the jack-o'-lanterns come riding the storm through the darkness, and go dancing over the bog?'

'How will he come?' I asked.

'On the west wind,' she answered.

'We must search for him,' I said, sticking to my point, which it seemed harder and harder to do.

'Aye, search,' she said, and went off again into peals of her wild laughter, which rang far over the bog and frightened the curlews.

'How could he get to Tir-nan-Og?' I asked. For if there was any chance of finding him, it would have to be done quickly, and she would not see that it was serious at all. I spoke to her all the more impatiently for the fear that I soon should believe her, and do nothing at all. And one ought to do something.

'He'd go by the way of the bog till he came to the sea,' she said. 'Didn't he know the way well?'

'And then?' I asked.

'There'll be a boat there, lifting and dropping with the lap of the tide,' she said; 'and eight queens to row it; queens that have turned from Heaven, and yet slipped away from damnation. Hell has not their souls, nor the earth their dust.'

'How could he know they'd be there?' I asked her.

'How could he know?' she said. 'I told him.'

But that made things no clearer. Then she gazed away over the bog and went on talking: '"Hell would have me, mother," he said, "if I stay here." And when I saw he was bent on leaving the world, I said I'd help him; for he knew the way over the bog to the shore, but he'd never been on the sea. And I went one stormy night to the bog, when the wind was in the West and all the people of Tir-nan-Og were riding upon the storm, and by the edge of the water where they were flashing and admiring their heathen beauty, I called out to them: "Ancient People, there's a man that would share your everlasting glory; and Hell wants him, because he has turned his face to the West. How shall he go to find you?"

'And with tiny voices they answered me through the storm, voices shriller than the cry of the snipe and small as the song of the robin, they whose voices rang once from hill to hill over Ireland; and they said: "To the sea, to the sea."

'"And then?" I said, "Oh ancient and glorious people?"

'"What would you have of us?" they asked.

'And I lured them nearer, by a power I have, and said to them: "By that power, I need your help over the sea."

'And they said to me: "When will he come?"

'And I answered: "One of these days," which is the only time we know with the future, and all we ever will know, till it is dated and mapped as is should be.

'And they repeated one to another, with their small voices, "One of these days," till the message passed out of hearing. And I made my compact with them out there on the bog, swearing by turf and heather, as they swore by blossom and twilight. For a danger threatened the bog and I swore to guard it, and they swore to carry Tommy over the water and bring him to Tir-nan-Og. Eight fair girls, they said, that were queens of old in Ireland, would bring him over the water, waiting for him where the bog ran down to the shore, upon the day that I said. And Tommy would know them, apart from their beauty and apart from their crowns of gold, by the light that would be gleaming along the sides of the boat; for the boat would be made from the bark of birches growing in

Tir-nan-Og, and the twilight that shone on them in the Land of the Young would be shining upon them still. And whether it was night in the world, or whether noon or morning, the twilight of Tir-nan-Og would be shining upon that birch-bark.'

I tried to picture a boat glowing gently in twilight while it was noon all round, with the sun bright on the water; or, more wonderful still, the birch-bark iridescent in the soft light of the gloaming, while all around was night. But thinking of this only drifted me from my purpose, which was to find a number of men and search the heather for Marlin. I was in two minds; one was the mind that listened to Mrs Marlin telling of Tir-nan-Og, of which I had already learned so much from her son; the other, a more disciplined mind, told me that the bog must be searched for Marlin whether there seemed any hope of finding him there or not. The more useless this appeared the more I clung to it, lest Mrs Marlin should lure me to forget it altogether, and a duty remain undone.

'We must search for him,' I repeated.

'Aye, search,' she said indulgently, as though the search were some trivial rite that custom idly bound me to. And I think she knew from the tone of my voice that I somehow had not my heart in it. 'Would they fail me?' she went on. 'Never.'

And I saw from her far gaze westwards, and the light in her eyes, that she was thinking of those eight queens.

We came to the bog's edge, where deep fissures ran down out of sight, as though the vast weight of the bog were too much for the banks that bounded it; and from that high edge I looked over the land lying round Marlin's cottage that had always seemed so magical to me, the land over which the old willows brooded in winter and were like an enchantment in spring, and I could have wept at what I saw. And what I saw is well enough known: I need hardly describe it: a large number of small houses meanly built, and all exactly the same, denying any difference between the tastes of one man and another, nor caring anything for any man's taste, nor expressing any feeling or preference of builder or owner. It was as though men without any passions had built them all for the dead.

They were barely finished, but men were already living in some of them, and work had already started on building the dam and putting in the wheel that was to be turned by the water and which would set the machinery clanking in the ugly house they were building. The world is full of such things, little need to describe them; the only concern that this story has with them is to tell that they came down dark upon that spot to which first my memories went whenever I was far from Ireland, racing there quicker than homing pigeons, or bees going back to the hive. And not only had they spoiled the magic that lay over all that land, deep as mists in the autumn, but they were there for the purpose of cutting the bog away; not as the turf-cutters take it, with imperceptible harvests, slowly, as years go by, a few yards in each generation, but working it out as miners work out a stratum of coal.

It was to these men that I now appealed, calling out to them from the high edge of the bog and telling them that a man was lost out there in the heather. They came at once, and I soon had about thirty of them, some of them English and some the men of Clonrue. 'Begob,' said one of the latter to me, 'if you set English-men walking the bog it's soon a hundred men that we'll have to look for, and not only one.' But oddly enough it was the English-men that took charge as soon as we started off, though they got very wet over it.

'We'll find your son for you, mam,' said one of them. 'Don't you worry.'

But she looked fiercely at him and only answered: 'Do you know the way to World's End?'

'I expect we could find it, mam,' was all he said to her.

Her eyes were blazing, and then she burst into laughter. 'And you'll only be half-way to him then,' she said.

Then we all spread out to about half a mile and walked in the direction of the deep part of the bog, from which Mrs Marlin and I had just returned, and heard her laughter still ringing in mockery of the thirty men that were trying to find her son.

We went back over the grey moss, about twenty-five yards apart, the bog-cotton flowering round us, a bright patch at the tips of the rushes, the skylark high above us singing triumphantly on.

'It's got on her mind a bit,' said one of the men, as Mrs Marlin's laughter rang out behind us.

'I'm afraid it has,' I said. For I could not explain Mrs Marlin to an Englishman.

'We'll find him all right, sir,' he said.

But he only saw that the heather was not high enough to hide anyone lying there from a searcher passing within twelve yards: he did not know the deeps of an Irish bog.

'Don't step on the bright mosses,' I said.

We went on till Mrs Marlin's laughter faded from hearing, and the only wild cries we heard were the cries of the curlews.

When I came again to that waste of water and moss, where trembling waves ran through the bog from every footstep, the line of men drew in from either side to the edges of that morass, each man seeming drawn towards it without anyone saying a word; and we all looked over the water and brilliant mosses in silence. I realised then that in bringing these thirty men over the bog I had done a conventional duty in which there was no meaning whatever.

We turned round and each man took a different line to the one by which he had come, so as to cover more ground on the way back, but nobody searched any more. I knew that they were not searching, but said no word to them, for my thoughts were in Tir-nan-Og.

CROTTY SHINKWIN

A. E. Coppard

'Crotty Shinkwin' is the story of two fishermen who actually discover a legendary island just off the Irish coast and learn to their cost that all the wonderful dreams about such places which have haunted their fellow countrymen for centuries may not be quite as true as they had expected. Anglo-Irish author A. E. Coppard (1878–1957), who became famous after the publication in 1921 of his best-seller, Adam and Eve and Pinch Me, has a highly individual approach to the myths and legends of Ireland, and his knowledge of tradition and his fine ear for the speech of ordinary people have set his stories head and shoulders above those of most of his contemporaries in the fantasy genre. The story of 'Crotty Shinkwin', which was originally published in a limited edition in 1932, has been praised for being reminiscent of the best of J. M. Synge as well as suspiciously like a semi-allegory. Whatever else, it is one of the finest modern short stories of an Irish wonder voyage.

*   *   *

This was a little man I'm telling you, Crotty Shinkwin, a butcher once, with livery eyes and a neck like a hen that was not often shaved. He knocked out a sort of living by the coast of the cliff and the sandy shore of Ballinarailin, a town full of Looneys, Mooneys and Clooneys, the Mahoneys, Maloneys, the Dorans, Horans and Morans, but if you were to ask what was their scheme of life it could only be said they were seen gathering weeds from the sea and stones from the shore, which is poor stuff anyway to be passing the time of day on.

In his young youth Crotty bought cattle alive and sold it dead. You would see him going into the kitchens with the large hack of meat in one hand, a saw in the other, and a great coulter of a knife in his mouth, and when he came out again you would observe there was the less meat on him to be carrying. But he was married ten years to Eva Clohesy, a hard woman, and so he was forced to give up that kind of life—it was too much altogether for a man that did not know the wishes of herself from one moment to another.

'Why,' says he to Peter Sisk, 'if you ask me what she likes, or what she wants, you have me beat. *She* could not tell you. It would take the help of God Almighty to keep up with her. Napoleon couldn't do it; he could not.'

So Mr Shinkwin took to fishing or to looking after the holy well, and little handicrafts like that, for there was nothing else to turn a hand to in that drifty place.

'Holy and sacred medallion!' says she to him then, 'and what are you about at all?'

She was glaring at him with her two cat's eyes, but a fine woman, one of the Clohesy's she was, as brisk as a Connemara cow, and two hairy arms.

'I am not well,' says he.

'What's on you?'

'And I never could be well again,' he says, 'not in this mortal world, and what's more—I will not.'

'Och! For a man that's about to be dying there's a deal of talk and porter in it yet!'

Crotty looked at her: 'The devil knows, you strap, and everyone knows I've a drowsiness in my bones and a creepiness in my stomach. I'm sick and I'm bad. It's wrecked I am.'

'O, you goat!' says she. 'You shanandering goat!'

'But . . . but I endure it,' Crotty said, 'as a man I endure it; I do not give in to it. By my soul, you can't daunt me, and I do not sink to my bed.'

She gave a great spit, like a man with a quid:

'The kingdom of heaven be yours, little or much.'

'And if I should come,' he continued, 'to my expiration, do not go for to put your hands on me and rouse me again.'

'The devil a hand,' says she. 'Let you walk out to the rocks now and catch me a couple of crabs, or by the harp of the Jews it's your corpse itself I'll be lathering with holy water this night.'

So Crotty would go perch himself on a stone to watch the half mile of surf roving in from the bay, and the nuns from the convent bathing in it. Giddy and gay they would be, bobbing up to their ribs and groaning, but they were dressed in blue sacks of night-gowns and long baggy trousers and offered no nice allurements to Mr Shinkwin's eye. If they took an orphan down to bathe with them, it should undress and dress on the stones outside the bit of a box they dried in, and though it blew hearty and crisp the child could not come into their holy boudoir.

'It would be queer and all,' thought Crotty, 'if the child was the nuns just now, and the nuns was the child!'

And here was Tarpy Ryan and his ass cart loading weed, and far out in the bay was Inniskalogue, a big hump of an island with nothing on it but grass, and smooth as a button. No one lived there, neither priest, peasant nor gentleman; nobody visited it— it had the bad name; no one owned it and nobody wanted it. If you asked a fellow about Inniskalogue he would twist his eyes, or he would shake his head and scratch it (or his haunches) until you wished you had not enquired of him. But it lay on the blue bosom of the sea, the sunbeams glistening, a fine sparkling pasturage with the gap of a cliff here and there.

One fine day Crotty and young P. J., a handsome lad, sailed over the bay in a yawl, and in about an hour they got so close to one corner of Inniskalogue that they could see the stones, but not a bird on it or any any other living sign. And P. J. cast anchor there for to do a little fishing. Down went the hook, the cables leaping and growling after it and after it until there was no more cable, and still they had not got a hold.

'By my soul, there's a power of deep water under us!' said P. J.

Just then, down comes a draught of air from a cloud and it puffed the yawl out round past the corner of the island. They went roving round to the far side with the anchor trailing, till they felt a jerk and the little boat shook.

'She's got a hold,' cried P. J.

And by the souls of the sainted martyrs, she had! The wind gave a great twist, the yawl reeled, and there was that island, hooked underneath by the anchor, tearing after them and following them.

'What is it and all!' Crotty shrieked, for his seven senses had gone black on him, and P. J. was too dazzled to loosen the sheet. They could not see the mainland for the island hid it from them, hundreds of acres it was, and it moving like a cork on the hills and hollows of the sea. They fell on their knees in the boat and prayed to God.

'Sir,' gabbled Crotty. 'We are perishing! For the love of heaven, mercy! Throw back that walking world and sweep the head off me, for my soul has no thirst for the waves of water. Jesus, Joseph, and Mary! Sir, if you please! Amen.'

Then, in the very nick of destruction, the island stopped, and the boat stayed and began to move backwards until it was rushing backwards towards the island. As they looked at it the island itself heaved up and twirled over like a great plate on a hinge until it was upside down. It turned as easy as a porpoise, casting no splash, with only showers dripping off it, but the great black half moon of it when it was up-ended, was as much as a side of the whole world falling, and threw a cold shadow across the yawl. It stayed upside down, and there the boat stayed too, anchored fast and the sail throbbing, and the sea rocking gently as a cradle now.

'We're stuck!' cried P. J., heaving on the rope. 'Crotty, we're stuck!'

'O, God alive!' Crotty said, pointing. 'Will you throw an eye on that!'

And he did so. The island was topsy-turvy now, its green hump was below and the roots of the island had come up from the ocean; they could see a neat little town sitting amid the drainings of a flood. The water was sweeping from it like sand from a barrel, but it dried on the moment. The weeds began to become grass and pretty fuchsias and long creepers to hang over the walls. Some big fishes that had got caught gasping in the hedges flipped into the fields and changed into sheep and went crying for their lambs. There was a little church with a steeple chiming—the bell had a pitiful note like the chink of two stones—and a score of cabins but no people seen.

'Will you tell me, Crotty, what is that there now?' P. J. was pointing toward the church steeple.

'What?' said Crotty.

'On the cross of the church? Do you see it?'

'I do see it.'

'It's my anchor!'

'God's fortune!' said Crotty, 'and how did it climb there at all?'

'And the rope of it stretching from us across the fields.'

It was true enough. The anchor had hooked in the cross of the church itself when it was upside down, and they had pulled it right over.

'I can't lose my anchor,' said P. J., 'it's Andy Mullen's anchor.'
'It is,' Crotty said.

They hauled on the anchor cable until the slack was dripping above the sea, and they pulled themselves right ashore against a path that ran up to the church.

'Go and get the anchor, Crotty.'

'O,' grumbled he, 'I was never that sort of climbing man, I haven't a wing to my elbows.'

P. J. went on coiling up the cables and readying the boat, and spitting in the sea, and staring at the island.

'Go and get the anchor, Crotty.'

Crotty, sitting on a thwart, gaped at the church steeple with repugnance. It was a small steeple, but still it was high and the anchor was on it like a crow's nest in a tree.

'I'm thinking,' said he, 'there's a bank of bog between this and that; a man would murder himself going there. And what's a bit of a hook? I'll take a pull on it, anyway.'

He pulled and pulled on the anchor rope until he was sore and tired.

'Go and get the anchor, Crotty,' said P. J. again.

Crotty sighed and sat down. 'A deceitful island,' he mused. 'No one knows the half of it, sleeping or waking. Am I alive, or is it dead we are? Is my head my head, or is it my rump?'

'Go and get the anchor, Crotty.'

'Ah, to hell with the anchor,' replied he.

P. J. stood up. 'I wonder,' said he, 'if there's a police barracks in this place.'

'Maybe,' Crotty said. 'Maybe there's a booking-office and a train to Dublin!'

P. J. took off his hat and flung it ashore.

'There goes my hat,' said he, 'and where it goes I must follow.'

So saying he stepped on the gunwale and leaped to a rock.

'God save all here!' he cried.

No one answered, but Crotty scrambled over and stood beside him. P. J. walked towards the little road, but Crotty kept still and called out: 'P. J.! Let you take a sniff round first!'

P. J. paused: 'Come on with you! Here's a notice on a board. Come and read it.'

Crotty went and read it out to him.

NOTICE

RATEPAYERS WHO HAVE FAILED TO PAY THEIR RATES NOW DUE
FOR SOMETIME ARE HEREBY INFORMED THAT STEPS ARE ABOUT TO
BE TAKEN IMMEDIATELY TO ENFORCE PAYMENT

(*Signed*) CROTTY SHINKWIN

'By the powers above, P. J., or the powers below, 'tis a disgrace
to my native land. I've seen the like of that notice before, barring
the name. I never thought my name was so common, I did not.
The buttons on your coat are the one buttons with mine, but your
name is not Shinkwin, and my name is not your name. Who is
this nigger-driver of a tax-man? Or am I doomed to a watery
grave, is it? Will I be collecting the rent from a few shrimps, d'ye
think?'

'Come on with you!' said P. J.

They went on, but they did not use the road going to the church;
they took a step aside on the turf that led them up a hill, good
honest turf, a little damp maybe, but thrifty and sound. Up, up
they went, and what with the steepness of it and the sun's warmth
Crotty was soon wishing they had never come that way or met
such a contrary island, or gone in a boat with such an ecclesiastical
turn of hook.

'I've a drought on me would blind a salamander.'

Looking here and looking there he saw no sign of life or laughter
till they came to the top, and there it was a high cliff they were
on, it dropping to the sea sixty or seventy or eighty fathoms down.
Behind them and below were the church, the cabins, the sheep,
the flowers; patches of field, and a wood of thorns; they could see
all over this turned-up island. And all round it was the tranquil
sea, but there was not a sight of the mainland or Ballinarailin
anywhere in the quarters of the hemisphere, nothing but the sea
only and the place they were on. They were stricken with the
surprise of that, and the fear of that, and the silence of it; the
power of the wind would not have loosened the flax from a ripe
thistle.

'Where in the world is the world?' moaned Crotty.

From the edge of the cliff they watched the blue seas move,
white gannets diving, and three porpoises rolling slowly along.
Halfway down the cliff a dead pig lay tumbled on a rock, a white
pig with a long red burst in its belly.

Crotty was timid as a sheep, but P. J. was staring like a man well on the road to heaven.

'Peace to my soul,' he murmured softly. 'This would be the grand place to live in with the woman you wanted and she loving you at all times. It is planted with sweet herbs, and the air is gentle with the kiss of their blossoms.'

'What is it? What is on you, P. J.?'

'Here, on this cliff for my holy tower and the wide sea shining, to go in strength and virtue like the fleet and careless birds. Or to walk with the burden of love till I might find her sleeping on the shore.'

'Ach!' growled Crotty, 'and she glaring at you with her two cat's eyes.'

Just then they saw the little man; he was sitting on the cliff with his legs dangling over. They walked up to him.

'The blessing of heaven on you, good man,' said P. J., 'but that's the queer place to be fishing!'

The man did not answer. He had the face of a weasel, and fingers like the claws of a crab.

'Is it deaf you are?'

The surly man took no heed of them at all, but was pulling up a long stout cord from the sea below. Over and over he coiled the white cord, a mighty stretch of it, until it dripped with sea, and there at the end of it was hooked a fish. The man gave its head a clout and cast it into a creel by his side. As soon as he had stuck a mussel on the hook he threw down the cord again and sat still as a stone. Presently he looked round, but he said nothing. It was as if he did not see them, although they were standing so close they could notice a flea was feeding on his ear.

'Is it blind you are?'

And Crotty bent down to tap him on the shoulder, but when he did that his two fingers sunk into nothing, as if the man was but a vapour.

'Jesus, Joseph and Mary!' yelled Crotty. 'Let me out of this!' And he ran off so fast you could not see his two feet moving at all. When he came to the boat again P. J. was beside him, laughing:

'Wait, Crotty! D'ye hear that, you stag!'

Crotty heard the church bell clinking faintly.

'There's the little anchor to fetch,' said P. J.

Back he turned up the road that led from the sea to the church, and Crotty could do no more but follow him. They hurried along the road past the wood of thorns to the village itself that had a shop and some houses, but not the sign of another soul did they see, and they got to the church where Crotty took a good dab at the holy water. Then they stood under the rope, taking a strong squint at that anchor hung on the cross of the steeple.

'I'll get that,' said P. J. 'I'll get it.'

So they went and opened the door of the steeple and saw a chimney, with a ladder of wood rearing up to the bell-chamber, all covered with barnacles and hairy weeds.

'Go out and hold the rope, Crotty, till I throw the anchor down.'

And he did that.

Crotty stood holding the rope amongst the gravestones and they leaning this way and that in the churchyard. There were pools of water round the gravestones and the leaning ones looked as though they were peering down to read their own inscriptions in it. One stone near him gave Crotty a twist of the heart when he had spelled out its words:

Eva
the faithful wife of
Crotty Shinkwin,
sometime of
Ballinarailin.
'Sweet heart of Jesus,
be thou my love.'

He let out a great cry but his comrade did not hear it, for he was crammed in the steeple.

'God rest her soul,' said Crotty, bending over the stone. 'Did a man ever see the like of that! God rest her soul—and soften it, too,' he added. 'Bad it is, for the grass grows on her tomb, and there's muddy water between her and heaven. But good it may be, for the world is made of a roguish nature, and wouldn't it be hard if there was no profit on misfortune at all! I was wearing out my life with both hands, waiting on her tooth and nail, and when I'd a mind to rest she would glare at me with her two cat's eyes!'

He looked round fearfully, as if he might see her tracking him even there. A voice cried: 'Mind yourself, Crotty, she's coming now!' But it was only P. J. pushing his head and arm through a hole in the steeple to take a grab at the anchor. The bell stopped clinking, and down came the anchor at Crotty's feet. Without waiting a moment he heaved it on his shoulder and ran off alone to the boat and cast the anchor aboard. Then he coiled the cable and readied the boat and set the sail. By and by he saw P. J. come stepping along with a bundle under his arm.

'Hurry on,' he shouted, 'hurry now!'

'Be easy, Crotty,' replied his comrade. 'I've the treasure of the world in my arms.'

'What is that, P. J.?'

And P. J. showed him the bundle was a pig's bladder, blown up like a balloon and tied at the throat with a blue ribbon.

''Twas hanging high up in that steeple. 'Tis a bag of air from the garden of Eden itself. A saint brought it away.'

'A saint! What saint?'

'Some holy man, Crotty, but he's gone dead with the hundreds of years.'

'And what's the virtue of it?' Crotty asked.

'Sure,' said P. J., 'and we'd never sink with this aboard. Mind yourself. I'm jumping.'

He took a good leap and landed in the boat. At once there was a terrible scrambling noise in it.

'What! What!' they both cried, stiff with the fear. For the anchor had taken a great jump on to the shore, like a thing alive, it was tearing up the road back to the church, and the rope rushing after as a long snake would.

'It's the anchor!' screamed P. J., and he made a grab at the runaway rope, but as he did so the skin of air from Eden's bower caught in a hooky nail and burst with a noise. Like a big gun, it was. Zip! And P. J. was blown up until he was no bigger than a pin, and then Crotty saw him no more, for the air let out from that bag was like the blast of fifty storms congealed in the crash of one gale. It tore the buttons off his coat and left the roots of thread dangling.

Away rushed the yawl on the crown of the sea, with Crotty alone and the island following him, for the hook was in the steeple again. The wind soon slightened, but Crotty's wits were all scattered and they went journeying upon the waters of the world for two days or three before the gossoon had the sense to cut the rope. And then he cut it. And when he cut it the island stopped, it heaved up in the sea again and turned right over to its own old shape and pattern; the church, the steeple, the pleasant fields, and the wood of thorns, sank in the heart of the ocean and you could see no more than the bare hump of pasture it had always been. The yawl sailed on, and Crotty heard a bird piping. He scanned the sea, and by the safety of God, there was the mainland again, and Ballinarailin again, and Inniskalogue was where it always had been! He set course and—signs on it!—it was not long before he was there where the nuns were bathing, and Tarpy's ass-cart was loading weed.

He fastened up the boat, and he hurried home with the look of decent grief upon him, but by the suit of Satan it was not grief at all when he met Eva Shinkwin at the door, as sleek as an eel, and she glaring at him with her two cat's eyes! It was like the cold nose of a calf pushed in the small of his naked back. He wished he had been able to buy her the makings of a costume, or something.

Where in the name of the king of thunder had he been? Devil and all, what traipsing females had he been after ruining now?

Well, if she *wanted* to know, he could tell her. O yes. Give him a civil word or two, and he would tell her. And it would be the truth. And the whole truth. And nothing but the truth. It would form the formation of all he had to say.

But, holy and sacred medallion, she could never believe a thing like that!

THE ARK OF CASHELMOR

T. H. White

No more curious Irish wonder-voyage has been envisaged than that in 'The Ark of Cashelmor', an episode from The Elephant and the Kangaroo *by T. H. White. The Archangel Michael has appeared at the farmhouse of the O'Callaghans and warned them of a new deluge that is about to befall Ireland and urges them to build an Ark. A resident with the family is Mr White, a dilettante and atheist from England, who is instantly converted by the message from the Otherworld and puts himself in charge of the plans for the voyage to come. The building of the Ark from an old barn, and the selection of those humans and animals to be saved, are the focus of the episode.*

Terence Hanbury White (1906–1964) is of course famous for his reworking of the Arthurian legends in the four books ultimately published as The Once and Future King *(1958) and now regarded as a modern classic. For a number of years White lived in Ireland, the home of his ancestors, and drew on his experiences—as well as his knowledge of the country's mythology—to write* The Elephant and the Kangaroo *(1947) which, despite (or perhaps because of) its satire on uncritical belief and Irish culture is unhappily neglected today. The following pages should prove that it well deserves rediscovery.*

*　　*　　*

The farmhouse was of the late eighteenth century. It had belonged to a squireen who had expected his yearly invitation to Dublin Castle, and who had been a friend of a mythological Irish character called Major Sirr. It was orientated according to eighteenth-century ideas, so that no single point of the compass was satisfactory. The company rooms faced north, so that they were in perpetual gloom, but they did not face to the true north, for fear that any of the other walls might face to the true south. The wall which ought to have been south, the one which had the green-house, was in fact a bit to the south-east, so that it only took the sun until four o'clock in the afternoon in summer. Moreover, this partly south wall had been built with no windows, for fear that any of the rooms in the house might have been sunny or dry. The stone of which the walls were built made dryness impossible, but the orientation made assurance doubly sure.

In the drawing-room there were: a beautiful piano, so far as the wood was concerned, but it had not been tuned for twenty-three years and the walls of Burkestown were made of a sweating stone which transmitted the climate freely; a stuffed badger in a case; two stuffed pheasants and a curlew on the piano, in a bower of dusty pampas grass arranged in pink glass pots; a whatnot with three black velvet cats on it and some dozens of china knick-knacks; nine photographs, mainly of departed priests, in frames made of sea shells (*chenopus pes-pelicanus*); a piece of needlework like a sampler, dated 1889, with a black border, in memory of a departed bishop; a gramophone with a scarlet tin horn and four-teen records, including 'Phil the Fluter's Ball' and 'Angelus' sung by Clara Butt; a sofa and two armchairs; a Berlin-work fire screen, wonderfully well done by an auntie of Mikey's; a mantelpiece looking-glass, framed in faded velvet, with mauve flowers painted on it and a retrieving dog, also done by the aunt; a papier-mâché clock, painted with gold paint, which had stopped; a nest of tea-tables holding lucky slippers, china cats, horseshoes, etc.; an oval table with pot containing a defunct primula in red crepe paper; a Second Empire circular mirror with eagle; six amateur oil paintings of horses and lunar landscapes, one of them good; an enormous cheap print of Jesus Christ pointing at His Sacred Heart; a plain mahogany table which served for an altar when they had a Station; and a card table for playing Spoil Five. The wallpaper was mil-dewed because of the stone, but it had been discovered that the pictures could be saved from the mildew by propping them away from the wall, with corks out of whisky bottles.

While on the subject of furniture, it would be fair to describe the dining-room. It was only that they had been furnished at different periods, one of which was, for the time being, too recent to seem as hallowed as the other.

In the dining-room, which suited the date of the house, there was a quiet, formal wallpaper, and a priceless Nelson sideboard with table and chairs to match. There were also: a lovely writing desk combined with bookshelves, which had secret drawers (still a secret to Mrs O'Callaghan) and oval-paned glass doors, most of the panes being broken; a good deal of imitation silver, wedding presents to Mikey and his bride; three attractive china plates commemorating a Eucharistic Congress, their Sacred Hearts exploding into flames like bombards; a set of Queen Anne teaspoons which Mr White had rescued from the kitchen where they had been put since some Woolworth spoons had been bought; a wireless set on a good nineteenth-century side table; a dead hydrangea on a bad twentieth-century circular table; a self-portrait of Mr White, done in the drawing-room mirror, the flowered one; an imposing black marble clock broken by Mikey, as, indeed, all the clocks at Burkestown had been broken by him, his method of repair, after he had overwound them, being to insert a turkey feather through any visible aperture and to twiddle it about; an excellent carpet, firedogs, and nineteenth-century grate; five mezzotints after Morland and Constable; bookshelves containing the whole of Everyman Library, imported by Mr White; severe grey marble fireplace; and, on the Nelson sideboard, the Infant of Prague.

The transference of the Wincharger to its temporary casing on the drawing-room chimney took two days. Luckily the distance from the roof of the hay barn to the point of entry was the same as the distance from the chimney to that point, so that no alteration was necessary in the cable. The erection took two days because it was a constructive job, and in this case Pat Geraghty had to do everything twice.

The dismantling of the hay barn went faster, because it was destructive. The advantage of destructive work was that Geraghty could not do it again. Once a corrugated sheet was off, it was done. Even if Mr White had taken it off, Pat could scarcely put it on again in order to do the same thing. They started from the far end, next to the cow-sheds, so as to leave their line of retreat open.

Brownie deplored the barn. She could not climb from the table and chair to the fluted roof, and spent the time sitting in the yard, groaning with disapproval.

Mrs O'Callaghan sent up tea to Mr White at intervals of a few hours.

Mikey took the pony trap to Cashelmor, to do the shopping. His real object was to escape the harvest.

Philomena turned her attention to Mr White's cravats, which he wore on Sundays with peculiar Victorian tiepins, and which her twenty-three brothers and sisters tied round their stomachs as a specific against lumbago.

Tommy Plunkett ran the farm as best he could.

When a sheet had been unbolted and lifted off, it was handed down to the Slane Meadow, which was the field behind the hay barn. The river Slane flowed at the bottom of this field, and Mr White said that even if the Flood was to be augmented by a general subsidence of the earth's crust, yet it was likely to begin in the bed of the Slane, at least in its initial stages. This meadow was also clear of trees, which made it a suitable location for floating off the Ark, and therefore for building it there.

The roof was not bolted to the girders. It was secured to them by galvanized clips. These, with the nuts and bolts, were put aside for reassembly.

It took only a day to dismantle the roof. The next stage was to take down the arc-shaped girders, of which there were four.

They twisted strong hay ropes for this job, with a twister, as the ironmonger in Cashelmor had nothing stronger than rope reins. They began with the two middle girders, because the two outside ones thus gave them a natural scaffolding from which to sling them. When the middle girders were down, the outside ones completed the square of the framework at the top, and this was the next thing to tackle.

It was more difficult. They had to tie the remaining girders— those of the sides and ends—to the upright supports before unbolting them. Then they had to untie them at one end, and lower that end with a hay rope, after which they untied the other end, and lowered that. The girders weighed about a hundredweight, and could be carried round to the Slane Meadow by hand.

Finally the upright supports had to be sawed off without dropping them, and without killing the person who did the sawing. They did not like the idea of dropping cast iron eighteen feet to cobbles. It was a poser, how to get them cut and lowered.

In the end they had to go the whole hog, dismantle the barn

completely, lower the uprights by slinging them from one another and from the roof of the cowshed, and saw them on the ground. It took two days extra, but it was worth it. They realised that they would have been forced to dismantle the whole thing sooner or later, in order to get the sheeting from the lower sides which was to be used to deck the Ark, when ready.

For the first few days the barn looked as if it had been bombed out. Then it got to look less and less as if it had ever been a barn at all. One day it was gone completely, and the yard was different. It was airy and strange. There was something missing, like the gap of an extracted tooth into which the owner puts his tongue with unfamiliar surprise.

*　　*　　*

It was evening. The three sat round a scrubbed table in the white-washed kitchen, under the electric light. Mr White had insisted on making lists.

Mrs O'Callaghan had a ruled copybook, a pen with a crossed nib, and an ink bottle with one millimeter of crust at the bottom. Mr White had an enormous folio notebook or ledger, and a fountain pen with green ink. They had given Mikey a piece of brown paper and a six-H pencil, which was the only one that Philomena had left in the house. Mikey had broken the point off, but continued to write with the wood, with much the same effect.

Their lists were headed: ANIMALS.

Mr White had decided that they would make different lists each night, pool them, and talk them over. One night it was to be Animals, the next night Tools, the third night Seeds, the fourth night Provisions, and so on. He was writing fast. Mrs O'Callaghan was writing intermittently, in the round, laborious characters which she used for shopping lists. Mikey was writing like an artist. That is, he touched his word up now and then—he had written only one—by putting a dot, or another letter, or by changing an established letter for another one on top of it.

Brownie was sitting in a corner, eating the latest glue. She was an animal who suffered from crazes, like her master. They say that wise men grow to resemble the creatures they are interested in, and that Darwin ended by looking like an ape. This is true conversely, at any rate, for most animals grow to resemble the masters they are interested in, and Brownie was no exception. She had put up with so many snakes, falcons, goshawks, merlins, ravens, ants, goat moths, hedgehogs, and other assorted fauna collected by Mr White that in the end she had taken to collecting herself. For instance, she was keen on week-old chickens. Every spring, when these came round, she attended all their meals. She also caught them in her mouth, without hurting them, and carried them into the dining-room, where she liberated them under the table and watched them run. The hens, ever after, in adult life, fled upon the approach of Brownie. Another of her interests was the insect world. She spent a good deal of time catching flies, or taunting the bees in the hall. She was a student of wood-boring wasps, which she would watch on the workshop window-sill all day long. She had been the proud owner of a wild baby rabbit, which she used to take to bed with her, in her master's bed, and also of a young leveret. Neither of these had been much pleased at having to sleep with Brownie and Mr White, and the rabbit particularly had often flown into a passion at the general perversity of the situation, and had bitten them both. People seem to think that wild rabbits are charming little balls of fluff, but they are really very choleric animals, with no tolerance at all. Other pets kept by Brownie included ducks, turkeys, and an orphan lamb. She was interested in the swallows on the tool cupboard, and devoted to hedgehogs, for which she had a special bark. She did not like puppies.

The craze for Nature Study, however, was not the only one she had. Mr White possessed varied interests, and so did she. There was carpentry, for instance, which was perhaps the latest of his digressions. Poor Brownie could hardly saw or hammer, but at least she collected the spare pieces of wood, and kept them under the dining-room table. So far as gardening was concerned, she collected most of the root crops and tubers, which she also stored under the table. She had, besides, a rubber ball.

Her master was a second-rate writer, and that was the way in which he earned such living as he had. It was the only occupation she was unable to share. When he sat at the typewriter, Brownie sat beside him and groaned continuously—perhaps she was doing her best to imitate the machine. When he wrote with a pencil, in an armchair, she sat on his lap and sighed, in order to be in it as much as possible.

The glue must have been due to the Ark. It was used in construction. Mr White had been trying to boil it in a soup tin, because he had no gluepot, and she had discovered it, in the solid state, at the bottom. This was what she was eating. Being at the bottom, it was almost out of reach of her tongue. However, she had bitten dents in the tin all round, and she could reach some of the glue, and it made her froth at the mouth.

It is only fair to add that she was good at her own profession. She was the rarest of all creatures, a steady retrieving setter. Everybody had told Mr White that it was quite impossible to train a setter to retrieve without losing steadiness, which had been sufficient to make him determined to do so, and he had done so; except, of course, that it is really the dog who trains her master, not vice versa.

Mr White had spent a busy day. The Wincharger was dismantled, and there was part of the casing already bolted round the drawing-room chimney. It had four holdfasts. There was enough charge in the batteries to give them light for a hundred hours on one twelve-watt bulb.

His list said:

> Nancy and colt, not by her.
> Friesian cow and bull calf ditto.
> Nellie and male piglet ditto.
> Sitting turkey and clutch.
> Ditto hen.
> Ditto duck.
> Ewe and hogget, mountainy.
> Diamond and Tiny (the farm dogs).
> Brownie.
> Titsy, I suppose.
> Item, we ought to take a dove. I think it must really
> have been a homing pigeon, or else it would have sat down
> on the branch instead of carrying it home. It will need a
> mate or eggs.
> Are rats really necessary?
> Mice ditto.
> What about fleas?
> Are lice any use?
> Bats . . .

But it would be tedious to give the list at full length. It ran to fifteen folio pages, and included such rarities as ladybirds—to eat the greenfly; dragon-flies—to eat scale insects; gulls—to eat the daddy longlegs; shrew mice—to eat slugs; and stoats—to keep down the rabbits. If asked where the pests were coming from, Mr White would have said that he was taking no chances with stowaways. He would have added that he would probably take them himself, to keep down something else.

Mrs O'Callaghan's list said:

> Mr White
> Miky
> Titssy
> Browny
> Nancy
> Nely
> Magy
> Dimon
> Tinny
> The Bisshop

Except for the first two and the last, these were the names of various cows and other animals on the farm. Mr White firmly crossed off the bishop.

Mikey's list said simply:

TABAKKEIGHE

'I suppose you think tobacco is an animal?'

Mikey looked guilty but obstinate. He liked it.

'How much do you smoke a week?'

'Four ounces.'

'Then we should have to take a couple of hundredweight or more, to keep you going for the next twenty years. Do you know how much that would cost?'

'It would cost a pound or two.'

'It would cost,' said Mr White, feverishly multiplying 240 by 16 on the margin of his list, 'exactly one hundred and ninety-two pounds at one shilling an ounce, and you can't get it for that.'

'Oh, Lor!'

'And yet—wait a moment—we do not know what kind of climate we shall come down in. It might be suitable for growing tobacco. Remind me to take a lot of tropical seeds, when we begin the next list.'

Mrs O'Callaghan said earnestly: 'What does this Flood be for?'

'For?'

'Well, why is it?'

'I suppose God must have got fed up with the human race—or the parts of the animal kingdom which we shall forget to take. He wants to start again with a clean slate, I suppose.'

'It doesn't be much use starting wid us.'

Now this was a point which our hero had been trying not to face on the roof during the day. Mr and Mrs O'Callaghan were childless, and past the work.

He said firmly: 'Perhaps the Archangel Michael does not want to continue the human race. Perhaps It is purposely sending us because It does not want more humans. We would be needed to build the Ark and to navigate it and to look after the animals at first, but after that we may be intended to die out.'

'You ought to get married, Mr White.'

'If the Archangel Michael wanted a married man, why didn't It choose one?'

'Think of all the little babies,' said Mrs O'Callaghan.

He thought of them. After the swallows and other animals, he would not have minded. It was the wife that had him terrified.

THE DEVIL AND DEMOCRACY

Brian Cleeve

The one voyage no one would wish to take is to Hell—but in this story the Devil, another familiar figure in Irish myth and legend, makes the trip in the opposite direction—to Ireland itself. The author, Brian Cleeve (1921-), for a while a familiar voice on Radio Telefís Eireann from Dublin and known more recently as a best-selling suspense novelist, here pits the Evil One against some typically resourceful Irish folk. It is a story of the downtrodden and the use of protest in the style of the best legends, which Cleeve himself suggested would fit into the theme of Ireland's heroic past— 'with a slight stretching of the word "heroic" perhaps!'

*   *   *

'Your lowness is always Left,' said Belphagor, absent-mindedly taking the needle-sharp little soul of a TV producer out of his lapel and starting to pick his fangs. 'But I think you ought to see them.'

'I will not,' snarled the Devil. 'I've been master here since before the Creation. D'you think I'm going to let this crawling little worm of a fifth-class sinner come down here and unionise Hell? I will not see them. I will not deal with them. I will not recognise them. And if that picket isn't off Hell's Gates inside ten minutes I'm going to—' and he lashed his tail so violently that he swept half a hundred weight of Kitchen Cob Souls straight out of the soul scuttle into the fire. They sputtered damply and began to smoulder with a rather nasty smell.

'I asked you for Bright Household Nuts,' said the Devil in a low, dangerous voice.

Belphagor shrugged.

'That's all there is. And when they're gone—' He shrugged

again. 'It's going to be extremely cold.' He stuck the TV producer in the corner of his mouth in a rather vulgar manner and spread out his hands in front of the smoky mass of bankers, politicians and armchair generals. 'If the electricians join in—' As he said it the bulbs began to dim and fade in the great crystal chandeliers. The photographers' models, boutique owners, cardsharps and motorcar salesmen inside the bulbs stopped glowing white, turned dull red, faded and vanished in the general gloom. Only the fire still burned an unhealthy blue at one end of the vast throne room. 'I really think you ought to see them,' Belphagor said. 'After all, just seeing them needn't commit you to anything. And it might get the lights back.'

Three hours later they were facing the union organisers across the black basalt conference table in the Third Circle of the Executive Suite. And a nastier group, thought the Devil, he had never seen since the Fall. Imps, trolls, fiends, illiterate demons; not a decently educated devil in the whole pompous bunch. Bad breath and worse manners, picking their noses with their tails, belching and scratching and trying to look as if they were used to sitting in leather armchairs instead of squatting on red hot buckets. 'Why am I doing it?' the Devil thought. 'Why don't I just retire to the country and forget all this? Lilith would love it. She's been at me for centuries—'

But Belphagor was knocking on the table. 'We are delighted to welcome you, gentlemen. If you have a spokesman?'

From the depths of an armchair upholstered in genuine Storm Trooper, a fat, slubberly, oily-faced imp wearing a dirty boiler suit clambered to his hind paws, and wiping the back of a thick, hairy front paw across his snout said in an atrocious accent, 'Our spokesman is Brother Grunge,' and sticking his paw into the pocket of his boiler suit pulled out a raucous, shouting, gesticulating little soul carrying a picket's banner in one fist and a red bandana handkerchief in the other.

'Brothers!' screamed Grunge, obviously continuing from the point where he had been stuffed into the imp's pocket a few minutes earlier. 'I've been fighting the employer-class for forty-seven years, and I know them like a dog knows fleas. They're yellow, I tell you, yellow all through—'

The slubberly imp tapped Grunge on top of his head with a horny claw. 'That *is* the employer.' He himself had the decency to blush a dark shade of black, but Grunge was unabashed. 'An exploiter if ever I saw one,' he shouted. 'We haven't come here to bargain. We've come here to tell you. We've got solidarity! We've got brotherhood! And we're going to stick this out till Hell freezes over. You can lock us out. You can starve us. But you'll never beat us. We're going to have justice here or you can sell this plant for a pig farm. Isn't that right, brothers? Am I speaking for us all?'

The row of ungainly imps nodded and growled agreement.

The Devil lurched unsteadily to his feet. From the moment that Grunge had first appeared, bilious green and sweating, out of the dirty pocket of the leading imp's boiler suit, the Devil had begun to look extremely reactionary, and the effect of Grunge's opening remarks had been far from beneficial. He had begun to swell and change colour in a marked manner, and by the time the imps had signified their agreement with Grunge, the Devil looked dangerously near having a stroke.

'Tell them to go away,' he whispered, clawing at the collar of his reptile green suit, which had grown extremely tight. 'The meeting is over. Get me my pills.'

'But you can't!' screamed the leading imp. 'We have to discuss—'

'I don't,' said the Devil, holding on to the gold dragon's head door handle for support.

'Fascist!' screamed Grunge. 'Close the plant! Pull out the maintenance men! One for all and all for one, eh, brothers?'

The Devil felt his way out of the room, and as Belphagor followed him, Grunge began leading the imps in the first bars of the Red Flag. Five seconds later all the lights went out. Outside the Palace crowds of working-class imps were standing about in sullen idleness, staring up at the now darkened windows of the conference room. Grunge, waving his red bandana, appeared on a window sill, put there by the leader-imp. 'Brothers!' screamed Grunge. 'Lay down your forks! The day has come! Justice! Liberty! Freedom! Let imps and sinners stand shoulder to shoulder in the fight for democracy! The bosses have divided us! Exploited us! Told us our interests are opposed! Give them the lie brothers! Let sinner and imp clasp hands in deathless brotherhood. Let the fires go out. Unity! Equality! I proclaim the Eternal Liberty of the Imps and Sinners Soviet Republic. This isn't a strike any longer, comrades, this is War, this is Revolution, this is the March of History!'

An ugly roar of approval rose from several thousand scaly throats, counterpointed by the shrill piping of an even larger number of souls just liberated from the furnaces.

'It's the end of everything,' whimpered Belphagor. 'If only you'd given them the ninety-six-hour week when they first asked for it—'

'Rubbish,' said the Devil, who had taken three of his heart pills in a glass of blood and was both looking and feeling very much stronger. 'All we need is strategy. Inside a week I'll have them begging for mercy.'

They slipped out of the back door of the Palace disguised as scullery imps. Grunge was still shouting. Belphagor shuddered. Sinners were lolling around at their ease. Younger imps were playing hopscotch or blindman's bluff. Older imps were playing cards on top of the cooling gridirons or lying asleep in the still warm ashes of the furnaces. Not a punishment was in progress. Not a sinner was screaming. The chute from the upper regions gaped over its empty bin. 'Look,' whispered Belphagor, awed by a sight that no devil had seen since Eve bit the apple. 'It's empty. The top-side staff have struck as well!' A cold shiver of fear ran through his tail.

'We're going to fix Grunge,' said the Devil, restraining himself with super-devilish control from kicking the nightlights out of an unwholesome looking stoker-imp who was playing three-handed stud with two souls from the Fourth Circle. 'We're going to send him back. Up Top.'

Belphagor stared at his Master open-mouthed. 'Up Top! Back? But you can't! Why—'

The First Law of Damnation learned by every imp and juvenile devil in third grade forbade it. It was unthinkable. 'What comes down can't go up.' QED. Quod est Damnatum.

'Watch Me,' said the Devil. 'I haven't built this place down to see it taken over by a bunch of stokers. Stick close behind me and shut your snout.'

They threaded their way through the crowd towards one of the lesser Gates. Already things were taking an even uglier turn. In the distance they saw a senior devil surrounded by jeering imps, who were forcing him to sing the Red Flag. On the far side of the

Palace there was a sound of breaking glass as if windows were being smashed. 'They'll be looting soon,' whispered Belphagor. 'Oughtn't we—'

'Let them,' snarled the Devil. 'Tomorrow is another century.' They slipped out of the unguarded Gate, threw off their repulsive and humiliating disguises behind a convenient bush, and spread their wings.

'Where are we going?' Belphagor said timidly.

'Belmuck,' said the Devil. 'Rapesprocket's parish.'

An instant later, if you calculate such things by earthly time, the Devil and his henchman landed in a small cave in the fair and wholesome parish of Belmuck. As you'll know, if you are at all versed in Infernal Theology, every Christian parish—and for all I know to the contrary, every pagan parish as well—has a Devil's Hole, through which, a moment or so after death, the souls of the unhappy damned are tipped to their eternal doom by the Resident Imp of the parish, the infernal counterpart of the parish priest. The Resident Imp of Belmuck was Rapesprocket, and a lazier, more unsatisfactory, more inefficient R.I. it would be hard to find in the length and breadth of Christendom. In centuries no parishioner of Belmuck had been tipped down the Hole. Even on the infamous occasion when the two O'Shaughnessys had killed each other over the widow Hegarty's cow, Rapesprocket had let them both slip out of his hands simply by being asleep at the crucial moment. Only family connections and the almost feudal conservatism of Hell had allowed Rapesprocket to retain his Care of Souls. Now, the Devil was extremely glad of it.

'Look at him,' he said to Belphagor with grim satisfaction. 'As usual.' And indeed, Rapesprocket's condition was all too usual, disgraceful as it was. An empty poteen jar lay under his head in the guise of a pillow. Another, almost as empty, lay in the crook of his fat and hairy arm. A clay pipe drooped from the slack and rubbery lips of his sack-like mouth, and out of the black vents of his snout came the soft snores of a far too contented sleep. Rapesprocket was both drunk and incapable.

'Shall I kick his head in?' Belphagor said hopefully. The Devil restrained him.

'Not yet. Not for another twenty-four hours. First we want a soul. Any one will do, so long as we get it in a nice state of mortal sin at the appropriate moment. Then we get Rapesprocket to throw it down the Hole.' He was clearing away a thick tangle of cobwebs from the mouth of the Hole as he was talking. 'Even Rapesprocket ought to be able to do that if we put it into his hand first.'

Belphagor gaped at him. 'What good will that do?'

'My dear Belphagor,' said the Devil wearily, 'there is a strike on at the bottom? Agreed? No souls are going down. No Resident Imp will agree to send one down because of the strike. Am I making myself clear? Except Rapesprocket, who as you see is obviously incapable of having heard of the strike, let alone joining it. Therefore, if we can induce Rapesprocket to send down a soul, this will be whitelegging? Am I going too fast for you? Down below they will refuse to process the soul, or even to receive it, and there will therefore be a discrepancy in the books between us below, and—' He coughed gently as he always did when he mentioned the Opposition—'and Them above.'

Belphagor still gaped. The Devil closed his eyes, and thoroughly unpleasant sparks came out of his ears and turned into fireflies. 'Someone give me patience,' he murmured. 'We go back down and negotiate. We agree to absolutely anything they want. And at a certain moment this matter of Rapesprocket's whitelegging is bound to come up. They'll demand the scab-production soul be sent back up Top. And—' He coughed gently—'the Opposition will have to agree in principle that we be permitted to send one soul back up the chute. *They* don't want to see us close down anymore than we do. And when I've got that permission—' His eyes glittered ferociously, and he swelled so large that he suddenly filled the cave and bruised himself badly on a knob of rock—'then I send one soul back up the chute the very next instant. But it won't be Rapesprocket's little capture. It will be Grunge.' He clicked two clawed fingers together like a pistol shot. 'Let's see how long the strike lasts without *him*.'

And followed by Belphagor in an admiring silence, he set off down the hillside toward the innocently sleeping village of Belmuck.

Unfortunately for our two fiends Belmuck believed in 'early to bed' if not in 'early to rise,' and on reaching the village the Devil found not a light lighting nor a soul stirring nor even a mouse nibbling cheese, and he and Belphagor had to occupy the next nine hours by disturbing and tormenting the sleep of any sleeper who caught their impatient and devilish fancy. Even old Concepta Hennigan, who was a hundred and six, had such dreams as startled her out of her white woolly bedsocks, and she woke up with such an appetite for breakfast and such a bright, hopeful eye as astonished her great-granddaughter, Rose Ann McCarthy, into nearly spilling the tea on her great-grandmother's coverlet.

'Watch what you're doing, gerrul,' quavered the old crone, but instead of telling her to be glad of any class of breakfast at all, even with tea in the saucer, Rose Ann simply smiled delightfully and emptied the spilled drops into the geranium pot on the window sill. 'Yer'll kill me geranium!' screeched Concepta, and Rose Ann merely patted the white pillow into its proper shape behind her great-grandmother's nearly bald head, set the tray on her lap, and buttered the homemade bread for her before cutting it into little, delicious morsels for the old woman's convenience. The Devil, who was watching all this sickening display of virtuous patience in the guise of a bluebottle perched on the geranium, ground his front feelers together and obliterated a small, innocent fruit fly which got in the way.

To see virtue in daily use was bad enough, but to see it in such a toothsome shape as Rose Ann McCarthy was infinitely worse. In fact it was intolerable, and then and there, almost forgetting the main purpose of the visit, the Devil determined that the soul he had come for should be the soul of Rose Ann and no other. 'I'll have her,' he snarled, gnashing his saw-edge proboscis over the mangled remains of the fruit fly. 'I'll have her inside the day.' And taking off from the geranium he buzzed round her dark and luscious head like an undertaker measuring a prospective customer. Although such a customer would surely have melted the heart of any undertaker and made him regret his mournful calling.

Her hair shone like brown silk of the darkest shade, thick and curling, with the warmth of the sun and the beauty of the moon in its deepest shadows. Her teeth were like white hawthorn flowers behind the red promise of her mouth, and the blush and flush on her cheeks was like the warm down of a ripe peach. And this would be only the beginning of the short description of the heads and chapters of her beauty. The soft throat of her, with hollows under the rounded chin where a bird could nestle; the sweet breast like modesty itself under the starched and pleated linen of her blouse—for what so beautiful as modesty in a young girl?—the supple promise of her waist that would scarcely fill a man's two hands unless he squeezed them tight—and who wouldn't, unless he was a Carmelite?—all this that I'm bashfully describing was merely the outermost revelations of her charm.

Let you watch her walking and guess at the hidden mechanism of her beauty, and I warrant that if you hadn't already, why then you'd fall down in the same fit of passionate attachment as had taken half the boys in the village, the other half being freed from it only by emigration. But however passionate your attachment was, it wouldn't be likely to be half so passionate as that of Desmond Sorley Boy O'Shaughnessy, the postman's son. He had only to think of her to go into cantrips and calamities of passion, and if he got more than two glimpses of her in any one day he had to steady himself that night with enough poteen to slaughter an ox or he couldn't have slept. Indeed it was in a slightly poteen-induced sleep that the Devil had found him, and through his tortured dreams of longing and love had got wind of the apparently impregnable state of Rose Ann's virtue.

'Get rid of that nasty fly!' screeched Concepta, and obediently Rose Ann picked up a tightly rolled copy of the *Cork Examiner* kept precisely for such purposes, and caught the Devil a terrible smack on the left side of the head. Thirty seconds later, and about thirty feet from Concepta's open window, the Devil came to his senses in the middle of the road and narrowly avoided being obliterated by a passing donkey.

'Yerrah damn,' said Belphagor in the shape of a wasp, alighting beside his master on a convenient lump of the donkey's droppings. 'That was a formidable belt you got from that lassie. I'd leave her alone if I were you.'

Most of what the Devil said in reply is completely unprintable, even with stars and asterisks, and all that can be safely repeated here are the last two words, 'follow me,' as the noisome pair flew off to meditate and scheme in the little shed behind Concepta's cottage. 'Now,' said the Devil, when they were comfortably settled, 'I mean to have that girl if it takes me till Doomsday, or at least till this midnight, and if you're unable to assist in bringing about this simple consummation, I suggest that you don't bother to return below with me, because if you do, by the red hot horns of my Throne I'll make you wish you'd stayed bleating and harping with the—ahem—Opposition.'

Belphagor polished his sting on the wooden seat in a rebellious manner, and eyed his Master with something close to exasperation. 'Why do you always want things the difficult way? Why not the old woman? Why not Shoneen James, the publican down the road? I've been watching him water the whiskey. He'd be a pushover.'

'It's Rose Ann I want,' buzzed the Devil, 'and Rose Ann I'll have. And I think I know how. Come back out to the road.' And back they flew, and a mile out of the village, where down a quiet boreen they transformed themselves in less than an instant into two of the sleekest, most persuasive travelling salesmen that had ever travelled the quiet roads of West Cork. And if you don't know the district, then you must merely accept my word for it that that's saying a great deal. Belphagor wore a camel's hair overcoat in spite of the warm June weather, and a green velours hat with a narrow, curly brim, and a pink bow tie with chocolate stripes, and a shirt to match, and a pearl cuff link just peeping out of the sleeve of his tasteful green suit. A pair of pink fluorescent socks and dark blue suede shoes completed the genteel ensemble.

But if Belphagor knocked the eye out of the day with his tasteful splendour, the Devil put it back again. A pale yellow suit with the faintest white checks in it would have made any onlooker realise at once that whatever else He was, He was a gentleman, by the sheer masterful cut of his double-breasted waistcoat with its sharp lapels and little gilt buttons. His socks were lavender blue, and his shoes were black and white, glistening like a wet heifer in the June sunlight.

His jacket was of the Italian cut, with cuffs to the sleeves and four buttons down the front. He wore a pink rosebud in his lapel and a four-in-hand tie of purple silk with a large gold stickpin to match his waistcoat buttons. His hat was purple to match his cravat and surrounded with a narrow white silk ribbon with a gold buckle. You might well have described him as dripping with splendour, and an ugly glisten of jealousy crept into Belphagor's eye at the sight of him.

'Now for a motorcar,' said the Devil, rubbing his hands, and there, shining with chromium plate and glory, was a new American roadster of the most opulent appearance: white leather upholstery, salmon pink body work, radio aerials, fog lights, automatic transmission, power steering, 384 brake horse power, a cruising speed of ninety-seven m.p.h., a built-in cocktail bar, a record player with stereophonic sound, and a collapsible rubber dinghy in the boot, not that the Devil cared about that.

In our villains got, with the Devil driving, up the boreen with them, round into the main road—main is it, God help it, nineteen-feet wide at the best, but yerrah, who'd pay the rates to widen it?—up the main road then, and coming to a whispering rest outside old Concepta's cottage. Out hops the Devil and knocks on the little rose-covered door. 'Musha,' says he when Rose Ann comes to the door, 'glad I am to be the bearer of such good tidings to the like of you, Rose Ann McCarthy asthorre.' For he was under the impression that this was how everyone in Ireland talked, no real Irishman having condescended to go below to him for some considerable time.

Rose Ann gapes at him, as well she might, what with his language, and his Dublin accent, and his grandeur, and the sight of Belphagor lifting his green velours hat and grimacing politely at her over the Devil's shoulder. 'It *is* Miss Rose Ann that I have the honour and pleasure of addressing, isn't it?' said the Devil anxiously.

'Why yes, sir,' trembles Rose, 'but—'

'Say no more,' says the Devil. 'Am I right in thinking that you are a constant user of Sinko soap'—a question to which he already knew the answer, having flown through the kitchen that morning—'and have you by a lucky chance an open packet of that incomparable soap powder in your kitchen at this moment? For if you have—'

'Why yes,' said Rose, a tiny flutter of cupidity disturbing the innocence of her mind. 'As a matter of fact, I have.' And on twinkling feet and dazzling ankles she flew to get it. Little and slight the start of the slope! So back she comes with her bright blue packet of Sinko Powder, and the Devil throws up his hands in delight. 'Now for our question,' he cried. 'Tell me, what is the name of the capital city of England?'

A faint shadow crossed the perfect surface of Rose Ann's forehead as she strained to think. 'L-o-n-d-' whispered Belphagor, mouthing and eyeing her from behind his Master's back.

'Why—London!' cried Rose Ann as if she had immediately thought of it herself. Oh sorrow! Oh alas, alas, that second step, that steepening of the slippery path! Oh poor lost innocence!

'Brains as well as beauty,' cried both the Devil and Belphagor, 'what a happy combination!' And the Devil snapped his fingers. 'Belphy, my dear chap, get Miss Rose Ann McCarthy her splendid Sinko Summer Dress with ruched pleats and pannier pockets and don't forget to slip that crisp new five pound note into one of them.'

Back to the car sped Belphagor, where lying on the back seat in its transparent plastic-wardrobe-carrying-bag lay the beautiful dress, little embroidered flowers on the hem, and the crispest, most wearable blue and white linen bodice and skirt that a girl could desire. 'Here, my dear!' cried the Devil, lifting his hat once more. 'Well may you wear it, and if a stranger may make so bold, may you soon wear it in'—he dropped his musical voice an octave—'in agreeable company. At the dance tonight in the next parish, perhaps? A little of that five pounds expended on potable enjoyments for your aged great-grandmother would make her sleep so soundly that she would never note your absence, why not even if it was prolonged until midnight.' But whether he said that aloud or merely whispered it into Rose Ann's receptive mind it would be beyond the wit of man to say.

Suffice it that tripping down later that morning to Shoneen James's Public House, Rose Ann bought her great-grandmother a medicine bottle full of watered whiskey and allowed it to tran-spire in passing that she had a new dress and that if anyone was of a mind to ask her she might even consider accompanying him to the dance in the next parish that same night.

And all this she said over the counter to Shoneen James in the full knowledge that, as she could see by the mirror behind and to one side of Shoneen James's head, Desmond Sorley Boy O'Shaughnessy was drowning his desires in the public bar next door to the Off-Licence department where she was transacting her business. Oh wirra, how far and fast the innocent can fall when once they lose their footing. Deception on deception. Oh alas. The Devil, again in the unsightly guise of a bluebottle sipping spilt beer on the counter, almost choked with satisfaction. 'I'll have her,' he spluttered, 'I'll have her surely.'

And round the corner he buzzed to fill the mind of Desmond Sorley Boy with unspeakable thoughts. And all the rest of that day till nightfall he and Belphagor left neither of those two unfortunates in peace or tranquillity, but first one and then the other had displayed to them the fruits of vice and the shameful joys of dalliance, until putting the two of them together on the same yard of road leading to the dance hall that night was like putting a magnet against a needle. They weren't two steps up the road but they were holding hands.

And they weren't ten steps further again but Desmond Sorley Boy was slyly and covetously slipping his arm round Rose Ann's waist, and finding the resistance to it no more than the merest formality. While at the same time his mind and mouth were filled with words of a passionate persuasiveness such as Rose Ann had never heard in her life and he himself was unaware that he was capable of framing. As no more he was, the poor thick, the Devil sitting on his shoulder all the while and whispering them into his ear one after the other, blarney upon blarney, enough to melt stone let alone the heart of a girl in a new summer dress with flowers on the hem and the change of a five pound note tucked safely in the Post Office Savings account.

And all the while wasn't Belphagor perched on her warm and delicately rounded shoulder in the shape and form of a money-spider, whispering to *her*? 'What's an arm round the waist after what you see in the films and on the television,' he was whispering—and then, as they came to the shady trees hanging over the road a quarter mile further on—'Suppose he was to try and kiss you?'—and the hot flushes and blushes nearly scalded his spidery foot as he trod on her bending neck. And Rose Ann near fainting with the persuasion she was receiving from two sides, and Desmond Sorley Boy near losing his footing on the stones of the road with unbridled passion—yerrah, damn is it any wonder that inside another ten steps he was kissing her like a starving man with a dish of pig's feet, and she—oh, how can a decent man write down the whole of it, she wasn't resisting him at all?

Everything she'd ever been told by her great-grandmother, and by her grandmother on her father's side (her grandmother on her mother's side being nothing much and dying at sixty-three of an accident), and by her mother, and by her aunt the good nun Mother Mary of the Angels, and by Father O'Byrne in Confessions and Retreats, and by the good Bishop of Cork at her Confirmation, all, all of it might have been so much smoke on the wind for all it did for her, and they weren't half way to the dance—Holy

Heaven, if it had been coming back from the dance it might have been another thing, but going to the dance, not even getting there—where in the world are girls coming to at all, I ask you?—they weren't half nor a quarter of the way to that unhappy occasion of sin, the Belcladder Parish Friday night dance with a late extension till two a.m. of a Saturday morning, when their feet inclined of their own accord it seemed down a little side turning, and from the side turning into a gateway, and from the gateway into a field full of the softest meadow grass and the most fragrant daisies and buttercups and cowslips, and from walking slower and slower, with their arms entwined and their lips meeting, didn't they—

But human pen refuses to continue. Let the Devil watch—as indeed he did—you and I can only avert our shocked eyes and withdraw into some more decent place. And having withdrawn, neither you nor I can know or say exactly what happened during the next hour or so in that misfortunate meadow, or why at the end of the time the pair of them came out looking shame-faced and down cast and brushing grass and cowslips off of their crumpled garments. But I fear the worst. And the Devil was sure of it.

'We have her,' he cried to Belphagor, the pair of them resuming their disguise as salesmen, behind the wheel of their powerful car. 'Not a second to lose.' And throwing the car into one of its powerful gears, the Devil hurtled down the boreen at seventy miles an hour with the lights out, or at least out until the last second. The unhappy lovers stumbled into the little lane through the gateway to be suddenly blinded as the ferocious headlights pierced the dark. A scream, a shadow, the thump of a bumper against yielding humanity, and all was done. Leaving Belphagor to park the car, the Devil leapt out of his seat, and his human shape, grasped the fluttering soul of the just-murdered Rose Ann McCarthy, and crushing her in his cruel grip, flew off to where Rapesprocket still lay stretched and snoring beside the long-unused Devil's Hole.

'Let me go!' cried poor Rose Ann, or rather her poor tarnished but still beautiful soul. 'Let me go! I am innocent!' But alas she lied, or the Devil Himself for all his dreadful powers could never have matched his noisome strength against her weak innocence. She lied indeed, and with a swift swing of his long arm the Devil pitched her like a baseball into the gaped and snoring mouth of Rapesprocket, waking him up in a choking paroxysm of coughing.

'Garrrh, Wugggh, Grummppff,' Rapesprocket gargled, and

poor Rose Ann all but disappeared down his black throat into his
unspeakable interior. But he coughed her out onto the palm of
his paw and stared at her as if he had never seen a condemned
soul before. Which as a matter of fact he hadn't, at least for several
hundred years. 'Whar? Who? Wharramarrer?' he said, breathing
poteen fumes all over the poor trembling sinner.

'Throw her down the Hole,' shouted the Devil impatiently.

'The Hole?' gaped Rapesprocket, staring round in alcoholic
befuddlement. 'Wha' Hole? Whug? Oh, the Hole?' And then,
even more befuddled, 'Who said tha'?'

The Devil began to dance with frustration. 'Throw her down!'
he screamed, for to achieve his full and ultimate purpose against
Grunge it was not enough that Rose Ann, or any other sinner,
should merely descend the chute into the waiting bin Below. She
must be sent down by an officially accredited Resident Imp, holding his Residence and Parish by feudal enfeoffment from His
Satanic Majesty, and now, by the progress of Democracy,
unionised by Grunge. In other words, by an Imp who ought to be
on strike, but wasn't. In short a whiteleg.

'Throw her down,' mumbled Rapesprocket dizzily. 'Ummm,
ahh.' He peered round him, lumbering unsteadily to his webbed
feet, searching for the black and gaping Hole beside him. So
unsteadily in fact that he nearly fell down it himself.

'Help!' cried Rose Ann to the surely not indifferent but still
helpless sky. 'Save me!'

Rapesprocket sniggered, belched, pawed her in a most indecent
manner while folding her into a convenient shape for throwing,
and prepared to fling her down the chute. The Devil smiled. Belphagor, who had joined him, clasped his dreadful claws in triumph.
Up went Rapesprocket's unsteady arm. One white hand struggled
between his gripping claws to appeal uselessly to the lost world of
life and hope. 'Down she goes,' snarled the Devil.

'In with you,' cried Rapesprocket, and hurled her into the
entrance of the Pit. When out of the Pit came pouring imps and
demons, trolls and greasy, unshaven fiends, carrying banners with
clumsily written messages scrawled on them: DOWN WITH THE
DEVIL-CLASS; DEATH TO THE FASCIST MONSTER
SATAN; ANGELS GO HOME; TO HELL WITH SANCTITY;
UNIVERSAL FRATERNITY OF IMPS AND SINNERS; SIN-
NERS OF THE WORLD UNITE! YOU HAVE NOTHING TO

LOSE BUT YOUR PAINS; and similarly subversive slogans.

One of the upsurging marchers saw Rose Ann's poor soul flying toward him in a downward curve, swung his banner with a practised ease that told of far too many hours wasted playing baseball behind the furnaces when he ought to have been tormenting sinners in front of them, and batted her straight back over Rapesprocket's head, over the Devil's head, over Belphagor's head, and although that was no part of his impish intention, right back into the boreen where a minute or so before she had been knocked senseless and apparently lifeless by the Devil's motorcar.

She opened her eyes to find Desmond Sorley Boy bending over her and murmuring the most extraordinary promises of future virtue and abstention from alcohol and other matters if only she would open them, and it is amazing proof of the resilient qualities of the human frame, and particularly of the young female human frame, that apart from extensive bruising in an indelicate (but given the full circumstances, perhaps an appropriate) place, and a resultant lameness that confined her to her bed for a penitential month, she suffered no lasting ill effects from the night's adventures. Unless her eventual and in fact somewhat hastily arranged marriage with Sorley Boy could be considered an ill-effect. She certainly seemed quite reasonably contented the last time I saw her.

As for the Devil and Belphagor, I am really not at liberty to say what has happened to them, these matters being *sub judice* and even *sub rosa* and *sub sigillum*. But I would advise you that if two extremely well-dressed men should come to your door asking if you by any chance have a packet of Sinko soap in your kitchen, you should close the door sharply in their ingratiating faces and have nothing whatsoever to do with them. Nothing.

THE LAST WARRIOR QUEST

Peter Tremayne

Two of the most famous sites in Irish mythology are featured in this final quest story by one of the the country's leading fantasy novelists, Peter Tremayne (1943-). The first is Tara, the fabled capital of ancient Ireland and the seat of the High Kings. This heart of the old world, parts of which have been dated back to 2000 BC, was named after the goddess Tea, wife of Eremon, the first Milesian High King, and the remains can still be seen today in County Meath. The second site is the Cave of Cruachan, the grim entrance to the Otherworld, often referred to as the 'Gate of Hell', through which it was said all the powers of darkness could be unleashed upon Ireland.

Tremayne (a pseudonymn of Peter Berresford Ellis, the noted writer on Irish history and author of the indispensable Dictionary of Irish Mythology) *has utilised his research into the country's pre-history to write a number of short stories specifically based on Irish myth, as well as three novels:* Raven of Destiny *(1984),* Ravenmoon *(1988) and* Island of Shadows *(1991). Peter is at the forefront of the Irish writers at present drawing on their own mythology to meet the demand for fantasy and 'Sword and Sorcery' fiction. He wrote this story of the ageing warrior Dara Mac Dalan and his dangerous mission to the Cave of Cruachan especially for this anthology, and his knowledge of Irish legends, combined with his ability to tell an engrossing story with a final twist, brings the book to a fitting climax.*

*   *   *

The warrior morosely stirred at the fire with the point of his sword, sat back on his haunches and stared at the dancing sparks before letting out a troubled sigh.

'Without doubt, Foltor, this will be my last warrior quest.'

The younger man addressed as Foltor sat in the forest clearing on the opposite side of the fire, roasting a hare over a makeshift spit made of a forked branch and a sharply pointed stick. He gazed across the top of the flames and smoke in the dusk-shrouded evening and stared thoughtfully at the etched grey lines of the face of the elderly warrior.

He had served as charioteer to Dara Mac Dalan of the Uí Duach for fifteen years, ever since he had reached the age of choice, when he was but a lad of seventeen summers. Yet Dara Mac Dalan was still old enough to be his father; a stocky, muscular man whose black hair was streaked with grey; his skin was fleshy with age, his stomach protruding and his face carried the creases of the unkind passage of the years.

'It's true for you,' replied Foltor, in his soft, considered voice. 'But no one at the court of Cashel would argue with your right to claim the hero's portion even now.'

Dara Mac Dalan grimaced wryly and threw some more sticks onto the crackling flames of the fire.

'But soon they will. And soon these teeth will not be able to cope with the meat of the hero's portion. Five decades is old enough in any man's life let alone to be a warrior. When we return I shall retire to Osraige and live my final days under the shadow of Sliabh mBladma.'

'Who then shall I drive for? Who then shall I sing a warrior's praise for?' Foltor demanded, his thoughtless younger mind considering his own future rather than that of Dara.

Dara Mac Dalan raised an indifferent shoulder.

'There is always another. That is the circle of life. And when you have been reborn in the Otherworld, another charioteer's voice will be heard in this world singing the praises of the warriors of Cashel.'

'But none so praiseworthy as you, Dara of Uí Duach!' Foltor realised his offence in the heavy tones of the warrior but his voice was perhaps a little too hasty in attempting to make amends.

Dara pursed his lips and ignored him.

Since Foltor had become charioteer to Dara he had, in all the fifteen years he had served him, never seen the grey eyed warrior smile. Behind his back the warriors and charioteers of the Nasc Niadh, the champions of the golden torque, bodyguard to the Eóghanacht kings of Cashel, had nicknamed Dara Mac Dalan

'Tróg', the miserable or wretched one. Yet they followed him joyfully in battle and no man would stand against him in single combat. Often had Foltor come to sing his praises before the great assembly in Cashel and thrice even before the High King himself at his stately palace at Tara. Yet no smile of achievement ever cracked the stony face of Dara or softened his permanent frown.

Grief cried from a deep cage behind his eyes, eyes cold, grey and brooding, like the Fomorian seas of the west. Yet what caused that grief none could say for certain. It was as if at some awesome and terrible moment in the life of Dara Mac Dalan, the rhythm of his heart had been abruptly stilled; had stilled and frozen his blood and never afterwards had it resumed its regular ebb and flow. Peace and content were alien concepts to the melancholy warrior.

Foltor knew this when he, as a young man, volunteered to drive Dara's chariot with its two night-black mares whose wild temperaments only someone with Foltor's special gifts for horsemanship could control, for was not Foltor the son of a charioteer and descendant of charioteers? Dara Mac Dalan had been the greatest champion of Cashel and that was why Foltor had ignored the man and sought to drive for the warrior.

Later, Foltor came to know that once Dara Mac Dalan had a wife named Grotach and a young son. It was whispered in the heroes' halls that the woman was voluptuous and wayward, sensually seeking pleasure from any who might please her; flitting, as her very name betrayed her, from one man to another. Dara had been besotted by her, so the whispers went, and allowed her every licence. Then, when his son was three years old, wife and child disappeared. A strange young warrior from Luachra had ridden through Cashel. His dark looks, and rich accoutrements, promised excitement for the woman. That was all. So the story went, anyway. From that very moment, Dara Mac Dalan had become like a man whose soul had been ripped from his body; never smiling, never enjoying life but always grim faced and resolute, without mercy in all his combats so that no man dared challenge him for his seeming invincibility. Foltor could witness that after every quest, the chariot of Dara would return to Cashel bedecked with the severed heads of Dara's enemies. Yet the souls of those venerable dead, reposing in the heads, did not enhance the spirit of Dara, nor give him joy in the accomplishment.

How often had Foltor, after each return, gone to the sweat bath for ritual purification before sitting down to the rite of the *dercad*, or meditation, by which to achieve the state of *sitcháin*, or complete peace of mind? How often, during the *dercad*, had he found his mind wandering and even questioning the sacred belief that in taking the heads of one's enemies, their souls, those souls that reposed in the heads, would inspire and strengthen one's own soul? No one could touch the dark soul of Dara Mac Dalan.

The breaking of a dry branch under someone's heavy footstep caused Foltor to come abruptly out of his reverie, trained as his mind was to be always alert for danger. But as quick as his reaction was, Dara Mac Dalan was already crouched, sword ready, eyes examining the gloomy surrounding woods. Foltor quietly reached for his bow and strung an arrow ready.

Whoever was approaching, he thought, was surely no enemy coming stealthily to catch them unaware. Here was someone with heavy footsteps not caring where they trod. In fact the steps sounded heavy and uneven as if . . . Foltor bit his lower lip. The approaching stranger was staggering. He glanced quickly at Dara, who still retained his position of readiness.

The crack of twigs, rustle of shrubs and now the audible gasp of anguished breathing, came clearly to their ears.

The dark outline of a figure was perceptible. It was bent double and its path erratic.

It suddenly crashed through the bushes, faltered a moment, and then with outstretched hand and a cry of pain it measured its length upon the ground.

Foltor stood, bow still ready strung, listening to the deep silence that followed the collapse of the figure that now lay on the ground before them. Moments passed and then Dara Mac Dalan seemed to uncoil and lay down his sword.

'There is no one else approaching. Come, let us see what this means.'

Foltor unstrung his arrow and laid his bow aside before joining Dara, kneeling by the side of the figure.

'An old man, wounded,' muttered Dara.

It was true that the figure, lying face down, had long white hair and his robes were streaked with blood. Carefully they turned him over on his back.

Foltor gasped.

The head of the man was shaven at the front, the hair being cropped back from the forehead to a line which stretched from ear to ear.

'The man wears the tonsure of a Druid,' he whispered.

'That much is obvious,' replied Dara tightly. 'And the gold circlet around his neck and the richness of his robe confirm as much.'

Foltor ignored the rebuke for Dara hated any wasting of words. If something was obvious, why bother to speak of it?

The front of the old man's robes were saturated in blood. Foltor without hesitation ripped at the clothing to discover the cause, noting that the old man's breathing was barely audible and shallow, rattling softly at the back of his throat.

It needed no expert to spot the three great cuts in the old man's chest. The spurting blood from one of them told its own story.

Foltor glanced at Dara and slowly shook his head.

'Let us make his last moments comfortable,' the warrior said without emotion, returning to the fire and fetching from his bedroll a container of *cuirm*, a strong liquor distilled from barley, from which he poured a small amount into a drinking horn. Then he brought it to the old man's cracked lips. Meanwhile, Foltor had sought to stem the pumping artery by pressing against the wound with a pad of cloth from the old man's robe.

Cradling the head with one arm, Dara attempted to moisten the pale, thin lips with a little of the *cuirm*.

The old man coughed a little, then his eyes fluttered open, pale and with fading life, trying to focus. When they did, they suddenly widened in fear and a tension caused his frail body to shudder.

'Have no fear, old one,' Dara said grimly. 'Tell us how you came to this sorry state?'

The old Druid turned his pale, watery blue eyes to the warrior, frowning as he searched the grim face.

'Who speaks?' His voice was no more than a whisper which Foltor had to lean forward to catch.

'I am Dara Mac Dalan of the Nasc Niadh.'

The eyes widened slightly.

'You are the champion of the kings of Cashel?'

'I am Dara.' There was no vain boast in Dara's voice.

The old man's eyes closed and his breath was a tortured sigh.

Dara raised the drinking horn to the lips of the Druid again.

The old man's thin lips twisted into a painful smile of gratitude. 'Who dared raised his sword against a wearer of the tonsure?' pressed Dara again.

'A warrior possessed of evil,' whispered the Druid. 'He has terrorised the land of the Uí Arada and none may best him in combat. We have all become his slaves.'

The Uí Arada dwelt among the mountains of this south west peninsula of Mumhan. Indeed, the Uí Arada were the very reason for Dara and Foltor's quest in this land. The clan were under obligation to pay an annual levy of seven milch cows to the king of Cashel. Two years had gone by without the payment and the king had dispatched Dara Mac Dalan to the chieftain of the Uí Arada to discover the reason for the discourtesy of the clan.

Dara was frowning.

'Who is this warrior?' he demanded.

'He is named Olc and he possesses no other name.'

'Evil the name, evil the nature,' observed Foltor dryly.

Dara's lips compressed.

'Is this Olc the chieftain of your people?'

The Druid was seized with a spasm of coughing blood. After a while, he answered: 'No assembly elected Olc to the chieftainship. He established himself over us by power of the sword.'

'And he did this to you?'

'I decided that our only hope was to appeal to the king of Cashel. In secret I set out hoping to persuade the king to send warriors from his élite Nasc Niadh, the champions of the golden collar, to save us. There is now no time to be lost.'

Dara was perplexed.

'No time to be lost? What makes you say this, old man?'

The Druid had another paroxysm of coughing and blood spurted from mouth, chest and nose. His time was close.

'I go to my rebirth, warrior . . . swear that you will destroy Olc . . . before . . . before it is too late?'

'I will swear,' agreed Dara. 'But too late, for what?'

The Druid's eyes started to glaze. His voice lowered to a breath so that Dara had to press his ear close to the man's lips.

'Olc has . . . gone to kidnap The Domna . . . the Keeper . . . the Keeper of the Word . . . He seeks entrance to the Cave of Cruachan . . . He will release the evils of the Otherworld . . . into this one . . . unless he be stopped. Swear you will stop him . . . ?'

Dara had no hesitation. His voice was firm and resolute.

'I swear! By the gods and by my ancestors, I swear that Olc shall die by my sword, unless the sky fall and crush me, or the earth open and swallow me or the sea rise and overwhelm me. I, Dara Mac Dalan, say this.'

He stared down at the old man still cradled in one arm. The Druid's eyes were closed, the skin of his face was mottled.

Foltor reached forward to touch the Druid's wrist.

'He is in the Place of Truth now, Dara,' he said softly.

They buried the old Druid in silence in the clearing, feet towards the west so that he might travel more easily there, westward to the House of Donn, where the souls gathered to be transported by the god of death, and again westward to the Otherworld, the Land of the Ever Young, to Hy-Brasil itself.

When the dawn light crept out of the eastern skies, Foltor cut the cold meat of the hare for the breaking of their fast before harnessing the team to the chariot. Dara nibbled morosely at the meal before stamping out the ashes of the fire and gathering his accoutrements. For a moment he stood with bare head at the head of the grave of the Druid, and then he swung up into the chariot behind Foltor.

The charioteer flicked the reins and the two night-black mares moved obediently forward.

'Do we still head to the ráth of the Uí Arada?' Foltor asked.

'That we do.'

Foltor bit his lip. He wanted so much to talk about the implications of the Druid's death.

'Have you heard before of this warrior named Olc?'

'I have not.'

Foltor sighed deeply but he pressed on.

'What did the Druid mean when he said that Olc had to be destroyed before it was too late?'

Dara's face was expressionless.

'Have you never heard of the Keeper of the Word?'

Foltor shrugged.

'Only as a tale for children.'

'Then remember that tale. For in the primal beginning there was only the Word and once it was uttered, Dana, the sacred water from heaven, poured down and fertilised the barren earth. The waters nurtured the seed of Bilé, the great oak god, and from

Dana and Bilé was born The Dagda, Father of the Gods. All this was accomplished by the Sacred Word.'

'I remember the story.'

'Good. From time immemorial there has existed a sacred hereditary priestess who was sworn to keep the holy Word for the knowledge of that Word gave untold power to all who possessed it. The Domna, Keeper of the Word, is said to dwell among the Uí Arada. None knows who she is or from where she derives her powers.'

Foltor chewed his lip thoughtfully.

'Yet if the words of the Druid were true, then this warrior named Olc has kidnapped the Keeper of the Word?'

Dara's lips were tight.

'And if the Word is in the possession of Olc, the five kingdoms of Ireland are in great danger for the Druid says he means to unlock the way through the Cave of Cruachan, the gateway to the Otherworld.'

'Does the Cave of Cruachan exist?'

'It does, Foltor. That act would unleash all the powers of darkness into this world.'

'And the stories are true?'

'As truth is to the Word.'

Foltor swallowed hard. He knew now why the Druid was so desperate to urge them to find Olc.

'Olc would make himself master of the world through the suppression of good?'

'Through the destruction of good,' affirmed Dara.

They emerged from the great forests and Foltor urged the horses forward along a broad coastal path with the granite mountains of Mumhan stretching up on their right side and down a short distance to the sea on their left side. The tang of the salt-scented air was invigorating to the breath. Foltor stared at the blue-grey vista with the white-crested choppy waves stretching almost as far as the horizon. Heavy rain clouds hung in patches and there was dampness in the air.

A little way along the roadway stood an aged stone dolmen of grey granite on which some Ogham letters had been cut.

Foltor reined his horses to a halt and bent to decipher the inscription.

'This is the country of the Uí Arada,' he interpreted confidently across his shoulder to Dara.

The warrior made no reply but Foltor knew that the keen grey eyes of the man were examining the terrain, searching out features in the landscape, points of danger from which ambush might be launched.

'We will proceed slowly,' he said at last. He had no need to add any warning or exhortation for Foltor to be watchful.

The charioteer flicked the reins and the black mares impatiently strode forward. Only the firm hands of Foltor kept them from breaking into a faster pace.

They followed the coastal path for some miles before sighting a great grey circular shape on the hillside above them.

'The ráth of the Uí Arada!' Foltor said softly.

He heard the soft exhalation of annoyance from Dara and pressed his lips together. There had been no need to identify the obvious. The fortress of the chieftain of the clan of the Uí Arada rose firm and strong in its large granite blocks of stone, circular in shape and dominating the countryside.

Foltor examined it with narrowed eyes.

There was no sign of movement along its battlements nor around the large gates into the fortress. The gates stood open and yet there seemed no warriors to guard them. Nor were people passing in and out. An air of desolation hung over the place.

Foltor drew in the reins and halted the chariot again. He glanced over his shoulder towards Dara and raised an eyebrow in question.

The warrior, who had also been examining the fortress, merely nodded.

Foltor reached forward and unhooked a horn from the side of the chariot, raised it to his lips and gave three long blasts.

The notes echoed back from the surrounding hills and then faded into silence. Nothing but silence answered the sound of the traditional signal of a warrior approaching a fortress with no evil intent.

Foltor bit his lip for a moment.

'Forward,' ordered Dara quietly.

Foltor reached a hand to the stand on the side of the chariot and checked that the three spears which stood in it were loose and ready for use. The chariot moved forward, Foltor allowed the horses to trot quickly as he swung the vehicle up the winding path towards the open gates of the fortress.

The first sign of danger was a faint sound of vibrating gut and a soft hissing of displaced air which gave Dara no more than a split second to raise his shield, identify the flight of the missile and cover himself before the arrow struck. With a soft clang of metal against metal the arrow bounced from his shield.

Foltor saw the bowman, already stringing another arrow to his weapon and he flicked the reins against his horses ears, letting them speed forward.

As he did so, Dara seized a spear and had leapt forward, out of the car and on to the central pole which yoked the horses to the chariot. With an uncanny skill he moved along the pole, balancing between the galloping horses, spear in one hand, shield in the other, as carelessly as if he were walking on a steady roadway. When he reached the heads of the pounding beasts he stood, swaying, his balance placed well, and brought back his spear arm. It was a favourite position from which to cast his weapon for it gave him an uninterrupted view of his assailant and allowed him to cast his spear with precision.

Foltor steadied the chariot for the turn even as he saw the bowman raise the flight of his arrow to eye level.

Then it was all over.

The spear of Dara had transfixed the man, sending him staggering backwards to the ground. The bow and arrow slipping out of his grasp.

Foltor halted the chariot by the man's body as Dara leapt down, sword in one hand, shield in the other, and glance downwards. With the spear stapling the assailant to the earth, there was no need to ask whether the man was dead or not.

Dara was already examining the rest of the deserted fortress.

Foltor left his chariot, bow strung ready, and gave a cursory examination of the bowman.

'He is not of the Uí Arada,' he said.

'Perhaps one of the followers of Olc,' replied Dara in annoyance. 'But where are the people of the Uí Arada?'

'Where you will not find them, stranger!' cried a voice which made Foltor jump.

From out of a door of one of the buildings there had emerged a burly, giant figure of a man, accoutred as a warrior but his face was coarse, his hair ill-groomed, his clothes dirty. He carried a shield and a great sword.

Dara swung round to face him, his face graven.

'Are you named Olc?' he demanded.

The burly man chuckled throatily.

'I have the honour to serve my lord, Olc, stranger. His enemies are mine. Even more so since you have killed my brother, who lies yonder.'

'Where do I find this Olc?' Dara demanded, unmoved. 'It is he that I quarrel with.'

'But you must quarrel with me first, stranger. Tell your charioteer to stand off.'

Dara nodded to Foltor, who returned to stand by the heads of the snorting horses.

With a great bellow, the burly giant rushed down on Dara. Foltor sighed sadly. The tall man was but vain; he thought with his muscles rather than with his brain. It was all over within a moment.

Dara stared down at his blood-stained body in disgust.

'It is not even worth claiming his head,' he said tightly. 'He was no warrior, but one who thought strength could overcome skill. He has learnt his lesson now; like a sheep to the slaughter!'

He spat in distaste.

'Unhitch the horses,' he continued after a moment, 'and we will search the ráth for sign of the Uí Arada and this strange warrior Olc.'

The search was not a long one. The great fortress was entirely deserted. Not even a dog whelp or cat inhabited the grey granite walls. Here and there, however, were ominous signs of blood.

Dara bit his lip and indicated with his sword.

'The spots of blood seem to form a trail. We shall follow it.'

He set off without another word.

Foltor could see that he was right. Outside the fortress the grass was flattened as if by several feet and blood stained a pathway away from the fortress along to where a small headland jutted precipitously above the foaming seas. Here the trail ended.

There was no need to ask what had taken place.

Foltor joined Dara as he stood at the edge of the overhang, staring down at the rock-strewn foam below where the seas pounded against the granite ramparts.

'All or just the wounded?' Foltor asked briefly.

Dara grimaced with distaste.

'Whether Olc ordered all the people of Uí Arada to be thrown over into the sea or simply the wounded, their blood is on his hands and he will answer for it. This I have sworn to the old Druid.'

He turned and began to walk swiftly back towards the fortress.

'Where will we find Olc now?' demanded Foltor, hurrying after him.

'He must be heading for the Cave of Cruachan.'

'Which is where?'

'No one knows for certain, simply that it is in the west. And we must find it within three days.'

Foltor frowned.

'Three days? Why three days?'

'Because in three days' time it will be the feast of Samhain, the one night when the Otherworld becomes visible to this one. Olc will use that time of vulnerability to force the Keeper of the Word to open the portals so that evil may flood our world.'

Foltor swallowed hard.

'But the west is so vast, the mountains many, the valleys too numerous to search and the lakes and islands beyond counting. How do we start?'

Dara's grim face betrayed no emotion.

'The odds may be against us, Foltor, but unless we start out we have no hope at all.'

Dara strode back to the dead bowman by the gates of the fortress and with a twist, wrenched out his spear and wiped it on some nearby grass, turning to replace it in its stand on the chariot.

It was Foltor whose keen ears caught the sound, even as Dara was retrieving the spear.

As Dara replaced the weapon in its stand, Foltor leant close to him and whispered.

'I heard the intake of breath. To your right, among those tall thorns.'

'Many?' queried Dara.

'One person. No more.'

Dara drew his sword and, like a cat, sprung forward without warning.

A sharp cry of surprise and fear broke the air as the warrior plunged among the bushes and dragged forth a slim, struggling form.

Both men's faces mirrored their astonishment.

A tall, well proportioned young girl, with waist length red-gold hair, battled fiercely to gain the release of her wrist from the hard grip of the warrior. Her green eyes flashed in fury.

'Identify yourself, woman!' demanded Dara.

'Identify yourself, first,' spat the girl, renewing her attempt to escape.

'Dara Mac Dalan of the Uí Duach,' replied the warrior.

'Another whelp of Olc, I suppose?' she sneered.

'Whelp of no one, be he man or god,' replied Dara firmly.

The girl stopped struggling, hesitated and frowned nervously.

'You deny Olc?'

'I have sworn a sacred oath to kill this Olc,' Dara rejoined solemnly.

The girl's eyes widened a little and she bit her lip. There was no doubting Dara's sincerity.

'Name yourself,' Dara insisted.

'I am Fithir, daughter of Gamal, chieftain of the Uí Arada.' She flung back her head with defiant pride.

'And where is Gamal?' interposed Foltor.

The girl threw him a look of anger, almost of hatred which caused the charioteer to recoil a step.

'You have just observed his last resting place!'

She threw out her hand towards the cliff edge from which they had just come.

Foltor's lips compressed.

'You'd better explain what has happened here,' Dara said quietly, finally releasing the girl's wrist.

'Isn't it obvious?' she demanded.

'Generally, yes. Specifically, no,' Dara replied calmly. 'Tell us that we may track down this man named Olc the more quickly.'

The girl stared hard at him. Foltor realised that she was struggling to hold back her tears and he reached out a hand to her. But she jumped back, almost wincing at his nearness. He halted and pointed to the chariot.

'Take a seat on the edge there,' he invited 'and I will get you a drink to help you tell your story.'

Reluctantly she went forward and sat down.

He gave her a drink of *cuirm* and after a while she began her story.

It had been two years since Olc had come to the land of the Uí Arada and established himself by means of his sword as overlord. He had attracted to him many unsavoury bullies, outcasts who lived by their wits and swords. These, at Olc's orders, helped keep the people in conditions of subservience. Olc demanded loyalty or death and many a young warrior of the Uí Arada had died in attempting to rid the countryside of his curse.

Then came the news that Olc had dared to defy the most sacred of the sanctuaries and had led a raid northward to the holy island in mist-shrouded Loch Léin where he had expected to find The Domna, the Keeper of the Word. The Domna did not reside at the sanctuary of Loch Léin but Olc was able to extract from a dying Druid that the priestess dwelt among the Uí Arada where her identity was secret even from her own relatives. Only the previous Keeper knew to whom the sacred office was passed. So Olc returned to the Uí Arada and set out to find who The Domna was. He was not subtle in his means.

The Uí Arada had, for two years now, bowed to the power of Olc. But this desecration of the holy of holies, this defiance of the power of the gods themselves and the threat of the destruction of the very world, caused Gamal and his advisers to stand up to Olc. Eolas the Druid volunteered to go secretly to seek help from the king of Cashel. A day passed before Olc came to Gamal and boasted that Eolas was dead. Gamal and the Uí Arada were given a choice. Give up The Domna or die.

Gamal refused, saying it was not in his knowledge or power to give up the Keeper of the Word and was the first to meet Olc's wrathful steel. Ten more of the Uí Arada, both men and women, followed Gamal's example. Olc merely wounded them and then had his men drive them to the cliff top, Gamal mortally wounded among them, and had them thrown to their deaths. The girl's voice was hesitating with emotion and no more could Fithir tell them, except that many Uí Arada had been slaughtered by Olc until a young girl, Dubailte, came forward and confessed that she was The Domna in order to stop the slaughter.

Then Olc demanded that the people accompany him to the sacred Cave of Cruachan in order to clear the passage to the cave for rock falls had sealed the entrance. He needed people to clear these rocks. Olc was daring to open the sacred portal to the Otherworld.

With the capture of The Domna any further resistance that the Uí Arada may have contemplated was broken.

They were rounded up, men, women, children—even the old ones—so long as they could heave rocks, and they were marched away.

'All except you,' Dara pointed out.

'Gamal, my father, told me to hide at the approach of Olc.' The girl coloured furiously. 'Olc has long looked at me with eyes of surreptitious lust. Since he went away to kidnap the Keeper of the Word I have come to the age of choice. My father wished to hide me lest a terrible fate overtook me.'

Dara nodded in understanding.

'So you hid?'

'I hid among the thorns where Gamal, my father, thought none might look.'

'And you saw what took place?'

'I did so. I saw the slaughter and saw the others being marched off.'

'Why were the two men left behind?' asked Foltor, motioning to the bodies within the gates of the fortress.

'Because Olc knew that I was hiding somewhere. But he could not wait. It lacks but three days to Samhain by which time he needs to clear a path to the Cave of Cruachan. So he left two men to wait until I emerged from hiding.'

Foltor frowned.

'When did this happen?'

'This morning.'

'So we are not far behind this warrior Olc?'

The girl nodded emphatically.

'I waited and time passed and then I heard your arrival. But I knew not who you were. I dared not emerge.'

'But when you saw we slew Olc's men . . . surely that showed we must be enemies of Olc?' queried Foltor.

Fithir shook her head.

'Olc has been known to slaughter his own before now merely for amusement.'

Dara was frowning, reflecting on the girl's story.

'If Olc rounded up the Uí Arada as labour to help him clear a path to the entrance of the Cave of Cruachan, then surely the cave is situated nearby?'

Fithir inclined her head.

'Of course. It is four miles north of here in the Valley of Lost Souls.'

Her voice was matter of fact as if it were common knowledge.

For the first time, as far as Foltor recollected, Dara's face showed some sign of surprise.

'You know this valley?'

The girl raised an eyebrow.

'Are not the Uí Arada the hereditary guardians of the Cave of Cruachan, ensuring that none may profane it?'

'I did not know.'

The girl sighed.

'Why do you think that The Domna dwells among us, though none may know her? Gamal only knew she did so, not who she was. Why do you think that he and those of his council paid so high a price to attempt to stop Olc?'

'Will you take us there, Fithir?' Dara demanded. 'Will you help us stop Olc from this terrible deed?'

There was little hesitation from the girl now.

'I will show you the way. But Olc has a score of warriors with him.'

'If Olc's warriors are of the same mettle as these,' Foltor boastfully said, indicating the bodies of the two who had been slain in the fortress, 'then we need not fear them.'

The girl examined his face thoughtfully.

'Perhaps. But Olc is made of sterner stuff and he is accompanied by a woman who advises him, his mistress some have said, who has the gift of cunning council.'

Dara's lips compressed.

'Then our first task is to slay Olc and this woman. If we can succeed perhaps the remaining men of the Uí Arada will help us deal with Olc's men. A score of warriors, did you say?'

'No more than a score,' Fithir assured him.

'Then the sooner we start for the Valley of Lost Souls, the sooner we shall arrive there.'

The girl and the ageing warrior clung to the rails at the back of the chariot as Foltor urged the two black mares forward along the winding pathway which twisted through the granite mountains carpeted with sodden brown bracken and tenacious reddish heather. The hills rose stern and forbidding on all sides as the charioteer guided his vehicle through the narrow defiles that led upwards.

The steepness of the hills seemed to preclude the midday sun and shrouded their path in deep shadow.

They spoke no word. Dara Mac Dalan's mouth was a thin bloodless slit and his eyes were stony, without emotion. The pale face of the girl still reflected the horror of her experience and her hands were white as they clung to the rail of the side of the chariot, white and twisting.

Upwards twisted the pathway so that the hills reformed as towering mountains and they passed through dark narrow valleys so deep that no warm ray of sun penetrated and they saw the mist of their breath before them on the cold air. Even the haze of sweat rose from the shanks of the two impatient mares and Foltor eased the pace a little, shivering in the icy atmosphere.

No word passed between them except for an occasional muttered direction from the girl, who indicated the path whenever it divided and Foltor hesitated.

Eventually they passed from the dark defile and moved into a broad valley where the grass was greener in its centre and where wild fuchsias bordered the pathway.

The girl cleared her throat.

'We are near the Cave of Cruachan now.'

Dara Mac Dalan sighed, shook himself and peered forward.

'Where does it lie?'

She raised a slim, pale arm with the finger extended.

'At the end of this valley the track will divide. The left hand path twists upwards into a high mountain valley. That is the Valley of Lost Souls and in that valley lies the Cave of Cruachan.'

Dara bit his lip in thoughtful reflection for a moment or two.

'We had best leave the chariot at the end of this valley and proceed on foot.'

Foltor nodded agreement.

Dara turned to the girl.

'You will wait for us in the chariot.'

The girl's chin came up in annoyance.

'I am Fithir, daughter of Gamal, who was chieftain of the Uí Arada. Those are my people who have been led in slavery to the Cave of Cruachan. I must help to divert this evil from them.'

Dara's eyes narrowed dangerously, staring into the girl's defiant features. He saw fear in the girl's eyes, but there was determination too; a determination to overcome her fear.

He grimaced.

'Very well, Fithir, daughter of Gamal. But only one can command in a time of danger. Do you acknowledge my right to command?'

She frowned, hesitated and nodded.

'There is no time to give in to vanity, to pride born of privilege,' went on Dara softly. 'Forget you are the daughter of a chieftain. Do you acknowledge that I will command?'

She flushed as he read her thoughts correctly.

'I do,' she replied sullenly.

'Then stay closely by me and when I say something obey it and do not think about it.'

The girl sniffed disdainfully.

Dara spoke no more for the time being.

Foltor eased the horses to a halt in a natural enclosure at the end of the valley but he did not unyoke them. If they needed to escape quickly then such an action would be dangerous. He took his bow and slung his quiver of arrows on his back and then he took Dara's two throwing spears and shouldered them.

Dara was walking towards the exit for the valley, followed by Fithir. Foltor joined them.

The girl pointed to the path.

'It is as I have said, we follow this left hand path up among those high rocks.'

'How far is the Valley of Lost Souls from here?' asked Foltor breathlessly as he hurried along.

The girl shrugged.

'I have only been here once in my life. It is a valley on which a *geis* is placed, which is taboo. None are supposed to enter it. I think, however, the entrance is no more than five hundred yards along this path through a narrow defile. That is where the Cave of Cruachan is sited.'

Dara exhaled softly. His trained eyes travelled the terrain.

'How confident is this warrior named Olc?' he mused softly. 'Would he have posted guards?'

Foltor smiled, more a grin of impishness.

'I know a warrior who was always guided by the maxim that

you presumed an adversary is intelligent and will do the unexpected. Even in his confidence, this Olc may post guards.'

Dara nodded slowly.

'So be it. We shall proceed on the basis that he will have guards.'

Keeping to the shadows of the walls of the defile, they followed
Dara's lead in moving stealthily forwards. Indeed, it was just as
well, for they had traversed some two hundred yards when Dara
halted, turned swiftly and placed a finger on his lips.

Ahead of them, squatting on a stone, bow with arrow strung,
carelessly held in his hands, was a rough-looking man. He had
clearly been left on guard but he was so confident that no danger
lurked nearby that he was half dozing, scarcely interested in his
surroundings.

Dara glanced to Foltor who nodded. There was no need to
exchange words. He raised his bow. The first arrow pierced the
man's throat to prevent him crying out, the second sank deep into
his heart. Olc's guard fell without a sound.

Fithir, the girl, suppressed a shiver of horror at the casualness
of the deed.

Neither Dara nor Foltor could spare the time to moralise with
her.

They moved swiftly onwards.

The valley was little more than a large granite depression on
top of the mountain. True, its walls were steep sided, almost hiding
the sky by large overhangs which prevented grass, heather or similar vegetation growing across the floor of it, even if there had been
soil enough to put down roots. It was a bare, grey valley at whose
end stood the dark mouth of a cave entrance.

Dara signalled them to press back into the shadows of the valley
entrance.

Warriors stood in watchful positions around the valley, no more
than a hundred yards in length and fifty yards across. Lines of
haggard-looking, bloodstained people were moving to and from
the dark cave entrance. Heading out of the cave entrance was a
line of people, men, women and children, bearing great rocks and
pieces of granite which they piled to one side before joining the
other group heading back to the cave. Thus were the people of
the Uí Arada being pressed by Olc to clear the entrance to the
Cave of Cruachan to allow the Keeper of the Word forward to
unlock the fiercesome mysteries of the Otherworld.

A group stood near the cave.

Foltor could identify Olc at once. A tall, muscular young man clad in the regalia of a warrior, his golden torc on his neck. The face was handsome yet, even from this distance, the young man looked arrogant and cruel. At his feet, slumped on the ground, was what Foltor took initially for a bundle of rags. When he peered more closely he saw that it was a young woman in bloodstained white robes.

Fithir leant forward.

'That is Dúbailte,' she whispered.

Foltor could see the girl was scarcely beyond the age of choice, a youthful, simple-looking female. The charioteer's eyes rose in surprise. He had been expecting the sacred Keeper of the Word to be different somehow, to look different . . . more mature and filled with wisdom. He opened his mouth to speak. But Dara turned and frowned, motioning them both to silence with a warning glance.

Behind Olc stood another figure, that of a woman wearing a hooded cloak which hid her features. Her stance, however, was both arrogant and commanding.

A thickset man with a whip emerged from the entrance of the cave.

'Lord Olc,' they heard him call gruffly, 'we are nearly through. A few more stones and the entrance will be cleared.'

As if in punctuation to this statement there came the rumble of thunder from the skies. Many looked nervously up at the blackening storm clouds which seemed to be gathering across the valley.

The young woman at Olc's feet let out a thin wail as if of despair.

'Do you not know what you are about to do, Olc?' came her shrill, penetrating voice. 'Once evil is abroad in the world you can never return it to whence it came.'

The young man chuckled. There was something cold and frightening about the sound.

They could hear his voice distinctly though he spoke quietly.

'What care I of that, girl, so long as power is my reward for loosening it?'

Dara turned quietly to Foltor.

'Can you send a single arrow into this Olc's head?'

Foltor strung his bow silently and took aim.

The arrow was loosed.

Then it seemed in that moment Olc's head cocked into a listening position and swiftly he raised his shield, deflecting the arrow away from him.

He stood smiling evilly in their direction.

'You will have to improve your aim if you wish to kill me!' he called.

Foltor stared in disbelief.

'By the gods,' he whispered, 'what manner of a man is this?'

Dara grimaced angrily.

'A man only. But a trained warrior who could hear the flight of an arrow. He is skilful. That much I shall say in his favour.'

The warriors had swung round, weapons ready while the lines of the Uí Arada had stopped their drudgery, expressions of hope on their faces. The young woman, too, had turned to see if a saviour was at hand.

There came another ominous rumble of thunder just as the stocky man with the whip re-emerged from the entrance of the cave. He seemed unaware of the drama outside and he shouted to Olc.

'We are through. We need only the saying of the Word, Olc, and . . .'

He faltered, staring at the silent tableau.

Olc was standing still smiling in the direction where Dara, Foltor and Fithir were concealed behind the rocks.

'We have visitors. Come hither whoever you are.'

There was yet another rumble of thunder which seemed to shake the very mountain.

The man with the whip stared over his shoulder uneasily and then up at the threatening skies as if, in his mind, the two were connected.

'My lord Olc . . .' he began nervously.

Olc motioned him to silence.

Dara Mac Dalan hesitated only a moment and then drawing his sword and raising his shield he stepped forward, just as lightning lit up the sky.

'Olc,' came the shrieking of the young woman, The Keeper of the Word. 'Can't you see that the gods grow angry at your blasphemy? Cease now before it is too late.'

The arrogant young man kicked at her, his eyes never leaving the figure of Dara.

'Take her into the cave,' he snapped to the tall woman who stood behind him.

The woman wearing the hooded cloak moved forward and dragged the younger woman upwards, propelling her forward towards the dark entrance of the cave.

Once again the thunder reverberated and lightning momentarily lit the sky.

'Well, well,' there was a sneer in Olc's voice as his cold gaze swept over the figure of Dara Mac Dalan. 'An old man dressed as a warrior. From what stone did you crawl, old man?'

Dara Mac Dalan never replied to insults. Many warriors would boast of their talents before a contest to awe their opponents but not so Dara of the Uí Duach.

Olc motioned to his warriors who then began to move steathily towards the solitary figure of Dara, raising their weapons as they did so.

Foltor knew what he must do.

In swift succession three arrows embedded themselves in the chests of the three leading warriors. They fell with cries of pain, causing the others to pause and look uncertainly for the source of the silent death.

'Call off these jackals, Olc,' cried Dara. 'Or you may lose more of them. Is the contest between the two of us or do you lack the stomach for single combat?'

The young man's chin came up defiantly, hot blood coloured his cheeks. The sneer obviously stung his ego.

'Stay back, then,' he called to his warriors. Some with clear relief on their faces withdrew back a step or two.

The thunder rolled and cracked across the hill yet again as the storm developed, causing the people to blink and cower at the livid white flashes that preceded its ominous roars. The sky became dark, an ever changing visage of swirling blacks and greys.

Olc glanced around.

'Old man!' he called. 'Have I your word that your hidden assassin will not shoot any more?'

'My word, Olc, that he will not shoot if he has no cause to do so.'

Olc moved forward. He held his sword and shield easily. The sneer on his face became apparent.

'So, old man, you have only one to support you?'

Dara gestured to the three warriors sprawled on the ground.

'Yet your force has decreased by six men, Olc,' the old warrior's voice was soft and even.

Olc frowned.

'Six? I count only three.'

'You left two men on guard at the fortress and one on guard in the valley behind.'

The young man smiled thinly.

'That is true. Well, I still have plenty more.'

His voice was matter of fact, as if the snuffing out of life was of no consequence.

There came a swishing sound and a man standing on an outcrop of rock gave a cry. Dara's eyes flickered up and he saw the man toppling, a bow falling from his hand and an arrow partially strung. Dara's eyes returned to those of the younger man.

'Seven now. The figure will decrease, Olc, every time you resort to subterfuge to overcome me. Stand and face me like a man. Tell your men to lay aside their weapons lest those who accompany me grow nervous of their intentions. When you have done that, we will test our mettle in settlement of this matter.'

Olc bit his lip in sudden annoyance.

'It seems that I underestimate you, old man.'

Dara shrugged without emotion.

There came another flash of lightning and crash of thunder.

'The Fomorii gods are waiting to be loosed into this world,' laughed Olc, moving closer, and sliding into a crouching position, shield forwards, the point of his sword circling wickedly.

'No!'

The girl's voice was still shrill, almost edged with hysteria.

Dara stared towards the Keeper of the Word who had broken loose from the grip of the hooded woman.

'I am The Domna, Keeper of the Word. There is blasphemy here. Put up your swords!' The young woman was standing suddenly imperiously tall.

The elderly warrior hesitated and then called to her.

'I am here to help you, Domna.'

The young girl hesitated, then avoiding the stretching hands of the hooded woman she suddenly tore herself away, scrambling up the rocky side of the valley, leaping like a gazelle from one isolated rock to another. No one moved at the sudden motion, as if spell-bound by the rising storm and drama.

'I will say what is to be done!' cried The Domna, pausing to regain her breath, standing overlooking them.

The young warrior, Olc, seemed disconcerted. He snapped something to the hooded woman. The woman started upwards after the young girl. The Domna gave another shriek, it was one of hysterical laughter which shocked both Olc and his men, as well as the gathered Uí Arada and Dara. The young girl was moving rapidly higher among the rocks, scrambling with ungainly movements upwards towards the rim of the valley. The thunder rolled ominously and loudly and a bright white fork of lightning made them blink as the storm moved directly above them.

The two women, the hooded figure chasing the Keeper of the Word, continued to scramble upwards to the rim of the rocky valley, watched uncertainly by everyone.

Dara was confused, unable to understand why the Keeper of the Word had apparently lost her reason. Then there was a terrifying crack. For a moment everyone was blinded by the light. Then there was darkness. No, not quite. The Domna, the Keeper of the Word, stood illuminated on the rim overlooking the valley, hands outstretched as if in supplication to the heavens; strangely illuminated she was as if emitting some ethereal blue light. They all imagined her shriek rather than heard it in reality. For a moment or two it seemed that she stood wrapped in flames. The thunder cracked again and then it was as if the storm clouds were racing away towards the distant horizon as the wind began to rise and howl.

For a while the people stood stunned. There was no need to ask if the black, smouldering pile of clothing held any life within it.

Then both Olc's warriors and the people of the Uí Arada dropped to their knees and began intoning prayers to the god Taranis the Thunderer that he might spare them from the fury of his lightning bolts.

Dara saw the hooded woman, who had given chase, now rapidly descending, casting nervous glances at the heavens. Olc observed her too—was there momentary relief on his features?—before turning back to the elderly warrior with his features suddenly twisting into a snarl of rage.

'You will not thwart my design, old man!'

There was sharp anger in his voice as he ran abruptly forward, his weapon at the ready.

Dara's trained eyes saw that the young warrior was certainly no novice. Whoever had trained him had trained him well. The first few feints told him that.

Metal struck metal in their first exchange, a quick, breathless exchange of blows before they stepped backwards, pausing to assess each other's ability.

The face of Olc had grown more grim as he realised that he was not confronting some ageing amateur. His features were more concentrated now.

Dara was aware of the Uí Arada huddling together with hopeful faces while the remaining followers of Olc had drawn aside, nervously putting down their bows, lest they emulate those of their company who now lay dead.

By the mouth of the Cave of Cruachan the hooded female companion of Olc had halted now, her shoulders heaving, her stance uncertain. The sacred Keeper of the Word, whose knowledge could destroy the world, was no more; nothing but a smouldering heap of charred flesh. Taranis, the god of thunder, had destroyed her. Only revenge was left.

All eyes were on the old man and young man as they warily circled each other.

Where the young man had youth and energy on his side, Dara had the years of experience, and both elderly and young warrior were equally matched in their grim determination. To and fro their contest raged, metal resounding against metal and now and then the spurt of blood as the sharp blades found soft flesh.

The end came unexpectedly, as all ends must come. Dara's heel struck a loose rock and he stumbled backwards off balance. With the gleam of victory in his eyes, the young man, Olc, raised his sword and lunged forward for the death blow. The blow was never delivered. Olc had let his anger overcome his judgement and opened his guard for that blow.

Dara's weapon stabbed out under Olc's guard. The sharp blade struck into the flesh under the arm, cracking through the bone of the ribs and finding the throbbing muscle of the heart.

The young man's eyes went wide, wide with shock and bewilderment. There was only a moment of realisation before the eyes glazed and the young man fell at Dara's feet without a sound.

For a brief second or two there was a stillness in which a pin falling to the earth might have been heard.

Then a shriek of rage echoed and re-echoed through the rocky valley. The sound was unexpected and caused everyone to freeze with shock.

The hooded woman scrambled across the rocky floor to the fallen young man's form and dragged at the head with her two hands, shaking it as if trying to shake awake a person who had fallen asleep.

'No! No! No!' came the vehement sobbing of the woman.

Dara stood, bloodied sword in hand, gazing down with features transfixed in a curious expression.

The woman was in a paroxysm of sobbing, beating futilely at her breast, her head rolling back and uncontrolled sounds coming from her twisted lips. The eyes were ablaze with hatred. They turned to Dara and the hood fell back, revealing a woman of middle age; a woman whose features had once been of beauty but were now twisted with grief and rage.

Even as the silent, amazed watchers looked, the woman rose and took a long knife from her belt.

Dara stood there staring at the harridan with a ghastly expression, his sword point never rising from the ground.

Foltor cried a warning to the warrior but Dara Mac Dalan of Uí Duach seemed transfixed, standing motionless before the rising weapon.

Foltor raised his bow. Within the space of a man's breath two feathered shafts stuck out from the woman's breast and without a cry she slumped across the body of Olc.

The silence that followed erupted after a moment into pandemonium. The surviving warriors of Olc were fleeing for their lives and cries of gratitude and cheers were rising from the lips of the surviving people of the clan of the Uí Arada as they saw Fithir emerge from cover behind the rocks with the young charioteer Foltor by her side.

Foltor cast a worried glance to where Dara was still standing motionless staring at the two bodies. The charioteer turned with an uneasy glance to where Fithir was smiling and acknowledging the joy of her people. They were acclaiming her as their chieftain.

'Little cause of joy,' Foltor observed heavily, raising his gaze to the rim of the valley where The Domna, the Keeper of the Word, had been blasted by the lightning stroke of Taranis. 'The Keeper of the Word has perished. Humankind is the poorer.'

Fithir chuckled curiously softly.

'Not so, charioteer. You and the warrior Dara deserve to know the secret but no one else. It is I who am The Keeper of the Word. I who am The Domna.'

Foltor's eyes widened in astonishment, his jaw dropping a little. The girl nodded solemnly in reply to his silent question.

'I am The Domna, hereditary Keeper of the Word,' she confirmed. 'When I heard from my father that Olc's intention was to seek out The Domna, I persuaded Dúbailte to pretend that she was The Domna until we could be sure what his reason was. At least Dúbailte's pretence saved many lives.

'Alas, my father Gamal, not knowing I was The Domna, had forced me to hide, otherwise I might have confessed. Poor Dúbailte, she was not of a strong, calm mind. Had she not been prone to hysteria, she would have been safe from any harm.'

Foltor was nodding slowly.

'But how safe? Didn't Taranis, the god of thunder, strike her down for blasphemy? A punishment for daring to claim to be The Domna?'

The girl shook her head sadly.

'If she had not run for the high rocks, she would have been safe from harm. The hills here have been mines for generations, the source of iron ore. The rocks are full of it. Iron attracts the lightning stroke as surely as day follows night. Small wonder that lightning chose to strike around this spot. Do you not understand why the Cave of Cruachan is located here? Iron is the symbol of purity and one has to journey through purity to the Otherworld.'

Foltor shook his head slowly before turning back anxiously to Dara.

The elderly warrior had not stirred but now, suddenly, he heaved his shoulders and sighed deeply.

The whistle of his sigh was troubled, like an exhalation of a bitter anguish from the very depths of his soul.

'You are the victor again, Dara Mac Dalan,' cried Foltor. 'Why is your face so troubled?'

The pained grey eyes of the warrior turned to face Foltor and then travelled on to the face of the young girl, Fithir.

'My task is done, Keeper of the Word,' he said softly.

The girl inclined her head in reply.

'Evil has been destroyed,' interposed Foltor.

Dara's lips compressed.

'And perhaps good with it. There is both good and evil within us all, only circumstance dictates which path we must follow.'

The girl reached out a hand and laid it on the elderly warrior's arm.

'I understand. I will gather my people now and return them to the ráth of my father for there is much to be done rebuilding this devastation.'

'But the Cave of Cruachan?' interposed Foltor. 'What of the sacred word?'

Fithir smiled somewhat wryly again at the young charioteer.

'The sacred word will keep now . . . until the end of time, I hope.' Then returning her gaze to the graven face of Dara she inclined her head in the direction of the bodies of Olc and the woman: 'They have already gone into the Cave of Cruachan to meet that which lies beyond. However, I shall have their earthly bodies taken into its protection.'

Dara bowed his head.

Foltor stood bewildered.

'But shall I not sever the heads to hang on your chariot of victory as is the custom?'

Dara's grey eyes glinted. For a passing moment his lips twitched before he said in even tones: 'No. We will be on our way back to the court of Cashel. There has been no victory for me in this place. No symbols of victory will hang from our chariot, Foltor.'

Dara raised a hand in farewell to the girl. He hesitated, glancing again at the bodies and only Foltor at his side heard the soft whisper: 'Farewell, Grotach; farewell, Olc.'

'May the road rise with you and the wind be always at your back,' the girl called softly as Dara Mac Dalan turned on his heel and strode away.

Foltor, frowning, made a hurried farewell to Fithir, and followed the elderly warrior. Foltor would have liked to stay, have spoken more with the attractive young Fithir, but the girl was already surrounded by her people, touching her hand and crying her praises. She would be their chieftainess now. Alas, Fithir was beyond his worldly grasp for, moreover, she was The Domna, The Keeper of the Word.

He caught up with Dara Mac Dalan as he entered the larger valley where they had left their tethered two black mares and chariot. Silently, Foltor replaced his quiver of arrows and his bow and the two war spears in their stand in the chariot and climbed into the car. Then he sighed in annoyance at Dara's grim-faced silence.

'You knew that woman's name,' he said accusingly. 'Olc's woman, I mean.'

Dara blinked slightly.

'Olc's mother.'

'Well, where did you know her from? Who was she?' Foltor made his voice sound aggressive in an attempt to force the information from the warrior.

Dara Mac Dalan gazed calmly at him a moment, his face set and grave. His voice was studied, devoid of emotion.

'Her name was Grotach. Once she was my wife. Olc was therefore my son, though I have never seen him since he was three years old. As I said, there is good and evil in all of us. There must have been some good in him for he was my child. Only circumstance dictates which path we will choose in life. Speed the horses towards Cashel, Foltor, for this has been my last warrior quest.'

It was then that the young charioteer noticed that tears were streaming unchecked from the elderly warrior's eyes

ACKNOWLEDGEMENTS

The editor would like to record his especial thanks to Peter Berresford Ellis and W. O. G. Lofts for their help in assembling this collection. He and the publishers are also grateful to the following authors, publishers and agents for permission to reprint copyright stories: John Murray Ltd for 'The Call of Oisin' by Lady Gregory; Macmillan & Co Ltd for 'Laughing Stranger' by James Stephens, 'The Return of Cuchulain' from *King Goshawk and the Birds* by Eimar O'Duffy and 'A Fable' by Mary Lavin; *The Dublin Magazine* for 'Balor and the Wonder-Smith' by Ella Young, 'The Outlaw' by Joseph O'Neill and 'The Woman Without Mercy' by Maurice Walsh; Orion Publishing Group for 'The Death of Macha Gold-Hair' by Dermot O'Byrne; The Harrigan Press for 'Earth-Bound' by Dorothy Macardle; Random Publishing Group for the extract from *The Sun Dances at Easter* by Austin Clarke, 'Midir and Etain' by Sir Shane Leslie and 'The End of the Rainbow' by Lord Dunsany; A. P. Watt Literary Agency for 'Legend for a Painting' by Julia O'Faolain; C. J. Fallon Ltd for 'A Prince in Disguise' by Sinead de Valera; Pilot Press for 'The Bewitching of Fursey' by Mervyn Wall; The Estate of A. E. Coppard for 'Crotty Shinkwin'; Little Brown for 'The Ark of Cashelmor' from *The Elephant and the Kangaroo* by T. H. White; Abner Stein Ltd for 'The Kiss' by Michael Scott; A. M. Heath & Co Ltd for 'The Last Warrior Quest' by Peter Tremayne; Brian Cleeve for his story 'The Devil and Democracy'. While every care has been taken to clear permission for the use of the stories in this book, in the case of any accidental infringement, copyright holders are asked to write to the editor care of the publishers.